D1606134

The Secrets of Darcy and Elizabeth

A Pride and Prejudice Variation

Victoria Kincaid

ISBN: 978-0-9975530-0-0

Chapter 1

London, 1803

Darcy was drunk.

He was inebriated. He was soused. He was foxed.

He had imbibed too much, and he knew it. Carefully, he set his empty glass on the table only to realize he had actually set it on the air *next* to the table, causing it to tumble to the floor and shatter. Darcy exhaled some oaths. He thought about summoning a servant to clean up the mess, but it seemed like too much effort—and all the servants were asleep. Better to simply avoid that part of the floor until morning.

He gazed around his sumptuously appointed study: the mahogany bookshelves crowded with his favorite books, the handsome stone fireplace, two quite comfortable wingback chairs flanking the fireplace. The ancient wooden desk had been in his family for years, but it was now piled high with papers he was trying to ignore. It was a handsome room, and he loved it, but it did nothing to soften his mood.

Perhaps the room's best feature was the crystal decanter of port resting on the shelf behind his desk. Swaying a little, he poured himself another glass and then shakily made his way back to a wingback chair. There was no fire in the grate in early June, but he found the chair more comfortable than sitting behind the desk regarding the work he should be doing.

He had started with wine at dinner and moved on to port only after Georgiana retired for the night because she should not see him like this. Of course, she would witness the aftermath in the morning, but he could pass it off as a headache. Or with luck he could sleep so late that she would be out when he arose. He drank deeply from the glass. This had become the only way he could achieve a whole night of sleep. One or two more glasses and he should be able to achieve oblivion.

But he was not there yet. He could still see Elizabeth's fine eyes shining and imagine the exquisite texture of her dark curls…the way her mouth quirked up when she laughed. But then these images dissipated as he recalled the sound of her voice: *You could not have made me the offer of your hand in any possible way that would have tempted me to accept it.* Shaking his head, he tried to rid himself of the memory, its pain almost as fresh as the day of the disastrous proposal.

The vision of her face, white with rage, haunted him. *Why with so evident a design of offending and insulting me, you chose to tell me that you liked me against your will, against your reason, and even against your character?* What had possessed him? But he knew the answer. *I believed I was being frank and honest with her about my misgivings,* he mused bitterly. *I was so proud of myself. But I never gave a thought for her sentiments.* Instead he had hurt her by relating sensibilities he had better left unspoken. *She was correct in refusing me,* he thought desolately. *I do not deserve her.* This realization warranted another glass of port. This time he poured with more care, and all of the tawny liquid made it into the fine crystal glass. As he took a sip, he smiled grimly.

Suddenly, the door burst open, causing Darcy to spill port on his shirt in surprise and curse vividly, glaring at the intruder. Colonel Fitzwilliam strode nonchalantly through the door and paused to survey the scene before him. "Port? What an excellent idea!" After pouring himself a snifter, he peered dubiously at the broken glass littering the floor, cautiously walked around it, and settled comfortably in the other wingback chair next to the fireplace.

"Richard," Darcy greeted him irritably. He had dismissed the servants specifically so no one would witness his dissipation. "I do not recall inviting you into my house or my study."

"I have a standing invitation and a key to your house," Richard reminded him, holding the port up to the light. "This really is excellent port. You should consume it more slowly and respectfully."

Darcy was certain Richard had a purpose in being there at that time of night but was equally certain he did not want to know what it was. His brain moved sluggishly, and he knew he was no match for his cousin tonight. Carefully keeping his glass level, he took an unsteady step to the door, hoping—rather than believing—that his cousin would simply let him depart. "It is past time to retire. If you will excuse me…"

Richard stood in one fluid motion and blocked Darcy's path, gently pushing and toppling him back into his chair. "What do you want, Richard?" Darcy's voice was edged with irritation.

"This is not a simple social call, Cousin," Richard revealed, gazing steadily at Darcy.

"Imagine my surprise." Darcy emptied his glass in one swallow. *If Richard is determined to be difficult, I am not nearly foxed enough.*

"A few days ago, Georgiana asked me to talk with you. I requested that she notify me the next time you did this." As he gestured to encompass the room, Richard's tone was brisk and matter-of-fact.

"Georgiana?" Now Darcy was surprised. "How—?"

"You truly believe it eluded her that you get foxed several times a month?" Richard's tone was light, but there was steel in his eyes. "She is anxious about you. Now that I see you, I am as well."

Darcy put down his glass on a small table with a little more force than necessary. "There is nothing to be anxious about. I am perfectly fine. Leave me alone."

Richard was undeterred, regarding his cousin skeptically. "It is nothing? Since we returned from Rosings, you have been closeting yourself in your study and stalking around the house like someone died. Georgiana tells me you refuse most invitations, never going out and barely speaking to anyone. Have you looked in the mirror, man? You seem to have aged ten years!"

Darcy felt anger rise but struggled not to lash out. His cousin deserved better. "Very well. There *is* something bothering me, but you can do nothing to help." Darcy thought his voice sounded calm and controlled under the circumstances. "I would rather not discuss it."

"I am here to listen. Sharing your troubles may lessen them." Richard's tone was no longer mocking.

"No." Darcy stood again to leave.

"So I should leave Georgiana alone to cope with this?" The thought of his sister stopped Darcy cold. "I know your inebriation is not accidental."

"No," Darcy readily conceded. "But it is only an occasional indulgence." Richard snorted in disbelief. Darcy's tolerance was ebbing. "Go home. Leave me alone." He turned to eye his cousin. "I shall be better in the future."

"If it were simply your well-being at stake, I would not hesitate to let you stew. But unfortunately for you, I am Georgiana's guardian as well; what affects her concerns me." Richard poured himself another snifter of port as Darcy stumbled back to his seat, fearing he would fall over if he did not sit. He held out his glass for a refill, but Richard pushed it away.

"I hardly think my moods are within the purview of a guardian," Darcy said acidly.

"On the contrary." There was more anger in Richard's tone than Darcy expected. "She is despondent over your behavior, but apparently you have not noticed. If you will not talk to me for your sake, do it for hers. Otherwise, she will persist in believing she has caused your despair."

Now Darcy was shocked. "What? This has nothing to do with Georgiana!"

"If you confide in me, I can reassure her of that." Richard watched his cousin closely, but Darcy fell silent. Georgiana was the one thing in his life that still mattered, his one point of vulnerability. He had believed he could keep his despondency from affecting her but was ashamed to discover how wrong he had been.

Slumping into his chair, Darcy regarded Richard through half-closed eyes, unwilling for his cousin to realize how shaken he was by the news about Georgiana. "I can see you will not grant me any peace until I have revealed all."

"Now you are talking some sense."

Darcy grabbed the bottle of port from the table next to Richard and quickly poured himself another glass, quelling Richard's incipient protest with a glare. He would not tell the humiliating story without fortification. But after sipping his port, he fell silent, reluctant to relive the farce.

"Well?" Richard prompted.

"I…proposed to a woman, and she turned me down.…Something many a man has had to grapple with. Not much to tell actually." He strove to keep his tone matter-of-fact and his voice steady.

"What?" Whatever Richard had expected, it was not that. He simply stared at Darcy. "You—?"

"Yes." Darcy found his cousin's shock oddly disturbing, as if it confirmed the enormity of his failure.

"I cannot believe it! All of London has been holding its breath waiting to see who you will marry. For eight years, you have not favored a single woman. You have been leaving a trail of broken hearts in your wake—"

"I hardly think…"

Richard ignored his protest and barreled on. "She refused you? Who in the world would do that? Who did you propose to? A princess?"

"Believe it, there are women in England who do not care about my fortune. At least one. She refused me because she does not care for me." *She was right to do so*, a voice in his head whispered.

"She does not like you? Darcy, who is this paragon who has seen through you?" Richard meant it as a light-hearted jest, but it struck Darcy to the quick. He scowled; that was exactly what Elizabeth had done.

"Does it matter?" The words came out almost as a groan. Darcy rubbed his face, realizing how tired he felt. Hopefully, Richard would leave soon so he could stumble up to his bedchamber.

"Yes, because I am dying of curiosity." Richard sat up straighter in his chair.

"I think I would rather let you perish." Darcy no longer attempted to conceal his irritation.

"Wait, is this Miss Bennet we are discussing?"

Darcy sighed. "Yes."

"I noticed you were in a foul mood when we departed Rosings, but I believed that was because you wanted her but thought she was beneath you." Richard's teasing tone disappeared, apparently sensing how seriously Darcy took this situation.

"It appears *I* am beneath *her*." Darcy gave a mirthless smile.

"Come, it cannot possibly be that dire. I know she found pleasure in matching wits with you at Rosings. What reasons did she give for her refusal?"

"I am proud, arrogant, and insensitive." Darcy ticked the points off on his fingers. "Also, her opinion of my character was shaped by conversations with our great friend George Wickham....And....I helped persuade Bingley to separate himself from her sister."

"That was *her* sister you told me about?" Richard groaned. "I am afraid I conveyed that information to Miss Bennet." He appeared genuinely contrite.

Darcy waved this concern away. "It does not matter. No doubt she would have discovered it another way."

"These do not seem to me to be insurmountable obstacles. You can explain the truth behind your dealings with Wickham and fix the situation with Bingley. Then you only need to be nicer to her...I know that will be the hardest part." He gave Darcy a wicked grin, his teasing nature resurrecting itself.

Darcy stood and started pacing, rather unsteadily, on the carpet before his desk. "I already refuted Wickham's lies in a letter to her. I also confessed my sins to Bingley two weeks ago. Hopefully, he will forgive me someday."

"That was well done." Richard nodded approvingly. "Will he return to see the sister?"

"I believe he will visit Netherfield next week." Darcy stared bleakly at the pattern on the carpet.

"You should accompany him. Perhaps you can change Miss Elizabeth's opinion of you." Richard's voice was full of hearty encouragement.

Darcy considered it for a moment; perhaps his letter had altered her view of his character, but, no, it could not possibly change enough. He shook his head in despair. "I am afraid it is a hopeless cause. She made that abundantly clear."

"Surely there is some small reason for hope."

"She said she had not known me a month before she knew I was the last man in the world she could be prevailed upon to marry. I defy you to find cause for hope in that."

Richard gave a low whistle. "That is...impressive...."

Darcy raised his eyebrows in appreciation of Richard's reaction. "Indeed."

Richard rubbed his chin with his palm. "Well, she is a spirited woman with decided opinions."

"Yes." *That is why I love her.*

"So, may I ask, what purpose does the port serve?" Richard's voice was gentler and less teasing. Did he sympathize with Darcy's despair?

"The theory behind the port is that it dulls the pain and causes me to forget, at least for a little while. It also helps me sleep. And then the following day, I feel so awful that I cannot think of anything else."

"So that is the theory. How does it work in reality?" Richard asked.

Darcy shook his head, realized that it made the room sway, and stopped. "A life in tatters with drink is still a life in tatters."

"Surely it will get better with time," Richard said encouragingly.

"So I believed as well, but I have yet to see it."

"You need a distraction, something to take your mind from her," Richard mused. Then he stood suddenly. "I know! Some friends and I are going to Paris in two days' time. You should accompany us. It will provide exactly the distraction you require."

"Paris?" Darcy's port-soaked brain was having difficulty absorbing the rapid shift in the conversation.

"Yes, since the treaty was signed, English visitors have been flocking to the city. We will spend two weeks seeing the marvels of Paris. Come with us!" Darcy had to admit that his cousin's energy and enthusiasm were contagious.

However, the thought of going anywhere was anathema in his present condition. "No. I would—"

"You would rather brood and cause Georgiana distress? Come with us! A change of scenery is just what you need. Maybe you will meet some beautiful English heiress doing her Grand Tour." Enthusiastic about his plan, Richard walked restlessly about the room.

"No, I will never love another." *I will never get married. It will be up to Georgiana to provide an heir for Pemberley.* He knew this truth in his heart but did not voice this thought out loud.

"Fine, my friends and I will attend balls, and you can visit museums. Come with us!" He gave

Darcy a calculating look. "You know I will hound you until you agree."

Darcy shook his head, unequal to the task of arguing with his cousin. There were good reasons not to visit France, he knew, but at the moment he was having trouble marshalling those reasons to his cause. "Very well." He sagged in his chair. Maybe it would do him good. At least he could get drunk in France just as easily as in London.

***

Darcy stared out of the window at the passing scenery. Picturesque hills and gardens rushed past the window. He wished to be excited about the view and the prospect of visiting a country that had been all but closed to English citizens because of war. But instead his mind fixated on Elizabeth, musing about how she would enjoy the scenery and fantasizing about having her accompany him on his travels. Again and again, he recalled her arch glances and bright smiles.

Darcy still wondered why he had acquiesced so easily to Richard's blandishments, although the thought of being in a different country from Elizabeth was very appealing. Perhaps the English Channel was wide enough that it could dispel some of his heartache.

I need never see her again, he reminded himself. But then he recalled that he must surely encounter her when Bingley and her sister inevitably wed. *What if she has found someone else by then?* He tormented himself with the thought that she might be engaged the next time he saw her.

He had often entertained the uncharitable hope that Elizabeth was languishing at Longbourn regretting Wickham's perfidy. *But what if she never read my letter? What if she did not believe it?* Or, worse yet, maybe she still cared for Wickham despite everything. One horrible night, it occurred to Darcy that if she had not read his letter, she might marry Wickham. But, he consoled himself, she had no fortune, so Wickham would not pursue her. *I hope.*

This thought led inevitably to the recollection of her words when she refused him and the expression of her countenance. Before the day of the proposal, he had seen her teasing, happy, even offended, but he had never before experienced her white-hot anger. *From the very beginning of my acquaintance with you, your manners impressed me with the fullest belief of your arrogance, your conceit, and your selfish disdain of the feelings of others.* He grimaced, musing that he seemed to have a special talent for calling forth rage from an otherwise amiable woman.

Not for the first time, he wondered what had possessed him to propose to her in such an offensive way, although in the past week, he had achieved some small measure of understanding. *I occupied my time thinking about my own attachment to her and devoted no time wondering about her regard for me.* He had assumed she would be honored and pleased by his offer. If he was honest with himself, he would have to admit that he had expected her to accept him because of his fortune. Any hesitancy she might experience about his character would be overcome by the honor of his addresses and the material benefits he could bestow on her and her family. The irony was not lost on him. After shunning fortune hunters for years, he had presumed that his fortune would win him the woman he loved. *Has it so warped my very soul?* Had he actually begun to believe he was irresistible after experiencing years of women fawning over him?

He had believed Elizabeth liked him. All those teasing conversations…now he realized she employed humor to cope with uncomfortable circumstances. But he had never considered her emotions at any great length. This had been, he realized, only one of many miscalculations. *I wanted her to love me, but I never stopped to wonder if she did.*

He shook his head to clear away a vision of Elizabeth welcoming him with a warm smile; such love would never come to pass. Before the proposal, he could never escape thoughts of her, and such musings had been a guilty pleasure, but now these visions caused nothing but pain.

He shifted uncomfortably in his seat, drawing his cousin's attention as he glanced across the carriage with concern. It was a mark of how distressed Darcy must appear that his cousin had been more anxious than teasing with him over the past few days. Darcy managed a wan smile for his cousin but knew that it had not reassured Richard; the concern did not leave his eyes.

Darcy returned his gaze to the passing scenery. France was truly a lovely country, and the early June weather meant that the farmland was green and lush. They were nearing Paris, where they would join two of Colonel Fitzwilliam's friends, Major Broadmoor and Colonel Wilkins, whom Darcy had met previously and knew would be good traveling companions.

"So, what shall we do tomorrow?" Richard asked conversationally.

"My first object is a visit to the Louvre. What are your plans?" Throughout the trip, Richard had complained about Darcy's silence, so he found it easier to pretend an interest in conversation.

"I suppose I could accompany you to a museum, but my first stop is a patisserie." He rubbed his stomach in appreciation.

"I should have known! You came all this way just for the French pastries."

"*Mais oui*," Richard responded with a grin. "Is there any superior reason?" Darcy gave him the ghost of a smile. "I received a letter from my mother's friend, Mrs. Radnor. She is married to a Frenchman, Robert du Plessy, who is now an advisor to Bonaparte himself. They have a grand house in a fashionable part of Paris."

"Your mother associates with one of Napoleon's advisors?" Darcy arched an eyebrow skeptically at Richard.

"We are no longer at war, remember?"

"Old enmities are not easily forgotten. Many people in London do not believe the peace will hold."

"So it is fortuitous we are visiting Paris while we can, eh?" Richard gave Darcy a rakish smile. "Mrs. Radnor has invited us to a ball she is holding at her townhouse the day after next. Would you like to attend?"

"A ball full of the *beau monde* of Paris?" This was precisely the type of social event he had been avoiding in London.

"I believe it will be populated mostly by visitors like us or Englishmen living in France. Lady Radnor wrote that she grows lonely for her countrymen and holds balls to bring them together."

"That is no inducement. I do not want to attend a ball." Darcy scowled at the thought. "I left England to escape them."

"I thought you left England to escape Miss Bennet," Richard promptly replied promptly.

"I still do not wish to attend any balls," Darcy said firmly.

"Perhaps you will be introduced to a comely English lass."

"Poor girl."

"Or perhaps a fun-loving French lass." Darcy simply frowned at this suggestion, but Richard grinned, not at all discouraged. "I have not conceded defeat. We will improve your spirits somehow."

"You shall have to find another means of doing so. I will not attend any balls."

***

Darcy surveyed the ballroom at Radnor House. *How did I let Richard talk me into this?* he wondered for the hundredth time. At one time he had felt that he was master of his life, but now— between Elizabeth's rejection and Richard's machinations—everything seemed to spiral beyond his control.

It was quite a crush; all over the ballroom, ladies in glittering dresses and gentlemen in brocaded waistcoats and lace cravats were jostling and maneuvering just to edge their way from one place to another. It was hot. It was loud. Everyone had to raise their voices to be heard. It was exactly the kind of event Darcy hated. Watching the milling throngs, he contemplated strategies that would allow him to depart early.

Balls were particularly painful because they could only remind him of Elizabeth. Elizabeth laughing at him behind her fan at the Meryton Assembly. Elizabeth lightly grasping his hand during the dance at Netherfield. He even thought fondly of Elizabeth's rejection of him as a dance partner at Lucas Lodge. *I would give anything for a glimpse of her—even that angry and impertinent Elizabeth!* He sternly reminded himself that a glimpse would do him no good. She would never be his; she was destined to be some other man's bride. Angrily, he attempted to push that thought, and its accompanying despair, away.

As he watched the revelers, he realized he had been foolish to believe that Paris would help him forget Elizabeth. Everywhere, he experienced reminders of her: a yellow bonnet on the street; the melodious sound of a woman's laugh; a clever turn of phrase by a traveling companion. Even the sight of a lavender ribbon in a shop window had sent him into an emotional whirlwind. *If Richard knew the extent of my infatuation, he would give me up as a lost cause immediately.* Even as he watched the crowds of revelers, he noticed a woman with a hairstyle similar to one Elizabeth had worn. For a moment, his pulse accelerated, but then he glanced away, angry at himself for his reaction.

Chastising himself, Darcy threaded his way through the crowd to where Richard and his two army compatriots were talking with a few other men about the state of the peace between England and France. "I do not believe Parliament will ever consent to surrender Malta to France. No matter what the treaty says," said Major Broadmoor with a shake of his head. "Its strategic value is too great."

"They already agreed. Do you believe they will not honor the treaty?" Monsieur du Bois was a Frenchman to whom Darcy and his friends had been introduced by Mrs. Radnor. He spoke excellent, though heavily accented, English. "If they do not give up Malta, they will violate it."

"Napoleon has already violated terms of the treaty. He has not quitted the Batavian Republic," noted Colonel Wilkins somewhat emphatically. "Many in England believe he never intended to honor his promises."

"You may be correct," shrugged du Bois. "I do not agree with all of the emperor's actions."

"If both nations do not meet the promises set down in the treaty, we will be at war once again," said Major Broadmoor with a sigh.

"Yes, I am afraid so," conceded du Bois. "The emperor has already threatened war if Malta and Egypt are not evacuated."

"Yes, and Parliament is recruiting more men for the navy," put in Wilkins.

Broadmoor shook his head sadly. "If you ask me, Napoleon is simply taking this time to consolidate his hold on power and organize his army."

"Hopefully, the treaty will hold for some time, though. I am thoroughly enjoying my visit to your fair city and would hate to cut it short," Colonel Fitzwilliam said to du Bois, apparently attempting to steer the conversation onto less gloomy—and less controversial—topics.

"I am always pleased when visitors enjoy the city. Have you visited Notre Dame?" du Bois seemed to welcome the change in subject.

Darcy left to collect more punch as the conversation turned to visiting the city's sights, of which he was already weary despite the fact that over a week of traveling still remained! Not that he yearned to return to England; here, at least, he was relieved of the burden of pretending to Georgiana that everything was fine. Darcy ladled punch into a cut-glass cup and then stood to admire the view from the window. Half an hour more, he calculated, then he could claim fatigue and leave.

"Darcy!" He turned to see Colonel Fitzwilliam approach with a lovely woman on his arm. She had blonde hair, blue eyes, and a very young face. "Here you are!" Richard said jovially. "I was explaining to Miss Howard how you yearned for an English woman to partner for a dance."

Darcy's eyes shot daggers at Richard, who smiled innocently. "I have it on good authority from her brother that she is quite an accomplished dancer. And she was born in Cornwall, so she is undoubtedly English." Miss Howard tittered appreciatively at the joke.

Darcy suppressed a grimace. He had specifically told Richard that he had no wish to dance or to be introduced to eligible young ladies, but his cousin was convinced that socializing would lift his spirits. Sighing, Darcy conceded defeat. "Miss Howard, would you do me the honor of the next dance?"

Miss Howard blushed. "Thank you, yes." They talked politely until the next dance formed, when Darcy led the young lady into position opposite him. It was an enormous ballroom and dancers were plentiful, Darcy saw with dismay, realizing it would be a long set.

As the music started, they danced in silence for a few minutes. Believing it was incumbent upon him to offer conversation, Darcy cast about for an appropriate topic. "Do you miss Cornwall?"

She appeared confused. "How could I miss such a place when I can enjoy the pleasures of London and Paris?" She blushed. Apparently she blushed whenever she answered a question.

Darcy decided on a different strategy. "Do you enjoy reading?" he asked as they moved through the complicated dance figures, grateful that at least she was a fairly skilled dancer.

"Oh yes!" Her enthusiastic response was followed by another blush.

At least we have a common topic! Darcy thought with relief as the steps of the dance drew them apart again. "What do you prefer to read? Poetry? Novels? Plays?" he asked when they came together once more.

"Not so much." *What else? Surely she does not read many history books!* "I prefer to read fashion magazines. Did you know that this season the fashion will be for long sleeves?"

"No, I did not." Darcy suppressed an inner groan. *I will be revenged on Richard for this!*

They held hands and turned in the steps of the dance. "Indeed! Why you should see the illustrations in Godey's! Long sleeves everywhere. And sheer overskirts in very light colors on almost every page! I said to my mother, can you fathom such…?"

Miss Howard continued in this vein without any encouragement—or even participation—from Darcy, who found his thoughts wandering. At least her enthusiasm for the topic had chased away her blushes. Far from making him forget Elizabeth, this girl was making him appreciate his love's intelligent conversation all the more—and reminding him of what he had lost. *When did Elizabeth become the standard to which I compare all other women?*

As he awaited his turn to twirl his partner in the middle of the line, he saw another young woman standing on the edge of the dancing, attempting to catch his eye, and smiling coquettishly over her fan when he noticed her. Undoubtedly, many of the English visitors here knew his identity, and he was certain he would be subject to fortune-hunting women and their avaricious parents. He averted his gaze; he had no interest in playing such games.

With an effort of will, he pulled his focus back to the intricate steps of the dance. Realizing that she should allow him to contribute to the conversation, Miss Howard blushed and inquired about his opinions on music, agreeing completely with everything he said.

Elizabeth had never simpered and agreed with his every opinion. Too late he realized it was simply that she did not desire his good opinion. He so rarely encountered young, eligible women who did not want his attention that he had not recognized her feelings for what they truly were. *I must cease obsessing about her!*

The dance seemed to last forever. Darcy and Miss Howard moved down the line of dancers, encountering a couple with whom that they had not yet danced. Darcy stepped forward to take the hand of the new woman in the opposite corner and gazed up into her face. It was Elizabeth!

Chapter 2

Now I am hallucinating! he thought at first. *My longing for her has addled my wits.* But when he glanced up once more, he knew the woman was definitely Elizabeth. She appeared as shocked as he felt. "Mr. Darcy!" He had not hallucinated that.

Paralyzed by shock, Darcy faltered on the next step in the dance. A man from another couple inadvertently crashed into him, muttering an oath. "I beg your pardon," Darcy murmured as he swerved to the side, only to trample a poor lady's toes. With another apology, he finally retreated to his proper place and sought out Elizabeth, but she was swept away from him by the tide of the dance.

Mechanically, Darcy continued dancing, relieved that it was a dance he knew well, but he could not refrain from continually peering down the line of dancers to Elizabeth. She seemed flushed with surprise but had managed to keep pace with the dance. Darcy glanced at her partner, a man of perhaps forty. *He is much too old for her!* The surge of jealousy caught him off guard.

Darcy tried to make sense of her presence here. *What is she doing in France? How long will she stay? More importantly, how will she receive me?* Occasionally, he had fantasized about encountering Elizabeth by accident, but now that he was faced with her actual presence, he lacked confidence that he could change her opinion of him.

Will she even speak with me? He entertained the hope that she had softened in her opinion of him after reading his letter, but he had to be realistic; it was equally possible that she had torn up the letter without reading it.

However, he knew one thing for certain: he must attempt it. *Proceed slowly,* he cautioned himself. *You should be content if she treats you with civility.* Stealing another glance at Elizabeth, he recognized her yellow silk dress as one he had seen before, a very becoming frock that flattered her figure and caressed her curves. Clearly the intervening time had not diminished his attraction to her.

After he had neglected to answer several questions, his partner had given up attempts at conversation. When the dance ended, Darcy barely remembered to take her hand to lead her from the dance floor as he craned his neck to search the crowd for Elizabeth. There she was! She was glancing around as well. Was she searching for him? He tried not to raise his hopes, but they were acquaintances, so she would be rude not to greet him.

She glimpsed him and approached on her partner's arm. Part of Darcy's brain was rejoicing at her sheer nearness while another part was frozen with panic, certain that he would do or say something to chase her away again. His whole body was flushed with warmth and seemed to be suffering from a sudden loss of coordination, even his tongue.

"Mr. Darcy! What a surprise!" She smiled, but her eyes slid away from his almost at once.

"Indeed." It was all he could manage.

"May I introduce my uncle, Edward Gardiner?" *Her uncle! Of course, not some new suitor.* Darcy smiled with relief.

"Mr. Gardiner, it is a pleasure to make your acquaintance." Under the circumstances, Darcy was happy he had managed a coherent sentence.

"Likewise, Mr. Darcy."

There was a pause, and Darcy realized he must introduce his partner. "Mr. Gardiner, Miss Bennet, allow me to introduce Miss—" His mind was a blank; seeing Elizabeth so unexpectedly had addled his wits. What was her name? He could not remember it at all! *Could this get any worse?*

"Miss Howard," his partner supplied, and the others returned her greeting. Apparently giving Darcy up as a lost cause, Miss Howard mumbled something about finding her partner for the next dance and hastened off. There was a long pause as Darcy silently berated himself. *Say something!*

In the weeks since the disastrous proposal, he had envisioned what might occur if he were to encounter Elizabeth. He imagined being angry and cutting—or proud and superior, demonstrating all of the advantages in life she had forsaken in refusing him. Then, later, as he began to acknowledge the truth in some of her reproofs, he fantasized about being amiable and dashing, impressing her with his good qualities. And always he had dreamed of kissing her, removing the pins from her hair and…he stopped those thoughts before they went too far.

However, he had never imagined being tongue-tied and awkward.

"M-Miss Bennet. I must say I did not expect to find you in France." There, that was an unexceptionable statement.

Elizabeth seemed uneasy and would not meet his eyes, instead looking down to fiddle with a button on one of her gloves. Was that because she wished to be away from here, talking to anyone else but him? "I had no such plans the last time I saw you," she explained. "I was planning a trip to the

Lake District with my aunt and uncle, but then unexpected business called my uncle to France. They generously asked me to accompany them for the voyage." Miss Bennet's facility with words had not deserted *her*, he thought enviously. Perhaps she was not as anxious as he since she had no concerns about earning his good opinion.

There was a lull in the conversation, and he knew he should fill it. "Your parents are in good health?"

"Yes, they are all in excellent health."

He cast about for another innocuous topic. "How have you liked France?" When Elizabeth glanced up at him and blushed, Darcy realized he was staring at her rather warmly, but he could not draw his eyes away from her. He was like a thirsty man in the desert, and she was his water. After such a long deprivation, he could not readily relinquish the sight of her.

"I have liked it very well indeed. It is quite different from London in many ways, big and small. And it is simply enchanting at night." Elizabeth managed a smile. Was it for him or for the city?

"What brings you to Paris, Mr. Darcy?" asked Mr. Gardiner.

What could he say? *I was trying to overcome my despair at never marrying your niece?* "My cousin, Colonel Fitzwilliam, invited me to accompany him and a few of his friends. It was all very sudden. I had no thought of it a week ago."

"Where are you stay—" Mr. Gardiner was asking when a young man appeared at Elizabeth's elbow.

"Miss Bennet, the next set is forming." The man was fair and slender and carried himself well.

His clothing was well-made and very fashionable. Darcy hated him immediately.

Elizabeth appeared flustered, once again not meeting Darcy's eyes. "Yes, of course. Mr. Darcy, are you acquainted with Lord Lennox?" A chill went through him. He had a rival already!

"No." The two men gave each other perfunctory bows of greeting. When Lord Lennox took Elizabeth's hand, Darcy had to fight the impulse to grab her and remove her from his vicinity. Every fiber of his being screamed against allowing the other man to lead her away. Instead he struggled to keep his tone even as he focused on Elizabeth. "Might I have the honor of the next dance?"

"Certainly." She smiled, but the smile seemed cold and formal to his eye. Then Lennox whirled her away into the dance, leaving Darcy to wonder about her reaction upon seeing him again. Did she hate the sight of him? Had she already given her heart to another?

***

As Elizabeth danced with Lord Lennox, her feet remembered the movements, but her mind was occupied with thoughts of Mr. Darcy. She managed to reply distractedly to the conversational forays of her partner but essayed no topics for discussion herself.

It was beyond belief that he should be here in Paris; she felt stunned and quite unequal to the task of conversing with him. Elizabeth had fully expected to never see Darcy again. His letter had quite altered her opinion of the man, and she was ashamed to realize how grievously she had misjudged him. Encountering him again had resurrected her embarrassment at the words she had flung in his face at Hunsford. She would not have blamed Mr. Darcy if he had wished to discontinue the acquaintance or even pretended not to know her, but he had been all amiability to her and to her uncle, who was in trade and lived in Cheapside. He had denigrated such connections before but tonight evinced no discomfort.

Lord Lennox took her hand as she twirled in a circle, but her thoughts were abstracted. What had caused such a change in Darcy? Dare she believe he had altered his behavior because of her earlier reproofs? That thought led to an uncomfortable sense of responsibility toward him. Or was it simply that he was all politeness at a ball among his peers? That was most probable. He would likely revert back to his proud behavior when next she saw him.

Why had he not greeted her coldly and politely, as she expected? She glanced over and saw him conversing amiably with both Gardiners. Surely he was as embarrassed about the incident at Hunsford as she. Why, then, would he wish to further the acquaintance? He could simply greet her, chat for a moment, and continue on. Why was he lingering and asking friendly questions?

He had seemed…she could not immediately give a name to his unusual behavior: hesitant and tongue-tied. Although he frequently appeared a little ill at ease upon occasions such as this, she had never seen him quite at such a loss for words. Of course, they were both unsettled by the unexpected encounter, but it was more than that. Nervous! That was it; he seemed nervous! But why? Surely *she* did not inspire such anxiety.

If she was honest with herself, she was not sure how she felt at seeing him again. They had parted on such unfriendly terms at Hunsford, and she thoroughly despised herself for how wrongly she had judged him, so she was grateful he seemed desirous of reestablishing a friendship. This was an opportunity to show him that her opinion of him had changed—and yet, it was an extremely uncomfortable situation as well.

Elizabeth joined hands with Lennox for a promenade. They had fallen silent, but she could think of nothing to say. Certainly she did not wish for more than friendship with Mr. Darcy. Although she realized she had been incorrect in many of her suppositions about his character, he was still a sometimes proud and disagreeable man. She could not imagine forming a tender regard for him, but perhaps in time they could be friendly acquaintances.

How could I have been so wrong about him? she asked herself for the hundredth time. *He offered me his love, his life, and I threw it back in his face. It is a wonder he can even bear to speak with me!* In addition to guilt, she felt pity for the pain he had undoubtedly experienced. *I owe him an apology for my behavior at Hunsford.* She glanced over at Darcy, who was smiling and nodding his head at something her aunt had said. *I just hope I have an opportunity to deliver it.*

***

With great effort, Darcy tore his gaze away as Elizabeth and Lennox commenced dancing, only then realizing that Mr. Gardiner was still by his side. He struggled to think of something—anything—to say, but he was still stunned by Elizabeth's presence. *She is here! In the same room!* Part of him exulted while the other part struggled to maintain some semblance of rationality.

He was painfully conscious that Elizabeth's uncle was one of the relatives he had maligned during his disastrous proposal. Although he was not averse to talking with the older man, he felt the awkwardness of it. The silence stretched too long; he must say something. He turned to Mr. Gardiner. "How long have you been in France?"

With this innocuous beginning, they commenced a conversation. To his relief, Darcy found Elizabeth's uncle very amiable and of good understanding. Mr. Gardiner introduced Darcy to his wife when she joined them, and the couple described their travels so far. They were guests of Mrs. Radnor, who was a longtime friend of theirs from London, a fact which suggested to Darcy that he had misjudged them. Although she spent most of her time in France now, Mrs. Radnor had traveled in the best society in England. Despite his position in trade, Mr. Gardiner was obviously well connected.

The Gardiners and their niece planned to stay another week before returning to England. Mr. Gardiner also revealed the sad intelligence that business called him to Rouen, so they would be leaving Paris in two days. Darcy felt a pang; he had already envisioned how he could occupy Miss Bennet's every waking moment. *Do not get ahead of yourself. You do not know whether she will welcome your company at all.*

As he watched Elizabeth dance with Lennox, Darcy found it difficult to focus on the conversation with the Gardiners. In her yellow silk dress, her cheeks brightened by the exercise and her dark curls bouncing, she was simply bewitching. He noted with dismay that Lennox cut a fine figure and was an accomplished dancer. *Would that he were another Mr. Collins.*

Whenever Lennox touched Elizabeth's hand, hot waves of jealousy rushed through Darcy. He told himself fiercely that he had no right to jealousy, that Elizabeth was not his. *But she should be*, came the whispered response from the deepest recesses of his mind. Simply glancing away from the dancing couple did nothing to alleviate the sensations since he still felt his pulse quicken and his muscles tense as if his body was preparing to fight Lennox. Darcy gave up his attempts to ward off the jealousy and surrendered himself to the pain.

"I do not believe I am familiar with Lord Lennox," Darcy said to Mr. Gardiner, desperately hoping that Lennox was an impoverished nobleman who needs must marry a wealthy tradesman's daughter to sustain his way of life. Then Elizabeth would be safe.

"His family is from Surrey," Mr. Gardiner supplied helpfully. "They own a large estate there. His father is the Earl of Westfield, and we have done some business together, but it has been some time since I saw his family. Lord Lennox is the earl's oldest son and is taking his Grand Tour. He is recently arrived from Italy. Imagine my surprise to find him here!"

"Indeed." Darcy concluded sadly that Lord Lennox likely had plenty of wealth and could marry whomever he wanted. Nor did he seem overly troubled by distinctions of rank. Damnation! The last thing he needed was a rival. How had Elizabeth managed so quickly to attract the attention of someone who could actually offer *more* than Darcy by way of material advantage? And a title as well!

Maybe he was dancing with Elizabeth out of politeness, Darcy thought desperately as he watched her laugh at something Lennox said. On the other hand, *he* probably did not have a history of offending her and denigrating her family. That was definitely to Lennox's advantage.

"When did you encounter him here in Paris?" Darcy inquired.

"Two days ago, directly after our arrival. We espied him during a walk in the park. He has been to call twice since then, and he secured us an invitation to the Foxcrofts' ball yesterday," answered Mrs. Gardiner. Darcy made a polite response, abstracted in his own thoughts.

*Clearly Elizabeth is not just a passing fancy for him. Worse and worse. Why should he not be interested? She has everything he would want in a wife: wit, vivacity, intelligence, beauty...*Darcy had to stop the cataloguing before he drove himself insane. He reminded himself sternly that Elizabeth had rejected him in no uncertain terms. He had no right to impose himself on her again, but this reminder did nothing to stop the yearning. Every inch of his body longed to touch her, kiss her, make her his.

Mrs. Gardiner seemed to be watching Darcy very intently. Did she suspect his affection for Elizabeth? Had he been that transparent already? *I must stop staring at her.* But his eyes did not want to cooperate with this resolution. Since Hunsford, he had tried to convince himself that he had exaggerated her charms, but now he realized his memories had not done her justice. He was exactly as entranced as he had been at Rosings.

Darcy and the Gardiners watched the dancers swirl past in a riot of color. He reminded himself that all the enchanting behavior Elizabeth had exhibited prior to the disastrous proposal at Hunsford was not flirtatious. At Netherfield and Rosings he had been so certain that she was flirting with him, that she matched wits because she recognized his interest in her and was encouraging it. Her reaction to his proposal had proved how sadly he had misjudged her.

Bitterly, he mused that it would be better for Elizabeth if he quitted the field in favor of Lennox, especially since it would not be difficult for her to think better of him than she did of Darcy. When they spoke earlier, she was probably simply being polite to an unpleasant acquaintance, he thought, as the image of her angry face spurning his proposal swam before his eyes—accompanied by a familiar sense of despair. Did it even matter that she was in Paris? She still disliked him and that was unlikely to change. *Perhaps I should leave now before subjecting myself to further dashed hopes.*

No, I cannot abandon the ship. I must apologize to her. I owe her that much. Only a glimmer of hope remained that perhaps she had changed her mind—or could be persuaded to change her mind—about him, but that hope kept him rooted to the spot.

Finally, the dance ended, and Lennox returned Elizabeth to her aunt and uncle. Her eyes were bright from the exertion, and she was simply breathtaking as she floated toward Darcy. *Stop! She is probably enamored of this Lord Lennox fellow.* Then Elizabeth returned his gaze and smiled brilliantly. Hope, which had lain like a dying thing in his breast, staggered to life.

"Miss Bennet." Lennox bowed over Elizabeth's hand, kissed it, and grinned intently at her. Darcy stiffened involuntarily. She smiled at Lennox, but to Darcy's eye, it was a pale imitation of the look she had bestowed on him. Only once Lennox had departed did the muscles in Darcy's back and neck relax slightly. Now Elizabeth was his—at least for the space of the next dance. As their hands touched, Darcy felt a surge of energy, like an electric current travel up his arm—a sensation no other woman had ever created. As he glanced over at her, he wondered if she could sense it as well, but if so, she did not betray herself.

They exchanged a few pleasantries as he escorted her onto the dance floor. The room had grown even warmer, and as a result, there were fewer couples waiting to dance.

As the music started to play, Darcy tried to guess at Elizabeth's sentiments upon seeing him. Was she angry that he dared to present himself to her again? The memory of her words at Hunsford caused Darcy's blackest thoughts to close around him again. No, he must nurture the small flame of hope that had been kindled. Perhaps he could alter her opinion of him—if he was not an idiot again! But what was the hope of that?

He pulled himself out of his reverie. If he never spoke to her, he could never change her opinion. "Miss Bennet, I should demonstrate to you that I have attended to your reproof at Netherfield by displaying my skill at conversation while dancing," he said. She colored slightly at this reminder. "Your parents are in good health?" As soon as the words were out of his mouth, he recalled that he had asked her already. What was it about this woman that made him such a fool?

Although a smile quirked the side of her mouth, she did not tease him for his *faux pas*. "Yes, they are in excellent health, thank you."

"And your sisters?"

"They are all well. My sister, Lydia, is gone to Brighton to visit friends."

No other topic occurred to Darcy, and he fell silent, cursing his inability to carry on light conversation in general and his propensity to be tongue-tied with Elizabeth in particular. The dance drew them back into opposite lines, putting a temporary stop to conversation. Instead he enjoyed the sight of Elizabeth dancing, finding every move, every gesture, every flush on her cheek utterly enchanting.

The dance brought them together once more, and Elizabeth spoke. "I received a letter from my sister, Jane, this morning. She wrote that Mr. Bingley returned to Netherfield and has been to visit at Longbourn."

Darcy smiled slightly. "Yes, he told me he might."

Elizabeth's gaze was penetrating. "Did you encourage him? To return to Netherfield, I mean?"

Darcy was intensely uncomfortable revisiting a topic that had caused such strife before, but he should explain his attempts to rectify his officious interference. Hopefully, Elizabeth would take good intentions into consideration. "I believe Bingley had some thoughts of giving the house up, but I suggested he visit it again before making such an important decision."

"Very sound advice indeed." Her smile for him was genuine, and his heart felt buoyant.

"I am pleased you approve. I merely suggested he should see the house in a different season to see if it still suited him. And if he still suited…it."

"You speak about the house almost as if it were a person!" She was laughing now.

"In this situation, I believe the comparison is apt. It is, after all, a very *personal* decision." Darcy felt lighter than he had in a long time. She was teasing him again!

"Yes, very personal." Her eyes were shining, and he basked in her approval.

As they danced, Elizabeth felt the warmth of Mr. Darcy's gaze on her. She had forgotten how intense his stares could be. Before the proposal, she had believed he watched her with disapproval; now that she knew his gaze was filled with desire, she was uncomfortable for a different reason. Naturally, she was flattered, but the warmth of his desire alone was not enough to recommend him.

With relief she noted that he appeared as willing as she to pretend the proposal had never taken place. Still, she recalled his saying that his good opinion, once lost, was lost forever. Was it possible that his good opinion of her had survived the accusations she had hurled at him? She found it hard to credit that idea; it was far more likely that he was simply showing how he had overcome his previous regard for her. Recalling his confession of a resentful temperament, she had often envisioned him nursing his resentment.

Their conversation soon turned to their travels and the sights each had seen or hoped to see. Elizabeth allowed herself to relax slightly and began to enjoy herself. All too soon, the dance was over. As he led her from the dance floor, Darcy asked, "Colonel Fitzwilliam is here. Would you like to see him?"

"Yes! Very much."

Darcy tried to quell an uprising of jealousy in his breast at her enthusiastic response. He reminded himself that Richard could not afford to marry a woman with no fortune, nor would he pursue someone for whom Darcy had expressed an attachment; however, if she harbored tender feelings for his cousin, all would be lost.

They collected the Gardiners and made their way slowly through the crush of people. Darcy's superior height allowed him to spy his cousin; when they came upon him, he was still immersed in political discussions with his friends. His back was to them, and he was making some point with an energetic wave of his arm when Darcy drew up beside him. "I encountered someone of your acquaintance, Cousin."

"Indeed?" Richard turned, and his jaw dropped open at the sight of Elizabeth. "Miss Bennet!"

"Colonel, it is a pleasure to see you again. May I introduce my uncle and aunt, Mr. and Mrs. Gardiner?"

After the introductions had been effected, Darcy and Fitzwilliam offered to collect drinks for the thirsty revelers. Darcy had been relieved to see that Elizabeth had shown no more than polite pleasure at Fitzwilliam's presence. As they moved toward the refreshments, Richard shook his head at Darcy. "You are a very lucky man. You have another chance."

Darcy grasped his cousin's meaning but said, "I am not certain it *is* another chance."

"You had better seize it, or I will personally throttle you," Richard said with a growl.

"That hardly seems a throttling offense," Darcy countered, smiling.

"I am serious." Richard turned to his cousin with a sober expression on his face. "Do not squander this opportunity, or I will never endure your drunken self-pity again."

"If I squander this opportunity, *I* will never forgive myself." Darcy looked back to catch a glimpse of Elizabeth through the milling throngs of people. "But I do not know if she will grant me another chance. Back in London, if I had truly believed she would forgive me, I would have traveled to Hertfordshire immediately. Her presence in Paris does not mean she is willing to excuse my transgressions."

"But you do plan to pursue her again?" Richard followed Darcy's gaze.

"Yes. I must. I have no choice." Darcy ran his fingers through his hair and tried to quell the edge of bitterness in his tone. "But I have no idea how to go about it. I believed she liked me before when she despised me. How am I supposed to gauge how she responds to me now?"

"Perhaps you should give it up. It seems a hopeless case." Richard watched closely as his cousin responded to this sally.

"No!" Darcy's answer was immediate and vehement.

"'Twould be the rational thing to do," Richard suggested with the air of someone playing devil's advocate.

"Rationality has never played much of a role in my feelings for Eliz–Miss Bennett." He shook his head. "No, I must attempt it. I knew that the moment I saw her here." He paused, searching for words. "She already haunts my dreams...invades my every thought…I cannot be in the same city and not attempt to change her opinion of me."

Richard was silent for a moment, shaking his head. "I do not believe I have ever seen you like this…so agitated and unsure of yourself. You are totally lost."

Darcy's voice was a harsh whisper. "Yes, I know." As he turned to go, Richard caught his arm.

"May I make a suggestion?" Richard asked. "You need to court her."

"Court her? How?"

Richard shook his head in exasperation. "You are too accustomed to women throwing themselves at you."

"Miss Bennet does not—"

"Yes, I know she does not. Which is precisely my point. Most men needs must take at least a few actions to make themselves pleasing to a woman. Take her for walks. Give her compliments. Bring her flowers. Write her poetry."

"I cannot write poetry!" Darcy exclaimed.

"Maybe not, but it would be amusing to see you attempt it!" Richard's eyes sparkled with humor. "I am merely saying that you must exert some effort to be amiable and demonstrate that you desire her favor."

"I have been doing that!"

Richard shook his head. "Not in any concerted way. You must show her you are dedicated to the cause." There was silence while Darcy assimilated these suggestions. "I, for one, hope you will make progress with her," he said with air of a man making a pronouncement.

"Why?"

"Because despite your air of uncertainty and anxiety, you appear far happier than the man who walked into this ballroom." Then he added waggishly, "And you are far better company."

"Hope will do that to you," Darcy admitted, hating the vulnerability this discussion created. "But it could easily be false hope."

"She seemed fairly happy a moment ago," Richard observed.

"Yes, but that could be because she was happy to see *you*," Darcy said with a note of despair in his voice. "I am certain I remain the last man in the world she would marry."

"Maybe you have moved up the ladder a few rungs. Perhaps she would now consider marrying you before, say, the butcher." Richard grinned broadly.

Darcy grimaced. "Great encouragement indeed. I thank you." Richard laughed as they took refreshments back to the group—and Darcy considered how to woo a woman who thought him proud, arrogant, and selfish.

Chapter 3

The next morning, Darcy walked to Lady Radnor's house, which was not far from his inn. He experienced greater optimism this morning. Although he would have to apologize to Elizabeth for his appalling behavior at Hunsford, perhaps then she would allow him to court her properly. If he could not win her after a proper courtship, he would know she would never be his—a thought that made him extremely anxious. He swallowed hard, trying to fend off the black despair such ideas evoked.

When he arrived at Radnor House, he found Elizabeth standing outside at the foot of the stairs leading to the front door. "Miss Bennet, how good to see you!" He bowed. "Are you on your way out?"

Elizabeth seemed startled at his appearance and did not answer his smile with one of her own, seeming more disconcerted than anything. Darcy felt a lurch in his stomach. During the previous sleepless night, he had feared that she did not truly wish to associate with him and had only been polite to him at the ball—and now she appeared to confirm this fear.

"Yes, we, umm...are going to see the Tuileries Gardens. I have heard they are very fine." She would not meet his gaze but glanced down the street anxiously.

He tried to fend off an impending sense of distress with the thought that she might simply be uncomfortable at their first private conversation since Hunsford. "They are very beautiful," he replied. "If you would like, I could take you and your aunt in a hired carriage. It is quite a walk from here."

She shook her head sharply and fidgeted with the strap of her reticule. "Thank you, that will not be necessary. We…" Her voice trailed off uneasily. *Leave now!* a voice in his head cried. *She does not want you here.* But he could not bear to relinquish the hope engendered by her presence in Paris. "We…ah…" Elizabeth seemed to be searching for an excuse while Darcy's hopes sank lower each second.

Then two things happened at once. The door to Radnor House opened, and Elizabeth's aunt descended the stairs. Simultaneously, a very fine coach appeared from around the corner, pulling up smartly in front of the house—and Elizabeth.

The door to the coach sprang open, and Darcy's mood grew even blacker at the sight of Lord Lennox, every bit the eligible young aristocrat. Now he understood Elizabeth's unease. She had been waiting for Lennox to escort them to the Gardens. "Are you ladies ready for the beauties of the Tuileries?" he inquired of Elizabeth and Mrs. Gardiner. "Hello, Darcy," he added as an afterthought.

"Lennox." Darcy's voice grated as he nodded a greeting.

Elizabeth turned to Darcy with a small smile that—to his eyes—appeared forced. "It was a pleasure seeing you again. I hope you will come to visit another time." Darcy nodded, trying to keep his expression neutral. She smiled at Lennox as he handed her into the carriage. Lennox helped Mrs. Gardiner in and then thumped on the side, and the coach was gone.

The street was almost empty as Darcy watched the carriage glide smoothly down the cobblestones and turn at the corner. He was aware of a hollow ache in his chest. *She is indifferent to me,* he thought. *She may already have an understanding with Lennox.* Yet even in his despair, he knew that he would come to Radnor House again; he had to. Silently, he cursed himself for letting the colonel talk him into visiting Paris. He did not need to have his heart broken all over again.

***

The next day, Mr. Gardiner once again departed the house early to attend to his business. Elizabeth and Mrs. Gardiner had hardly finished breakfast before Lord Lennox came to call. Although it was ostensibly Mrs. Radnor's house, the mistress herself was occupied with an ill child; however, it was clear this did not inconvenience Lennox.

After half an hour of conversation, they had already exhausted the topics of the weather and the various beauties of the city. Lord Lennox was an attractive young man, but Elizabeth found his conversation rather dull and, unfortunately, plentiful. He was recounting a winning hand of piquet he had once played at White's when the butler announced Mr. Darcy. At this information, Mrs. Gardiner's eyes slid sideways toward her niece; she clearly had her ideas about why both men were visiting.

Elizabeth stifled a sigh of dismay. It had been awkward enough when Darcy had appeared immediately before their departure with Lennox the day before, but must they both visit at once? It was likely to be most uncomfortable. She reminded herself sternly that neither man had set about to disconcert her, but the awkwardness still embarrassed her.

Mr. Darcy strode in, but when his eyes fell upon Lord Lennox, he stiffened perceptibly. Had the two men previously had unpleasant dealings? But, no, Mr. Darcy had said they did not know one another.

"I see you have company. I will come again another time," Darcy said. His expression was as black as that day at Hunsford. As he turned to leave, Elizabeth could not bear the pain on his face. Regardless of his proud and unpleasant manner, she knew she had treated him unjustly, and he deserved better from her. She feared that her discomposure from the previous day had appeared to be coldness to Darcy.

"Please, Mr. Darcy," Elizabeth said. "We had little chance to converse at the ball the other night." Darcy turned back, focusing intently at Elizabeth, who scarcely knew what to think. He seemed to be under the influence of strong emotion, but she was unable to discern what he was feeling. She was also unable to ascertain how she herself felt; Darcy caused the most confusing tumult of emotions in her.

Perhaps seeing that as a signal, Lord Lennox rose. "It is past time for my departure. I have another engagement." His exit helped Darcy to a decision; he took possession of one of the room's ornately brocaded chairs. Mrs. Gardiner engaged him in conversation, making the happy discovery that her hometown of Lambton was near Darcy's home of Pemberley. Elizabeth noticed how animated his face grew when he spoke of his home and observed how amiably he treated her aunt.

Nevertheless, Elizabeth could not escape a sense of unease in his presence. Every time he turned toward her, she recalled the horrible scene at Hunsford and reviewed all of the terrible words she had spoken to him—and she realized she colored almost every time he glanced in her direction. Although he did not engage her much in conversation, his eyes were often upon her and having the most disconcerting effect on her. At the ball, she had been able to forget some of the embarrassing memories from their earlier encounter, yet today her mind seemed fixated on them.

She was also at a loss as to the reason for Mr. Darcy's presence. Although she had enjoyed dancing with him, their encounter was by chance, and he was under no obligation to seek out her society, particularly two days in a row. Elizabeth had assumed he would avoid her company so as to prevent the further mortification that memories of their earlier encounters must provoke. Yet here he was in Mrs. Radnor's drawing room, impressing her aunt with his good manners. She had longed for a private opportunity to express her regret over her behavior regarding his proposal; perhaps he might also wish to apologize, although he was so proud that she could hardly credit that thought.

Having exhausted the topic of Lambton, Mrs. Gardiner turned the conversation to Paris. With a great deal of energy, Mr. Darcy turned to Elizabeth. "Have you taken a walk along the Seine? It is quite beautiful, and I know you enjoy walking."

"No, we have only been here four days," she explained, uncertain of his purpose.

"Perhaps we could go now. It is not far." His voice was level and his face neutral; she received no hint as to the motivation behind the offer.

Elizabeth glanced at her aunt, who nodded cautiously, regarding Darcy closely. "That would be delightful, Mr. Darcy," Mrs. Gardiner said. Uncertain whether she was happy or anxious about this turn of events, Elizabeth left to retrieve their bonnets.

It was a beautiful early summer day. The sun shone brightly, but it was not yet excessively warm. There was no hint of rain, and Elizabeth was free to enjoy the beauty of Paris. Everywhere, she saw new sights to delight her: here a lovely garden, there a beautifully designed building. *The French know how to make everything beautiful*, she thought.

They walked toward the river mostly in silence. Elizabeth was content to soak up the beauty of the city as they passed. However, she was acutely aware of Mr. Darcy, his nearness seeming to overwhelm her capacity for speech and her thoughts constantly revisiting the question of why he had sought her out. Occasionally, Mr. Darcy would point out a famous landmark or building. Although Elizabeth appreciated his solicitude, she had read extensively about the city before her visit and had already seen many sights. It was as if he regarded her as a country miss with no education.

After a mile of walking, Mrs. Gardiner, who was not a great walker, allowed that she required a rest. Elizabeth offered to sit with her, but her aunt insisted that the two continue on and return for her later. Reluctantly, Elizabeth agreed. They settled her on a bench and set out at a brisker pace than previously.

They soon reached the riverbank and started to stroll along its length. Mr. Darcy did not offer her his arm; was he afraid she would not take it? Instead he took long strides with his hands clasped behind his back, and she struggled to discern his mood. She knew she must convey her apologies to Mr. Darcy, but it was so awkward. The whole situation was very anxiety provoking. Mr. Darcy paused near a pier on the river and pointed. "Along there is the left bank, and here is the Ile de la Cite, 'Island of the City.'"

Elizabeth's anger flared at his continued assumption of her ignorance. "I know, Mr. Darcy. We have been here some days," she said with some asperity. "Despite my lack of formal education, I do speak fair French."

Darcy grew pale, and his eyes darkened, but his face did not cloud with anger as she expected. "Yes, of course, you do. My apologies, Miss Bennet," he said immediately and resumed walking, his eyes downcast.

Her first reaction was amazement that he apologized so readily. Her second was embarrassment that she had overreacted to his completely benign attempts to show her the city. Were they always doomed to be at odds with each other?

As they continued to walk, his face was a pale mask. Finally, he spoke. "I did not intend to imply—"

Elizabeth forced herself to meet his eyes. "No, I know. I am sorry. I am afraid I am too sensitive in this matter. I do know some French but not as much as someone who has studied it in school. It troubles me upon occasion," she confessed.

"No, I am the one who should apologize. I do not wish to appear condescending," he insisted, glancing out at the boats on the Seine, the vendors lining the walkway—anywhere but at her. Silence fell as she struggled for an appropriate reply.

This was the opening she had been waiting for. Taking a deep breath, she spoke. "I actually owe you an additional apology."

"Miss Bennet?" His eyebrows rose in surprise as he turned toward her. She stopped walking and forced herself to meet his eyes.

"When we talked at Hunsford...I said many terrible and unjust things...and I believed lies I had been told." Her face grew hot with mortification, but she forged ahead. "I cannot tell you how sorry I am. I am exceedingly grateful that you do not appear to be bearing a grudge."

"What did you say of me that I did not deserve?" Darcy smiled bitterly. "I *was* arrogant and condescending. Even ungentlemanly." He gave a short, mirthless laugh. "I had always thought of myself as a gentleman. No one had ever accused me of failure in that regard. Although, goodness knows, others had undoubtedly thought it."

"But I never should have—"

He gave an ironic half smile. "I eventually discovered that I was pleased you told me your true thoughts of my character, even if it was painful. Although it took some time to reach that conclusion."

"At least let me apologize for believing Mr. Wickham's lies. When I read your letter I was so horrified at myself for crediting what he had said. Never before has my judgment been so faulty..." Elizabeth's voice trailed off. She looked down at her feet, no longer able to return his gaze as she recalled the horrible sense of shame she had experienced when she realized the truth of her misjudgments. She did not dare tell him of her even greater shame: that she had spread her negative opinion of Darcy liberally among her friends and family. He did not know, and she did not wish to inflict greater pain.

"Please do not reproach yourself," Darcy said. When she looked up, he appeared to be scanning the river, but she noticed a tightness in his mouth. The sunlight on his eyes darkened their blue to almost black. "I confess I am relieved that you believed what I wrote. I was not certain you would—or even that you would read a letter so improperly delivered."

"I do not believe that anyone reading that letter would think you insincere. Only then did I realize my horrible error in—"

Darcy turned his head and captured her eyes with the intensity of his gaze. "Enough, Miss Bennet!" His voice was both emphatic and strained; he seemed almost angry at her apology. "Please allow *me* to apologize for my abominable behavior at Rosings. The memory of what I said makes me shudder. Please permit me to make amends."

Elizabeth wondered what kind of amends he had in mind. "That is not at all necessary, sir—"

"It is!" He said it with such vehemence that she was taken aback. Seeing her reaction, he instantly softened his tone. "It *is* necessary that I beg your forgiveness—if only for my own peace of mind."

She hurried to reassure him, alarmed at the depth of feeling he revealed. "Do not permit it to trouble you one minute further. All is forgiven and forgotten. I had long since forgiven you in my heart." The relieved smile he gave this declaration was almost blinding. Until that moment, she would not have believed him capable of such an open expression.

"You are generosity itself," he said.

Unable to bear his eyes on her, Elizabeth recommended her stroll, and they followed the path in silence for a minute. Elizabeth drank in the beauty along the river: the intense colors of the summer day and the soothing movement of the water. Would she ever see Darcy again, now that he had unburdened himself? Now that she had accepted his apology, would he part ways with her?

Then she remembered his stormy face when he saw Lord Lennox's carriage the previous day. Was it possible he still loved her? If so, how would she feel? During the last months, she had re-examined her assumptions about his character and reviewed all of their encounters in light of her new understanding, but it had never occurred to her that he would renew his addresses. *No, surely my rebukes at Hunsford destroyed whatever affection he had for me!*

Abruptly, Darcy stopped walking and swiveled to face her. "Miss Bennet," his words poured out in a rush, "I would beg of you an opportunity to recommence our acquaintance, given what we now understand about each other. I would like a new beginning, putting pride and prejudice behind us." Elizabeth was surprised at his words and attempted to decipher his agitated manner. *He is nervous again. Nervous about me!*

The thought struck her forcefully. How could she, Elizabeth Bennet from Longbourn, make a man like him nervous? He *must* still care for her! It was the only possible interpretation. He must be violently in love with her to consider renewing his attentions after such a disastrous proposal. This realization sent a thrill through her entire body, recognizing how he honored her with attentions, now that she knew that he was not only wealthy but also intelligent and honorable. But could she reciprocate those feelings? Once, the answer to that question had been a definite "no." Now she was not quite so certain, but she knew she was not prepared to say "yes."

Darcy waited in suspense for Elizabeth's answer. It had required all his courage to even ask the question. Now he felt so vulnerable to her disapproval, but he had to discover if he had a hope of winning her. That would be sufficient for now: just a shred of hope. He dared a glimpse of her face, which was serious and thoughtful, betraying no hint of how she would answer his question. The uncertainty was agony, creating a sense that he was completely at her mercy and engendering a sense of helplessness that was unfamiliar—and uncomfortable.

Fear gripped him when he thought of her possible refusal. She was honorable, he knew. If she thought he could never succeed with her, she would not accept friendship. If she refused him now, he would know there was no hope—and there would *never* be any hope that she would return his affections. Then he would have to leave Paris at once and…go where? Scotland perhaps. As far away from her as possible. But even as the thought occurred to him, he knew nowhere would be far enough. Nor would there ever be enough time to recover from Elizabeth.

As he regarded her, she tilted her head slightly to one side in a way that was utterly bewitching. He knew she was unaware of the effect she had on him, but her every movement, every glance and sigh, was a delight.

Elizabeth realized her long silence was causing anxiety for Mr. Darcy. He was frowning and glaring at the ground but quite visibly restrained himself from hurrying her response, and she found herself admiring his self-control. "I would like a new beginning," she finally said. Relief flooded his face, and he relaxed visibly. "However," she continued. His eyes rose sharply to her face. "I cannot promise I could ever reciprocate any deeper sentiment than friendship."

Darcy silently nodded his understanding of this caveat. "Thank you for granting me another chance." Deeply felt emotion colored his voice. "Friendship is all I ask—for the present."

She raised her eyebrows at that last statement. Sometimes his candor was unnerving. They resumed walking, but Darcy stopped again almost immediately. Taking a few steps away from her, he made a little bow. "I am Fitzwilliam Darcy, miss, pleased to make your acquaintance."

She laughed at his charade and made a small curtsey. "I am Elizabeth Bennet. It is a pleasure to meet you. I believe you are from England, as am I. Shall we walk?" Smiling at her jest, he offered her his arm, which she took without reluctance.

After a few minutes of walking in silence, Elizabeth realized her companion was quite agitated once more. Frowning deeply, he glared at the path before them. "Mr. Darcy, is something else is making you unhappy?"

At first she thought he would not say anything, but then he spoke in hesitant tones that suggested the words were dragged out of him. "Please tell me. I must know if you have reached some kind of…understanding with Lord Lennox. I know I do not have the right to ask, but—"

Her quick reaction forestalled his words. "Lord Lennox? No!" The very shock in her face seemed to reassure him. "Indeed, I have no reason to believe he is serious in his attentions to me. While it is true that he has visited almost every day, I think it is mostly because he is bored with Paris."

"I think you underestimate yourself, Miss Bennet." He gazed at her intently; clearly he never intended to create a fiction that friendship was all he wanted from her. "I can think of many reasons why a man like him might enjoy your company."

"Perhaps you should share them with him when next you meet," she suggested archly. "Then he might view me with greater seriousness of purpose."

Darcy exhaled a laugh. "That would be contrary to my self-interests."

Elizabeth laughed; it was lovely to see these glimpses of his sense of humor. However, as they resumed walking, she felt more sober, realizing that he did intend to renew his addresses to her—an eventuality she had hardly thought possible. Still, Mr. Darcy was far more relaxed, and she was pleased she had been able to bring him some small measure of peace. If the price of his peace was slight discomfort on her part, it was fitting penance for her earlier misjudgment of him.

After a few more minutes of strolling, Elizabeth noticed the height of the sun and realized it was close to noon. She turned to Mr. Darcy. "We have walked a long way. Perhaps we should turn back and find my aunt."

As the three of them were strolling back to Mrs. Radnor's house, Mrs. Gardiner broached the subject of their upcoming trip to Rouen. Elizabeth felt a pang of regret at the thought of leaving Paris in only three days since there were still many sights she had not seen. And now that she and Mr. Darcy had made their peace, she actually felt pleasure at the thought of spending more time with him. She chastised herself immediately for these regrets. Her aunt and uncle had been very kind in bringing her to Paris; she should not resent the exigencies of their schedule.

Mrs. Gardiner regarded Elizabeth closely. "It does seem a shame to remove you from Paris after so brief a visit."

"It is fine, Aunt."

"Well, it occurred to me that Mrs. Radnor might host you at her house while we are away. Your uncle's business will bring us back to Paris in a week. We could collect you then."

Elizabeth's heart sang with pleasure at this suggestion, but she felt the need to exercise caution. "I have to admit, I would be pleased to pass additional time here. However, I am loath to impose on Mrs. Radnor."

"I will ask her, but I do not think it would be an imposition. She enjoys your company." Mrs. Gardiner's voice was brisk as she strode on ahead. Darcy had said nothing during this exchange, but Elizabeth glanced over at him just in time to see a faint smile grace his features.

Everything was soon settled with Mrs. Radnor, who was delighted to have Elizabeth remain and promised the Gardiners that she and her husband would take excellent care of their niece. The next day, Elizabeth visited some shops with her aunt, marveling at the quality of the cloth and trims that could be had throughout Paris. When they returned, they found Mr. Darcy waiting. His visit was brief but pleasant.

The following day, he appeared at Radnor House early, bearing flowers for Elizabeth, and suggested a visit to the Louvre. As the group wandered through galleries of fabulous art,

Elizabeth noticed that her aunt and uncle lagged behind, granting her some privacy to talk with Mr. Darcy. They were not blind. They had recognized his partiality for her—and they must have approved of him or they would not have granted the two such leeway.

***

The next day, Elizabeth bade her aunt and uncle goodbye early in the morning but was not surprised when Mr. Darcy came to call a little later, suggesting a visit to Notre Dame Cathedral. Mrs. Radnor excused herself on the grounds that her son was still ill and needed attention, leaving Elizabeth without a proper chaperone, but Mrs. Radnor did not seem alarmed. Although she was English, she had been living in France for more than a year and took a more relaxed view of such matters.

As they walked toward the cathedral in companionable silence, Darcy glanced over at Elizabeth's profile. She was gazing about her in sheer delight at the sights of Paris; it was a thrill simply to observe her take such joy in the city. When she had accepted his offer to begin their friendship anew, he had been overjoyed, but since then some of his optimism had drained away. Elizabeth did not seem to find his company burdensome, but she was reserved with him. While her enjoyment of Paris was uninhibited, her behavior with him—every glance and gesture—was polite and formal. She occasionally joked with him and teased him, but she was, in general, far more constrained in his presence than she had been before his declaration at Hunsford. He cursed himself again for the stupidity of his misbegotten proposal.

He tried to reassure himself that he should be pleased she had agreed to friendship, which was more than he had any right to expect. Nor was she attempting to discourage his attentions. However, he thought with frustration, she was not doing anything to *encourage* them either. Her whole manner seemed designed not to reveal any feelings she might experience. He had accepted this state of affairs at first, but now he wondered if she would ever demonstrate a warmer regard toward him. What did it all mean?

Once they had arrived at the cathedral, Elizabeth expressed awe at Notre Dame's beauty and exclaimed over every stained glass window. She conversed with Darcy about the building's history and the history of Paris itself, and he appeared impressed with the breadth of her knowledge on the subject. Silently, she thanked the plentiful collection of history books in her father's library. Although she did not have the advantage of a wealthy gentlewoman's education, at least she had compensated for the deficit with extensive reading.

Mr. Darcy was extremely amiable and agreeable throughout their visit. She found herself wishing she might have glimpsed this side of his character earlier. Away from ballrooms full of people and the necessity of engaging in idle conversation, he was more at ease and less somber.

Near the cathedral they found a little patisserie and, after collecting tea and sweets, settled into seats on the sidewalk in front of the shop. The night before, Elizabeth had found her thoughts returning again and again to Mr. Darcy. She had reflected that in many ways he remained an enigma to her, so during a lull in the conversation, she asked a question that was designed to elicit more information about her companion's character. "What is Pemberley like?"

He appeared surprised. "What would you like to know about it?"

She shrugged. "Anything. Whatever you would like to tell me."

He described the house and the grounds. When she did not appear bored, he went on to explain the estate itself and his role in managing the estate and the tenants. She listened with great attention, noting that this topic rendered him more voluble than any other she recalled. It began to dawn on her how much responsibility he held and had been holding since a young age. Many a young man in his position was known as a dandy or a rake, with too much time and money to waste—and insufficient morals to guide them. This did not describe Darcy at all.

He wound down his recitation. "I have been monopolizing the conversation, and I fear I have bored you. Please excuse me." Genuine anxiety shaded his face.

"Not at all," she assured him, trying to put all her warmth into her words. "Your description caused me to think how great your responsibilities are. You take care of your servants, your tenants, and your sister. But who takes care of you?"

He was quite taken aback by the question, and she instantly realized how forward it was. "Well, of course, the servants see to my needs, but I do not need anyone to take care of me," he murmured.

"Everyone needs someone to take care of them." She smiled gently at him.

His gaze became abstracted, suggesting she had given him something new to consider. "I suppose I have become accustomed to being self sufficient…at least since my parents died."

As an escape from the intensity of the moment, she gazed down at her hands resting on the café's table. She suddenly realized that caring for him was what he had requested of her when he proposed. Perhaps some part of him realized he needed a wife's care, but was she the appropriate woman to provide it? She did not have a good answer to that question.

After finishing their pastries, they retraced their steps back to Mrs. Radnor's house, strolling unhurriedly along the street, past shop windows, manicured gardens, and picturesque houses. Her opinion of Mr. Darcy was improving, she realized, but it made her slightly uneasy. It had been simple to refuse his suit when she felt anger and contempt for him; admitting to his more admirable qualities could open her to more tender feelings about him.

Now she recognized Mr. Darcy as a witty, responsible, intelligent, caring, and, she had to admit, quite handsome man. His attentions gratified her vanity, she realized, but she wished to be careful not to confuse that sensibility with true affection. For the first time since she had met him, she glimpsed the possibility that she could give her heart to this man. That prospect was disconcerting. He was pleasant and amiable now, but would the cold, unyielding Mr. Darcy reappear?

For his part, Darcy still found Elizabeth to be a mystery. Although she had relaxed a bit in his presence today, she was still formal and careful. Her questions about Pemberley had demonstrated her interest in him and his life; he was grateful for the attention. Was he imagining that she exhibited signs of tenderness for him? Was she only being polite?

Would she ever care about him the way he cared about her? The sensation of not knowing was almost like physical pain, which mingled with the almost unbearable pleasure of being in her company. Careful of her sensibilities, he had been leery of exhibiting too much affection, and the restraint was exhausting. Displaying the full power of his attachment, he feared, would frighten her away— but he felt heat between them whenever they touched. Had she experienced it as well?

Perhaps if he relaxed his guard a little and demonstrated some tenderness, it might stir similar sentiments in her. They were passing a park where children raced toy boats in a pond, and she watched them with undisguised delight. "You are very quiet," he ventured.

She grinned impishly. "Are you implying that I am being *uncharacteristically* quiet?"

He laughed in appreciation. "While it is true that you have decided opinions, it is also true that your lively conversation is one of the things I treasure about you." She colored slightly but did not object to this affectionate statement. *Dare I try more?* he wondered.

The thought suddenly struck Elizabeth that he loved her—apparently had always loved her—just as she was, despite any flaws in her character or her family. *She* was the one who wished him to be other than he was. The realization made her slightly ashamed of herself.

Elizabeth thought about making a saucy comeback to his declaration, but that did not reflect her true reaction. Instead she opted for sincerity. "Thank you. You are too kind." Her statement reminded her of something that had troubled her since Rosings. "I must confess that I sometimes find it difficult to make out your character. Since you often argue with me, I had believed you were my harshest critic."

Darcy seemed surprised by her statement and then turned thoughtful. "No, I was never that. Do you not see? I would not have crossed swords with you if I did not regard you highly. I rarely debate anything with Miss Bingley." He grinned wryly.

They turned onto a street lined with shops and crowded with people. Now Elizabeth realized that she had completely misinterpreted his actions. It was true that he usually ignored people whose opinions he did not value; she had observed him simply turn away from conversations with Mrs. Bennet or Lady Catherine. But he most frequently engaged in spirited discussions with Colonel Fitzwilliam and Mr. Bingley, two men he counted as close friends. Viewing their previous conversations in this new light compelled her to recognize how sincere and longstanding his affections for her were. Guilt and shame washed over her anew; how had she not realized this before?

"I am honored." Although the words sounded sarcastic, she said them with breathless sincerity, daring to meet his eyes.

"I hope you know," he said softly, "there are many things that I treasure about you." They had stopped walking in the middle of the sidewalk. The intense emotions reflected in his blue eyes took her breath away. His very proximity was mesmerizing.

He gently pulled her to the edge of the sidewalk, next to the window for a dress shop, where they would be out of the way. *What does he intend? Will he attempt to kiss me? Do I want him to?* But he did not bend his lips to hers. Instead he raised her gloved hand to his mouth and kissed it gently, his eyes never leaving her face. She experienced that current of excitement she always felt when he touched her. Whatever he read in her eyes seemed to encourage him, for he turned her hand over and gently kissed the palm. Then his lips traveled to the bit of skin visible between her sleeve and her glove. A tingle of pleasure coursed up her arm, and she closed her eyes against the sensation.

When she opened them again, he appeared concerned. "My apologies, Miss Bennet, if I am being too forward."

"No, not at all," she said faintly. Then she blushed to realize her statement could be construed as encouraging behavior that brushed the edges of propriety, but she could not bring herself to discourage actions that pleased her so much. Her heart was beating so rapidly that she thought he might hear it.

When she glanced down, she realized he had unbuttoned her glove at the wrist and was removing it finger by finger. She gave a shaky laugh. "I had not realized that I was granting you license to indulge in further forward behavior."

Now less concerned about her disapproval, Darcy continued his intimate attack on her hand. "You need only say the word, and I will stop." His voice was low and hoarse as he kissed her palm and the inside of her wrist. Shivers of pleasure ran up her arm and down her spine. He glanced up at her. "Does that feel good?"

Good is a completely inadequate word. "Yes, it feels…" She could not imagine a way to complete that sentence without leading to impropriety, but he seemed reassured. Removing her other glove, he lavished the same attention on that hand. When finished, he simply held her hands in his and looked into her eyes. The weight of his gaze created excessive warmth throughout her body. Beads of perspiration—which had nothing to do with the temperature of the day—dampened the collar of her gown.

Darcy gave a little shake of his head, as if willing himself to behave. After one more kiss to her palm, he tucked one hand under his arm—without restoring her gloves—and they resumed walking. Something had shifted subtly in their relationship, she realized; her acceptance of his actions had become a tacit agreement to his attentions. Part of her objected that she must not permit him to go too far, but another part welcomed, even cherished, his tender affection.

When he bid her adieu back at the door to Mrs. Radnor's house, he kissed her hands gently and lingeringly before slowly restoring her gloves to their rightful place. A shudder of pleasure surged through her body. He lowered her hands but did not break the gaze that was locked with hers. His nearness was intoxicating; she did not want him to leave. At that moment, she knew that if he wanted to kiss her—here on the street—she would let him. *What is happening to me?*

"May I call on you tomorrow?" His voice was low and husky. She nodded, not sure that her voice would work at all.

When he released her hands, she immediately felt bereft. He walked her into the home's foyer, where she was greeted by Mrs. Radnor's butler. Darcy gave a short bow to her, turned, and exited the house. As she watched his departing figure, she mused that when she had agreed to a "new beginning" to their relationship, she had not actually anticipated ever developing sentiment greater than friendship. Now she was not certain what she felt.

Nodding hello to the butler, she slowly climbed the stairs toward her bedroom on the second floor. Then a thought struck her so forcefully that she stopped halfway up the steps. Since she had met him, Darcy had often been in her thoughts, albeit frequently in a negative light. After Darcy left Netherfield but before she saw him at Rosings, she had dwelt on the injustices Darcy had done Wickham. But she now realized that she had focused her thoughts far more on Darcy's ill manners than Wickham's pleasing flirtations. Now she recognized that her reaction to him had always been personal—and intense. Certainly her conversations with him had challenged her like no others. She enjoyed lively conversations with Jane and her father, but neither was inclined to exert great effort in teasing out or questioning her opinions. Not like Darcy.

Originally, she had believed her impertinent reaction to Darcy was the result of his satirical view of her, but she had been wrong about his opinion of her. Was she also wrong about her reaction? Was it rather because her heart had recognized a kinship and connection with him that her mind had not seen? Shaking her head as if to clear it of bewildering thoughts, she climbed to the top of the stairs. One thing was certain: she was confused about her feelings for Fitzwilliam Darcy. Life had been so much simpler when she was simply disgusted by his pride!

***

The next morning, Darcy was awakened early by a rapid knocking on the door to his room. He groaned as he sat up, wondering what could possibly justify such urgency when the sun had barely risen. Then he heard Colonel Fitzwilliam's voice. "Darcy! Open the door! I need to speak with you immediately."

Now alarmed, Darcy threw on a dressing gown and opened the room's worn wooden door. Richard strode in, already fully dressed and clearly agitated. "The treaty has been broken! England has declared war on France!"

Chapter 4

It took Darcy a moment to absorb the news, and then he sank into the room's only chair in dismay. "How did you learn of this?"

"A messenger arrived from General Norland a few minutes ago. Napoleon wished for Tsar Alexander's assistance in negotiating a new treaty, but Parliament would not agree. The English navy is again blockading the French coast. We all must return to England at once. English visitors will be most unwelcome in France."

Darcy admired his cousin's gift for understatement. "Indeed." His mind rapidly considered the implications of this news. "But, Richard, surely your danger is greater than mine. Any military officers will be suspected as spies."

Richard shifted his weight anxiously as he stood in front of Darcy's still-open door. "Believe me, it has occurred to us. Broadmoor and Wilkins are packing. We are also taking a Major Brent with us. We secured a carriage to take us to Calais immediately."

"Yes, you must leave at once." Darcy rubbed his face, attempting to rid himself of his early-morning stupor.

"I am afraid we have no space for you in our carriage." Richard's face was flushed with anxiety as he regarded Darcy.

Darcy waved that concern away. "I can fend for myself, Richard. The French government will be far less concerned with random English civilians."

"But you must not delay. You should hire a carriage for Calais immediately. They will soon be in short supply." Richard's voice was low and insistent.

Darcy ran his fingers through his unruly hair and envisioned all of the English visitors in Paris attempting to depart en masse. There had to be hundreds, placing a severe strain on the city's available carriages and horses. Many of those English visitors were as yet unaware of the outbreak of war, but the news would spread quickly. No doubt some travelers would be trapped in the city without any means of escaping.

Richard stepped back to the doorway but still watched his cousin anxiously. His hand gripped the doorframe tightly. "I will not rest easy until I know you have returned to English shores. Promise me you will not tarry." His eyes focused intently on Darcy.

Darcy shook his head emphatically. "No. Believe me, I recognize the advisability of a hasty departure."

A voice called Fitzwilliam's name from down the stairs, causing Richard to turn, but he seemed reluctant to depart. "I must go." His voice was full of regret.

"By all means. Go. Godspeed." They clasped hands briefly, and Richard was gone.

Darcy dressed quickly and started to pack his trunk. His valet, Haines, had remained in England because his mother was sick, but now Darcy regretted not having his assistance. As he folded and stowed his clothing in his traveling trunk, he reviewed the steps he must follow to ensure an expeditious departure: settle with the innkeeper, find a reliable carriage, and—

Then it struck him like a lightning bolt: *Elizabeth!* Why had it taken him so long to think of her? She would have no means of leaving the city. Even without the inherent dangers of a woman traveling alone in a strange country, she would barely have the means to hire more than passage on a post chaise, and those spaces were likely to fill immediately. Her aunt and uncle might return to collect her when they heard the news; however, they could not possibly return before tomorrow. How would she escape to England?

He closed the trunk with a bang and locked it. Shrugging on his coat, he rushed out of the room.

Twenty minutes later, he was on the doorstep of Radnor house. Elizabeth and Mrs. Radnor, hastily gathered to the drawing room by his arrival, seemed surprised at such an early visit. Had he interrupted their breakfast? If so, they were most gracious. Mrs. Radnor gestured him to one of her ornate upholstered chairs, but he remained standing.

"Mr. Darcy, what a pleasure to see you again," Elizabeth said, although her voice betrayed some anxiety at the sight of his agitated mien.

"I have come on a matter of great urgency," he responded somewhat breathlessly. Elizabeth had gathered some embroidery, but it fell, forgotten, into her lap at his response. "England has declared war on France."

Elizabeth's hands flew to her mouth in horror. "What?" cried Mrs. Radnor. "When?"

"I believe the treaty was broken yesterday. But I received the news only this morning."

"So that is why Alexandre was called to meet with the emperor," Madame mused. She settled back on the couch, but her hands twisted in her lap anxiously. Elizabeth absently retrieved her embroidery while her eyes, wide with shock, were fixed on Darcy.

Darcy addressed Elizabeth. "It will not be safe for English citizens to remain in the country.

Colonel Fitzwilliam and his compatriots have already departed. I have a carriage awaiting me at the inn, but I first wished to make you aware of the news." He tried to calm the nervous energy flooding his body; it was all he could do not to grab Elizabeth's hand and drag her out the door to ensure her safety.

Elizabeth appeared deep in thought but murmured, "I thank you. I appreciate your delaying your departure for my sake." Irrelevantly, Darcy admired her calm reaction to the news. What a wonderful mistress of Pemberley she would be!

Mrs. Radnor spoke slowly and thoughtfully. "I cannot leave without my husband…and the emperor will not wish him to leave. I must remain behind."

"But, Madame—" Elizabeth started to protest.

"No, Miss Bennet, we will be safe here. The emperor holds my husband in high esteem. However, you must leave as soon as possible." Mrs. Radnor's face appeared serene, but she was compulsively straightening the folds of her dress.

"Agreed. But how is such a feat to be accomplished?" For the first time, Elizabeth's countenance betrayed anxiety.

"I am afraid I do not know. My husband has our carriage and we will have need of it. We could send you by post, but those carriages are likely to be full already."

"What about the Gardiners?" Elizabeth asked.

"I thought about them," Darcy responded. "When they hear the news, they will undoubtedly return to collect you, but they are better off departing immediately for Calais. They are much closer in Rouen than they would be here."

"No, they should not return!" cried Elizabeth. "I would not have them expose themselves to danger for my sake!"

"They *will* return for you unless they are aware you have already departed," Mrs. Radnor said firmly. "I know them." Elizabeth said nothing, but her eyes revealed that she recognized the truth in the other woman's statement.

"May offer a solution to this dilemma?" The conversation had arrived where Darcy had expected it to. "I can take Miss Bennet with me to Calais in the carriage I have hired. She will be quite safe." Holding his breath, Darcy awaited the women's reactions. What he proposed was highly improper under the normal rules of propriety, but he had no desire to follow such strictures if the alternative was leaving Elizabeth in danger.

Mrs. Radnor shook her head emphatically. "I appreciate the offer, but I have been given responsibility for Miss Bennet's reputation as well as her safety. I cannot allow her to travel unescorted with an unmarried man."

Inwardly, Darcy cursed the dictates of propriety, but he had also anticipated this objection. "Perhaps you could spare a maid who might accompany us to Calais? I would gladly pay for her return passage on the post chaise."

The woman thought for a moment. "Yes, yes, that might do. I could send Celeste; she would probably like a little adventure, and Miss Bennet is familiar with her. That would do quite nicely." She stood abruptly and rang for a servant. "Excellent! We have a plan. Thank you, Mr. Darcy. I will have Marguerite pack Miss Bennet's trunk and will make sure Celeste prepares herself." The butler appeared in the doorway, and she exited into the hallway to talk with him.

Now standing, Elizabeth gazed at Darcy awkwardly. "Thank you for your generous offer." Elizabeth's eyes met Darcy's without flinching, but he saw a slow blush creep over her face. He had no doubt she was grateful, but the prospect of sharing a carriage with him did give her some unease. Darcy understood completely; he had no doubt he would find the trip most disconcerting.

"Do not be anxious. I will ensure your safety." Closing the short distance between them, he took her hand in both of his and attempted to appear reassuring.

"I am not anxious. Not for myself. But if something should happen to the Gardiners—they have four children, and Mr. Gardiner's business employs a number of people. It would be a tragedy if…" Her voice trailed away.

How like Elizabeth to think of others in a situation like this! "Perhaps you should send them an express explaining the circumstances," he suggested. "They must not return to Paris in search of you."

"Yes, indeed! That is an excellent thought." Elizabeth withdrew her hand from his and left the room hastily.

Within half an hour, they had departed in a hackney coach for Darcy's lodgings, accompanied by Mrs. Radnor's maid. However, once they arrived, Darcy discovered the carriage he had hired was no longer to be found. "I begged him to stay," the innkeeper explained. "But the other travelers offered him so much money, he did not wish to refuse."

Darcy swore with frustration, realized Elizabeth was standing next to him, and swore more softly. "I would have gladly doubled their offer if he had given me the opportunity!" He turned to Elizabeth. "I apologize for this inconvenience. I did not realize the carriage driver was so untrustworthy."

"You have nothing to apologize for, sir," Elizabeth said faintly, but he could see a small crease of worry forming between her eyebrows.

"Please remain here, and I will find substitute conveyance." He attempted to appear calm and reassuring.

Elizabeth and Celeste waited in the inn's common room while Darcy and one of the footmen from the inn scoured the streets of Paris for a carriage for hire. As they were disappointed time and again, Darcy's anxiety increased; every minute of delay would make it more difficult to escape the city. The sun had risen in the sky, and it was turning into a steamy July day. Covered in the dust of the street, Darcy was tired and hot.

In their wanderings, they had canvassed a goodly part of the city, and he had noticed many groups of disgruntled Frenchmen angrily exclaiming about "Les Anglais!" The situation was ripe for mob violence. *We must depart as quickly as possible!* As he watched the footman exit yet another stable with a grim expression on his face, Darcy sighed and cast about the street for another establishment where they could make inquiries. His eyes alighted on something, and an idea began to form…

***

Elizabeth had a pleasant conversation with Celeste over some tea at the worn table in the inn's common room. In her passable French, she asked the girl questions about her family and employment with Mrs. Radnor. Celeste's English was only a little better than Elizabeth's French, so the conversation proceeded slowly. Elizabeth found her to be an interesting companion, but as the morning progressed, she became worried that Celeste was unwell. Although the maid denied it, she seemed feverish, shivering in the warm room and rubbing her head as if it ached.

The longer they waited with no word from Darcy, the more Elizabeth's anxiety built. Obviously, he was finding it difficult to locate some means of escaping the city. *What will we do if no carriage can be found?* It would be very dangerous to linger even one more day.

Finally, she saw Darcy's tall figure in the inn's doorway, silhouetted by the bright noontime light. Despite her anxiety about their plight, she had to admire what a fine figure he cut. He sank wearily into a hard wooden chair adjacent to the table. "I apologize for my lengthy absence! I hope the innkeeper has been taking good care of you." Elizabeth nodded absently. "There are no real carriages to be had in this city. I believe we have searched everywhere. However, I have found something that will suffice to get us out of Paris at least."

He rose, and she followed him out the inn's door into the courtyard where she saw a curricle drawn by two horses. It was a small carriage, meant for pleasure jaunts around the city, and could hold no more than two people on a small bench; it did not even boast a roof to shield the passengers from rain. "I bought the curricle and horses from their owner, so he does not expect their return. My thought was that the curricle would get us out of Paris at least. Once in the countryside, we may be able to exchange it for more suitable conveyance." Darcy watched her anxiously, as if fearing she would chastise him for not providing the carriage he had promised.

"This will do quite well," she assured him, and he seemed to relax slightly. *Does my approval mean so much to him?*

Then Darcy raised another objection. "My concern is that there is space for only two people. We must send Celeste back to her employer."

"I understand," Elizabeth said. "But you are a gentleman. I know I will be safe in your hands." He blinked rapidly, seemingly surprised and touched by her confidence in him. "And we can hardly be expected to adhere to rules of strict propriety during a time of war. Please, sir, do not make yourself uneasy on my account."

"Thank you for being so understanding," he murmured.

The next few minutes were occupied with supervising the tying of their trunks to the back of a vehicle not meant to hold luggage. Darcy gave Celeste a little money and sent her with his thanks back to her mistress. Elizabeth breathed a sigh of relief that the maid would be able to rest at home rather than sicken herself by traversing the countryside with them. Within minutes, Elizabeth and Darcy were perched next to each other on the curricle's high seat and moving slowly out of the inn's courtyard.

The streets of Paris were thronged with the normal noontime traffic as well as hundreds of

English travelers seeking to escape the city. They made very slow progress, causing Mr. Darcy some anxiety as he constantly scanned their surroundings and slapped the reins to urge the horses to further speed. They often passed wandering knots of angry, shouting men who made Elizabeth feel very exposed in the small carriage's high seat.

After passing a particularly dangerous-looking mob, Darcy took both the reins in one hand and pulled something out of the pocket of his great coat: a small pistol. Elizabeth regarded it with surprise. "A precaution only," he insisted as he laid it across his lap. "I purchased it from the innkeeper. I have seen anti-English mobs all over Paris. A small incident could set off a violent reaction."

To ward off her sense of vulnerability, Elizabeth pulled her shawl more tightly around her and tilted her head so her bonnet hid more of her face. She had to fight a sudden impulse to huddle closer to Mr. Darcy.

The helpful innkeeper had recommended a route out of the city that was less traveled. As they made their slow way to the outskirts of the city, the people and carriages were sparser. Darcy had just gotten the horse up to a trot when he turned the carriage onto a new street and immediately spied some debris blocking the road ahead. Although no inhabitants seemed to be about, houses crowded the street on both sides. When they arrived at the blockage—broken furniture combined with tree branches in a haphazard heap—he pulled up the horses and alighted from the carriage. Frustrated at any delay, Darcy hastily began to clear a path wide enough for the curricle to pass through. Elizabeth also started to climb down from the carriage. "I can help."

He shook his head. "Please stay there. I may need you at the reins if I have to guide the horses." Moving one last branch, he surveyed his progress, hoping there was enough room for the carriage to pass. Suddenly, rough hands grabbed him from behind and spun him around. He received a blow to the stomach before he knew what was happening and went sprawling in the dirt of the road. "Les Anglais!" a voice spat out.

Chapter 5

The voice of his attacker continued with a flood of French, which Darcy's brain automatically translated even as he realized that several voices were shouting. "Don't let the English filth escape! Make them pay!" Still on the ground, he stared up into the faces of his attackers, a group of five rough-looking men glaring at him with anger and hatred. Darcy pushed himself to his feet, but two men immediately came forward and grabbed his arms. In French, he attempted to reason with them. "We are only trying to leave the city. We have no quarrel with you. Please, I have a frightened young lady with me." Several of the men leered at Elizabeth, and he instantly wished he had not drawn their attention to her.

While he spoke, he felt in the pocket of his great coat. With a sense of despair, he realized he had left the pistol on the seat of the carriage. He had to protect Elizabeth! But now he realized that in attempting to save her, he had led her into greater danger!

Attempting to formulate a plan, he thrust his hands further into his pockets, finding a few francs which he proffered in one hand. The sight of the coins distracted some of the men, as he intended. He dropped the francs on the ground, and two of the men raced to retrieve them; however, the other men's arms holding him held firm. *Not distracted enough*, he thought ruefully. He had additional money in his trunk and thought about bribing their way free, but the men had no reason to treat them well once they had the money; Darcy was in no position to bargain.

The biggest man, apparently the mob's unofficial leader, picked up a board with several nails still sticking out of it. Menace radiated from every inch of his body. He raised it over his head, preparing to strike Darcy, who struggled—to no avail—to escape his captors' grip. Staring at the jagged nails, Darcy braced himself for the blow.

Then he heard a woman's voice. "*Arretez!*" Elizabeth stood in the curricle, the pistol pointed directly at his attackers. "Let him go!" The men stared at her in astonishment. "*Maintenant!*" As she made an angry gesture, her face was fierce, and her manner was very commanding. The hands holding Darcy loosened their grip, and he quickly shrugged them off. He launched himself toward the curricle, knowing that now was the time to make good their escape before the thugs realized how they could use their superior numbers to overcome one woman with a pistol.

Elizabeth sank down to the seat as he climbed up into it. "Keep the pistol trained on them!" he hissed to her as he took up the reins, and she immediately made a threatening gesture with the gun at the men who stood in the road.

"*Deplacez*! Now! *Maintenant*! " The men stared at the gun but then slowly shifted out of the way. Their leader looked down and spat in the dirt, muttering to himself, clearly deciding it would not be worth the trouble to attack the English couple. Darcy slapped the reins and maneuvered the horse through the breach he had created in the barrier; for the first time, he was grateful that their conveyance was small and narrow. After they passed though the barrier, Elizabeth turned on the seat so she could point the pistol on any ruffians who might follow them. Darcy slapped the reins again, urging the horses into a run, and they soon left the thugs far behind.

Fortunately, the curricle quickly reached the countryside. There were few other carriages; the only people they saw were working in the fields far from the road. Darcy slowed the horses to a trot, not wanting to exhaust the creatures, as Elizabeth relaxed her death grip on the pistol, and it fell into her lap. It was only then that Darcy realized her hands were trembling violently. "I do not believe I have ever been so frightened in my entire life. Not even when Charlotte Lucas's brother tricked me into running through the bull pasture, and it chased me!" She laughed a little shakily.

What a woman! he thought. *Capable of making a jest even in these straitened circumstances.* Most women of his acquaintance would be having hysterics. *No wonder I fell in love with her!* "Thank you for your quick thinking. You saved my life." He noticed that his voice was low and husky with emotion.

"My thinking was not at all quick. It took me forever to recall the pistol lying beside me." She shook her head self-deprecatingly, rubbing the palms of her hands against her skirt in an attempt to dry them. Gingerly, she handed the pistol back to him, and he stowed it in his coat.

Darcy chuckled. "It was very timely as far as I am concerned."

"I was grateful they did not challenge me further," Elizabeth admitted, wrapping her arms around herself. "I have no idea how to fire a pistol. They would have laughed to see me attempt it."

"You were very convincing." He glanced over at her. Although her expression was resolute, he could see that she was trembling all over. It was all he could do not to take her in his arms and embrace her until the shaking subsided. He wanted to pull down her hair, bury his face in it, and kiss her neck… *I must quit this line of thought before it spins out of control. She trusts me to be a gentleman!* She had no idea how much her simple statement of trust back in the inn had affected him. In that instant, he had resolved to live up to her trust in him. Given her recent fright, she did not need to fend off a too ardent—and perhaps unwelcome— admirer. Still, he watched her clasp her gloved hands shakily together and wished he could help her quell her nerves.

Daringly, he held the soft leather reins in one hand while reaching over and enclosing one of her hands in his. She stiffened perceptibly, and he thought she would draw her hand away. Then she relaxed a little and smiled, but she did not turn in his direction or meet his eyes. "Mr. Darcy, I believe you are trying to take advantage of my discomposure to flirt with me!"

The pert tone in her voice told him she was not truly offended. "Am I not permitted to provide you with one shred of comfort?" He tried to match her light tone.

"Comfort? I do not believe etiquette books for young women cover the topic of comfort!" She gave a little laugh that he found completely endearing.

"A serious deficiency," Darcy said solemnly.

"Indeed, I believe I will write to the author of my mother's favorite book and suggest that he discuss appropriate behavior when escaping an angry mob in France with an unmarried gentleman. That subject was sorely neglected in the last edition!" She smiled at him mischievously.

Now he laughed aloud and again fought an almost irresistible impulse to take her into his arms. Her ability to notice the absurd and humorous in any circumstance delighted him. At the same time, he attempted to remind himself that even though she accepted a modicum of comfort, it did not mean that her opinion of him had changed. Regretfully, he released her hand, not wishing her to believe that he was taking advantage of their circumstances.

Silence stretched between them as the horses continued at a sedate trot. Although Elizabeth had made light of the situation, he could not help but dwell on the impropriety: unrelated single men and women should never travel together. If word of this journey reached England, everyone would assume he had compromised her, and her father would demand that Darcy marry her. That would not be such a bad fate as far as Darcy was concerned. But, no, he did not desire her consent under those circumstances. He could not imagine her reaction to be coerced in such a way, but it would not be good.

What was her true reaction to traveling with him? She had joked about it, but the humor could mask discomfort. Perhaps she had been uncomfortable when he took her hand. He cleared his throat. "I…apologize for the impropriety. I wish we could have brought Mrs. Radnor's maid for your comfort."

She gazed steadily at her hands clasped in front of her. "Please do not apologize again for circumstances beyond your control. I know you would never take advantage."

She would not be so sanguine if she knew some of the fantasies I have had about her, Darcy thought. Nevertheless, he was touched that she voiced her trust of him so forthrightly and decisively. *Dare I hope her opinion of me is improving? Perhaps I now rank above a shopkeeper!* He smiled a little at the thought.

"Mr. Darcy?" Elizabeth glanced at him questioningly.

"I had viewed our time in Paris as an opportunity to demonstrate my better nature," he explained. "Instead I have displayed a talent for getting you alone."

This brought no laughter from her; instead she seemed pensive. "On the contrary, I believe you have shown a loyalty and resourcefulness that are quite admirable. I could never have escaped Paris on my own." Her compliments spread warmth throughout his body.

He smiled at her. "I should denigrate myself more often just for the pleasure of hearing you sing my praises. Perhaps I should describe myself as unpleasant and ugly?"

She laughed aloud at this until she gasped for breath. "And to think I once believed you had no sense of humor!" *Her opinion of me* is *improving,* he thought happily. Hope surged through him.

"I am afraid you have not always seen me at my best," he confessed, keeping his eyes fixed steadily on the road.

He sensed her eyes were watching him. "I am beginning to understand that." He turned slightly to gaze into her face. The intimacy of her tone made him shiver a little, and her fine blue eyes were so captivating that he thought he could never tear his away. Suddenly, he wished they were in a drawing room somewhere and not on a carriage seat where he could not view her easily or take her in his arms. *Just as well I do not have the chance to do something foolish and impulsive.* For a moment, he considered pulling the curricle to the side of the road so they could talk, but he knew they could not afford to waste time. He thought of the irony. *I have longed for a chance to get Elizabeth alone and uninterrupted but not under circumstances such as these.*

***

Several hours later, silence had fallen over the travelers. The sky was gray and overcast, suiting Elizabeth's mood. Although the countryside was pretty enough, it was unvarying—mostly farmland—and she was weary of it. She watched Darcy's large capable hands handle the reins and wished she could decipher the puzzle this man represented. Although his letter had compelled her to modify her worst opinions about him, she had still considered him proud and difficult. After all, his harsh words about her family had been heartfelt, if tactless—although she was forced to admit he had not been entirely wrong either.

When she had encountered him at the ball in Paris, he had been amiable but still proud and reserved. Now, however, she was seeing a very different side of him. When not surrounded by other people, he was more quick-witted and relaxed. She was conscious not only of the honor of his attention but also the depth of caring he exhibited for her. Although she liked to think of herself as independent and capable, she recognized that she had needed his help to escape Paris, and she found his devotion to her protection—even to the point of jeopardizing his life—somewhat thrilling. It filled her with warmth to think that he valued her that highly.

Her thoughts about him were quite different from what they had been when she had arrived in France. She no longer experienced anger or antipathy or even wounded pride. In their place she felt admiration and affection, but was there more in her heart? She had never been in love. How did it feel?

Darcy's hand brushed against her arm as he shifted on the hard wooden bench, and again she felt that familiar tingle of electricity, a physical rush of energy that she had experienced with no other man. What did it mean? All of these questions were causing a headache; she rubbed her forehead with her hand.

She studied Darcy's profile as he gazed intently at the road ahead. What did Darcy experience when their hands touched? Did he sense the same electricity? A little shiver passed through her. His proximity and sheer masculinity were a little intimidating but also somewhat exciting. *What is happening to me? I never used to have such thoughts!*

When he had proposed at Hunsford, she had not believed that he truly loved her; rather he had seemed infatuated with a concept of how he wished she would be—if she were separated from her family. Recently, however, his constant devotion and sensitivity to her comfort had convinced her that his love for her was genuine. And his conversation had convinced her that he understood her far better than she had given him credit for.

She must take his affection seriously, but she had been more comfortable when it could be easily dismissed. What had she given him in exchange for his devotion? He had risked his life and reputation for a woman who had refused his proposal in an angry and insulting manner. Had Elizabeth even granted him hope that her opinion might change? Or shown him that it had already altered somewhat? Did he believe that he was risking his life for a woman who would still angrily refuse him? She contemplated whether there was some way to demonstrate how her thoughts had changed.

Slowly and deliberately, Elizabeth put her hand on the bench between her and Darcy. He did not seem to notice at once, and it rested there a moment, but she discerned a slight stiffening in his posture. Then he unhurriedly placed his hand on top of hers. Elizabeth blushed and smiled but did not turn toward him, unready for that step. Darcy had a small smile on his face as well, and when she did not pull her hand away, he consolidated his hold by further intertwining her fingers with his. Elizabeth found the small gesture both thrilling and comforting.

***

Later in the afternoon, their conversation turned to books, discovering that they shared many common interests in poetry, history, and the plays of Shakespeare. When they discussed contemporary novels, Darcy had some strong opinions about their value, and they were not complimentary. While Elizabeth allowed that many novels were lurid or overly sentimental, she maintained that many were well worth reading. Darcy took the opposing view, apparently without having read many of the books in question.

When she discovered the potential conflict, Elizabeth said amiably, "Well, it appears we cannot agree on this point. Have you read the latest volume of Wordsworth?" Darcy was silent for so long that Elizabeth feared she had offended him somehow. "Mr. Darcy?"

Her inquiry roused him from his reverie, and he peered at her intently. "I have never known you to retreat from an argument before."

"Are you asking me to quarrel with you?" She shifted on the unyielding wooden seat. Every muscle in her body now ached like her head, and she had no energy for her usual verbal sparring.

"Not on principle. However I would hope you are frank with me when your opinions differ from mine."

Elizabeth weighed her response for a moment before replying. "When I have been frank with you in the past, I have made some hurtful declarations. I have many sins to atone for."

"Must you do so by agreeing with me?" An ironic smile quirked up one side of his mouth.

Elizabeth forced herself to think clearly through the fatigue that clouded her mind. "Earlier in Netherfield and Rosings, your good opinion did not matter to me." His face darkened at this reminder, and he shifted his gaze back to the dusty road. "Now it does. Furthermore, you are risking your life to save mine. Surely that deserves some consideration."

"Find another way to show it." The words came out almost as a growl. Now she was certain he was offended, but she reminded herself that she had misunderstood him before. His commanding ways did not always demonstrate disapproval.

"You truly wish me to disagree with you?"

"I wish to hear what you are truly thinking. I know you are capable of that." He sighed, struggling to articulate his thoughts. "I receive very

little frankness from most of the people in my life."
She suddenly recalled that he did not regard Miss
Bingley as worth arguing with.

"You wish to know what I truly think?" This
conversation was important; she pushed herself to
focus on it.

He suddenly seemed very wary, every muscle
in his body tense, but he nodded. "Yes."

"I think you are a very good man." She could
see his profile as he started a little and then turned
to see if she was serious. They locked eyes for a
moment, and then he gave a small smile.

"Thank you, Miss Bennet."

She shrugged. "You asked me to be honest."

Silence fell between them for a few minutes.
Elizabeth was quite eager to quit the carriage. As
she adjusted her bonnet, her head felt too large and
swollen all out of proportion. The sunlight was
weak on a cloudy day, but it still seemed too bright
to her. She had never experienced such a headache!
Was it the weather? It had been cool and damp all
day. Pressing at her temples, she wished she could
somehow relieve the pressure in her head.

"All you well?" Darcy regarded her with
concern.

"Just a headache."

"We shall arrive at a small town in about an
hour. Hopefully, we can exchange these horses for
fresh ones. Perhaps we may rest for an hour and
obtain some tea."

She nodded, but even that small movement hurt.
What was wrong with her head? As her foggy brain
pondered this question, she felt the first fat raindrop
land on her arm. "Oh dear!" She peered up at the
low-hanging clouds in dismay as the first drop was
followed by a multitude of others. In a matter of

minutes, her clothes were soaked. She pulled her shawl around her head, but it provided little protection.

Darcy regarded her with alarm. "Please take my coat." He made a move to shrug it off.

"No. Please, I cannot."

"I insist. I also have a waistcoat and shirt. You have only a dress."

"You are driving this carriage. Our well-being depends on your ability to guide the horses. My well-being is not so essential."

"On the contrary, your well-being is absolutely vital," he said through gritted teeth. She shook her head but said nothing. He appeared about to argue further, but she set her chin, waiting to counter his arguments. He finally just sighed. "In town I will search out an inn where we can await the passing of the rain." She nodded, attempting not to think about how cold and wet she was.

Darcy was growing increasingly concerned about Elizabeth. Over the past hour, she had fallen into a kind of stupor, saying nothing, staring into space, and only moving in occasional violent shivers. He recalled that Mrs. Radnor's son had been ill, and the maid Celeste had appeared unwell. Elizabeth could easily have contracted a fever or other illness, which the rain had then exacerbated.

He turned his gaze away from the endless road and toward Elizabeth. Her eyes were closed, and her head was drooping, but he could not imagine she could sleep under such circumstances. Then, even as he watched, she began to sway alarmingly, coming perilously close to pitching off the edge of the high carriage seat. Putting the reins in one hand, he quickly flung the other arm around Elizabeth before she could topple out of the carriage altogether.

She awakened instantly. "Mr. Darcy!"

The last thing he needed was for her to believe that he was taking liberties! "You were about to pitch off the seat. I believe you fell asleep."

Her tense muscles relaxed a little under his arm. "It is possible, I am quite tired. I am not sure why." She shivered violently. "It is so cold." It had stopped raining, although the sky was still overcast. Darcy refrained from observing that it was a rather mild July day.

"Perhaps we should get rooms for the night at the next town."

She brushed hair impatiently out of her eyes. "I thought we would attempt to reach to Calais today."

"We have not made as good time as I had hoped, and the roads are now muddy. We are still quite a ways from Calais. It would be better if we rested and started fresh tomorrow."

"But—"

"Miss Bennet, you require rest," he said in his firmest voice.

"You are accustomed to people doing what you tell them, I can see." Her smile took the barb out of her words.

"No…well…yes." He smiled a little at her riposte. "However, in this case I am correct. I believe you are ill."

She immediately straightened up on the seat. "I am fine."

"Are you in the habit of falling asleep on carriage seats?" His voice was acerbic.

"Well, no…"

Without asking permission, Darcy stripped off his glove and put his hand to her forehead. She opened her mouth to protest the impropriety but then closed it again at the alarmed expression on his face. "You are burning up! We must get you to an inn at once and find a doctor!"

He slapped the reins and urged the horse into a brisker pace, causing Elizabeth alarm. "Additional haste is not required! I am certain it is just a trifling cold. We should do nothing that will delay our departure."

"We shall see what the doctor says." His face was implacable.

***

Half an hour later, Elizabeth was sitting on a battered chair in the crowded common room of a little inn while Darcy talked with the proprietor. Grudgingly, she admitted to herself that she was not at all well. Her body was exhausted and seemed to ache all over. Her head pulsed with pain, and the thought of lying down was very appealing, although there was no space. Nonetheless, she found Darcy's devoted attention to be somewhat embarrassing. She wished to cause him no further trouble, but he insisted that she needed a doctor. *If I could only sleep a couple of hours, I would be much improved*, she told herself. Darcy was worrying himself needlessly, she was certain.

She glanced around the busy room; it was full of weary travelers, many of them English. The noise was overpowering as was the stench of unwashed bodies, making her wish she could return to the cold, wet seat in the curricle. It occurred to her that Darcy might not find a room to let; there had been a large number of carriages resting in front of the inn when theirs had pulled up. Undoubtedly, the news of the war had caused many people to rush to Calais, and since this inn was on the route, it would be popular.

Finally, Darcy sank wearily into the other chair at her table. Resting his elbows on the scarred surface, he shook his head. "There is no room at the inn."

"Indeed, I suppose I should be happy we are not traveling by donkey," she intoned solemnly.

For a moment, Darcy thought she was delirious with fever, and then he laughed. "Yes, although Joseph and Mary did not need to contend with rain-soaked roads or war."

To his eye, her answering smile seemed forced. *She wishes to hide how ill she truly feels.*

"Are there other inns in the town?" she asked.

"No," he said, regret coloring his voice. "It is a very small village, and there are no other towns nearby."

"I suppose we will simply ride to the next village." Placing her hands on the table, she pushed herself into a standing position, smiling bravely.

"Not necessarily. I had a thought. When I saw the name of this village, I recalled that a friend of mine lives nearby." Listening, she sank back into her chair. "Thomas Whitmore. I know him from Cambridge. He became a clergyman but then married a Frenchwoman whose family owns some property near here. I corresponded with him when I planned this trip, and he invited me to stay with him. When the war erupted, I thought circumstances would prevent my visit, but he would be happy to offer us hospitality."

"But he is not expecting us!"

"Under the circumstances, I think he would understand. I just hope that he is at home. He wrote in his letter that he would need to travel to Toulouse soon. But I think we need to attempt it; he is our best hope for accommodations tonight." He said nothing about how badly Elizabeth appeared to need such assistance.

***

By the time Darcy pulled the carriage to a stop in front of Whitmore's home, Elizabeth's condition had deteriorated. Her face was deathly pale, and she was in a stupor; with every mile, Darcy's concern for her health grew.

Whitmore's home was a large chateau whose grand entrance fronted a sweeping circular drive. In the gathering dark, Darcy could see little of the grounds, but they appeared extensive. Darcy drew the carriage as close as he could to the main entrance so Elizabeth need not walk far, but when he pulled the exhausted horses to a halt, she appeared to be sleeping once more despite the lack of support provided by the high carriage seat. Darcy descended to knock on the door. He explained to the butler who he was; within moments, Thomas Whitmore was striding across the foyer to greet him.

"Darcy! You are here! What an unexpected pleasure." The warmth of his tone conveyed how genuinely pleased he was to see his friend.

Darcy was extremely relieved to find Whitmore in residence. "I apologize for appearing on your doorstep unannounced. The news of the war disrupted my travel plans."

"Of course. I am happy to see you no matter the circumstances." He turned and spoke to the butler in excellent French. "Henri, please see that a room is prepared for Monsieur Darcy." The butler bowed and left.

"Actually, Thomas, I am not traveling alone." Darcy strode out the open door with Whitmore on his heels. He gestured toward Elizabeth slumped in the carriage seat with her shawl around her shoulders. "This is—" At that moment, she slouched still farther and began to topple sideways off the seat. Darcy rushed forward to catch her before she hit the ground. Her body landed heavily in his arms, but she still did not awaken. Holding her, Darcy could sense the warmth of her fever-wracked skin through the thin muslin of her dress.

"Oh my goodness!" Whitmore exclaimed, perusing Darcy's burden.

"I am afraid she is ill and can travel no further. The inns were full—"

"I am so happy you came here," Whitmore said reassuringly. "We will do everything we can for her. I will send for a doctor immediately."

Darcy carefully carried Elizabeth into the house's marble-trimmed foyer, thinking how little she weighed; she had eaten almost nothing that day. Whitmore gave orders to the servants to bring in their trunks and to summon a doctor. Darcy took her up the stairs and into the guest room Whitmore indicated, a large room dominated by a grand, carved four-poster bed. Laying her gently on the fine linen covers, Darcy noticed the pallor in her face. She had not stirred at all as he carried her, a very worrisome sign.

Some of Elizabeth's hair had come free of her neat bun, and Darcy smoothed it unconsciously. Whitmore observed him closely. "I did not know you were married."

"I am not." Darcy's hand froze as he realized what he was doing. Suddenly, it occurred to him that Whitmore would wonder how he came to be traveling with a woman who was apparently unrelated to him. "This is Elizabeth Bennet. Her father is a gentleman in Hertfordshire, and I recently became acquainted with her family. I encountered her in Paris, but when news of the war broke, she had no means of leaving the city, so I offered to…"

As he spoke, Darcy stood and turned toward Whitmore but did not venture from Elizabeth's side. The other man's face had lost its warmth, and he regarded Darcy with disapproval. "I would never have thought that you of all people…with a respectable woman…a—"

Darcy was exhausted and losing his patience. "She is not my mistress, blast it! We are simply traveling together. We are just friends."

Whitmore narrowed his eyes at Darcy, who looked down and noticed he was holding Elizabeth's hand. "I do admit to having…some affection for her," he admitted grudgingly. As much as he disliked laying bare his sentiments for another's scrutiny, he knew he needed to give some explanation—an honorable explanation—for his actions.

Whitmore's glare softened. "That much is obvious. We will take good care of her. I will send a maid to help her undress. We shall put you in the room next door. I am certain you will wish to change your clothes."

Darcy was reluctant to leave Elizabeth, but he could do little for her at that point. Furthermore, propriety dictated that he should not visit her bedroom alone. Before he left the room, he took one last glance at the pale, still figure, very small in the huge bed.

An hour later, Darcy's disposition had improved after having washed and changed his clothing. He joined Whitmore and his wife in their sumptuously appointed dining room. "Darcy, this is my wife, Marie," Whitmore introduced her. Marie was a pretty, petite woman of about five and twenty with dark hair and a heart-shaped face.

Her smile to Darcy was quite warm and gracious. "Welcome to our home, Monsieur Darcy. I am pleased to finally meet Thomas's friend. Though I am sorry it is not under better circumstances." Her English was excellent, with only a slight accent.

"I greatly appreciate your hospitality," Darcy returned. "It is providential that your home was so close."

They enjoyed a pleasant conversation during the delectable but simple country dinner. Darcy explained their situation and described their travels, but he found he could give his hosts only half of his attention. At every moment, he wondered how Elizabeth fared and if there had been any change in her condition. Whitmore smiled knowingly when Darcy once again lost the thread of the conversation. "The doctor should arrive soon. Do not worry. Flouret is the best to be found in the neighborhood."

"If it is only a fever, we can hope it will pass quickly," Marie ventured. Darcy tried to smile at their reassurances, but it turned into more of a grimace.

***

The doctor arrived while they were finishing their meal, and Darcy followed as Whitmore escorted Monsieur Flouret to Elizabeth's room.

Then he stood in the hallway, hovering around the room's entrance while the doctor examined her. When Flouret had finished, he met Darcy in the hallway. "Monsieur, your wife is very ill."

"She is not my wife," Darcy corrected automatically.

The doctor cleared his throat uncomfortably. *Damn, now* he *thinks she is my mistress!* Darcy reminded himself that it hardly mattered what the doctor thought.

Flouret continued, "She has a high fever, and her pulse is weak. I gave her some medicine and will return in the morning to see how she fares." He could see that the doctor was speaking slowly and enunciating every word to ensure Darcy's comprehension.

"What can I–we do for her comfort?" The French came very naturally to Darcy after being in the country for so long.

The doctor's eyes were downcast as he made notes in his notebook but continued to give instructions. "Cool compresses for the fever. If she is awake, she should drink water or weak tea so she will not become dehydrated."

Darcy thanked the doctor, and the man left. When Whitmore came upstairs a few minutes later, Darcy was again sitting in Elizabeth's room holding her hand. Darcy was aware of his friend's scrutiny but could not bring himself to take his eyes off Elizabeth's face, which was flushed and beaded with perspiration. She did not sleep restfully but rolled her head from side to side and shifted listlessly every few minutes.

Anxiety closed around his heart. What he would not give to see her fine eyes open and smiling at him! All he wanted was to see her alive and well, even if he could never have her for his wife.

When Darcy finally met Whitmore's eyes, the other man's face was full of sympathy. "Are you planning to ask Miss Bennet to marry you?"

"No…well…yes. It is complicated." Darcy was so worn down by exhaustion and worry that it actually felt good to unburden himself. "I hope she will someday accept me."

Whitmore raised his brows at the uncertainty in Darcy's tone. "You must love her very deeply."

"I do. She is a remarkable woman." Darcy fell silent, his throat suddenly constricted.

Concern was reflected in Whitmore's face. "You should rest. I will send in a maid to stay with Miss Bennet during the night. She will awaken you immediately if there is a change in her condition."

"No!" Darcy realized right away that his exclamation had come out more fiercely than he intended, and he moderated his tone. "Thank you, Thomas. I…I could never rest easy if I could not see her myself and know how she was faring. And when she awakens, she will not know where she is. You can have the maid stay as well if you wish."

"Even with a chaperone, Darcy, you cannot stay in her room," Whitmore said gently. "She is not your sister or your wife."

"I would never take advantage of a sick woman!" Darcy hissed.

"I know that, but she is under my protection. I am concerned about her reputation." Whitmore's voice was soothing, but Darcy was in no mood to be calmed.

"And I am thinking of her *life!*" Darcy spat out. He stood abruptly and strode to the window. The moon was rising, casting shadows on the surrounding grounds. Taking a deep breath, he tried to calm his disordered nerves. Once he was in better control of his emotions, he continued in a more conciliatory tone. "No one need know of it save you, Marie, and your staff." Whitmore was still shaking his head, and Darcy swore. "Unless you summon your footmen to remove me bodily from this room, I am staying!" Darcy swung around and regarded Whitmore challengingly.

Whitmore returned his gaze steadily for a moment and then sighed. "Very well. I do trust you, Darcy, and I suppose what occurs here is unlikely to affect her reputation in England. I will have a maid wait in the hallway. Let her know of anything you need."

"Thank you," Darcy said gratefully, watching as Whitmore left the room, closing the door softly behind him. Darcy settled himself into the brocaded chair near Elizabeth's bedside. It would be a long night.

***

Darcy woke with a start. He had fallen asleep sitting in the chair but with his head resting on the bed by Elizabeth's side. He heard noises, but it took a moment to pinpoint the source: Elizabeth was thrashing violently in the bed covers and calling out.

"Oh…oh…the French…the soldiers! Papa, we must run! Help! Papa, please hurry! Where are Lydia and Jane? Papa!" Her tone was frantic, and her face was creased with worry.

Darcy realized she was in the throes of a feverish nightmare. He laid his hand gently on her arm, hoping to shake her out of her delirium. "Miss Bennet, it is a dream. You are perfectly safe." She did not react to his touch or the sound of his voice but continued to thrash and moan. Hoping his words would penetrate the fever, Darcy continued to talk in soothing tones.

Suddenly, she sat bolt upright in the bed, startling him. "William! William! Where are you? They cannot capture you. I need you!" She screamed the last word so loudly he feared she would awaken others in the household. He tried to shush her gently, wondering—somewhat jealously—who this "William" was. Suddenly, the realization penetrated his sleep-fogged brain: she meant him! Few people in his life called him by his given name, and most called him Fitzwilliam. He had never heard Elizabeth call him anything other than "Mr. Darcy," but perhaps she thought of him as "William" in the privacy of her own thoughts. Despite the seriousness of the situation, he smiled to himself, thinking that maybe she did harbor some positive opinions regarding him.

She cried out again, and Darcy grabbed her shoulders, staring into her flushed face and unfocused eyes. "Elizabeth, it is just a bad dream! It is only a dream!" But she gave no indication that she heard him. He released her shoulders, and she sank back on the pillows, continuing to toss and turn and mutter, although the words were barely coherent.

The maid had brought a basin of water earlier, so Darcy took a rag and bathed Elizabeth's forehead. "So hot," she murmured. He could sense the skin through the thin cloth of her nightgown; she was burning up. Pulling down the covers, he pushed up the sleeves of her nightgown to cool off her arms. He bathed her hands and throat in cool water, wishing that propriety allowed him to access other parts of her skin. Perhaps he should get the maid...

With the cooling water on her skin, Elizabeth quieted somewhat. She no longer thrashed, though she moved restlessly and rolled her head from side to side. With the sheets no longer covering her, Darcy could not help admiring her beautiful figure. He envisioned her in his great bed at Pemberley, her dark, curly hair spread on the pillows just as it was now...her eyes shining with love for him. Welcoming him...

Shaking out of his reverie, he chastised himself for thinking such thoughts about an ill woman. There were many reasons why such a vision might never come to fruition. He should not torture himself with it.

***

Darcy was awakened again by a shaft of early morning sunlight shining in his eyes. He glanced quickly at Elizabeth, noticing that her hands were moving restlessly as she plucked ineffectually at the coverlet. Her eyelids fluttered, but her eyes did not open. He took her wrist and felt her pulse, which was still weak. Instead of replacing her hand, he held it in his own. Perhaps in her current state she would be comforted to feel her hand in his—or she might be appalled at the liberties he was taking.

Her dark tresses spilled out across the pillow. How often had he longed to touch her hair to discern if it was as soft as it appeared? Almost of its own volition, his hand reached out and stroked one of the curls. How he wished he could do this when she was awake!

Her eyelids fluttered open, and he jerked his hand away guiltily. She gave no indication she had noticed his actions but looked rather dazed. Her eyes flitted around the room until they rested on him. "Will–Mr. Darcy!" He wished he could ask her to address him by his Christian name, but this was not the time. "Where—?" The words came out weak and breathy, totally unlike her usual energetic and pert tone.

"We are staying at the home of my friend, Thomas Whitmore. Near Montdidier."

"We must get to England!" Her voice was only a hoarse whisper, and she appeared to be fighting to keep her eyes open. Violent shivers wracked her body, and he pulled the covers further up around her neck to keep her warm.

"We are perfectly safe," he said reassuringly. "Mr. Whitmore has offered his protection. No one will seek us here."

"But, we must—"

"You are ill. We must remain here until you recover."

Her head shook weakly. "It is not safe. I cannot...you cannot risk yourself for me—"

"I will not risk your health. Nor is there any reason to believe we are in danger now that we have left Paris. Mr. Whitmore has heard nothing of soldiers seeking out Englishmen in the countryside." She said nothing but glanced down to where his hand still grasped hers. Darcy colored at the liberty he had taken, but she did not appear dismayed. Nor did she pull her hand away. Darcy returned his eyes to her face. "You must put your energy into recovery. How do you feel?"

"I am...good." The weakness of her voice belied her words.

Darcy noticed the alarming pallor of her skin. "Please tell me the truth."

She smiled wanly. "I can see from your face that I must seem very ill indeed."

"I have seen you looking better," he allowed.

"You are all politeness." Her voice was a little stronger, and her smile a trifle broader. "I will admit to being somewhat tired and weak." Another shiver shook her body.

Darcy persuaded her to drink some water, but she would not eat. Soon she fell into a shallow sleep. He took the opportunity to awaken the maid, who sat with Elizabeth while he visited his room to change his clothes.

Time crawled by slowly in the sick room. Darcy had perceived Elizabeth's early morning coherence as a hopeful sign, but she grew steadily worse throughout the day. Darcy took breakfast in her room and did not leave her bedside. Rationally, he knew there was little he could do for her, but he could not bear to be away for any amount of time. By dinnertime, her skin seemed, if possible, even hotter, although she no longer thrashed while she slept. Instead she lay very still and pale in a way that Darcy found extremely disturbing. Her breathing had become more labored, and he could hear every breath she took. The doctor came twice during the day and left medicine, but he observed little improvement in her condition.

***

Late in the afternoon, Whitmore visited the sick room. He found Darcy pacing back and forth before Elizabeth's bed. He stared distractedly at Whitmore. "If only there were something I could do! But there is nothing." He ran his fingers through hair that was already disheveled. "I hate this…this…helplessness!" He flung himself into the chair. "I shall go mad!"

Whitmore regarded him sympathetically. "You have been confined too long. Your mind needs distraction. Come down to dinner. I will have the maid watch over Miss Bennet."

"No, I cannot leave her. What if she needs me?"

"My friend," Whitmore said softly, "there is nothing that you can provide that the maid cannot. Driving yourself into exhaustion will do her no good. For Miss Bennet's sake, please take some sustenance."

Darcy thrust himself out of the chair and paced the length of the room until he stood by the window, peering out into the gathering twilight. "Very well. But please tell the maid to summon me if there is any alteration."

Darcy joined his hosts for dinner but was unable to provide much conversation and had little appetite. Perfectly comprehending his mood, Marie and Whitmore carried the burden of the conversation, telling him about their life in France. They lived a quiet country existence away from the glamour of the capital city. In response to Darcy's question, Whitmore admitted that he sometimes encountered hostility against Englishmen, but the prominence of Marie's family among the local notables protected him, and he had never felt threatened.

They socialized with a few other families who numbered expatriate English men and women among their members. Whitmore was sometimes called upon in his capacity as an ordained minister of the Anglican Church to perform weddings and baptisms for English citizens who resided in this predominately Catholic country. Darcy tried not to think about the possibility that Elizabeth might need Whitmore to perform last rites. *No,* he told himself, *she was strong and healthy before this fever took hold. There is no reason to think it will strike her down.*

After dinner, Whitmore and Darcy arrived at Elizabeth's room to find Monsieur Flouret examining the patient. When he was finished, he met the men out in the hall. He asked Whitmore to translate as he talked to Darcy, a request that made Darcy apprehensive; before they had struggled along with Darcy's imperfect but acceptable command of French.

"He says the infection is in her lungs, and she struggles to breathe," Whitmore explained, his face full of concern. "Her pulse is very weak." Whitmore paused and listened to the doctor's torrent of French. "I am sorry, Darcy. You must prepare yourself for the worst. He does not believe there is much hope she will survive."

Chapter 6

Darcy felt as though a deep hole had opened suddenly under his feet, dragging him down into the earth. There was darkness around the edges of his vision, and he heard the doctor's voice as if at the bottom of a deep hole. His mind struggled to understand what he was hearing.

"No—" The word came out like a moan.

Whitmore put his hand on Darcy's shoulder in sympathy. "I am so sorry."

"NO!" Darcy tore away savagely from Whitmore and rushed into Elizabeth's room.

A few minutes later, he was staring at the too-still form on the bed. Sitting in the bedside chair, he gripped the smooth linens of Elizabeth's bed like a lifeline. Whitmore had dismissed the doctor and entered the room, hovering near the door. "What else can I do for you? I want to help."

"Find another doctor for her. I do not care about the expense. Summon someone from Paris if necessary!" Darcy's voice crescendoed from a harsh whisper to a shout.

Whitmore nodded. "Certainly, there is another doctor over in Noyon. We shall send for him immediately." He turned to depart but paused and glanced back at Darcy. "Perhaps you should write to Miss Bennet's family?"

Darcy shook his head slowly. "I considered it, but I fear members of her family might attempt to come to France and place themselves in danger. Besides, they would probably arrive too late." He gazed longingly at Elizabeth's pale face. "It is a shame. She would certainly find comfort in her sister's presence." He had sent letters to Georgiana and the Gardiners when they had arrived at

Whitmore's house to let them know where they were and that they were safe. "Safe!" he muttered, thinking that the word now mocked him. If she were to die, the Gardiners and Bennets would be completely unprepared for such ill tidings.

"I understand." Whitmore nodded and left the room. Darcy continued to stare at Elizabeth's face, trying to absorb the possibility—the reality—of her death. He had not shed a tear since his father's death nearly seven years before, but now he felt wetness in his eyes. How could he continue to live? How could he inhabit a world with no Elizabeth? Far better to see her wed another man! If she were to die, he did not know how he could survive a single day.

The evening dragged on. The other doctor, a short, stout man, arrived. After examining Elizabeth, he provided her with additional medicine but could not render a more optimistic conclusion than Flouret's. Darcy had not believed it was possible for his spirits to sink even lower, but they did. He alternated between frantic pacing back and forth in front of the bed and sitting as he stared in despair at the bed's inhabitant. Whitmore visited him around eleven o'clock before retiring for bed, but Darcy was not disposed to conversation.

Around midnight, Elizabeth's fever rose higher, and she began again to thrash and moan. Darcy bathed her face and arms in cool water. Peeling away the sheets drenched with sweat, he pulled the damp nightgown away from her calves so cooler air could circulate. He even untied the top of her nightgown and bathed her neck and shoulders. Bitterly, he remembered how he had fantasized about viewing and touching these parts of her body. Now those dreams seemed to mock him.

What will I do without her? He imagined how empty his life would be. It would be even worse than after the disastrous Hunsford proposal when he was sure she would never be his. How could she be taken from him now when he believed he had achieved some small progress in improving her opinion of him? Envisioning the prospect of living another thirty years without Elizabeth in the world, he dropped his head to the edge of the bed and sobbed.

When he awoke, his head was resting on the bed, and his neck was very stiff. The weight of Elizabeth's hand pressed on his hair. It felt so pleasant and natural, but then her hand drifted away again. He straightened up, thinking Elizabeth might be awake and aware of his presence, but her eyes were closed. She seemed much the same as before, although her breathing was more labored, and he heard a rasping in her lungs that he had not noticed before. A fresh wave of despair washed over him as he realized there was little to pin his hopes on.

It was still night. Moonlight streamed in through the window, creating eerie shadows in the room. Darcy stood, but his muscles were so cramped that he almost toppled over. Hours spent sleeping in the chair had wreaked havoc on his body, which seemed to ache all over. He gazed at Elizabeth. It was a large bed, and she occupied only a small part. Her skin had cooled some, so he pulled the coverlet over her once more. The bed was very inviting; the pillow would be very soft under his head. He could lie down next to her. He could hold Elizabeth to him, just once.

Before he could change his mind, he removed his boots and lay down on top of the covers, rolling to his side so that he was pressed up against her back. He was still wearing breeches and a shirt, and she was swathed in her nightgown and the sheet, but he was attuned to her physical presence. Tenderly, he drew his arm around her waist and kissed the nape of her neck. It was damp with perspiration, but it smelled wonderfully of Elizabeth. Soon he had fallen into a deep and dreamless sleep.

When he awoke, it took him a minute to recall where he was. He was still cuddled up next to Elizabeth. The weight of her in his arms was so good and so right. *But,* he thought with chagrin, *it would be a different situation if she awakened and found me here.* Despite her illness, this was beyond the bounds of propriety. What had he been thinking last night?

Carefully extricating himself from the bed, he walked around to Elizabeth's bedside. It was dawn, and the early morning light was peeking through the room's sheer, lacy curtains. Elizabeth's condition had not changed from the night before. Darcy sighed. He had hoped for some evidence of improvement, but thus far her illness had progressed just as the doctor had predicted.

He gazed at Elizabeth's beautiful, full lips, thinking how soft they might be and how they tempted him. He had never even kissed her. Now he might never get the opportunity.

Quietly, he leaned over and pressed his lips briefly to hers before pulling back. Her lips were as soft as rose petals, just as he had imagined. It was pleasant but not the same as kissing an awake and happy Elizabeth who might kiss him back. Then he smiled at his foolishness. Did he think he was a prince who could awaken the lady with a kiss? *This is no fairy tale,* he thought bitterly as he stood, shaking out his stiff legs. Walking to the window, he pressed his face to the cool glass.

***

Elizabeth awoke from confused dreams where she was first in empty, desolate fields of dying crops and then standing in rooms that were crowded with people who ignored her and spoke in a language she could not understand. When she finally struggled to some kind of alertness, she realized that the experiences had been dreams. She must have had a fever. This was her room in Mr. Whitmore's house, she realized, and it was early morning, judging from the yellowish-red light shining from behind the drapes.

A huge weight seemed to have settled on her chest, making it an effort even to breathe. Each breath was only a shallow gasp, and she could hear a raspiness deep in her lungs. Her body seemed to ache everywhere at once, and her skin alternated between being too hot and too cold. Even as her hands pulled at the covers, she was uncertain whether she wished to pull them further up or push them down. The covers stubbornly remained where they were; the muscles of her hands were numb and would not obey her.

As she glanced around the room, she noted that even small movements of her head caused pain. Mr. Darcy was leaning on the window frame, gazing out. "Mr. Darcy?" Her voice cracked with disuse.

He whirled abruptly and strode to the side of the bed, his face a mixture of trepidation and hope. "Eliz–Miss Bennet. How are you feeling?" Elizabeth was shocked at his appearance, taking in his rumpled clothing, his lack of cravat, and the fact that he was wearing no coat at all. Even his hair was in disarray. Despite the circumstances, she felt herself coloring a little; she had never seen any man so informally attired except for her father.

However, most shocking of all, Darcy's eyes were red-rimmed as if…as if he had been crying. No, that was not possible! Surely the redness was from exhaustion. But then, even as she watched, he discretely wiped his nose with his handkerchief. She was certain he had been crying. *He must have received some terrible news*, she thought. *Had something happened to Georgiana or Colonel Fitzwilliam?* But how would any news have reached him here? Surely no one knew where they were.

She recalled that he had asked her a question. "I am…" She had anticipated reassuring him but realized he could easily discount any false claims to improved health. "To own the truth, I have felt better," she finally admitted. "Could I please have some water?"

He hastily poured a glass for her, but when she attempted sitting up to drink it, she realized how incredibly weak she had become. Darcy needed to put his hand against her back to help her into a sitting position and then steadied the glass in hands that shook too much. The half-glass of water she could manage was cool and refreshing on her dry throat, but even that small effort exhausted her. She shook her head slightly when he offered more and sank back on the pillows.

"You should drink more," he insisted.

"Later." Her voice came out in a croak. She scrutinized him again. "How do you fare, sir?"

"Me?" Surprise colored his voice. "I am fine, although I suppose I am somewhat tired."

"No." She was too weary to be anything but direct. "Something has distressed you, I can see. What has happened?"

"Nothing. Truly, I am fine. Please do not concern yourself with me. You need your strength to recover." He projected reassurance, but his eyes would not meet hers, instead fixing on a spot above her right shoulder.

Suddenly, Elizabeth realized the source of his distress. Why had she not recognized it before? It was her! It was her illness that troubled him. But surely circumstances were not so dire that he should weep over it. Surely he was worrying needlessly. Then she considered how her body felt: it was difficult to breathe, as if each breath had to be dragged from the bottom of her stomach. The muscles throughout her body seemed incapable of supporting her or undertaking even the smallest movement. In all her life, she had never felt the like.

"What…what did the doctor tell you about me?" Her eyes focused directly on Darcy.

Darcy flinched, and she knew all she needed to know. His eyes drifted to the window. "He says the disease is serious, but you can fight it."

"He does not think—he thinks I will d—" The realization was shocking, but she found herself more concerned about the effect it had on Darcy than on her own reaction. Then she thought about her family. *Oh my God! What terrible grief it will inflict on all of them.* "I am so sorry." She attempted to catch Darcy's gaze, but his eyes were now fixed, staring at nothing.

Her apologetic tone shook him out of his lethargy, and he turned his gaze earnestly on her face. "Please, do not distress yourself. You need your strength to recover. To—" He paused and swallowed hard. "The doctor himself explained there is much they do not know about fevers of this type. You are young and strong…"

His words faded away as his façade began to crack. She knew he was a painfully honest man and found it hard to profess reassurances he did not feel, but it made no difference; he had confirmed her worst fears. At the same time, she was oddly pleased that he had not lied to her.

Her sluggish brain returned to her previous realization: Darcy had been crying. He had been crying because he feared she would die. For the first time, Elizabeth felt tears leak from the corners of her own eyes.

What had she done to him? If she had not misunderstood him so horribly at Hunsford—if she had not said such hurtful things—events would have unfolded differently. They probably never would have come to France, and she would not have fallen ill. *I am the cause of his pain*, she realized. *I refused him and caused him pain—and now I will die and bring more anguish into his life. He deserves better—far better.*

"Oh, Elizabeth…" He found a clean handkerchief on the bedside table and tenderly wiped her tears away. The soft cloth felt good against her skin.

Unable to bear her sorrow and guilt, she glanced down at her hands. "I am so sorry," she sobbed.

"For what? For falling ill? You can hardly accept the blame for that." He managed a little smile.

"No, I never should have…" Her words trailed off. She attempted to force her fever-clouded mind into some semblance of coherence. What should she have done? With a shock, she realized that she regretted not accepting his proposal. She wished she had accepted it—wished it with all her heart! When had these emotions stolen over her? When had she fallen in love with Mr. Darcy? And why had she only realized it now, when it was too late?

This realization made her weep more, which in turn troubled Darcy further. Murmuring reassuringly, he attempted to wipe away the tears as they fell. The fine linen handkerchief was now quite damp. Her hand reached out to grasp his.

"I am so sorry..." She wished to put the conviction of her sentiments into every word. However, it took great effort to speak at all.

Darcy shook his head vigorously. "You have nothing to regret. I told you—"

"No! Listen to me!" Darcy closed his mouth abruptly. "I...am sorry I did not—" If only she could articulate everything she was experiencing, but her heart was so full that it seemed to choke her words. "We have wasted so much time! I apologize...*I* have wasted so much time."

Confusion creased his brow. "I am afraid I do not—"

She had neither the time nor the energy to be circumspect and ladylike in her words. "I regret that I did not say yes at Hunsford, Mr. D—William." A brief smile curved his mouth at the sound of his given name on her lips. "I regret that more than I can say. If I had not abused you so abominably, we might be—be..." Her hoarse voice trailed off.

"Married?" he whispered.

"Yes. It is *all* my fault." It was so hard to breathe; she struggled to emphasize each word so he would believe that she meant what she said.

Darcy shook his head. "No, darling, I was the one in the wrong. You were correct to—"

She cut him off with a feeble wave of her hand. "Nevertheless, we have wasted all that time when we could have been happy—together. And I only just realized it. And you knew. I think you have always known deep down. I should have understood it before; even in Paris I did not see." Her tears had dried, but she could hear the despair in her voice.

"See what?" he asked gently.

"How much I love you." The words came out almost in a whisper. "I was blind to it before—I was blind!" Tears were shining in the corners of his eyes, threatening to spill out. "I am sorry we wasted so much time," she repeated.

"Thank you for telling me." His hand gripped hers harder. Even in the midst of sorrow, she could see that he was happy about her revelation. "I am not angry with you. I love you." He looked down at their hands as his thumb began to caress her palm.

"I do not understand why. Silly man!" She gave him a wan smile, and he returned it with such an attempt at cheer that it hurt her heart.

"Well, if that is truly how you feel about me," he said, "then I absolutely forbid you to…to…" The word seemed to choke him.

"I do not believe it is my decision—or yours."

"Believe me," he said fervently, "I have said many prayers."

"Well, if God will do His part, I will do my best as well." But even as she said this, she recognized that it was growing more difficult to breathe; her words were coming out in gasps.

"That is all I can ask."

Elizabeth felt darkness pull her down as the edges of her eyesight became foggy and black. "I love you, William."

"I love you, Elizabeth." Then all was dark.

***

Darcy kept holding her hand. Now that she was asleep, he allowed two tears to trickle down his cheeks. He was uncertain if it made it better or worse to know how she felt about him. No, he realized, he was happy to know she returned his love. Even if the worst happened, it was better to know. At the same time, the thought of losing her caused him to mourn a life with her that might never be. Terror blossomed in the pit of his stomach as he thought about a future without her.

He tried to convince himself that her recent coherence was a positive sign for her recovery, but he understood from past experience that she was usually at her best in early morning. Later in the day she would worsen, he was certain, and released an audible moan at the thought.

The day passed with agonizing slowness. Darcy did not wish to lose one moment with Elizabeth, refusing all offers of meals until Whitmore insisted that he at least eat a tray in the room. The doctor visited and perceived no change in his patient's condition. In the late afternoon, her fever rose to the highest Darcy had yet seen it. She was burning up and thrashing as her breath came in harsh, slow gasps.

It was agony seeing her in such distress. Darcy did everything he could to make her comfortable, applying wet compresses to her warm forehead and propping her up on pillows to ease her breathing.

But he could do pitifully little to ease her discomfort. Every gasp of breath pierced his heart as he wondered if it would be her last. If she delayed taking a breath, panic would grip him. At one point, when she was breathing easier, he leaned in close and whispered into her ear, "I love you, Elizabeth. Remain with me. Do not leave me, please!"

Around dinner time, he perceived a change. Sweat started pouring out of every pore in her body. Perspiration soaked her pillow and the bed's coverings, so much so that Darcy asked the maid to change the sheets and her nightgown twice because they were wet through. Around midnight, he was carefully tucking the soft linen sheets around Elizabeth's still form when he realized the import of the perspiration. Perhaps the fever had broken! Gingerly, he felt her forehead and then her arms, noting that her skin remained excessively warm, but it was far cooler than in the days past. Hope started creeping back into his breast. Was it possible she had survived the worst of the illness? Still huddled in the chair next to her bedside, he kissed her much cooler brow, fervently hoping and praying. Eventually, he settled his head on the bed next to Elizabeth and slept.

Much later, he awoke to the sensation of someone stroking his hair. It was very pleasant. No one had done so since his mother had passed away. Then he remembered where he was. *What is happening?* He straightened up with a start.

Elizabeth yanked her hand away as if burned. "Mr. Darcy, I apologize!"

"No…" He attempted to shake himself into some sort of coherence. The room was still dark, so it was still deep into the night. "Do not be sorry…I…" Capturing her hand, he gently kissed the tips of her fingers and peered earnestly into her face. Her color was definitely better: neither pale nor fever-flushed. Suddenly, he realized he was simply staring at her. "Would you like some water?" Assisting her into a sitting position, he handed her a glass. This time she was able to hold it, although she needed both hands.

When she was finished drinking, he recaptured her hand and asked, "How are you feeling?"

She considered for a moment. "Better, actually. But so tired and weak…" Her voice was stronger but had a wheezy quality that reminded him that she was still far from recovered.

"Understandably."

"I am afraid I will be deprived of my deathbed scene after all. I had so hoped to give a grand speech and then perish like a heroine in a novel!" She smiled, and he chuckled.

"I am just as happy to be denied my role in such a scene." His hand held hers in a death grip; he never wanted to let it go again.

Her eyes sought his. "Thank you …for caring for me…for everything." Her eyes were so clear and free of fever that he wanted to cry for joy.

"You are welcome, but I did little. You had the true fight."

She laid her head back and closed her eyes for a long moment. Darcy believed she had fallen asleep, but soon she opened her eyes again and regarded him steadily. "I find it very comforting when you hold my hand, but I do not expect you to do so over the course of hours."

"I do not mind—" he began, but she shushed him.

"I know. However, you are exhausted." He started to protest, but she shook her head. "You should return to your room and sleep. I can summon a maid if I need anything."

He shook his head vigorously. "I cannot leave you alone."

"I am feeling far better."

He gazed down at their clasped hands and then up into her eyes. "I can see that you are better, but you are not completely recovered. I cannot be sanguine until I see further improvement—and I expect I would be unable to sleep in my room."

She sighed. "I thought you might say something like that." Then she gestured to the vast expanse of bed next to her. "I have all this space; please, lie down."

"No…I cannot…it would not be proper—" *Yes!* his baser nature urged, but he knew he must fight the temptation.

Elizabeth gestured impatiently. "Forget propriety. No one will be the wiser—and you require rest." He shook his head again. "Please? For me? I will be comforted to have you lying beside me." She had unerringly hit on the one argument he could not deny.

In a moment, temptation had conquered all his objections. "Very well." He silently climbed in next to her but did not get under the sheets. With his clothing on, he would be warm enough to sleep without covers. She rolled on her side, near the edge of the bed. He dared not put his arm around her waist as he had when she was asleep, but he did cover her hand with his where it rested on her hip. A contented sigh escaped her.

Darcy held himself rigidly, afraid he would accidentally initiate more contact; however, he soon heard the steady rhythm of her breathing, still quite raspy. She was sleeping, but it was a much quieter, more restful sleep than before. Smiling with relief, he realized he did not want to surrender possession of her hand for all the world.

The sounds of floorboards creaking in the hallway awoke Darcy in the early morning. His arm was flung over Elizabeth in a most compromising position. Flushing, he saw gratefully that she seemed deeply asleep. He slid off of the bed and anxiously viewed the patient, who seemed to be sleeping peacefully. Darcy exhaled a sigh of relief; for a horrible moment, he imagined that he only dreamed she had improved. She had developed a worrisome, wet, hacking cough, but she was so exhausted that no amount of coughing could awaken her.

The doctor arrived shortly thereafter. While he examined Elizabeth, Darcy went to his room to wash up and change his clothing. He spoke to Flouret in the hall. "Quite a remarkable change. I believe Miss Bennet will recover completely, although it will take some time. I think she still has a fever, but it is slight. Her breathing has improved remarkably. The coughing is something we must watch. It could develop into pneumonia. Be sure she does not exert herself too much. She needs rest to recover her strength." Darcy agreed wholeheartedly to adhere to every admonishment, and the doctor departed.

When Darcy returned to the room, he found Elizabeth awake and sitting up, displaying a heart-melting smile when he entered. At that moment, he knew he would do anything for her.

***

Over the next few days, Elizabeth slowly regained her strength. Of all her symptoms, only a nagging cough persisted. She spent most of her time in bed, but two days into her recovery, the doctor allowed her to stand and walk about for a few minutes. The first day, this minimal activity exhausted her to such an extent that she was compelled to agree with the doctor that she was not yet ready to resume a normal schedule.

Originally, she ate nothing but broth and gruel and exhibited little appetite. But then the doctor allowed a greater variety of foods, much to Elizabeth's delight. By the fourth day, she was eating normal foods, although her appetite was still greatly diminished. Alarmed at how much weight she had lost, Darcy encouraged her to eat at every opportunity, even badgering Whitmore's cook to supply her favorite foods.

Darcy delighted in every sign of progress, no matter how small, even greeting with enthusiasm her demands for bread instead of gruel and complaints about her lack of a bath. A rosy color returned to her cheeks, and energy returned to her conversation. He was particularly pleased when she began again to tease him; he had missed her arch comments and pert asides, but he still shuddered when he recalled how close he had come to losing her altogether.

Elizabeth enjoyed the company of Whitmore's wife Marie, who was a quiet and thoughtful woman. She would bring Elizabeth flowers from their garden—something the invalid cherished. They talked of their lives, and Marie told them of the news from the outside word. The two women became fast friends. Whitmore was an infrequent visitor; being in a lady's bedchamber was simply too uncomfortable for him, but he did visit long enough to make Elizabeth's acquaintance.

With so little activity, Elizabeth soon became bored. She read and worked on some of the embroidery she had brought to France, but she was by nature an active woman, and the enforced inactivity chafed at her. Most mornings, Darcy read to her, usually the poetry of Byron or Wordsworth although he alternated with the plays of Shakespeare, and discovered again how similar their tastes in reading were. Elizabeth was even interested in books of history and eagerly devoured the latest reports on the war against Bonaparte, a kind of active curiosity he had not seen in most women. But then she was not most women. Elizabeth even cajoled him into reading a contemporary novel, which he had previously disdained, but he found he rather liked it.

Now that the anxiety of Elizabeth's illness was past, Darcy found himself enjoying their relative freedom and seclusion. He had no estate business to address and no social obligations to fulfill. He simply spent time with Elizabeth; what more could he ask?

On the other hand, he felt uncertainty about how matters stood between himself and Elizabeth. She had never referred to their conversation on that horrible night when he feared she was about to die. That night, she had told him she loved him, and he treasured that memory. But the terrible thought had occurred to him that she did not even recall the conversation. Or did she remember it merely as a fevered dream? Worse still was the thought that she had only said those things because she thought she was dying. Had her attachment for him changed upon more sober reflection?

He tried to reassure himself that she was undoubtedly happy in his presence and seemed to desire his company. Despite the impropriety of his continued presence in her bedchamber, she never objected. He had visited her when she was sick, and he saw no reason to discontinue the practice now, but he lived in fear that she would tactfully admit one day that his presence was uncomfortable to her. She had reverted to calling him Mr. Darcy, and he no longer called her by her given name, which had fallen so easily from his lips when she was sick. Now that she was improving, such intimacies felt inappropriate.

Nevertheless, Darcy longed to discover the truth of her sentiments but feared distressing her and interrupting the smooth progress of her recovery. This did not prevent him from experiencing an agony of uncertainty. That terrible night, he thought he had won her regard, but now he was not so sure. Every day he feared learning that her feelings about him had changed once more and that she desired nothing from him but friendship. He wanted to discuss it with her but was unsure how to broach the topic. *By the way, one night in a feverish delirium you said you love me. Did you mean it?* It was awkward, to say the least.

***

After five days of recovery, one evening Elizabeth was well enough to go down for a very pleasant dinner with Whitmore and Marie. Elizabeth admired everything from the luxuriously appointed dining room to the delicious roast while

Whitmore related the latest news regarding the war. "No battles have been joined, but there has been much posturing on both sides. Unfortunately, the English navy captured two French ships. Napoleon has retaliated by ordering the arrest of all Englishmen between eighteen and sixty years of age who still remain in France."

Elizabeth gasped and shot a panicked look at Darcy.

"You are both safe here," Whitmore reassured her. "Marie's family is an important one, and her uncle lives not far away. They have been enough to protect me for years. No one will arrest me or a guest under my roof, and our servants are loyal; they will not reveal your presence here."

Darcy nodded slowly. "The danger will be when we leave here to seek passage across the Channel."

"Just so," Whitmore concurred reluctantly. "And I am afraid Calais is where they will expect to find the most Englishmen. You must find passage to England from somewhere else. I will investigate your options."

Elizabeth grew ghostly pale. "Then we must leave as soon as possible. Departing will only grow more difficult with time."

Darcy shook his head emphatically. "No, the doctor said you could not travel for several more days." The stricken look remained on her face. Darcy cast about for ways to reassure her. "Do not worry. We will find a way home. I might be required to hire a fishing boat, but we will arrive safely."

Elizabeth had a stubborn set to her mouth as she voiced her objections. "We should leave immediately. I am so much better. I would be fine on a trip; traveling by carriage is not so fatiguing."

Darcy knew how determined she could be but knew he could not give in to her on this issue. "I cannot live with the thought that I might risk your health." Whitmore immediately voiced his support for Darcy's position.

She considered for a moment. "I will ask the doctor about it in the morning." Darcy sighed, but he was satisfied; he knew the doctor would support his assertions. "If he will not allow me to travel," she continued, fixing Darcy with her gaze, "you must leave without me."

Darcy started in shock. "That is not an option!"

Elizabeth appeared ready to argue, but Marie stood, signaling the end of dinner. Fortunately, Darcy had been seated next to Elizabeth, so he noticed her sway when she stood. He caught her just as she crumpled to the floor. She awakened immediately in his arms. "Oh, Mr. Darcy. I suppose I fainted."

"Yes, I believe so." The look he gave her betrayed both concern and amusement.

"Thank you for catching me." A blush crept over her cheeks.

"You are most welcome, but I want to hear no more about being well enough to travel."

She bit her lip with a small smile. "I suppose it did undermine my argument."

"Yes, I think it did." He smiled as he carried her to her room, enjoying the novel sensations of her in his arms. When they arrived at her room, he knew the gentlemanly act would be to set her down on the bed at once, but he did not want to. It felt so right to be holding her thus. If only he could stand there forever, enjoying the sensation of her body touching his. Finally, he laid her on the bed but caressed her thigh a little with his thumb as he withdrew his hands. She started and blushed but did not protest, and he gratefully took that as a small sign of acceptance. Before he completely removed his arms, she straightened up and gave him a small kiss on thecheek, causing his heart to skip a beat.

Reluctantly, Darcy realized that now was not the time to begin a more serious discussion. "I will have Whitmore summon the doctor. Your fainting spell could be a sign of a more serious problem." She shook her head feebly but did not say anything. "You should sleep." Already apparently fatigued, she nodded, and he silently left the room.

***

Two days later, Darcy agreed to escort Elizabeth on a brief walk in Whitmore's formal French garden. There had been no recurrence of her fainting spell, and her improvement had been steady, but she chafed at being confined inside. Although Darcy had taken occasional walks, he felt the lack of exercise as well. The weather had turned warmer, as sunny weather had overtaken two weeks of rainy and overcast days. It was a beautiful clear day, not too warm, and perfect for walking.

Elizabeth indulged in a deep breath of fresh air. "Oh, it is so lovely not to be indoors! What beautiful gardens." She stopped to admire and smell a rose while Darcy admired her. "This is infinitely superior to lying in bed."

Darcy delighted in watching her experience the garden. "I would expect so."

They walked in silence for a few minutes, Darcy enjoying it when Elizabeth took his arm and leaned on him lightly for support; however, the scent of her—like lilacs and summer days—and her sheer physical proximity threatened his self-control. It was all too easy to imagine pulling her toward him and ravaging her mouth with his. Caressing her hand, he enjoyed the soft silkiness of her skin and tried not to imagine the texture of the skin elsewhere on her body. The possibility that someday he might have the opportunity to touch every inch of her was tantalizing; his whole body quivered with barely contained longing. He could not live with this uncertainty much longer. He emerged from his reverie to find Elizabeth regarding him quizzically. *I have been silent for quite a while*, he realized, praying that he was not blushing. *I hope she cannot guess what I am thinking.*

To cover his discomposure, Darcy asked a question that had long been on his mind. "How much do you remember of the time when you were ill and feverish?"

Her eyes gazed at nothing as she thought for a moment. "I remember mostly bits and pieces, but it is difficult to know which things are real and which were the product of a delirious imagination. Although I am pretty sure that the talking lion who offered me tea was not real." She smiled archly at him.

He chuckled. "I never saw such a creature in your room, so I believe you are correct." Taking a deep breath, he asked the question that had occupied his every waking thought since her recovery. "How much do you remember of the night before your fever broke?" He held his breath while waiting for her answer, and his heart pounded so loudly that he was sure she could hear it.

Looking down, he noticed that his hands were trembling.

She blushed furiously, which told him that she must remember *something*. "Please forget what I said that night." The words came out in a rush.

Darcy's heart sank. *She had changed her mind. She did not love him!* "Why?" he asked.

She looked everywhere but at him. "I was much too…bold…The fever, I am afraid, loosened my tongue…and I said some things…and made assumptions…about your feelings…" Her eyes raised anxiously to his.

Darcy exhaled a relieved breath. Apparently, she did not seem to regret the sentiments themselves, merely the voicing of them. He gazed intently into her delicate, brown eyes, willing his eyes to radiate the warmth he felt. "You made no assumptions that were not correct. My affections and wishes are unchanged." Elizabeth seemed overwhelmed and soon looked away.

He had no way to read her face; her expression was inscrutable. It was agony not knowing what she thought. "My concern," he continued, "had to do with whether your sentiments had changed. I would not hold you to something you said—"

"While delirious?" She finished the sentence for him, although her eyes were still fixed on her feet. "I had a fever, but the expression of my sentiments was…accurate." Finally, she looked up, gazing steadily into his eyes. "I do love you."

Darcy's heart swooped with joy. "Oh, Elizabeth!" He crushed her to him in a fierce hug that evolved into a tender, lingering kiss.

How could such a simple act create so many sensations everywhere at once? Elizabeth wondered. She tingled all over; in every place their bodies touched, she felt a warm energy spread through her skin. The same sensation she had earlier experienced when he touched her hand now hummed along the entire length of her body while in the pit of her stomach she experienced a pang, a deep longing. Too soon, Darcy pulled away to look down at her, but he still held her firmly in his arms. "Miss Bennet, will you do me the honor of becoming my wife?"

She smiled at him as a warm serenity spread through her. "Mr. Darcy, I will."

He reclaimed her lips with a kiss that was more urgent and desperate than the last. His hands rose to her face and then her hair, exploring the curls and threatening to dislodge her hair pins. She did not understand how the simple, gentle sensations from his fingers—while exquisite—could travel through her body, making her weak in the knees and hot all over her skin. Her body pressed against him almost of its own volition, apparently wishing to mold to him until there was no space between them and they felt like one body. They separated only when Elizabeth found herself gasping for breath.

Darcy stared at her in wonderment. "There are no words to describe this moment. 'Happy' is completely inadequate to describe my feelings."

Elizabeth smiled tenderly at him, enjoying the gentle pressure of his arms still clasping her waist. "I know." Then she felt suddenly dizzy. Taking a few unsteady steps, she seated herself on one of the garden's stone benches.

"Forgive me." Darcy was instantly concerned. "I forgot about your illness. Would you like to return to the house?" Carefully, he settled next to her on the bench, watching her guiltily.

"Please, do not apologize for kissing me like *that*! No woman could possibly object." He chuckled. Unable to resist, she reached up and kissed him briefly. Inwardly, she wondered at her own boldness; not only did she want his kisses, but she also wanted more—much more. These sensations were completely wanton, but kissing him felt so good—so absolutely right—that it was hard to resist.

When they separated, Darcy asked, "When would you like to be married?"

She leaned her head on his shoulder, sensing the warmth of his body through his coat. "As soon as possible."

"I am absolutely in accord." The enthusiasm in Darcy's voice was unfeigned. "Perhaps a fortnight after we arrive in England? That should provide sufficient time to make arrangements."

"*If* we make it to England," Elizabeth said, anxiety surging through her again.

"Do not worry." He squeezed her hand reassuringly. "I will ensure we arrive home one way or another."

Elizabeth said nothing but gazed out over the garden's perfect rows of flowers. To Darcy's eye, she seemed a little melancholy.

"Darling, is something amiss?"

"No, no…It is simply that…it will be another week until we can leave, then a day or so of travel…and then another fortnight…" Her voice trailed off.

"Yes?" he prompted, not understanding the source of her distress.

"It simply seems so long to wait—too long." Blushing a little, she fixed her eyes on her hands.

Darcy's heart pounded with joy. He wanted to jump and dance. She could not wait to marry him! The thought flooded his entire body with happiness and set it afire with aching desire. "I am afraid it cannot be helped." The calmness of his words belied the wild excitement coursing through him.

She bit her lip in a way that he found completely endearing. Then she regarded him with an expression that betrayed her anxiety over his reaction to what she was about to say. "William…what if…we could get married here? Now?"

Chapter 7

"Mr. Whitmore could perform the ceremony," Elizabeth rushed on. Darcy was so shocked that he could not speak, his lungs robbed of breath. "We have waited so long…I do not want to delay any further. *You* should not wait. And we have days of travel ahead of us. It will make it easier to travel since we will need no chaperone."

Darcy's mind attempted to grasp the idea. "That is true…." A wry smile twisted his lips. "Everywhere we have traveled people have been assuming you are my wife or—" Too late he realized that he should not have pursued this line of conversation.

"Or—?" She arched her brow curiously at him.

He hesitated but forged ahead. "Forgive me, my mistress."

To his astonishment, she laughed. "This is precisely my point! From that perspective, a hasty marriage is far better!"

He smiled but still shook his head. "Elizabeth, everyone will assume that I have compromised you or that you are with child—"

Elizabeth sprang to her feet and started pacing, her slippers crunching the path's gravel. "Let them!" Then seeing his shocked expression, she said in a softer tone, "William, I almost died. It forced me to consider what is most important in my life—and understand what is missing. I do not wish to wait what society would consider an appropriate amount of time. I want to seize the moment!" She closed the distance between them, pressing herself against his chest. His arms wrapped around her of their own accord, reveling in her softness. With her in his arms, warm and alive, he found it difficult to think about anything else. "I want to start our new life as husband and wife immediately," she whispered.

He pulled away from her to gaze directly into her eyes. "But a wedding with no family, no friends..."

Her joyous expression faded slightly. "I will miss Jane, that is true, and my father would have liked to give me away. But if we marry here, it will be a moment just for the two of us. And, truthfully, we will be better off without certain family members..."

Darcy knew she was thinking of some of her more embarrassing relations, but he considered how grateful he would be to do without Aunt Catherine. "Are you certain?"

"I know that I do not wish to wait."

He bestowed a huge smile on her. "Very well. I will speak to Whitmore today."

Whitmore seemed a little surprised to find Darcy at his study in the middle of the day, but Darcy explained his purpose right away. "Elizabeth has consented to be my wife." He could barely contain his sense of ebullience; this moment had been so long in coming.

***

His friend evinced no surprise, but his face split in a wide grin. "Congratulations, man. This calls for some brandy. I know it is early in the day, but some occasions warrant celebration." He poured them both glasses.

"You do not seem surprised," Darcy observed, settling into a stiff-backed chair opposite Whitmore's desk.

"No one who observed the pair of you during the past days would be surprised. I have noticed how you watch her—and how she looks at you."

This remark took Darcy off guard. "Truly? Does Elizabeth truly—" He was still insecure enough in her love for him that this confirmation of her regard came as a surprise—and a reassurance.

Whitmore chuckled knowingly, refilling their glasses. "You might not have noticed, but Marie and I have. Miss Bennet is as smitten with you as you are with her."

"I am pleased you think so because I have a favor to beg. Elizabeth's brush with death has made her eager to…seize the moment. She would like to be wed as soon as possible, before we leave for England."

Whitmore choked a little on his brandy and set his glass down hastily, taking a moment to absorb the news. "And you concur?"

"I have been waiting for her for a long time. I would prefer not to wait any longer. Plus, being married would mean we could travel more easily. "

Whitmore eyed him skeptically. "What about your family?"

"Actually, there will be a great advantage in arriving home with the wedding a *fait accompli*."

Comprehension dawned on Whitmore's face. "You are thinking of your aunt?"

Darcy nodded. "And a few other relatives. I would prefer to avoid enduring their attempts to dissuade me because they believe Elizabeth is beneath me. She is infinitely my superior."

"She is a fortunate woman. I saw how devoted you were to her during her illness."

Darcy plowed ahead with the conversation. "The favor I would like to ask: we are hoping you would marry us."

Whitmore seemed to have anticipated the request. "When?"

"As soon as possible. Is it necessary to obtain a special license?"

Whitmore shook his head. "Not in France. I could do it tomorrow if you would prefer."

"That would be …excellent."

Whitmore shook his head, chuckling. "I was saying that in jest."

"I am in earnest, Thomas. The sooner we start our married life, the happier I will be."

"Very well. I will assemble the papers you need to sign. And I must tell Marie. She will never forgive me if I do not give her some time for preparations."

***

After another glass of brandy, Darcy left Whitmore and sought out Elizabeth, who was alone in the parlor reading a book on the fainting couch. Silently, he approached and gave her a kiss on the neck. After she started, she gave him a smile so blinding that he thought he would never recover. Such a short time ago he believed she would never look at him that way!

He perched on the edge of the couch next to her, and she laid down her book. "What did Mr. Whitmore say to our request?"

The smell of her filled his nostrils, and the sight of her filled his eyes while his hands longed to be full of the touch of her skin. Darcy tried to form a coherent sentence. "He was somewhat taken aback by our desire for speed, but not, however, with the fact of our engagement." Unable to stand it any longer, one hand reached out to caress her neck.

"Indeed?" She gave him an arch look that was so appealing he had to kiss her. Elizabeth responded ardently, curving her back to press herself against him. The sweet responsiveness was almost too much for him; he longed to strip off her clothing and make love to her right there. *But she is an innocent*, he reminded himself. *Do not scare her off before the wedding.* Reluctantly, he pulled away.

Attempting to divert himself from her all too distracting nearness, he resumed the conversation. "Thomas was not at all surprised. Apparently, we have betrayed ourselves to him and Marie."

"I am happy we could provide our hosts with such an amusing diversion." Elizabeth's tone was impish. "After all, I have been a very troublesome guest."

"Nonsense. I believe they were very pleased with the opportunity to meet you."

"So when can he marry us?"

"Would tomorrow suit you?"

Elizabeth gasped. "Are you in earnest?" He nodded. "It will be perfect!" Her joy at the prospect warmed his heart.

But he still experienced doubts. "Are you certain this is what you want, my love?" he asked, his voice going husky.

"Yes, William." Her tone was firm. "Are you having second thoughts?"

"No! Of course not." He fought the urge to laugh at the question. "I have loved you for the better part of a year. I shall not change my mind, but I want you to be certain. ...You have been ill...this is an overwhelming situation."

She gave him a playful look. "Mr. Darcy, I believe you are giving me reasons not to marry you!"

Before responding, Darcy walked to the window and gazed out over the extensive grounds. Then he turned toward her. "It is simply that this…situation is so new. I worry every moment that your feelings for me will change again. I cannot take anything for granted."

Her gaze fixed on her hands, Elizabeth was silent for so long that he feared he had offended her. What kind of idiot would accuse the woman who had just consented to marry him of inconstancy? He was on the verge of offering an apology when she spoke.

"I can understand this seems sudden to you, but it has been coming on gradually for me. My feelings toward you have been warming ever since the ball in Paris—well, even before, when I read your letter. Trust me when I say my sentiments will not wane. Once I have given my heart, it is given completely." As he noticed tears shimmering in her eyes, he thought of the devotion and care she demonstrated toward her family. She certainly understood love and loyalty; he should never have doubted her. Instead he should feel privileged to be in the select group of people she cared about.

Returning to the edge of the couch, he took her hand gently. "Please do not believe that I mistrust your affection…. It is simply so…sudden. Two weeks ago I despaired of even establishing a friendship with you. It is hard to believe my good fortune."

"Good fortune? Being hunted by the French government and trapped in a country house with a sick woman?" she asked wryly.

"I do call it very good fortune," he said simply. Then, overcome with love for her, he leaned forward to kiss her gently, more carefully than before. His heart was full of months of pent-up passion for Elizabeth, but he knew that he needed to go slowly. He feared demanding more than she was prepared to give, especially in her weakened state. Nor did he want to render her uncomfortable with his ardor. At Hunsford, he had made the mistake of believing he understood her degree of affection for him. If she required time to accustom herself to the physical side of marriage, he would give it to her. He broke it off slowly and regretfully, but her eyes were smoldering with a passion that threatened to shred his self-control.

It took every ounce of self-mastery to stand and prepare to leave the room, but Elizabeth captured his hand. "Please do not leave yet." He closed his eyes; how could he resist such an entreaty, one that was so much in accord with his own instincts? Yielding to the pull of her hand, he sank down next to her once more.

"Elizabeth," the word came out like a groan, "I wish to stay—very much. But you are recovering…"

"Yes; however, I am not made of spun glass! Besides, I am certain the doctor would consider this beneficial activity." She gave him a coy smile.

"You do not know how irresistible you are," he moaned as he leaned over for another kiss. This time she placed her hands around his neck and pulled him closer. He surrendered to the impulse to bury his hands in her hair, which felt softer and more luxurious than he had even imagined. His hands dislodged most of her hairpins, and he could feel some of her hair tumble down her back as he pressed her up against the side of the couch, enjoying the sensation of his firm body bearing down on her yielding softness. All he could smell was the intoxicating combination of lilac and Elizabeth. His hands, denied for so long, stroked all the available skin on her arms, shoulders, and neck, savoring how soft and smooth it was. Her responses to his kisses grew even more passionate, and he wondered how he could ever call a halt to this bliss.

He pulled back slightly, but Elizabeth raised her head urgently so their lips met once more. This time he lingered, deepening the kiss. *It is good the wedding is tomorrow. If she continues to kiss me like this, I might not be able to prevent myself from anticipating our marriage vows.*

Then they both heard the sound of the parlor's doorknob turning and instantly sprang apart. Darcy tried to straighten his clothes, but it was a hopeless endeavor; his cravat was completely askew, and his coat was half off. With a creased dress and hair spilling across the back of the couch, Elizabeth seemed exactly like a woman caught in a compromising position. Oblivious, Whitmore's housekeeper entered with a tea tray. "Miss," she said, "Madame Whitmore thought you would like some tea—"

She stopped short and gazed from Darcy to Elizabeth, her face perplexed. Darcy was sure they were both blushing, although he carefully directed his eyes away from Elizabeth. Comprehension dawned on the woman's face, and without a word, she turned and departed the room, still bearing the tray.

Darcy cursed himself silently. *Why could I not keep my hands to myself for one day? Elizabeth must be appalled at my forwardness! Or worse, chastising herself for bringing about such mortification!* He turned toward her, an apology on his lips.

The door clicked closed, and Elizabeth burst into giggles. After a moment, Darcy joined her, relief welling up in him. "Do you think she will report us to the master of the house?" Her laughter continued as she carefully twisted up her hair into a simple knot.

"Perhaps. Fortunately, he already knows my intentions are honorable. Hopefully, that will spare me a lecture." Darcy was pleased to hear the playful tone in her voice; however, he remained anxious. Perhaps she was appalled—or worse, intimidated—by his behavior but was putting on a brave face.

"At least tomorrow he will have no need for lecturing."

"Yes," Darcy said fervently. "I am even more grateful that we need wait no longer."

She gave a wry smile. "I suppose we just demonstrated the advisability of *not* waiting."

Capturing her hand, he brought it tenderly to his lips. "Please forgive my dishonorable behavior. I did not—"

She put a finger to his lips, silencing him. "There is nothing to forgive. You may have shocked the housekeeper, but you did not shock me. I believe I was an equal participant, so I share at least half the blame."

"No, the fault was mine. I—"

"I am quite capable of protesting if I dislike your behavior."

He paused to consider that statement, and then he allowed himself to believe her words, relief washing through him. She did not blame him! She enjoyed kissing him! His heart sang with love for the woman. He kissed her hand formally. "You are a remarkable woman."

"Thank you, sir."

"But you need to rest, and I do not believe that will be possible while I am here. So I will take my leave."

As he strode away from the parlor, he realized that he needed a ride. Yes, a long ride in the countryside, that was just what he needed.

***

So it was that Elizabeth Bennet and Fitzwilliam Darcy were united in holy matrimony in the chapel at Whitmore's manor home. Marie, beaming with happiness, served as the witness, having cheerfully donated her wedding gown to Elizabeth after a maid had altered it. Elizabeth carried a bouquet of flowers she had collected herself from the garden earlier in the day. Her face was framed by a delicate white bonnet, dark curls caressing her cheeks. Darcy thought she had never been more beautiful. As he watched her float down the short aisle toward him, he had a sudden sense of unreality. He still found it hard to credit his good fortune that she had consented to be his!

As Whitmore said the words of the traditional ceremony, Darcy gazed steadily into Elizabeth's eyes. He had feared to find doubt or hesitation in her face, but she was shining with happiness, and he could detect no traces of regret. As they prepared to say their vows, Elizabeth set her bouquet aside so they could hold hands and recite the time-hallowed words. Nothing could be more joyous or more perfect.

The ceremony over, they walked up the aisle, now husband and wife. Darcy reflected that when he had arrived in France he had not expected ever to see Elizabeth again and had not dared to hope he could ever win her friendship. How far he had traveled in a few short weeks!

After the ceremony, Whitmore and Marie treated them to a small wedding breakfast; Elizabeth then rested for most of the afternoon. When she awoke, the newlyweds took a leisurely stroll in the garden, afterward retiring to their rooms to dress for dinner. Dinner was an especially jolly occasion, with Whitmore proposing multiple toasts to the happy couple. The wine was excellent, but Elizabeth found it necessary to limit her consumption for the sake of her health.

Elizabeth thought Darcy seemed happier and more relaxed than he had appeared in a long time. It warmed her heart that she had brought him such joy. He had taken such scrupulous care of her during her illness and had suffered so much anxiety; at least she could bring him some measure of happiness.

***

That evening, rather than remain downstairs for a traditional gathering in the drawing room, Darcy and Elizabeth retired early, knowing that their hosts would understand. Whitmore's housekeeper had provided Elizabeth with a different guest room that night, one with a larger bed and attached sitting room. Darcy retained his room down the hall, following the custom of separate bedrooms for married couples.

Elizabeth had changed out of her wedding gown into a simple but elegant white nightgown she had brought from England. Darcy had already seen

more of her nightclothes than most grooms did
before a wedding, she reflected, but tonight the
atmosphere was entirely different.

Now she really was Mrs. Darcy. As she
brushed her hair, she searched her heart—as she had
been doing for the past week—for any trace of
misgiving about Mr. Darcy or the wedding;
however, as before, she found none. She had come
to understand what an exemplary man he truly was
and how fortunate she was that he loved her. His
anguish over her illness had demonstrated how deep
his love was and how loyal he was to those he let
into his heart. She could not have articulated *when*
she began to love him, but it had settled into her
heart by time her recovery had started.

Her only reservation—she could not call it a
misgiving—was that her family was not present to
share her joy on this day. She felt Jane's absence
most acutely, but she knew Jane would forgive her
when she understood the circumstances. Her father
would not be so understanding; however, Elizabeth
hoped his wrath would be short-lived. Of course,
her mother would be overjoyed that her second
daughter had secured such a wealthy husband, but
Elizabeth was happy she had spared Darcy the type
of marital preparations her mother would have
deemed appropriate, not to mention her effusions
about Darcy's fortune. No, although she loved her
mother, Elizabeth could not bring herself to regret
her absence. She did miss the Gardiners; they had
always provided her with good support and
guidance, but, like Jane, they would understand.

Elizabeth also regretted not having an
opportunity to get her aunt's advice on being a
married woman. Although she understood the
essentials of the marriage bed, much still remained

a mystery to her. Marie had sought her out the day before to talk with her, and her words had been very reassuring. Still, it would have been good to hear from someone with whom she had a longer acquaintance.

Her stomach fluttered nervously at the thought of the wedding night, a great unknown to her. But then she thought of the previous day in the parlor…how she had felt with his lips on hers and his fingers in her hair. She had felt no apprehension then, only desire. Surely tonight would be no different. She loved William and trusted that love; thinking of that, she began to relax.

She heard a soft knock on the door. "Come in." The squeak in her voice betrayed her anxiety. Darcy entered, giving her a frankly desirous look that warmed her inside. He wore his shirt and breeches but had discarded his coat and cravat. Drinking in the sight of him, she admired his naked neck and the firm chest outlined by the shirt.

When she raised her eyes to his face, she noticed that he appeared apprehensive. Elizabeth could not fathom any reason for his anxiety and experienced sudden uncertainty.

"Elizabeth," he breathed. "You are beautiful—a vision."

"Thank you." She was certain she had blushed a bright red.

He strode to her and positioned himself between her legs where she sat on the edge of the bed. Pulling her toward him, he kissed her very thoroughly. She responded with equal passion, swept up in the sensation of his hands exploring her curves through the thin fabric of her nightgown. But then he pulled back. "I do not think we should…tonight…we cannot take the risk that any activity could set back your recovery." She knew her face betrayed disappointment. "We can still kiss and enjoy each other's company," Darcy hastened to assure her.

"Am I to be consulted about the activities on my wedding night?" she asked tartly. "The doctor believes I will be fit to travel in two days. I feel well. I think I am strong enough for amorous activities!"

Taking her hand, he pressed it ardently to his lips. "I thought you might require some time to accustom yourself to the idea of…after all, we did not have a long engagement."

She gave a little laugh. "That is true. But, William, I…I want to consummate our marriage. I want to be your wife in all ways—"

"You should not experience an obligation. There is plenty of time for—"

"What I experience is not *obligation*. What I experience is…desire." As she exhaled the last word, she saw Darcy's eyebrows shoot up, but she persisted. "The kisses on the fainting couch were just a taste…I am greedy. I want more." She blushed and looked down as she said it, feeling very wanton, but it was true. Perhaps it was not wanton to express such desires to her husband.

He put a finger under her chin and tilted her head up to more easily view her face. "Truly?" He gazed into her eyes with concern but also hope.

"Yes." Boldly, she leaned forward and initiated a kiss that began innocently enough but soon turned passionate.

When they finally separated, they were both panting. Darcy gave a huge sigh. "Very well, Mrs. Darcy. Against my better judgment, you have convinced me that I must seduce you on our wedding night."

She laughed, but abruptly William stood and picked her up. He settled her gently in the center of the immense, mahogany, four-poster bed and then stretched himself alongside her. His bold, admiring look alone was enough to make her blush.

Darcy's hand idly touched one silken curl where it rested on a pillow. "I do not want you to be scared or nervous." His voice was low and husky.

"If you keep kissing me like that, I will not be at all nervous," she said with a little laugh.

"I cannot tell you how often I have imagined this, but I never thought it would come to pass," he confessed.

Their eyes locked. "I have imagined this as well," she said softly.

The information seemed to startle him. "Truly?" Such a response was far more than he could hope for. Then he gave her a warm smile. "I hope tonight will not fall short of your imagination."

She glanced down to see his hands undoing the ties on her nightgown. He leaned over and kissed her with undeniable passion, pressing her against the soft mattress. Then he sat up and divested himself of his shirt. Elizabeth gazed at his chest with unabashed admiration. "Mr. Darcy, I have every confidence you will exceed my expectations."

He laughed and kissed her again. Then they had no more time for talking.

***

The next morning, Darcy awoke from a confused dream and, for a moment, had trouble recalling where he was. But when he opened his eyes, he saw Elizabeth curled up next to him. As the events of the previous day flooded back to him, he felt a great rush of love for the sleeping woman. *It is not a dream! We are indeed married.* He was the most fortunate man alive!

Elizabeth stirred and opened her eyes, smiling when she saw him. He pulled her close to his chest, and before she could say anything, his lips were pressed against hers hungrily. No conversation had passed their lips, but he knew they were going to be late for breakfast.

***

Darcy and Elizabeth lingered one more day with the Whitmores, but then they reluctantly agreed it was time to leave. Dr. Flouret had examined Elizabeth and pronounced her well enough to travel, with the caveat that she should not exert herself excessively or allow herself to be chilled. The doctor was still concerned about her cough but was heartened that it had not worsened. *Nor has it improved markedly,* Darcy thought to himself.

He would be happy to delay until Elizabeth was stronger, but she was stubborn in her desire to depart. She worried that every day it would become more difficult to leave the country. Hostilities with England would only escalate, and Darcy was in more danger than she. The thought of leaving for England without him was intolerable to her.

Elizabeth had also expressed concern about her family. Darcy had sent brief notes to the Gardiners and to Georgiana explaining the reason for their delay, although he had not revealed how ill Elizabeth had truly been. But he had cautioned them against writing back; he did not want anything to

draw attention to their presence in France. The
Gardiners would have passed the news along to
Longbourn. Nevertheless, she was certain that all
the assembled Gardiners and Bennets would be
anxious until she was safely home.

The night of their final dinner at the manor,
Darcy and Whitmore discussed the safest method
for arriving in England. Whitmore insisted on
sending them in his coach with two footmen despite
Darcy's dismay. "I appreciate the offer, Whitmore,
but I cannot possibly put you to so much trouble."

Whitmore demurred. "It is no trouble at all. We
have another carriage we can use until our footmen
bring the other back after your departure. We can
easily spare the men." He casually helped himself to
some of the beef.

"Whitmore—" Darcy began.

Whitmore interrupted him. "I insist! I only
wish I could send more men to accompany you.
Who knows what kind of dangers you might
encounter on your journey? Marie and I will not rest
easy until we have done everything in our power to
see you safely on your way." Sitting next to him at
the table, Marie nodded emphatically in agreement.

Darcy sighed. "Very well. Where should we
depart from?" He stared at the fine linen tablecloth
but was visualizing a map of France.

"I have given it some thought. Calais is out of
the question; that is where they will expect to find
Englishmen. Instead you should consider Dunkirk.
It will be a longer trip from here, and it will take
you more time to reach England, but the Dunkirk
port has fewer passenger ships and more cargo ships.
You can probably find a cargo ship or fishing boat
that would take you to England for the right price. If

that proves too dangerous, you could consider Boulogne-sur-Mer."

"Which town is less likely to be full of soldiers seeking wayward Englishmen?" Darcy asked, taking a sip of his wine.

"Truly, I believe Dunkirk. Boulogne has some naval vessels, although it is not a major port."

Darcy considered for a moment. "Very well." He turned suddenly to Elizabeth. "Elizabeth, how is your Italian?"

"Passable, but not as good as my French." She appeared a little startled at the abrupt shift of topic. "Actually, I am at my best if I can sing it."

He smiled. "I do not believe that singing will be required. My plan is that if we are challenged by the police or military, we will tell them we are Italian, Signor Guillermo Rossi and his wife, Lisabetta." He raised his wineglass in a mocking toast.

Whitmore nodded his approval of the plan. "You would never be able to convince a Frenchman that you are a native. But they probably cannot tell if you speak Italian with an English accent."

"As long as we do not encounter any actual Italians," Elizabeth said with a wry smile.

Dinner over, they rose from the table. Elizabeth complimented Marie on the meal and on her cook's skills, but Darcy noticed she had eaten little. Whitmore clapped Darcy on the back. "You have thought this all through. It is a solid plan."

Darcy did not enjoy nearly as much confidence. "I hope it will be enough." The thought of leading Elizabeth into such danger was very disconcerting.

"Come to my study, and I shall show you my maps. The more you know about the geography, the better you can make decisions." Whitmore led

Darcy off to his study while Marie took Elizabeth to the drawing room for tea.

***

The next morning, they were up early and out the door after saying goodbye and expressing heartfelt gratitude to their hosts. They settled into the coach across from each other, as tradition dictated, and Darcy insisted on tucking a blanket around Elizabeth to stave off chills. Darcy rapped on the roof, and the coach started moving with a lurch. Darcy immediately moved so he could sit next to Elizabeth and hold her close.

Elizabeth watched the beautiful French countryside move past the window, attempting to appreciate these last glimpses of her first trip abroad. However, it was difficult to focus on the scenic beauty. Instead she was torn between anxiety about how they would escape to England and the very pleasurable distraction of Darcy's proximity.

When she thought about how they would escape France, she was more apprehensive on Darcy's behalf than on her own. The French government would most likely release her if they were captured together, but Darcy could languish in jail for however long the war lasted, perhaps years. That must not happen! But what could she possibly do if they were captured? Pondering the question, she drew closer to Darcy, who shifted on the leather coach seat and stroked her hair with his hand.

Dusk was falling as the coach rode into the small town where they would stay the night. The weather had been cooperative, and they had made good time, only making a brief stop to change horses and eat the meal that Marie's cook had prepared for them. They wanted to minimize their contact with the general populace; although the average Frenchman might not harbor animosity toward a traveling English couple, the two countries *were* at war. They could not take the chance that they might encounter someone who would alert the authorities.

They stopped at an inn that Whitmore had recommended, and Andre, the footman, went to secure lodgings for his "Italian" master, keeping Darcy from betraying himself with English-accented French. Their rooms were small but well-appointed and clean. Andre had asked for dinner to be brought up to their room, so they spoke very little to the inn's staff.

Darcy watched Elizabeth with concern. He could tell that the trip had fatigued her and that she was attempting to conceal the extent of her fatigue, although she could not hide the worsening of her penetrating cough. He had no doubt the travel was taking its toll on her health. She did not protest as he picked her up and placed her on the large bed's embroidered coverlet, and her face showed relief when he suggested they retire early. *Only one more day of travel and then we should be away to England,* he thought grimly. *If we are not captured first.*

Elizabeth awoke early as the golden light of dawn was just beginning to shine in. Darcy was still asleep beside her, and she took a moment to admire his sleeping form. It was taking her time to accustom herself to waking up beside him, but the sight of his face always made her smile tenderly. As if aware of her scrutiny, his eyes opened, and he gave her a warm smile. "How are you feeling today?" he asked, concern darkening his eyes.

"Well," she assured him. "And we are not due to depart for at least an hour. How *will* we pass the time?" She leaned in to kiss him, inhaling his deliciously male scent.

When they separated, he smiled at her. "I appreciate the sentiment, my love, but the walls in these inns are very thin. Other inhabitants are likely able to hear everything we say and do."

Elizabeth pondered this for a moment. He expected her to express dismay and was perversely disappointed himself that she merely looked thoughtful, but then she smiled impishly. "I can be *very* quiet if necessary."

"Mrs. Darcy," he marveled, "you are full of surprises." Likewise, Andre was surprised to find that the usually punctual Darcys were late departing from the inn.

***

The good weather continued all that day, and they arrived at Dunkirk in late afternoon. Knowing that no boat would undertake a voyage so late in the day, they spent the night at another inn, attempting to blend in with the other guests. The night passed without incident, and they reached the docks just as the sun was rising the next day. The port was crowded with fishing vessels, small cargo ships, and pleasure craft.

With the help of Andre and the other footman, Jean-Paul, they sought out small but seaworthy boats whose owners might be persuaded to transport them to England. Darcy tried to be careful about whom he approached since the wrong person might report them to the authorities. One fisherman had already turned Andre down rather brusquely despite what the footman assured Darcy was the offer of a very generous payment.

Darcy glanced around the port. Most of the boats were big passenger or cargo ships bound to far-distant ports. Before war broke out, there had been smaller sailing vessels that plied the waters to England and back daily, but no one would engage in such a dangerous activity now, at least not openly. The other boats of that size mostly belonged to fishermen. Darcy eyed the naval ships at one end of the wharf and hoped that they would not attract the attention of anyone on those vessels.

Andre started speaking with another fisherman, one with a boat that seemed in good repair. Darcy followed the progress of the conversation and could see that Andre had reached an agreement with the man. But as Darcy scanned the area, he noticed that the fisherman they had spoken to earlier was now talking to a group of men resplendent in the uniform of the French army. The man was gesticulating and motioning in Darcy's direction. *This does not look good,* he thought. *We should disappear.* He tugged on Andre's sleeve to pull him away from the negotiations, but it was too late. By the time the two had returned to where Elizabeth and Jean-Paul waited with the luggage, the soldiers, a group of five, were already approaching.

Andre intercepted them. In response to their inquiries Darcy heard him tell them that his employer was an Italian businessman who had interests in England and needed to travel there with his wife. The commanding officer, a hawk-faced man in his forties, was clearly skeptical. He sauntered over to Darcy, standing closer than was necessary, and asked some pointed questions about his name and business. Darcy had invented these details in the carriage ride, so he had ready answers, which he gave in Italian while Andre translated as best he could. Over the officer's shoulder, he could see Elizabeth's face as white as a sheet. If only he could spare her this anguish!

Darcy thought they might have the officer convinced. Several of his men seemed bored, anticipating no excitement from these "Italians," but suddenly the commanding officer leaned very close to Darcy and plucked a book from the breast pocket of his great coat. Darcy's heart pounded when he realized it was a volume of Shakespeare's poetry that he had been reading to Elizabeth in the carriage. Hardly the kind of book an Italian tradesman would possess. The man perused the pages and then glanced significantly at Darcy, a small smile curling his mouth. Dread seized Darcy's heart.

The man then sauntered over to Darcy's trunk and opened the latches, ignoring Darcy's protestations. He pulled out several documents and scrutinized them. Darcy knew what would happen next.

"*Il est Anglais!*" the man announced triumphantly, waving the documents around. Before Darcy could react, two soldiers grabbed his arms and held him in a vise-like grip. "I arrest you in the name of the Republic of France!" the officer said in heavily accented English.

Chapter 8

Darcy saw Elizabeth blanch even more and wished he could reassure her. At least she could return safely to England; they would not detain a woman. He would cooperate, giving them no reason to be angry; otherwise they might create some trumped up charges of spying against her, in which case they could imprison her indefinitely. He had heard reports of such things happening.

"Your wife may return to England, but we will keep you here," the officer said.

"No!" Elizabeth cried, all her anguish contained in the one word, causing the soldiers to shift their attention to her. Elizabeth drew a breath to speak but then started coughing, the longest fit Darcy had heard in days. *She is worse! She will have a relapse right here in Dunkirk!*

Even at this distance, he could hear the wheezing and rasping in her lungs as she coughed. Perhaps she was coming down with pneumonia; the doctor had warned of that possibility. Had all of the traveling triggered a relapse? Was the anxiety of the current situation worsening her illness? If she had to return to England alone, who would take care of her? Darcy turned these questions over in his mind, finding no satisfactory answers. There was no one who could travel with her. A woman traveling alone was vulnerable enough, but an ill one…he closed his eyes and tried not to think about it. She was safer in England…as long as she could reach England.

Elizabeth stopped coughing and approached the officer, her face drawn and wan. "May I speak to you, sir?" she asked in French, her voice a harsh whisper.

"Elizabeth, no!" Darcy did not know what she had planned, but if she said the wrong thing, they would arrest her as well—which would be far worse. A French prison would undoubtedly be horrible, but he could withstand it if he knew Elizabeth was safe, and there was the chance that his family could ransom him from the French government. Elizabeth glanced at him briefly, her face inscrutable, but ignored his plea. The commanding officer took her aside and spoke with her in low tones that Darcy could not discern, with Andre acting as a translator.

Darcy strained in the soldiers' arms, but their grip was unbreakable, holding him harder the more he resisted. He could do nothing but watch in anguish. Elizabeth spoke to the officer, but then she experienced another coughing fit, one that left her pale and gasping for breath. Andre was practically holding her up. Now Darcy was positive she was exhibiting symptoms of pneumonia, but how could she return to England alone? When she recovered sufficiently, she stumbled to Darcy's trunk and showed the officer something from it—a piece of paper. Darcy was puzzled about what she was displaying. Most of his papers were routine correspondence he had received in Paris.

She pleaded with the officer, and Andre nodded in support of her words. Suddenly, her voice started to falter, and she almost crumpled to the ground, rescued only by Andre's quick hands under her arms. Even the officer radiated concern as he helped Andre carry her to a nearby bench. Darcy attempted to lunge for her, but his captors only tightened their grip. Once at the bench, Elizabeth seemed to recover some and managed a seated position. But she was so weak and haggard that it was clear her recovery had been set back. *She will never make it to England alone!*

Focusing on Elizabeth, Darcy had not noticed the commanding officer, but suddenly the man stood directly before him. "I will release you, Monsieur Darcy. But you must leave French soil immediately." The man sounded resigned, as if he had no choice in the matter.

Darcy could not fathom what had triggered this change of heart but had no desire to question it. "I will. *Merci.*" The soldiers released Darcy's arms, and he rushed over to Elizabeth, who was still slumped on the bench. He seated himself next to her and placed an arm around her back to support her. "My love—"

She waved him off, appearing a little stronger than a moment ago. "Please, let us go to the boat."

Realizing they had no choice, Darcy quashed his reservations about her health. The officer wanted him out of the country. Even if Elizabeth had contracted pneumonia, they must leave. He wondered if he could pay the fisherman extra to get them there faster but realized they would be limited by the capabilities of his vessel. The boat did not even have an indoor room where he could shelter her from the fierce wind. Elizabeth leaned heavily on Darcy as they made their way slowly along the pier. The coughs decreased in frequency, but her steps were less steady.

He helped Elizabeth over the boat's gangplank as Andre and Jean-Paul loaded their trunks. While Elizabeth settled herself on a hard wooden bench, Darcy gave the two footmen his profoundest thanks and a generous gratuity. Watching them depart, Darcy noticed the French officer and his men standing on the dock, observing their progress.

Obviously, they felt the need to ensure that he left immediately.

The fisherman and his crew raised the sails, and the boat glided away from the pier, causing Darcy to heave a sigh of relief. The sun was shining brightly, but the wind was cold and cutting; Darcy wished for a blanket to wrap around his wife. Sitting next to her, he took her hand, regarding her with concern. "Elizabeth…"

She gave him a relieved smile. "I am well. Truly I am. My fainting fit was for the benefit of the soldiers." Relief washed over Darcy.

Darcy glanced back at the French soldiers, who were dwindling into black specks as the boat sailed into the Channel. "I admit to being quite bewildered by their change of heart. What did you tell them?"

"I showed them the wedding certificate and explained that we had only been married four days. Then I explained how ill I was and that the doctor thought I was unlikely to live." She winked at him. "I said I did not believe I could make it back to England without my new husband, who had never even met my family and who had married me despite my deadly illness." She leaned back against the boat's wheelhouse, looking satisfied with herself.

Darcy shook his head in admiration. "I did not realize I married such a talented actress! How did you devise such a story so rapidly?"

"Some of the story occurred to me back at Whitmore's estate. The French are very romantic, even the men. I thought they would dislike separating a newly married couple."

"Is that why you wanted to get married right away?" Darcy arched an eyebrow at her.

She tilted her head winsomely as she regarded him. "One of the reasons. I thought it would increase the odds of escaping France together. I also realized I have a very authentic-sounding cough, which I can trigger by breathing deeply. I thought I might use that to our advantage."

He drew her close to him, trying to warm her with his body. "I am full of admiration for your quick thinking. And even more pleased that you are not truly having a relapse! I was close to panic."

"I am sorry." She took his hand and held it warmly in hers. "I should have explained my plans, although some of it was the inspiration of the moment."

"All is forgiven, Mrs. Darcy. And soon we will be safely returned to England." He pressed an intense and relieved kiss on her lips.

Hours later, Darcy gazed out at the water of the English Channel; Elizabeth's head was in his lap as she slept soundly. She had been napping for more than an hour, he estimated, and was so beautiful he did not want to look away. It was good she had taken the opportunity to rest. Although she was not nearly as ill as she had pretended in Dunkirk, he could tell the traveling fatigued her. Her eyes had dark circles under them, and she had not regained any of the weight she had lost to the illness.

Darcy and Elizabeth formed an island of quiet amidst the activity on the ship. Around them the boat's crew hurried about, climbing up and down the rigging and shouting at each other.

He stroked her hair, wishing that he could free it from the hairpins and feel each silken curl, but the fishing boat's crew was all around. Although they were not paying him much attention, Elizabeth would not appreciate if he took such liberties in public. Still, maybe if he removed two pins, he could liberate a few curls…

Elizabeth opened her eyes and studied his face, no doubt seeing him grinning like a fool at her. "Sleep well?"

"Yes. I am better now." As she sat up, she straightened her clothing, wrinkled from traveling.

"I think we are about an hour away from Dover. I was concerned we might be stopped by the English navy since they are blockading the French coast. The boat's captain expressed some reservations about the trip for that reason. Fortunately, a couple more coins persuaded him."

"Perhaps the navy pays no heed to boats this small."

"I hope you are right," Darcy said. They sat for a moment, holding hands and enjoying the sight of sun on the water. Then Darcy broached a subject he knew they must discuss. "Elizabeth, we must determine what we will say to our families—and how."

She sighed. "I know. It has been so pleasant, just the two of us."

"Pleasant?" he said in amazement. "Fleeing Paris, fighting off brigands, contracting a nearly fatal fever, and tangling with the French army?"

She laughed. "But the other parts have been wonderful. I cannot even wish the dangers away because they helped to bring us together."

"Yes, the last four days have been my favorite part of the trip." He smiled at her. "It has been nice to free ourselves of the need for a chaperone."

Elizabeth frowned pensively. "I think we should not tell anyone about our marriage until we have an opportunity to tell Papa."

"I agree," Darcy said immediately.

"Good! I was concerned you would not want to wait until we could visit Longbourn."

"No, I have robbed your father of his chance to consent to the match—"

"*We* have robbed him. It was a decision we both made. And I am of age."

"I stand corrected. But he cannot consent, nor can he give you away. I think we should do him the courtesy of telling him first. Except that I would like to tell Georgiana."

"Of course! I am so looking forward to meeting her."

"She will love you," Darcy predicted confidently.

"I hope so." Elizabeth fell silent as she tried to bring order to her jumbled thoughts. "It will be difficult when we get to London. I shall have to go to the Gardiners and you to your home."

"Only for a couple of days, and then we can leave for Hertfordshire. Perhaps a few days' time will be beneficial. If we appear in public, the *ton* will assume I am courting you." He smiled rather whimsically at the thought. "We can establish the notion that I am showing you favor so the news of our marriage will not come as such a shock."

Elizabeth nodded. "That is an excellent plan."

"Just about no one knows how I feel about you, so we may benefit if they receive a little warning."

"If only we had time to do that in Hertfordshire," she said with a sigh. "I am afraid you will encounter many people at Longbourn who believe that I detest you."

"Including your father?"

"Yes." She regarded him apologetically.

"I have to confess, Elizabeth, when I was younger and envisioned asking for a young woman's hand, I never imagined a father who would be less than pleased." His smile was ironic.

She laughed. "No, I would suppose not. But to his credit, Papa is less concerned about material advantage than with my happiness."

He raised her hand to his lips. "*That* is something we have in common."

"Any disapproval on his part will pass with time," she predicted. "Once he knows what a fine man you are, he will appreciate you." Darcy fixed his gaze on the horizon and hoped she was correct in that assumption. He would be taking her far away from her family; he did not want to create a rift with them as well.

They arrived at Dover around dusk. After Darcy thanked the captain and paid him well, they stepped onto British soil with a great sense of relief. Darcy hired some boys to carry their trunks to a nearby inn that he had frequented before. Fortunately, the innkeeper had available a pleasant room with attached sitting room that was quite cozy. As they readied themselves for bed, Elizabeth thought with regret that this would be their last night together for at least a couple of days. While she hoped that their families would be happy for them, she knew that they would likely encounter some anger and disappointment. These days together, isolated from those cares, had been a very pleasant interlude. If only it could go on forever!

***

They woke early the next morning to hire a carriage to take them to London. Fortunately, it was not a long trip, and they found themselves pulling up in front of the Gardiners' house on Gracechurch

Street around mid-afternoon. The carriage came to a halt, and Darcy gazed onto a very respectable looking townhouse, not at all what he pictured belonging to someone in trade. But then he had been very impressed by the Gardiners when he met them in Paris; they were well-informed, genteel people.

Elizabeth peered out the carriage window at the townhouse and then back at Darcy. "I am going to miss you tonight."

"Only at night?" he teased. "I will miss you every moment of the day you are not with me."

"I will as well. But at night I will experience it most acutely." She tilted her head up at him in a clear invitation. He kissed her deeply and thoroughly, mindful that this might be their last kiss for a while. He did not want to let her leave his arms, but eventually he loosened his grasp with great reluctance, opening the carriage door and helping Elizabeth out.

As they approached the door, Darcy raised his hand to knock, but the door was suddenly opened by the mistress of the house, dressed in a bonnet and gloves to go out. Mrs. Gardiner started for a moment, then cried "Elizabeth!" and flung her arms around her niece. Her cries brought other inhabitants of the house, and Elizabeth was soon encircled by her uncle and the Gardiners' children.

Darcy retreated to a corner, watching this scene of domestic bliss and musing that his family was seldom so exuberant. He supposed that once he might have found such a display lacking in decorum, but now he saw it as a touching demonstration of how much the family members cared for one another. Visions of enjoying such tranquility crowded his mind as he pictured Elizabeth at Pemberley surrounded by children.

Soon Mrs. Gardiner had sent the children upstairs to resume their studies and ushered Darcy and Elizabeth into the house's respectable but not opulent drawing room for some tea. Mrs. Gardiner could not stop smiling at Elizabeth. "We were so worried about you. We should never have left you behind in France."

Elizabeth shook her head emphatically, wanting to ensure they suffered no guilt over their actions. "No, Aunt, you made the right choice. I could not have borne it if you had stayed behind for me and been harmed in any way."

"Did my messages arrive?" Darcy asked as he settled into a chair near Elizabeth. "Did you know why our departure was delayed?" Occasionally during their return voyage, he had expressed a concern to Elizabeth that his letters had been lost.

"Yes, we did hear about Elizabeth's illness. How are you feeling dear?" Mrs. Gardiner gazed on Elizabeth with concern.

"I am well." Elizabeth did her best to appear healthy.

Mrs. Gardiner scrutinized her more closely. "You have lost weight! And you look so tired. Are you quite recovered?" Elizabeth nodded vigorously, but Darcy shook his head.

"She may pretend otherwise, but Miss Bennet is still recovering and will need to rest here before she can travel to Hertfordshire." He glared at Elizabeth sternly, but she merely returned an angelic smile, trying to convey that she would cooperate with his orders to rest. "But she held up well during our travels. I am no longer fearful of a relapse," Darcy assured Mrs. Gardiner.

"The newspaper has been full of terrible stories about Englishmen being imprisoned in France," Mr. Gardiner interjected. He sat on the settee next to Mrs. Gardiner, holding her hand. "I must say it caused us some concern. Did you have any difficulties?"

Elizabeth exchanged a look with Darcy and then gave the Gardiners an expurgated account of their escape from Dunkirk. Darcy broke in at one point to explain that Elizabeth had used her illness as a reason she could not return to England alone. "That was quick thinking, Lizzy," Mr. Gardiner said.

"Now, tell us of the rest of the trip. How did you leave Paris, and how did you arrive at your friend's house, Mr. Darcy? Elizabeth wrote us that you were helping her return to England, but she did not mention such a stop." Mr. Gardiner's words were polite, but Elizabeth could hear a hint of steel underneath. She was cognizant of how inappropriate it had been for the two of them to travel alone, but Darcy did not appear angry at her uncle's suggestion that he had behaved improperly toward his niece.

Elizabeth had warned Darcy that her uncle had a very strict sense of propriety. They had agreed they wanted to avoid lying to their families, but as Darcy told the story, she noticed he skimmed over certain aspects of their journey, emphasizing their stay at a respectable clergyman's house and not mentioning their lack of chaperonage. When he was finished, she discerned that Mr. Gardiner had more questions about Darcy's behavior.

Elizabeth regretted that her relatives were subjecting Darcy to such suspicion. Her uncle opened his mouth to voice another question, but his wife put her hand on his arm, and he stopped. A look passed between them, and Elizabeth's uncle seemed to subside. Darcy's face reflected the relief Elizabeth felt at the thought that the Gardiners would give them time to reveal their relationship.

Elizabeth sensed the need for a change in the subject. "Now, tell us of the happenings in Longbourn. It seems like so long since I have been home, although it has not even been four weeks!" Her aunt and uncle exchanged a concerned look, and Elizabeth felt her heart contract in fear. Whatever news they had to convey, it was not good. "Oh no!" she cried. "What has happened?"

"Everyone at Longbourn is in good health, Lizzy. It is Lydia…" Mrs. Gardiner's voice trailed off.

Mr. Gardiner took over the story with the air of someone who wished to put an unpleasant task behind him. "She left her friends in Brighton and ran off with an officer almost three weeks ago. We have been unable to locate her."

Elizabeth gasped and covered her mouth with her hand, trying to comprehend this dreadful news. "They eloped?"

Her uncle shook his head. "As ill-advised as that would be, we do not believe they are married. Nor at this point does it appear that he is in a hurry to marry her." Elizabeth felt tears come to her eyes with each revelation, unable to bear all the implications of this news.

Darcy, too, was shocked. "Do you know the officer's name? Where his family lives?"

"His commanding officer said he had no family living. I believe he had some acquaintance with the Bennets when the regiment was in Meryton. His name is George Wickham."

Elizabeth heard Darcy's hiss of indrawn breath and felt that all the wind had been knocked out of her as she peered up at her uncle through the tears swimming in her eyes. "Wickham! Oh, these are the very worst sort of tidings! How is such a man to be worked on?"

"There are ways," Darcy said evenly. Elizabeth buried her face in her handkerchief, thinking how he must regret having allied himself with a family that was experiencing such disgrace. Would he come to wish he had not married her? She had vowed that she would never give him reason to regret the decision. Unfortunately, she could do nothing about her family's behavior.

"What has been done to recover her?" Darcy asked Mr. Gardiner in calm tones, but Elizabeth knew him well enough to be aware of how distressed he truly was. *This is the very worst sort of news! Why, oh why, could Wickham not have chosen someone else's sister?*

"My brother came up from Longbourn for a week since we had some information they were in London, and we searched for them." Her uncle was more troubled than she had ever seen him. "But we failed to discover them. We think they *were* in London, but recently one of his friends received word from a mutual acquaintance that they have left London to find cheaper lodgings. However, we have no information about where they have gone. I have hired an investigator, but so far he has found no trace." His face was a study in disappointment as Mrs. Gardiner gave his hand a reassuring squeeze.

"I may be of some assistance in that regard. I have had some dealings with Wickham in the past," Darcy said softly as if fearing to intrude. However, Elizabeth recognized the firm resolve underlying his words and knew her family would not be permitted to decline his assistance.

"I did not know that!" Mr. Gardiner's face registered his surprise. "Any help would be most welcome."

Elizabeth glanced over to find Darcy's eyes intent on her, but she could not discern his expression. Was he indeed regretting their marriage? *Why would he not? Lydia's disgrace will be shared by the whole family. No one will wish to associate with us!* He will want to leave the scandal behind him, but he cannot. At least, she consoled herself, no one knew of their marriage, giving the option of concealing it for the present so as to preserve his reputation. And he would have his sister's reputation to consider as well; they were planning her come out for the following year. Elizabeth felt a sharp pang of regret over the loss of the bright future they had planned as fresh tears fell from her eyes.

"How is everyone at Longbourn? How are they coping with this state of affairs?" Darcy asked the Gardiners.

"My sister had a fit of nerves and has taken to her room, as is to be expected," answered Mrs. Gardiner. "Jane writes that Mr. Bennet has shut himself up in his library and says little since his return from London."

The maid entered carrying a tea service. "How is Jane herself?" Elizabeth struggled to keep her voice as normal as possible while her aunt poured tea.

"Of course, she does not complain on her own behalf, but I believe these circumstances weigh upon her," her aunt replied. "Mr. Bingley was a great help to her in the first few days after the scandal broke, but then he had to return to London on business. She has not said so, but I think she fears he will not return to Netherfield." Mrs. Gardiner handed a teacup to Darcy, studiously avoiding his eyes. Of course, she knew Darcy was Mr. Bingley's friend.

Darcy frowned in concern. Would this scandal be enough to frighten Mr. Bingley away from Jane just when it appeared that they were doing so well? Elizabeth had been hoping to return from France to learn that they had become engaged.

Thinking some tea would calm her, Elizabeth picked up the teacup her aunt had placed in front of her, but her hands shook so violently that she spilled tea in the saucer. She abandoned the endeavor altogether.

"Perhaps I will see Bingley while I am here," Darcy said. In this simple statement she heard an unstated promise to straighten Bingley out if he had fallen victim to his sisters' fear of scandal. *Perhaps he does not regret our marriage so much after all!* Elizabeth gave him a warm smile. He seemed a little stunned by her approbation. Elizabeth sensed Mr. Gardiner's attention on them, and she turned her gaze to the handkerchief in her hands in an attempt to avoid betraying her affection.

"I regret that we must give you such dreadful tidings so soon after your return from France." Mrs. Gardiner's tone was warm with concern.

"I must return to Longbourn at once!" Elizabeth said with conviction. "They will need me at this moment of crisis."

"You cannot!" Alarm colored Darcy's voice. "You are not well enough for any additional travel. You must rest here for some days."

Shaking her head vehemently, Elizabeth was about to protest when Mrs. Gardiner joined her voice to Darcy's. "You are so pale and tired, Lizzy. And this news will undoubtedly make you feel even worse. There is little you can accomplish at Longbourn in any case. I would not have you jeopardize your well-being."

"But—" Elizabeth began. However, at that moment, the Gardiners' housekeeper arrived to tell her master that a Mr. Harris had arrived to see him. "Ah, that is the investigator!" Mr. Gardiner said. "I hope he has good news. Please excuse me."

After he left, Mrs. Gardiner tried to console Elizabeth with the thought that since Lydia had no fortune, Wickham must have some regard for her, but Elizabeth was not comforted. If Wickham did care for her sister, they would already be married. One glance at Darcy's face told her he did not believe that Wickham would honor his promise either.

Then the housekeeper returned, bearing the news that one of the children had a stomachache and was demanding his mother. Mrs. Gardiner excused herself. In the doorway, she glanced back at Elizabeth and Darcy a little apprehensively since propriety demanded they should not be left without a chaperone. However, her aunt must know they had been unchaperoned quite a bit in France. Apparently as a compromise, she left the door ajar and hastened away.

Darcy was positioned about as far from Elizabeth as the room would allow, and he watched tears trickle down her cheeks, burdened by the full weight of his guilt. *How she must hate me at this moment. I could have prevented it all!* Would she grow to resent being married to the man who had allowed her sister to fall into the hands of such a scoundrel?

Her red-rimmed eyes turned to him, and he felt a fresh wave of guilt wash over him. "I am sorry, Elizabeth," he said. "You must be so angry with me at this moment."

Her expression turned from distressed to puzzled. "Angry with you, why?"

Relief flooded him at the thought that she did not blame him as much, perhaps, as he deserved. "I am the one who allowed this to happen."

A small smile curved her lips. "You are? I thought you were in France at the time."

He stood abruptly and paced the length of the room. "But I could have prevented this!" he said bitterly. "If only I had been willing to lay bare my private affairs. I was too proud to reveal my family's business to the world. If everyone had known Wickham's true nature, this could not have happened."

"I am as much to blame as you. I could have revealed the truth as well."

"You wanted to protect my family's privacy. That is completely admirable!"

Unexpectedly, Elizabeth gave a little laugh. "We could stand here all day trying to take blame, but perhaps that would not be the best use of our time."

He stopped as he considered this idea and then sighed. "Of course, you are right." Watching her wipe her eyes with the handkerchief once more, Darcy was struck by the sudden revelation that she needed his comfort more than his self-recrimination.

Crossing the room in one stride, he gathered Elizabeth into his arms. "My darling, I am so very sorry." He kissed the top of her head and stroked her hair. "The entire time we were talking with your aunt and uncle, I longed to hold you and provide what comfort I could. If they had not left when they did, I might have given into the impulse to hold you—and provide your uncle with evidence to chastise me." He strove to keep his tone lighthearted in the hopes of lightening her mood.

"I am the one who should be sorry," she murmured as she cried against his shoulder. "I regret that you are attached to a family in such disgrace! What will people think of you allying yourself with our family?"

Is that what she truly believes? Darcy asked himself. *How could she think that of me?* Darcy pulled back a little so he could behold her eyes. "My love, there is nothing that could make me regret marrying you. Nothing!" His voice was rough and fierce with emotion. "Not even if you had four disgraced sisters!"

Unexpectedly, this declaration caused her to sob all the more. Hopefully, Darcy thought, with relief.

Then she turned her face upward for a kiss, so he obligingly caressed her lips with his. "It is an inexpressible comfort to have your love at a time like this," she said. He smiled and kissed her again.

He had pressed her against the room's door, which was now completely closed. Therefore, he was well positioned to hear footsteps in the hall and hastily maneuvered Elizabeth into a chair. When Mr. Gardiner entered, Elizabeth was sitting demurely on the settee, and Darcy was gazing out of the window next to the door. Her uncle glanced from one to another but said nothing. When her uncle looked away, Darcy saw Elizabeth discreetly smoothing down her hair.

Darcy turned away from the window. "Has your investigator found them?"

Her uncle shook his head. "Their one clue led nowhere, and I am at a loss. I do not want to abandon my niece, but we have no information about where she is to be found."

"I have some ideas," Darcy said. "Perhaps we should retire to your study to discuss them." Mr. Gardiner nodded gratefully and ushered Darcy out of the room.

Darcy was soon seated in Mr. Gardiner's study with a glass of port at his elbow. He had given the man the whole history of his dealings with Wickham, omitting only Georgiana's name in favor of "a close relative." If the other man guessed her identity, he said nothing.

"So where will you start your investigation?" Gardiner asked.

"I will begin with Mrs. Younge. She runs a boarding house in London where Wickham may have lodged while he was here. If so, she may have an idea where he planned to go. I will also see what can be learned from Wickham's associates near Pemberley."

"That seems like a sound plan." Mr. Gardiner nodded approvingly as he sipped his port.

"I will notify you immediately of any progress." Darcy started to rise, thinking of Elizabeth distressed and alone in the other room. However, Mr. Gardiner cleared his throat to speak, so Darcy stayed his movement.

"Mr. Darcy, I cannot tell you how grateful we are that you returned Elizabeth to us safely." Elizabeth's uncle would not meet Darcy's eyes.

"It was my pleasure, sir. I would never have forgiven myself if I had left her alone and unprotected."

"I would imagine that you had to lay out quite a bit of money to make good your escape. Doctor's bills, hiring a boat, not to mention carriages. However, I suspect you would not accept if I offered to reimburse you for those expenses."

"No, sir."

Mr. Gardiner shook his head, unsurprised by the response. "One other thing. I understand the necessity of fleeing Paris as you did—alone and unchaperoned—and the days you spent with her in your friend's house. Not to mention returning to England just the two of you." Darcy winced inwardly at this description of the continuous impropriety of their situation. "But not everyone would be so understanding. I know you are a man of good character, and Elizabeth seems to hold you in high regard—"

"I assure you, sir, that nothing improper took place." Darcy thought of this as a sin of omission rather than an outright lie. After all, what could be more proper than marriage? However, he was well aware that Mr. Gardiner might not see it in that light.

Elizabeth's uncle waved the assurance away. "I am sure. If my niece had felt herself wronged in any way, she has methods of making it known."

Darcy chuckled a little. "Yes, I believe so."

Mr. Gardiner gave the younger man a wry smile. "All I am asking is that you do not make the circumstances of your escape from France widely known. I am thinking of her reputation."

"Yes, sir. I had already come to that conclusion on my own. I would be loathe to be the instrument of injuring Eliz–Miss Bennet in any way. Rest assured, I plan to conceal it entirely, except perhaps from my sister."

Mr. Gardiner's eyebrows had risen when Darcy used Elizabeth's given name, but he did not comment. "Good, good. Especially in light of Lydia's behavior, the Bennet family hardly needs more gossip circulating."

"I could not agree more."

Mr. Gardiner paused as if hoping that Darcy would say more—perhaps a declaration of his intention to court Elizabeth. However, Darcy could not bring himself to take the deception that far.

The other man stood. "Well, let us rejoin the ladies."

After another half hour of conversation in the drawing room, Darcy reluctantly concluded that he needed to depart. In addition to informing Georgiana of his arrival, he had to set the wheels in motion to find Wickham and Lydia. Elizabeth escorted him out to the carriage to say goodbye, but he was well aware that anyone could be watching them from the house. Darcy wished he could kiss her, caress her, take her back to his house, and…well, there was no use in wishing; he would just have to be patient.

He confined himself to a kiss on her hand. "I believe your uncle is wondering what my intentions toward you are."

Elizabeth laughed a little. "I am sure he is. We will just have to leave him in suspense."

Darcy regarded her seriously. "I am afraid that the news about Lydia makes concealing our marriage even more imperative."

She nodded. "That had occurred to me. I would not want to give my father two unwelcome surprises in such a short time." She bit her lip. "I cannot help comparing my behavior to Lydia's. I am almost as bad as she, acting impulsively without thinking about my family—"

"No!" he said vehemently. "I will not allow you to disparage yourself in this way! We did the honorable thing in marrying. It cannot be compared to living without the benefit of matrimony for weeks. Lydia and Wickham have given no thought to the effect on your family. We have made every attempt at discretion."

"Yes, but I still picture how disappointed my father will be at the circumstances of our marriage." Her head was bowed as she gazed down at her hands.

"But just think how pleased your mother will be." Elizabeth gave him a sour look. "And I would like to think I have more to offer your family than Wickham."

She smiled mischievously at this sally. "I suppose Pemberley is a bigger advantage than Wickham's gambling debts."

"I am afraid must leave. I am sure Georgiana has been worried about me," he said.

He kissed her hand again. They said a lingering goodbye, and he stepped into the coach and left.

***

The carriage pulled up in front of Lord Matlock's house fifteen minutes later. Although Darcy missed Elizabeth with an almost physical pain, he was eager to see Georgiana. Despite the letters he had sent, he knew she would be worrying about him.

The butler admitted him and sent a footman to find Georgiana. Within a minute, she was flying down the stairs with a huge smile on her face and embracing her brother with all the strength her slight frame could produce.

"Brother! I am so relieved to see you. I was so worried!"

"I hope you got my messages about why I was delayed in leaving France."

Georgiana practically quivered with joy. "I did, but I could not rest easy until you were back in England. There have been so many terrible stories about what is happening in France. Englishmen have been imprisoned for no reason!" Darcy thought now was not the time to tell her that he had almost been one of them.

Georgiana recollected herself and said, "You must be famished! Let us retire to the drawing room, and I will ring for tea." She was so happy at the thought that he did not dare to tell her that he had already had tea.

Even before tea was served, Georgiana started peppering him with questions about the trip. "Did you see the Louvre? What was it like? Was it dangerous being about once the war was on? Were you frightened? How is your friend who was sick?"

Georgiana finally ran out of breath, and Darcy, smiling, answered just the last question. "My friend is much better, thank you. It was fortunate we were able to leave France when we did." He congratulated himself on negotiating the answer without using pronouns or names. In his letters to Georgiana, Darcy had not mentioned the gender or name of his friend, knowing that she would assume it to be a male friend. Although he would need to tell her eventually, she was still young and easily shocked, so he hoped to put it off—at least until after she had met Elizabeth.

As they sipped tea, he gave her an abbreviated account of his travels, including the ball at the Radnor residence. He recounted the tale of encountering Elizabeth quite unexpectedly. "I would love for you to meet her, Georgiana. She has a good understanding and a lively disposition. I think you would get on very well."

"She is the one who visited Rosings at Easter, is she not? I would love to meet her." Impressed that she remembered Elizabeth from his brief mentions in his letters, Darcy realized he had never before asked his sister to meet a woman of his acquaintance. She must suspect a partiality, but that was all to the good, he thought; it would lay the groundwork for his eventual announcement.

Lady Matlock sailed into the room upon Georgiana's last words. As always, she had a commanding presence and was dressed in the very latest fashions; however, Darcy thought he spotted shadows under her eyes and creases of worry in her face. He wondered what had occurred to disturb her usual equanimity. "Whom would you love to meet, Georgiana?" she asked as she gave Darcy a kiss on the cheek and settled herself into a tapestried chair. "Fitzwilliam, lovely to see you. I am so pleased you are not imprisoned in France after all," she murmured. Then she turned to Georgiana, awaiting her answer.

"Miss Elizabeth Bennet, Aunt," Georgiana said.

"Bennet! Is that not the name of the foolish girl who ran away with a militia officer?"

Darcy groaned inwardly. Since his family and Elizabeth's traveled in such separate spheres, he had hoped the news of Lydia's scandal would not have penetrated this far. "That girl is Elizabeth's sister. How did you come to hear of it?" he asked.

"Catherine wrote to me of it. The Bennets are related to her rector I believe."

Darcy shuddered to think how Lady Catherine and Mr. Collins had interpreted the event. "I hardly think Miss Bennet can be blamed for her sister's indiscretions."

"No, but the family…" Lady Matlock's voice trailed off uncharacteristically. "Especially now, we should not be associating with anyone…who…we should not associate with them for at least several months until the whole thing is less fresh in everyone's minds. You shall have to wait a while before forming such an acquaintance." His aunt's tone suggested Georgiana should relinquish the idea of ever meeting Elizabeth.

Although his aunt's suggestion was not unexpected, Darcy was confused by the hesitations in his aunt's speech; she was not usually so vague. "Miss Bennet will be in London only a couple more days," Darcy explained.

"Fitzwilliam, Georgiana probably has not apprised you of recent events. Now more than ever it would not be good to have your sister—or *anyone* in the family—associating with less than desirable companions." Her voice was emphatic but quivered with unexpected emotion.

Darcy took a deep breath and prayed for patience. "What has happened?"

His aunt's face colored, and he thought he had never seen her demonstrate so much embarrassment. She was the soul of rectitude and a premiere arbiter of fashion in the *ton*. "Well, I suppose I must tell you before you hear it from someone else. We have tried to keep it quiet, but you know how they like to talk…"

Darcy was rapidly losing patience. "What is it, Aunt?"

"It is Robert. He has married that…that…Williams girl." Her voice was full of disgust.

Darcy looked from her to Georgiana in astonishment. "The actress?" His aunt nodded. "My cousin married his mistress?"

Chapter 9

Lady Alice was one of the most indomitable women Darcy knew, but she was blinking rapidly as if holding back tears. "They went to Gretna Green just last week. I am certain many in town have not heard tell of it yet. Fortunately, it is thinly populated this time of year, but they will hear of it. They will."

The import of the news was beginning to sink in. His cousin, his uncle's heir, the future Earl of Matlock, had married his mistress. Darcy had never met the woman, but she was reported to be quite vulgaralthough very pretty. "Where are they now?" Darcy could now see the signs that Georgiana was also quite distressed by the news and her aunt's reaction to it.

"They are hiding up in Brookton. He sent us a letter when they returned from Scotland. At least he has the decency not to come to town!" She shook her head. "I knew he was always impetuous, but I never thought—an actress!" Dabbing at her eyes with a handkerchief, his aunt was the picture of mortification.

Darcy knew that some prominent peers had married actresses who were eventually accepted by the *ton*, but it had taken years to gain recognition— and those women were rather genteel. Robert and his wife might never be accepted. "I am so sorry, Aunt. That must have been distressing news to receive."

"Indeed." She twisted her handkerchief in her hands. "Your uncle has not yet stopped cursing under his breath."

"Aunt Alice believes it is incumbent upon all of us to put forth our best manners and hold our heads high." Georgiana's first contribution to the conversation came out as hardly louder than a whisper, a reflection of her own distress.

"Precisely! If our family is to live this occurrence down, we must ensure that not the slightest hint of impropriety tinges the Fitzwilliam name." Lady Alice's face was stony as she made this pronouncement and gazed meaningfully at Darcy.

So this would be a bad time to tell them I married a woman of no fortune. Darcy ran his fingers through his hair. This was another complication he did not need: first Elizabeth's sister, now his cousin. Their families seemed to be inadvertently conspiring to ensure that they could never publicly acknowledge their marriage.

"In fact, we are planning a ball for two days hence. I expect you to attend," his aunt added. The return of her authoritarian manner signaled that she had mastered her emotions.

"Aunt Alice, I completely understand and respect your wishes for our continued propriety, and I have no desire to cause additional scandal," Darcy said. "I will happily agree never to admit the Bennets' wayward daughter, Lydia, into my home or to Georgiana's acquaintance. But I am not prepared to shun a respectable family because of the poor judgment of a foolish young girl. It is important to me that Georgiana meet Miss Elizabeth Bennet." He knew that by insisting on the point, he was virtually declaring his intentions toward Elizabeth. But they had to know soon; there was no point in concealing his interest even if he could not reveal everything.

Aunt Alice's face resembled a bull's when confronted with a red cape. "But she is a nobody! Her family has no name, no fortune, and they are disgraced! Georgiana cannot associate with them, and you should not either!" In her indignation, her face had turned quite red.

Darcy sighed. "I must insist on this point. I am not about to discontinue my association with Miss Elizabeth Bennet, and you cannot forbid me to introduce her to Georgiana. *I* am her guardian. I will, however, happily abide by other directives that you deem necessary for the family at this time."

His aunt's eyes narrowed as she regarded him, enlightenment flashing across her face. "So that is how the wind blows, is it? I have thrown every eligible young lady of the *ton* at you for years, and you have never so much as danced two dances with a single girl. And now you are attaching yourself to a country miss?" Georgiana squirmed in her seat, obviously uncomfortable being present during such a disagreement.

"You should be relieved. You keep telling me I am waiting too long," he said with an ironic smile.

"I am *not* relieved!" she snapped. "This is an entirely inappropriate attachment. Especially now! I do not condone it."

"Miss Bennet is a completely respectable young woman. Her father is a gentleman in Hertfordshire, and she has excellent breeding."

"But much of her family is in trade, I understand, and her family has no standing to speak of. The scandal of her sister will follow her. No, it cannot be done. Not now!" His aunt gestured emphatically.

Darcy stood. "I do not need your approbation, madam. I am not a child!"

He was on the verge of stalking out of the room, but Georgiana touched his hand, and he peered down at her, knowing that she did not want dissension in the family. He took a deep breath. "I appreciate your concern for our family's reputation—and I share it. However, I am more concerned about my own happiness. It is, of course, your prerogative to not receive Miss Bennet or her family. But should you choose such a course, it will almost certainly result in your estrangement from me."

Lady Alice looked nonplussed for a moment. "You would create more scandal for the family—at this time? How could you?"

"I do not believe there would be scandal, nor do I wish to be estranged from your family. However, I will not compromise my own happiness."

His aunt sighed. "Very well. Visit with this Miss Bennet if you must. I will not perpetuate any unpleasantness, but I can do nothing to curb the gossip."

"I would like you to invite Miss Bennet and her aunt and uncle to your ball. Their name is Gardiner." His aunt was already shaking her head. "Would you like *me* to attend the ball? I believe I may have a previous engagement that night."

His aunt closed her eyes as if in pain, but she won the struggle to maintain her composure. "Very well."

Darcy smiled mirthlessly. "I think I can rearrange my schedule to accommodate the ball."

"Where do they live?" Lady Alice's voice came from between gritted teeth.

"Gracechurch Street. In Cheapside."

"Cheapside." The way his aunt said it, it might as well be a curse.

Darcy bristled. "They are thoroughly respectable, genteel people."

His aunt sighed. "Promise me that you will not make your attentions to this Miss Bennet too obvious, and you must dance with some of the other eligible young ladies. Perhaps someone more appropriate will turn your head." Darcy started to shake his head. "You promised to cooperate with my directives," she reminded him.

Darcy leaned back in his chair. "I will dance with them if you wish, but I can tell you that they will not alter my sentiments." *Thank goodness she does not know it is already too late!*

"We shall see." With that, his aunt arose from her chair and stalked out of the room. Georgiana still appeared distressed, so Darcy sat next to her, taking her hand and turning the conversation to more pleasant topics.

***

Later that day, Darcy was in his study, having finally returned to Darcy House and receiving a long overdue bath. His visit to Mrs. Younge had proceeded as he expected. With some financial persuasion, she admitted that Wickham had been in London for a week but departed because he could no longer afford lodgings. It was clear, however, that she did not know where Wickham had gone.

Immediately, Darcy proceeded to hire one of the famed Bow Street Runners. One investigator now had the names of Wickham's associates near Pemberley and would visit Derbyshire to see who had news of him. Without money, Wickham would need assistance from friends. Another investigator would try to pick up Wickham's trail in London. Darcy had also visited Colonel Fitzwilliam—who was very relieved to find his cousin back in the country—to ask for any help he and his colleagues in the army might provide. Darcy sighed, thinking that he should visit Pemberley to speak with Wickham's friends in person, but he could not bring himself to leave Elizabeth. *The investigator should be able to make progress with the information I gave him,* Darcy reassured himself.

Darcy smiled ironically at the thought that the best way to flush out Wickham would be to reveal his marriage to Elizabeth. Wickham would probably be on his doorstep the next day demanding payment in exchange for marrying Lydia. However, there were equally good reasons for concealing the marriage.

Darcy applied himself to the correspondence that had accumulated while he was in France. After he had worked for an hour, a footman arrived and announced Mr. Bingley's arrival. "Darcy!" Bingley bounced in as usual, but there were lines of care around his face that Darcy did not recall seeing before. "I only just learned that you had returned."

"I arrived this morning. Napoleon made it difficult to extricate myself from France." Darcy gestured his friend to a seat and poured Bingley a brandy, which he downed with alacrity despite the early hour. Pouring another, Darcy suspected some distress on Bingley's part.

"So I learned when I visited Georgiana and your aunt last week. I am eager to hear the complete story. "

"Another time, perhaps." Darcy set down his glass untasted. "It is long and involved, best suited to a leisurely evening with a glass of port."

"I look forward to it." Bingley fell uncharacteristically silent, and Darcy again sensed that something weighed on his friend's mind but gave him time to broach the subject on his own.

"I visited the Bennets in Hertfordshire last week," Bingley finally said. Darcy knew what his friend was leading up to.

"How were they?"

"They were good. That is, except—there has been a bit of upset over the youngest sister."

"Yes, I know about Lydia and Wickham."

Bingley's eyes widened in surprise. In retrospect, Darcy realized it was scarcely the kind of news he would ordinarily be privy to, especially on his first day back in London. "I learned it from Lydia's aunt and uncle, the Gardiners, this morning. I offered my assistance in locating Wickham."

Bingley's face continued to register astonishment. "That is very good of you. But why in the world were you visiting Lydia's aunt and uncle? I did not know you were acquainted."

Darcy traced one finger along the rim of his brandy glass. "I…um…met them in France. They were there on business."

"Oh, of course! Then you must have seen Miss Elizabeth as well." Bingley's open expression demonstrated that he did not suspect Darcy's regard for Jane's sister.

"I did have that pleasure." Darcy controlled his expression so it would not betray him.

"Has she returned from France as well? Jane was most concerned about her."

"Yes, she is recently returned," Darcy answered carefully.

Bingley frowned in perplexity once more. "But what was so pressing that you needed to call on the Gardiners as soon as you returned from France?"

This was a bit of an impertinent question, and Darcy considered saying something about ascertaining that the Gardiners had returned safely from France. But Bingley was one of his best friends and deserved to know the truth—at least some of the truth. "I was not visiting the Gardiners. I was there to see Miss Elizabeth."

"Whatever for?" Now Darcy was regretting how circumspect he had been about his affection; even Bingley had no suspicions.

"I am…I have developed…an interest in her…"

"What sort of interest?" Then Darcy saw understanding—and astonishment—dawn on Bingley's face. "But you thought the Bennets were—"

"Yes, I know. I was wrong as I mentioned when I apologized for my conduct earlier. It was partly my regard for Eliz–Miss Bennet that showed me how wrong I had been."

"Oh." Bingley fell silent as he digested this information, then sat up straighter. "So you are precisely the person I need to speak with about my circumstances." Darcy nodded encouragingly as his friend continued. "When the news arrived at Longbourn about Lydia's elopement, I wanted to be of assistance to the family. But there was deuced little I could do! I could offer Jane comfort, but she was occupied with caring for her mother. I thought my presence was more of a hindrance since Jane felt she needed to entertain me when she had other duties."

Bingley took a long sip, finishing off his brandy, but Darcy did not offer to pour him another. "Caroline and Louisa were staying with me at Netherfield. They were horrified about Lydia and thought the whole affair demonstrated the Bennets' bad breeding. They wanted to leave Netherfield and disassociate from the family. I agreed to bring them to London, in part because I thought it would help Jane to remove them from her vicinity. But I would not agree to stop courting Jane. Now I regret returning to London. Caroline has wasted no time informing everyone she knows about the Bennets' disgrace. I think she is hoping to shame me into giving Jane up, but *nothing* could do that!" Bingley made the announcement with uncharacteristic vehemence.

Darcy responded mildly. "Good. I am pleased you will not renounce the attachment over this matter."

"I explained all of this to Jane before I left, but she may have believed I was only trying to spare her feelings. Her countenance stayed serene, but she is good at hiding her true sentiments—and my history in this regard is not good," Bingley said with a bitter expression. Darcy winced inwardly; he knew Bingley was not reproaching him, but he experienced regret nonetheless. "What do you think I should do?" Bingley asked.

"Are you certain you want my advice? I have not proven a good advisor in the past."

"Yes, I am sure. In fact, you are the only person who could truly understand my dilemma. Since you and Miss Elizabeth—"

"Our circumstances are quite different actually."

Bingley ran his fingers through his hair, appearing about to leap out of the chair with nervous energy. "Yes, yes, I see what you mean. Miss Elizabeth is here, not at Longbourn. But even so, what do you think I should do?"

If only he knew how different their circumstances were! "What do you want to do?" Darcy asked quietly.

"I wish to be with Jane," Bingley answered instantly.

"Then you should and ignore your sisters' comments. They can remain in London. In fact, I will be visiting Hertfordshire in three days. I would be happy to have you accompany me."

"Good!" Bingley exclaimed. "You must stay at Netherfield. That is an excellent plan. Going with you gives me a reason to travel there. Thank you." Darcy smiled, happy that he could be of service to both his friend and Elizabeth's family.

***

Elizabeth had passed a restless night. *How quickly I have grown accustomed to Darcy's presence that now I ache for him when he is absent!* During the long night, she recited to herself the reasons for not revealing their marriage, but they seemed to pale in comparison to the longing she felt for him. She wanted his lips on her…his arms around her…his hands…no, it would not do to further fan the flames of desire.

Apparently, her listlessness was noticed at the breakfast table. "Are you feeling unwell? You seem peaked," Mrs. Gardiner asked.

"No, Aunt, thank you, I am perfectly well. Simply fatigued. The traveling wore me out a bit." Elizabeth attempted to butter her toast in a more lively fashion.

"You must take every opportunity to rest today," her aunt insisted. "I can see that you are still recovering from your illness." There was a knock at the front door; moments later, the housekeeper entered with an elegant, creamy white envelope, which she gave to Mrs. Gardiner. Elizabeth's aunt looked surprised, broke the seal, and opened it at once. "Oh my!" she exclaimed.

"What is it?" Elizabeth asked.

"The Earl and Countess Matlock have invited us—and you—to a ball tomorrow night." She looked bewildered. "I do not believe I have ever met Lord and Lady Matlock." Still frowning in confusion, she handed the invitation to Elizabeth.

"I believe they are Mr. Darcy's aunt and uncle," Elizabeth said as she perused the invitation. Experiencing a need to behave casually, she took a sip of tea.

"Oh, I see. He must have arranged for the invitation. How nice!" Her aunt was eyeing Elizabeth speculatively and then appeared to have made a decision. "I suspect Mr. Darcy of some partiality to you. Has he said anything of an attachment?"

Elizabeth blushed and set her teacup down quickly, thinking of the last time he expressed his affection forcefully. How much should she reveal? She was uncomfortable with outright untruths but could not allow her aunt to guess the truth. "He *has* expressed a warm regard for me," she confessed. There, it was not a lie but did not reveal too much.

Her aunt drew her breath in quickly. "Oh, Elizabeth, truly? And how do you feel about him? I know that once you disliked him."

"That is all in the past. I…experience affection for him…." she allowed. "He took excellent care of me when I was sick."

Mrs. Gardiner smiled as she regarded her niece over the rim of her teacup. "You may not be aware of the great honor of such a man's affections. His estate of Pemberley is very large, and the house is very grand—one of the grandest in England, I daresay."

The raptures of her aunt, who was not prone to exaggeration, had a peculiar effect on Elizabeth. She was eager to see Pemberley since Darcy spoke of it with such love, but now she reflected on the responsibilities of being his wife. Was she prepared to be mistress of such an estate? She took a deep breath, attempting to quell her apprehension. It would happen whether she was prepared or not; the decision had been made.

"Are you all right?" her aunt asked. "Your face suddenly became rather white."

"Yes, I am fine." Elizabeth attempted to calm herself by envisioning William's face: his slightly crooked smile, his beautiful dark eyes, and the way they twinkled when he was teasing her.

"There is no time to order you a new gown before the ball, but I have one that we could alter for you."

"Nonsense! I can wear the yellow silk I wore in France."

"No, a ball at an earl's house demands greater elegance. Plus, Mr. Darcy has already seen that gown. We shall visit the *modiste* once we have finished breakfast." Her aunt's tone was very emphatic.

Elizabeth sighed in acquiescence. It seemed foolish for her aunt to give up a gown in hopes of securing a man who had already become her husband. But, Elizabeth realized, this ball would also afford the inhabitants of the *ton* their first glimpse of her. It was important to give a good first impression. "Very well."

***

Only an hour later, Darcy brought his sister to the Gardiners for a visit. When he entered the drawing room, Elizabeth's heart fluttered, and she wanted nothing more than to fling herself into his arms. When they had devised the plan of concealing the marriage, she had not anticipated how difficult it would be to see him and desire him but be unable to act on it. *How have I become so brazen in only a few days?* She blushed at the thought. *But then we are married. Surely it is permissible to desire my husband.*

Darcy's eyes sought hers as soon as he entered the room, and he gave her a heartwarming smile. She returned it, trying to put all of her unspoken love into each glance.

Elizabeth enjoyed making Georgiana's acquaintance. She was a lovely girl, although painfully shy, and initially answered questions with the shortest possible sentences. However, Elizabeth diligently sought out subjects that would elicit some conversation from the younger girl and was rewarded with some longer answers. After a few minutes, she was freely speaking to Elizabeth about her school, her friends, and her love of music.

Whenever Elizabeth glanced at Darcy, she noticed approval on his face. During a lull in the conversation, Mrs. Gardiner took the opportunity to ask Darcy questions about his family and Pemberley. Elizabeth was happy that they were becoming better acquainted. After they had been there an hour, Darcy suggested a walk in the nearby park.

It was a clear day and not overly warm—ideal for a walk. After the four of them had been strolling a few minutes, Darcy and Elizabeth lagged behind the others, so he offered her his arm, and they took the pathway at a leisurely pace. Mrs. Gardiner was showing Georgiana a pond and other features of the park, providing the lovers with some privacy. Georgiana seemed content but did not respond as readily to the older woman as she had to Elizabeth.

Darcy shook his head in disbelief. "I have never seen Georgiana take to someone as quickly as she did to you. Usually, it takes her months to become comfortable with a stranger, if it happens at all. She has been especially reticent...after recent events."

"I thought her a very pleasant conversationalist," Elizabeth said.

He hugged her hand tightly to his side, wishing he could embrace all of her. "You have a unique ability to put her at ease. It gave me great joy to see you converse so freely. I believe you are destined to be great friends."

"I hope so," Elizabeth said. They walked in silence for a moment. Elizabeth soaked up the sunshine and enjoyed the tranquility of the park. "We received an invitation to a ball given by Earl and Countess Matlock tomorrow."

Darcy smiled. "I am glad it arrived." He turned his head toward her. "This will be an excellent opportunity for you to meet some of my relatives and acquaintances. At least they will know who you are when we reveal our marriage."

"I believe it will be a shock no matter how much preparation we give them," Elizabeth opined.

"Perhaps, but the ball will provide an opportunity to show my partiality for you." Elizabeth noticed a muscle in his jaw tighten.

"Is there a problem?"

He sighed. "A small one; nothing you need to worry about. My cousin, Richard's brother, apparently took it into his head to marry his mistress while I was in France. She is a former actress, and it has created quite a stir within the family."

Elizabeth imagined how the family must feel. "They must be very unhappy. And I thought they would be scandalized by me!" Darcy chuckled. "Was the marriage completely unexpected?" she asked.

Darcy considered his answer. "Perhaps not entirely. He was always very enamored of her, but my aunt and uncle thought he would outgrow the infatuation and marry someone more appropriate. The difficulty is that my aunt is particularly concerned about the damage to our family's reputation. Which means—"

"She is not pleased to have you associate with *another* family touched by scandal," Elizabeth finished for him. "Unfortunately, her reservations are completely understandable. Perhaps I should wait and attend a ball in a few months, when both scandals will have faded from memory."

"No!" Darcy's voice was fierce. "I have waited long enough for you. I will not wait one moment more than necessary." He brought her gloved hand up to his mouth and kissed it, causing her to wish he could kiss other parts of her body. As he stopped walking altogether, he gazed intently into her eyes. "At night I long for your touch. Just the memory of it …is sweet torture. And now…seeing you and being unable to touch you…"

Her eyes locked on his; she could not tear her gaze away. "I know," she whispered.

"We should continue walking or I will surrender to my desire to kiss you," Darcy murmured, and she chuckled.

As they resumed walking, she placed her hand on his arm, and he covered it with his. "I must tell you, my love: I insisted that my aunt invite you to the ball, but she was not pleased. In exchange, I promised that I would not be overly attentive in my attentions to you and that I would dance with other eligible young women. I am sorry." He regarded her anxiously.

"Well, if that is the price I must pay for seeing you at the ball, so be it," she said lightly.

"Thank you for understanding. Please know, they—these other women—will mean nothing to me. If I could, I would dance every dance with you."

"That *would* cause a scandal!" Elizabeth laughed. "Nor do I have the energy for every dance, I believe."

Darcy's face instantly reflected concern. "Will your health allow attendance at the ball? I do not want you to exert yourself too strongly and compromise your recovery."

Elizabeth shook her head. "I do tire a little more easily than before, and I slept quite late this morning! But today I am more like myself. Certainly I can survive a ball." Darcy appeared about to protest. "William, I do not want to miss it." He subsided but still looked concerned.

They walked in silence for a while. Seeing that she was tiring, Darcy invited her to sit on a bench and then took the place next to her. Eventually, Darcy spoke. "I have a reputation for never dancing with the same woman twice. I never wished to give rise to rumors or create false expectations, and there was no one I wanted to know better—until you." His smile warmed her.

Suddenly, she realized that while they were talking, Darcy's hand had worked its way around her back and softly caressed the nape of her neck. She blushed at the thought of her aunt's reaction to the impropriety. Fortunately, Georgiana and Mrs. Gardiner were far ahead of them, feeding bread to the ducks in the pond.

Her first impulse was to chastise Darcy or at least tease him, but when he ran his hand lightly along her shoulder, she shivered with pleasure and recalled so many other pleasurable touches. Closing her eyes, she simply enjoyed the sensations.

Then she opened them and tilted her head toward Darcy. "When I first met you, I thought you excessively proud and proper. Who knew that underneath you are completely lacking in propriety, sir?"

"I beg to differ. I was the soul of propriety before I met you, madam." He arched his brow at her.

She laughed. "So I have corrupted you? No, I do not believe that to be the case. I know I never before allowed a man to caress my neck in public." She gave him a mischievous look. "I am afraid you are an appallingly bad influence on my behavior— and not the other way around."

"Now that I think of it, I do believe I have talked you into some shocking behavior." Seeing Georgiana and Mrs. Gardiner turn and stroll back toward them, Darcy hastily removed his arm from around Elizabeth's back. As the two women were almost within earshot, he leaned over and whispered in her ear, "Mrs. Darcy!"

Her giggle caused her aunt to raise an eyebrow. Elizabeth schooled her face into a properly demure expression as they turned back to Gracechurch Street.

***

Darcy's aunt insisted on greeting each guest who arrived, apparently as part of her campaign to appear as if no scandal had touched the family. Unfortunately, she had also insisted that her husband, Colonel Fitzwilliam, and Darcy join her, although Darcy was last in the line and many people did not linger to talk with him. Because Georgiana was not officially out in society, she was spared this duty. *Lucky Georgiana*, Darcy thought. Darcy's eyes were drawn to the door each time a new visitor appeared. Instinctively, he knew he would be more comfortable with the whole evening once Elizabeth arrived, even if he could not spend every moment with her as he would prefer.

He glanced at his aunt and uncle; Aunt Alice held her head high as she attempted to appear above any gossip about her son and his mistress. His uncle appeared oblivious, which he probably was. He had been irate about his son's actions but often did not notice the ill effects of gossip. However, happily, very few people had declined the invitation to the ball, so Lady Matlock was in high spirits, seeing it as an indication that the earl's family had not slipped down the social pecking order. But Darcy saw signs of strain around her mouth and knew that they could not assume they had escaped scandal so easily.

Even as this thought occurred to him, Darcy noticed some women gossiping behind their fans and exchanging raised eyebrows. Clearly there was some talk about his cousin's behavior. Darcy could understand his aunt's insistence on avoiding further scandal at this moment, although he grimaced at the thought. He would have had no trouble complying with her wishes at another moment in time, but how long could he bear to be separated from Elizabeth?

There was a lull during which no guests arrived, and Colonel Fitzwilliam, who was standing next to Darcy, took the opportunity to scrutinize his cousin. "Well, Cousin, you do not seem nearly as melancholy as before we left for France." Darcy nodded briefly in acknowledgment but said nothing to enlighten his cousin. "Now you have a new sprightliness in your step. Care to reveal why?"

Darcy gazed past his cousin to the ballroom door. "No."

"I shall figure it out." The colonel grinned rakishly. "I would love to learn more about your escape from France. It is a thrilling story, I am certain."

"Yes, I will have to recount it when I have time to do it justice," Darcy said, trying to ignore Fitzwilliam's scrutiny.

"I had planned to apologize for luring you to France and entrapping you in a war, but perhaps it is not necessary."

Darcy gave him a sidelong glance that was full of irony. "Richard, have I thanked you recently for dragging me to France and entrapping me in a war?"

Fitzwilliam was still attempting to formulate an appropriate response when Darcy spied Elizabeth and the Gardiners entering the room. He hurried forward to make the introductions.

Elizabeth was stunning in a gown of blue silk, with a light blue ribbon woven into her dark curls. As he introduced them, Darcy could see his aunt taking the measure of the younger woman, having already dismissed the Gardiners as being unimportant. Now she pursed her lips in disapproval as she regarded Elizabeth, who nonetheless radiated charm and confidence, smiling and talking with apparent disregard of his aunt's mood. He wondered what the effort was costing her.

Darcy resumed his place next to Fitzwilliam as the Gardiners and Elizabeth made their way toward him. Elizabeth curtsied before the colonel. "Miss Bennet," he said, "I am so happy to see that you were able to escape France without harm."

"Thank you, Colonel."

"When did you arrive in London?"

"Only a few days ago." Fitzwilliam raised his eyebrows at this information but said nothing. "I did not expect to see you in London," she added.

"Yes, I have been assigned the onerous duty of defending the capital," Fitzwilliam replied with mock regret, and Elizabeth laughed. "Actually, I am currently serving as an aide to General Howell, but they may send me abroad soon. I hope I may have the pleasure of a dance tonight?"

"Yes, sir." She smiled winningly at him. "The first dance is reserved." Elizabeth's gaze slid to Darcy, her eyes sparkling since he had requested the first dance yesterday. "But you may have the second if you wish."

"Very good." The colonel's eyes traveled speculatively from Elizabeth to Darcy, who returned the look blandly.

Mrs. Gardiner had been standing next to Elizabeth during this exchange. "Elizabeth, you cannot do too much dancing, remember. If you fatigue yourself too much, you might suffer a relapse."

Annoyance flashed across Elizabeth's face and was gone. "I will be careful. May I present Colonel Fitzwilliam, Mr. Darcy's cousin?"

As the Gardiners conversed with the colonel, Elizabeth moved down the line to stand opposite Darcy, curtseying with an ironic gleam in her eye. "Mr. Darcy, so good to see you again."

"Miss Bennet, can I say you look lovely tonight? I daresay no other lady here can compare." He kissed her hand. It was pure torture. She was here—more beautiful than he had ever seen her— and he could not kiss her. He decided the rules of proper behavior had some serious flaws. "I look forward to our dance."

"As do I." Her smile was completely innocent, yet it made him want to forget every promise he had made to his aunt—to dance every dance with her, take her into his arms, and never let her go. He wanted, God help him, to announce their marriage to everyone at the ball so there would be no barriers between them.

The Gardiners greeted Darcy, and after a brief conversation, the trio moved away, Darcy watching Elizabeth until she disappeared into the crowd. Most of the guests had already arrived, and the two men had no one to greet. Colonel Fitzwilliam turned to his cousin with a speculative gleam in his eye. "I had not realized Miss Bennet had been ill."

With a sinking feeling, Darcy realized where this conversation was tending. "I believe she is mostly recovered," Darcy allowed.

"It is quite a coincidence," Fitzwilliam continued. "Georgiana said your letters from France explained how your traveling companion was ill and unable to travel. She thought it a little curious that you did not mention your companion's name but concluded it was because she was probably not acquainted with him. Now I wonder if he was a *she*." Fitzwilliam grinned at Darcy.

"Your powers of deduction are undimmed, Cousin," Darcy said, lowering his voice. He had known he would not be able to conceal the truth of his travels in France from his cousin for long. "Miss Bennet had no other way to leave France since her aunt and uncle were in another part of the country. When she became ill, I took her to the home of my college friend, Thomas Whitmore. Nothing improper took place, however. After all, she was ill most of the time."

Fitzwilliam waved this statement away as unnecessary. "Of course. I know you Darcy. Are you ever planning to enlighten Georgiana?"

"Eventually. She is so young and easily shocked, but I know she will be sympathetic to the necessities of the situation. I hope she will get to know Elizabeth better before I must lay out the full story." Darcy sighed inwardly at the thought of how much story there was to explain. "Out of concern for Miss Bennet's reputation, we have kept the details a secret."

"Rest assured, I will not say anything." Fitzwilliam resumed his speculative expression. "Did I perceive a softening in her regard for you?"

Darcy could not suppress a small smile. "There has been progress. Unfortunately, your brother has made it rather difficult to associate with a family touched by scandal right now. Not to mention the trouble caused by Lydia Bennet and Wickham."

Fitzwilliam shook his head in disgust. "Did my mother lecture you about your duty to the family? Are you going to let that stop you?"

"No, although I plan to be circumspect." Fitzwilliam nodded his understanding.

As soon as he finished greeting guests, Darcy procured a glass of punch and took it to Elizabeth, who was talking with Georgiana while the Gardiners observed. Darcy stood at Elizabeth's elbow, amazed how easily she conversed with his sister. It was probably the most he had ever heard Georgiana say to someone who was not in the family.

Soon the orchestra started playing some introductory notes, signaling the beginning of the dancing. He saw his uncle escort his aunt—every inch the countess—to the dance floor to open the ball. "I believe this is my dance, Miss Bennet?" He took her hand and led her to the dance floor. Colonel Fitzwilliam came to claim Georgiana as a partner. Since she was not officially out, Darcy's sister could only dance with family members, and Darcy considered this night to be a good rehearsal for her eventual debut. Next year, for her first season, she would be obligated to attend balls and dinners almost every night.

Darcy and Elizabeth beheld each other as they waited for the dance music to begin. He could hardly wait to touch her even though the strictures of the formal dance would allow only limited contact. The music started, and he took Elizabeth's hand as she circled around him. When she passed close enough, he murmured, "My bed was very empty last night." He was rewarded by a delicate blush coloring her cheeks, but then she looked pensive. As she circled again, she said, "What a coincidence. So was mine." He felt himself flush and then chuckled, realizing she had gotten her revenge.

As they negotiated the dance's intricate figures, Darcy felt more at ease than he ever had at a ball. Elizabeth's smiles touched his heart, and every time their hands met, he felt an electrical shock. His frustration at their limited contact was tempered by a deep satisfaction in the knowledge that she was his.

At first he danced in a haze of love, oblivious to anything outside their private world; eventually, however, he noticed an inordinately large number of people watching them. Young women stared while mothers and chaperones talkedg with great animation, no doubt wondering about the identity of his partner and her family. As his aunt had predicted, anyone he danced with would become an object of interest. He would find the whole thing laughable except that he was sure the news of Lydia and Wickham was circulating as well, and people would soon connect the scandal to Elizabeth's family. It could not be helped, but he vowed to shield Elizabeth from the vitriol as much as he could.

When he turned his attention back to Elizabeth, her beautiful eyes were full of concern as she recognized what all the whispering meant. As the steps of the dance drew them close, Darcy murmured to her, "Do not be concerned, my love. We will face it together."

"William, are you sure you do not—"

He knew what she was about to say. "I do not have one moment's hesitation about what we did," he whispered. "My only regret would have been if you had refused me a second time." His words were rewarded with a slow smile spreading across her face.

The first dance ended, and Darcy passed Elizabeth over to Colonel Fitzwilliam while he danced with Georgiana. Darcy found it hard to keep his attention on Georgiana, who fortunately did not seem to expect him to converse much. His gaze continuously drifted to Elizabeth and Fitzwilliam. He could not hear what they were talking about, but she was laughing and smiling. Darcy noticed every time his cousin's hands briefly touched her waist or her hand. *You have nothing to worry about; she has chosen you*, he reminded himself. However, the necessity of concealing their marriage meant it was difficult to believe in the reality of her choice. He was especially sensitive to Fitzwilliam's attentions since he knew his cousin had admired her at Rosings.

Then Darcy noticed Georgiana watching him watch Elizabeth, so he smiled reassuringly to his sister and focused his attention to her. The expression on her face suggested she had guessed his attachment to Elizabeth; he would need to tell her the truth soon.

When the second dance ended, Darcy handed Georgiana to Fitzwilliam and quickly strolled toward Elizabeth, intending to make sure she rested—and did not dance with anyone else, except maybe her uncle. However, before he reached her, he was intercepted by Aunt Alice. "Fitzwilliam," she said softly but firmly, "you promised me not to be excessively attentive to Miss Bennet and to dance with other eligible ladies." While she spoke, she put a hand to his elbow and guided him over to a young lady who stood waiting with her mother. She was quite pretty, he supposed, with blonde curls and blue eyes. Her dress was quite *au courant* and showed a pleasing figure; however, he knew that only one pair of eyes and dark hair would satisfy him.

"May I introduce Miss Penelope Maddox? Her father is the Earl of Colting," Aunt Alice said. "Miss Maddox, this is my nephew, Fitzwilliam Darcy." Miss Maddox curtsied, and Darcy bowed.

Time to pay the piper, he supposed. "Miss Maddox, would you do me the honor of the next dance?"

She lowered her eyes demurely and smiled slightly. "Yes, thank you."

For the next several dances, his aunt kept him well supplied with partners—as if she hoped she could erase her son's scandal if her nephew made a brilliant match. After a few dances, the women started to blur together: all were fashionably dressed, well spoken, and good dancers who conducted themselves impeccably…and he could not have been more bored. The ball would improve dramatically, he knew, when he could return to Elizabeth.

As he danced with his sixth—or maybe seventh—partner, he realized with alarm that he was failing utterly in his vow to protect Elizabeth from mean-spirited inhabitants of the *ton*. He could not deflect criticism if he was not with her. On the other hand, she might not be the subject of much speculation if he did not converse with her much. One dance—even if it was the first dance—might not be enough to stir gossip and jealousy, but all of him rebelled at the thought of leaving her to fend for herself.

The dance ended, and Darcy thanked his partner, although he could not remember anything they had discussed. He saw his aunt bearing down on him, but he preempted her. "I have danced enough for now. I need to rest."

She regarded him coldly. "I have already selected another lady." She gestured with her fan to a nearby woman whose profile Darcy recognized all too well.

"Caroline Bingley!" Darcy had not known the woman was at the ball or he would have taken pains to avoid her. Her party must have arrived after the receiving line ended. Darcy rounded on his aunt. "I have had plentiful opportunities to court Miss Bingley if I so desired. Her brother is my friend."

"I know," she smiled at him serenely. "Their fortune is in trade, so she is not the *most* eligible lady here. But her dowry is far better than what *some* women bring to the table." Darcy knew this was an oblique criticism of Elizabeth and wondered if arranging a dance with Miss Bingley was his aunt's revenge for his attentions to Elizabeth. *Ah well, best to get it over with...*

He approached Miss Bingley. "How good to see you again. May I have the pleasure of this dance?" She acquiesced with a smile that she probably believed appeared sincere.

As he led her into position, he asked, "Is your whole family here?"

She shook her head. "I came with my friends, the Winslows. Charles and Louisa are at home. So you will have to make do with me," she said with a simpering smile. Darcy clenched his jaw; it would be a long set. It was as torturous as he expected. She agreed with his every opinion and denigrated the Bennets at every opportunity until he finally growled at her to stop.

When the dance was over, Darcy returned Miss Bingley to her friends and was able to disengage from her attempts at further conversation. Before he could move toward Elizabeth, his aunt swooped in with a calculating gleam in her eye. Darcy relentlessly strode past her, determined not to fall prey to her schemes, and this time she let him pass.

He hurried over to where Elizabeth talked with the Gardiners and Georgiana and positioned himself at Elizabeth's elbow. During a break in the conversation, he asked in a low voice, "How are you feeling? Are you excessively fatigued?" He saw Mr. Gardiner regard him curiously and realized his tone was more suited to the familiar role of husband than the more formal and tentative tone of a suitor.

Elizabeth's arched eyebrow showed that she also recognized his *faux pas*. "Thank you, Mr. Darcy. I am quite well. I think it will take more than two dances to fatigue me!" Although her last words were teasing, her tone was formal, making Darcy cringe inwardly at having forgotten himself. The idea of pretending to be a courting couple had seemed simple when they had planned it, but it was much more difficult to execute than he had anticipated. He wanted so much more from her than propriety allowed him.

Mr. Gardiner made an observation about the ball, and soon the others were conversing about the impressive size of the crowd. Darcy said nothing, so intoxicated by Elizabeth's proximity that he noticed every move of her hand or tilt of her head. Everything was charming and graceful; he thought he could watch her all night.

He was close enough that he could reach out his hand and touch her back through her gown. Even that limited sensation would be close to heaven, but they were surrounded by guests on all sides who might observe him. *Maybe I could...no, I cannot risk it.* In fact, the logical part of him dictated that he should depart her immediate vicinity, but he could not bring himself to move a muscle.

The Gardiners went to join the dancing, and Miss Bingley promptly took their place. Darcy suppressed a groan since Miss Bingley topped the list of people he would like to keep away from Elizabeth. She knew about Lydia and Wickham—and had every reason to wish Elizabeth ill. His protective instincts surged before the woman said anything.

"Dear Georgiana! So pleasant to see you again!" She greeted his sister with such embarrassing effusiveness that Georgiana was immediately uncomfortable and quickly excused herself to greet a friend. Then Miss Bingley turned to Elizabeth. "And my dear Eliza Bennet! What an unexpected pleasure."

"Miss Bingley," Elizabeth replied, her tone carefully neutral.

"I want to tell you how sorry I was to hear of your sister's disgrace! That loss must be felt very keenly. My heart goes out to your entire family." Her words were warm, but her delivery could not have been falser. Darcy's ire rose immediately, but before he could say anything, Elizabeth responded.

"Thank you, Miss Bingley, I will take your words in the spirit in which they were intended." It took Darcy a minute to notice how barbed this response was.

Miss Bingley's false smile turned sour as she noticed the slight. "I am surprised you do not feel the need to be by your parents' side at a time like this. Your mother's nerves must be in a sorry state."

"I will be departing for Hertfordshire very soon," Elizabeth said serenely.

"I am sure you miss it very much. I have heard that many country-born ladies become very attached to the lands of their birth. And to be so far away from your family..." Every word she uttered dripped with condescension.

"I do miss Hertfordshire," Elizabeth said, "but I think I could live anywhere happily if those I loved were with me." She glanced sidelong at Darcy, and he returned her grin. A quick frown creased Miss Bingley's features; Elizabeth had scored a hit. Why on earth had he thought he needed to defend his wife from anyone? Georgiana drifted back to the group and appeared to notice the tension between the two women. Darcy was thankful that she had missed the conversation about Lydia's scandal, although he knew he would have to tell her about Wickham eventually.

Miss Bingley was quick to launch another attack. "I have the happy talent for being at home wherever I am. Why, I was in Paris five months ago and felt not the least bit of homesickness!"

Elizabeth rose to the challenge. "Yes, Paris is enough to make anyone forget their homesickness. I was there not a fortnight ago."

"You were in Paris?" Miss Bingley could not conceal her astonishment.

"Yes, I even encountered Mr. Darcy at a ball there. Did he not mention it to you?" Elizabeth radiated so much insincere innocence that Darcy was tempted to laugh. "He was such a great help to me in getting out of the country when all the unpleasantness erupted."

Clearly nonplussed by this information, Miss Bingley murmured, "Mr. Darcy is always a valuable friend."

"Indeed."

Darcy enjoyed how well Elizabeth had handled this attack. Now Miss Bingley would wonder *how* he had helped Elizabeth escape France and how closely they had associated. However, she would tell no one; exposing that he had possibly compromised Elizabeth's reputation would not serve Miss Bingley's purposes at all.

Finally, Miss Bingley said, "I think I will collect some punch. It is a little warm in here." She glanced at Darcy as if hoping he would beg her to stay, but when he said nothing, she quickly melted into the crowd.

Darcy leaned close to Elizabeth and whispered in her ear, "Well played, darling."

Georgiana watched Elizabeth with ill-concealed glee. "I hope sometime you can teach me how you do that." Darcy knew that Georgiana disliked Miss Bingley but feared her sharp tongue.

"It is not difficult," Elizabeth explained with a lively twinkle in her eye. "Although it does help if you find the other person very vexing."

Georgiana and Darcy were still laughing when his aunt arrived, giving Darcy a withering glance for associating with Elizabeth, although he found it hard to care. His aunt had another young lady in tow, and Darcy found himself obligated to invite her to dance. Her purpose accomplished, Lady Matlock retreated, undoubtedly in search of fresh women to foist on him.

After a dance with an unobjectionable lady whose biggest flaw was that she was not Elizabeth, Darcy returned to Elizabeth and the Gardiners. He was horrified to see Lord Lennox holding Elizabeth's hand. Jealousy surged through him. During their travels in France, Lennox had haunted Darcy's dreams nightly, always swooping in to claim Elizabeth before he had a chance to declare his love for her. In one of his dreams, Elizabeth had stared directly at Darcy and said matter-of-factly, "I have always wanted to marry a lord."

Darcy tried to master his emotions, telling himself that Lennox only held her hand because he was preparing to escort her onto the dance floor. However, the very idea of Lennox dancing with her was itself alarming. How had that happened? Why had he left her unattended even for a second?

He hurried over to the pair. "Miss Bennet, I apologize for leaving so abruptly. I had intended to ask you for this dance."

To his jealous eye, Elizabeth gazed at him rather coolly. "I am sorry, I have promised this dance to Lord Lennox. But the next dance is available." Darcy stood rooted to the spot, trying to restrain his urge to wrench her hand from Lennox's. At that moment, he would have happily thrown Elizabeth over his shoulder and carried her back to Darcy House. It did not help that Lennox gave him a triumphant smirk.

As the two passed him, Elizabeth gave a sudden lurch as if falling, causing Darcy to instinctively reach out to steady her. Her mouth came near his ear, and she whispered, "Do not worry. I am not planning to marry him!" An involuntary smile came to Darcy's lips.

"Sorry," she said to Darcy in a normal tone of voice. "My slipper caught in my hem. Thank you for your assistance." Then she put her hand on Lennox's arm and said lightly, "I promise not to be so clumsy on the dance floor!"

"You could never be less than graceful!" Lennox said gallantly and swept her away.

As he watched them dance, Darcy tried to retain the sense of reassurance her jest had given him, but it was short lived. He could not tear his eyes away from them, instead noticing every laugh and gesture they exchanged. Each time Lennox touched her, Darcy wanted to challenge him to a duel.

***

While she danced with Lennox, Elizabeth was aware of Darcy's eyes on her; whenever she turned in his direction, she saw him. Knowing the intensity of his affection made her feel very desirable, but she was also vexed with his behavior. She feared that his obvious jealousy would expose her to gossip and bring more scrutiny upon her family, the kind of scrutiny they could ill afford. And she was aware that his aunt had asked him to be discreet about his preference for her. Would Elizabeth now have to face his aunt's wrath?

Lord Lennox was very complimentary of her dancing and her appearance. At every moment, he seemed desirous of her good opinion, but she found it hard to focus on the conversation with him; her thoughts always returned to Darcy.

When the dance ended, Lennox thanked Elizabeth and kissed her hand, but Darcy appeared immediately to claim her for the next dance.

Lennox gave an ironic little bow to Darcy before departing.

Darcy took her hand immediately. "I believe this is my dance."

"William," she said softly, "I thought your aunt wanted you to avoid showing me too much attention."

"I do not care what my aunt thinks," he growled. "I am my own man and want to dance with my wife."

"Please keep your voice down!" she hissed.

The music started, and they moved somewhat stiffly into position. Elizabeth enjoyed this dance with Darcy less than the previous one. Although she still experienced a tingle wherever he touched her, she could tell his jealousy was getting the better of him. Perhaps this was the inevitable result of their constant need to avoid touching or otherwise betraying their affection. It was difficult to pretend to be almost strangers when she knew him so intimately.

As they danced, his hand lingered longer on her waist than it should, and he held her hand in a way that was not quite proper. She noticed these moments time and again and was certain that anyone observing them would as well. Since Darcy had favored her with a second dance, she would already be the subject of speculation. If only Darcy would be more discreet! She had no desire to make enemies among those guests who had hopes of him since her family's situation would already cause everyone to see her as a fortune hunter. They would gossip about her family, and that would inevitably trigger talk about Lydia and Wickham. *Oh, I never should have come!* she thought miserably.

She greeted the end of the set with relief and relaxed instantly when Darcy escorted her from the dance floor. He did not relinquish her hand immediately but instead said, "I think perhaps you should forgo dancing for the remainder of the evening. I would never forgive myself if you experienced a setback in your recovery." There was a sizeable crowd in their path, so they stopped where they were rather than return to her aunt and uncle.

"I thank you for your solicitude," she returned, finally removing her hand from his. "But I feel perfectly well. And I very much enjoy dancing."

Darcy leaned forward and whispered in her ear, "That is enough. I do not want you to fall ill again." She stepped backward so he needed to speak aloud once more. "I am certain your doctor would not want you to be out at such a late hour, let alone engaging in vigorous activity," he continued forcefully.

Elizabeth felt anger build inside her. She was well aware of the true reason he wished her to quit the dance floor but knew she had done nothing to spark his jealousy. It was difficult not to resent these high-handed attempts to control her. If he wanted a meek and obedient wife, he had married the wrong woman!

Curious glances were turned in their direction; her anxiety grew as she considered how they were drawing attention to themselves. "Unless my doctor is here personally, I will have to depend upon my own judgment. Thank you for your concern," she said coldly. Then she turned and stalked away to the room where they were serving beverages.

Darcy wanted to follow Elizabeth but was aware of the eyes on him. Their conversation had been soft and brief, so he doubted that anyone nearby knew its substance, but he had no doubt the tension between them had been obvious to bystanders. He schooled his expression into one of indifference and told himself that he could follow her in a few minutes when it would be less noticeable.

Casting about for a distraction, Darcy's eyes found Fitzwilliam, who came over immediately. "Is there a problem? Your face has that dark look again."

Darcy tried to make light of it. "Nothing of import. You know how Eliz–Miss Bennet and I are always sparring."

"I see." Fitzwilliam's tone was carefully neutral. "Was she chastising you on your lack of manners again?"

"In a manner of speaking," Darcy said stiffly. Fitzwilliam's face was skeptical, and Darcy recalled that his cousin was better at reading him than anyone else he knew. Sometimes that was an asset; however, at the moment it was a definite disadvantage. He had no desire to stay and undergo his cousin's inquisition. "I do believe I will avail myself of some of your parents' excellent punch," he said and strode away.

However, when Darcy arrived in the punch room, Elizabeth was not there. He returned and scanned the ballroom but did not espy her. There were more than one hundred revelers; she could be buried in the crowd. Then Darcy noticed a door near the punch table that led to the terrace. Following his instincts, he opened it and walked through. He did not notice Fitzwilliam follow him a moment later.

The terrace was quite large, running along one entire side of the house. The staff had set up a few torches outside, but it was not enough to illuminate the whole expanse, so much of the terrace was in shadows. Darcy scanned the area, noting a few other couples and clusters of partygoers cooling off and chatting in the relative quiet of the outside. Then, far down at one end, he could barely make out a solitary woman's figure. As he drew closer, he knew it was Elizabeth.

Elizabeth gazed into the darkness surrounding Matlock House, still seething with a mixture of anger and embarrassment. While part of her knew that jealousy was a common reaction for many men, she also knew that most married men at the ball were content to let their wives dance with other men. Why did Darcy have to treat her like his chattel? Was this a harbinger of future difficulties? That thought chilled her more than anything else.

Darcy's figure loomed out of the darkness. His expression was unreadable to her; she could not ascertain if he was contrite or angry. "My love, I am sorry I let my jealousy get in the way of my better judgment. Can we put this unpleasantness behind us?" Now there was pain on his face.

He reached to put his arms around her and lean in for a kiss, but she pushed him away. She could smell the wine on his breath and suspected he had drunk more than usual as a means of enduring a trying night. "No, we cannot!" she exclaimed with some heat. "It is not that simple to forget. I watched you dance with seven other women—all of them more elegant and wealthier than me—but I said nothing."

"That bothered you?" Darcy asked, sounding surprised. *Does he think that only he suffers from jealousy?* she thought furiously. He even sounded a little pleased, which enraged her further. Again he tried to embrace her, but she turned away so her back was to him.

"Naturally, it did!" Elizabeth stopped and swallowed, trying to modulate her tone. "But I know those women meant nothing to you. I know that you are not contemplating marrying them. And you know the same about me! I only danced with two other men all night, and yet you do not trust me! Is this how it will be for the rest of our lives?"

This last question seemed to strike him forcefully, causing him to stop and consider his answer. "No, of course not. You are not my—my possession!" Darcy put his hands on her shoulders to turn her in his direction, but Elizabeth stepped backward, breaking his hold on her.

"Then stop trying to grab me like I am something that belongs to you." Darcy instantly dropped his arms. "I am guarded like some precious jewel instead of being seen as a living, thinking woman. Why do you act so?"

Darcy's anger appeared to ebb. He rubbed his forehead and closed his eyes so he could think. "I should ask myself the same question. I do trust you, but I suppose I am still insecure of your love for me."

"Why?" Elizabeth was genuinely shocked.

"Because it is so new. Because I have spent so much time convinced of your indifference." Darcy struggled to articulate thoughts that he recognized only now. "I have a difficult time believing that this is real, that it will last. You held such a bad opinion of me for so long that I fear you will change your mind again. Such doubts result in behavior that confirms your bad opinion. I am so sorry."

"Oh, William…." His admission of insecurity did more to quell her anger than all of his fury had.

She was now heartily ashamed of her display of temper. *I should have understood what was underlying his behavior.* And, she realized, her angry rejection of him in the ballroom had exposed both of them to possible repercussions. *What if someone guesses the truth?* At least this end of the terrace was deserted, she reassured herself; no one could have overheard their conversation.

"I am sorry, too," she said softly. "I should have understood why you reacted as you did. This is a difficult situation. It is taking its toll on both of us."

"Yes." His voice was hoarse. "I never imagined how hard it would be to be away from you, or to be near you and not permitted to touch—"

"You can touch me now. There is nobody who will see," she suggested impishly.

"You minx!" He chuckled. "Does this mean our argument is over?"

She nodded slowly and seductively, causing Darcy to pull her to him roughly. Instantly, he was raining kisses on her lips, her neck, her shoulders. Every touch, every kiss felt like it left a trail of fire on her skin. Then his hands rose to explore her back, caressing her curves and pulling her more tightly against him. She moaned as he moved one hand to cup her breast.

Darcy was wondering what could be accomplished if he pulled her deeper into the shadows or even into the bushes when they heard voices approaching. As he reluctantly pulled away from Elizabeth, she turned away to straighten her clothing. Meanwhile, he stepped up to the terrace's railing as if he were simply enjoying the night air, knowing that merely being alone with Elizabeth would be enough to compromise her in some eyes.

He was relieved to see that the approaching figures were Fitzwilliam and an army friend of his, Lieutenant Preston. He knew Fitzwilliam would never reveal any possible improprieties or start rumors. The two men were talking rather loudly and laughing; Darcy wondered how much they had had to drink. "Hello, gentlemen!" he greeted them as they approached.

"So this is where you went," Fitzwilliam exclaimed, scrutinizing him rather sharply. "My mother was searching for you."

Darcy realized that he had been away from the ballroom longer than he had intended. His very absence could cause rumors, especially if people realized that Elizabeth was missing as well. He had taken such care to protect her reputation; he could not give rise to speculation now.

"Hello, Miss Bennet," Fitzwilliam said when Elizabeth emerged from the shadows. "Lovely night, is it not?" He did not seem at all surprised to find her here. Well, he might have suspected, knowing of Darcy's interest in her. Darcy hoped that nothing about Elizabeth's appearance revealed their activities.

"Yes, neither too hot nor too cold," Elizabeth replied blandly. "An ideal night for a ball." Her face did show a slight blush of embarrassment.

Fitzwilliam eyed Darcy again. "You really should get back to the ballroom. My mother will be livid and will send servants seeking you out." Darcy noted the unspoken warning in his cousin's words. "We can escort Miss Bennet back when she has finished enjoying the night air." Darcy was about to protest when he realized that his cousin was giving him an opportunity to belie any suspicions of a dalliance with Elizabeth. If she returned in the company of two soldiers, no one would suspect she had had a rendezvous with Darcy.

He bowed to the inevitable. "Yes, I should go. Miss Bennet, gentlemen." He bowed to each in turn and left. But every step that took him farther from Elizabeth tugged at his heart.

***

The next morning, Darcy worked in his study. The prolonged sojourn in France had left him sadly behind on his work for his estate. As he read his correspondence, he realized he would need to visit Pemberley soon. A footman came in to announce, "Colonel Fitzwilliam, sir," even though Fitzwilliam was only steps behind him. Richard threw himself into a chair as the footman closed the study door.

"Good morning, Richard. To what do I owe this pleasure?" Darcy glanced up from his paperwork and took in Richard's appearance for the first time. His cousin had a strange expression on his face; he was flushed, but his lips were pressed together in a thin white line. He was angry! Darcy tried to think of the last time he had seen this usually genial man so furious. Was it something Aunt Alice had done?

"How could you?" Fitzwilliam spat at him. He launched himself out of the chair and started pacing. "How could you impose yourself on her like that?"

Chapter 10

Darcy was bewildered. "On who?"

"Do not play the innocent with me! Miss Bennet! I saw you on the terrace with her last night," Richard practically shouted, leaning over Darcy's desk.

Damn! Darcy thought with a sinking heart. *This will not be an easy conversation.* "Saw but not heard?" he asked his cousin.

"I had no need to hear! It was obvious what was happening!" Fitzwilliam resumed pacing, agitation showing in every line of his body.

Darcy struggled to recall how he and Elizabeth had behaved as opposed to what they had said. At first he had attempted to embrace her, and she had shrugged him off—several times. He had to admit that it would appear potentially damning. "We had an argument—" he started to explain, but Fitzwilliam cut him off.

"That much was plain! I could see that she did not desire your attentions, but you imposed yourself on her again and again—until she finally acquiesced."

Now Darcy could understand what Fitzwilliam thought had happened but found his ire rising as well. "That is not what—"

Fitzwilliam had not finished. "And I could see that last night was not the first time this has happened. She knew she was in an untenable position and had to give you what you wanted eventually. What did you do to her? Is she accepting your 'favors' in exchange for your silence about how much you compromised her reputation in France? Or did she agree to become your mistress because she knew she was too compromised to be *anyone's* wife?"

"I did not—"

"To think I encouraged you to woo her! I thought your intentions were honorable! A woman like that...she deserves far better—"

As Fitzwilliam ranted, Darcy reached into a desk drawer and pulled out a piece of paper. He laid it on the desk in front of his cousin. "What is this?" Fitzwilliam's voice seethed with hostility.

"It is self-explanatory."

Fitzwilliam read the paper. "What is this?" This time he sounded stupefied.

"It is a marriage license."

"You got married?" Now his tone was bewildered.

"Yes, we were married in France. My friend, Thomas Whitmore, an ordained clergyman, performed the ceremony. And before you think I was imposing my will on Elizabeth, the wedding was her idea. Well, it was my idea to get married, but she was set on doing it immediately."

"But why?" Fitzwilliam sank into a chair, trying to absorb the information, anger draining away.

Darcy sighed. "For several reasons. She thought it would make it easier for us to travel since we had no ready chaperone. And she believed the French would be less likely to imprison me if I were a newlywed."

"What a clever woman. Was she correct?"

"Indeed. With creative theatrics she was able to convince some French soldiers not only that they should not separate a newly married couple but also that she was practically dying and could not return to England without me."

Fitzwilliam chuckled. "She is brilliant! What an actress."

Darcy's expression darkened. "Yes, although she almost did die, Richard. She almost died in France. I spent an entire night by her bedside believing that each breath might be her last."

"Good Lord!"

Darcy nodded. "That was the primary reason Elizabeth wanted to marry right away. The experience altered her perspective. She said we had waited long enough, and she did not want to wait any longer."

Fitzwilliam shook his head slowly. "I cannot believe this…you are married!"

Darcy nodded, experiencing relief at finally telling someone the truth. "The problem is that Elizabeth wanted to tell her father before anyone else knew. When we returned, we were greeted with the news about her sister and Wickham, which means it is even more important to maintain secrecy. So—"

"So you are a very frustrated man." Fitzwilliam nodded knowingly.

"I think we are both frustrated with these circumstances." Darcy smiled mirthlessly. "Still, it is preferable to living with the certainty that she hates me."

Fitzwilliam laughed at the chagrin in his cousin's voice. "So it turns out you were not the last man in the world after all. Quick work, Cuz."

Darcy grinned ruefully. "I suppose not. I shall have to remind her of that."

Fitzwilliam sobered. "I apologize for leaping to conclusions last night."

Darcy shook his head. "It is understandable given what you saw. I am afraid I let my jealousy overcome my better nature. These last few days have been difficult."

'Well, it is not like she will run off and marry someone else."

"Elizabeth reminded me of precisely that last night—rather forcefully."

"I can imagine," his cousin replied with a smile. "Now I am sorry I interrupted you."

"So that was intentional!"

"Yes, Preston was passing by, and after I saw what was happening, I convinced him to take a turn on the terrace. I believed I was protecting what was left of Miss Bennet's virtue." He shrugged. "But it was probably the only time you have had alone in two days. Sorry."

"Hmmpf," Darcy grunted. "What I require is the means to separate Elizabeth from her aunt and uncle for a couple hours."

Fitzwilliam gave a short laugh. "That would not be easy. I like her uncle, but he seems vigilant. That fortification might be too heavily guarded."

Darcy nodded glumly. "I suppose so. Though as a military man, please notify me of any strategies that occur to you. In the meantime, I am sure I do not need to tell you not to breathe a word of this to anyone, especially not your mother."

Fitzwilliam smiled cheekily. "Of course, you can rely on my discretion—and my fear. I hope I am safely on the battlefield when you tell my mother—and Aunt Catherine."

"Coward," Darcy muttered.

After Fitzwilliam left, Darcy finished up his work and then sat down to a late breakfast with Georgiana. He had wanted to explain his marriage to Georgiana since arriving in London, but the opportunity had not previously presented itself. So he took the opportunity to divulge the entire story of their travels in France while leaving out some of the more intimate moments. When he described the wedding, Georgiana clapped her hands in delight and informed her brother in no uncertain terms that she had been hoping to acquire Elizabeth as a sister. While she did regret having missed the ceremony, her enthusiasm at the news prevented her from holding it against him too much, and she assured Darcy of her secrecy on the matter.

Darcy was pleased with how easy it had been to explain the wedding to two of the people closest to him and felt his cares lighten now that he had unburdened himself. Georgiana and Fitzwilliam clearly understood that Elizabeth would make him happy. However, he knew that others in his family would not be so understanding and would place other considerations ahead of his happiness. Still, his sister's and cousin's reactions buoyed him, and he thought eagerly of the day when it would all be out in the open, and he and Elizabeth could live as husband and wife. Sometimes it felt as if that day would never come.

***

That afternoon, Darcy visited the Gardiners' house to see Elizabeth. She and her aunt would be leaving for Longbourn the next day, and she already anticipated missing him. As he sat with Elizabeth and her aunt making polite conversation, Elizabeth could sense his intense gaze on her even when she was concentrating on her needlework—and every time she looked up, his eyes locked with hers. Her aunt was hardly oblivious as to where his attention was directed, but she said nothing.

After a prolonged conversation about the weather and a discussion of the ball at Matlock House, Mrs. Gardiner observed that her husband had not had any luck in locating Lydia and Wickham.

"My Bow Street Runners have not turned up anything promising either," Darcy said with regret. "I wish I had better news in that regard. However, they have not yet spoken to all of the acquaintances of Wickham's who are on my list. Hopefully, somebody will give us a clue."

"Perhaps they are already married," Aunt Gardiner said hopefully.

Darcy pressed his lips together in a white line. "Perhaps." Elizabeth could tell he was not optimistic about that prospect.

"Poor Lydia." Her aunt sighed.

"We are undoubtedly feeling it more than she," opined Elizabeth. "She probably thinks of it as a great lark."

Eventually, Darcy and Elizabeth slipped out to enjoy a short walk in the park. He told her that Georgiana and Colonel Fitzwilliam now knew their secret, although he did not reveal the circumstances under which he had divulged their secret to his cousin.

Darcy gazed around the leafy green park, shimmering in the late afternoon heat. Since they were alone, Darcy removed Elizabeth's glove and his own and held her hand, tracing the back of it with his thumb and making Elizabeth long for more.

"I will miss you even though I know the time will be short," he told her.

"I will miss you as well," she said. "When will you arrive at Longbourn?"

"In three days. I will be bringing Bingley with me," Darcy explained. "He showed up on my doorstep the other day—torn between his sisters' expectations and wanting to be with Jane. I suggested that we both travel to Netherfield."

"Jane will be so pleased to see him. Does he know about us?" Elizabeth asked.

"I allowed that I had some interest in you but did not explain all the circumstances," he responded. "I was afraid Bingley might be somewhat shocked at how precipitous we were. He has dawdled quite a bit over this courtship business by comparison." Elizabeth smiled at this jest.

"As I recall *I* was the one who suggested marrying immediately."

"But I was not strong enough to object to the haste." As he clutched both her hands to his chest, his eyes were fixed on her lips. "I wanted it too much." Although Darcy knew they had good reasons for keeping their secret, at that moment he was hard pressed to name a single one. "How soon can we tell your father, do you think?"

"I do not know. I will have to see how he is— how everyone is at Longbourn. I shall have to judge my father's mood."

Grasping her shoulders, he stared intently into her beautiful brown eyes. "He will think I compromised you?"

"Perhaps. He believes I dislike you. I want to demonstrate how my opinion has changed before we shock him with the news of the marriage. Otherwise, he will believe I married you for your fortune or to avoid disgrace." He wished he could kiss away her distress, but they were in public.

He caressed the back of her hand with light strokes, and she shivered in response. "Well, you will have three days to assess the circumstances. When I arrive on Thursday, we may develop a plan."

"I cannot wait until this is all over, and we can just be husband and wife."

"Nor can I." Darcy suppressed another urge to throw caution to the wind and kiss her until she could not breathe. Reluctantly, they turned and went back to the Gardiners' house.

***

Elizabeth and her aunt had good weather for their trip to Longbourn and arrived in excellent time. The whole Bennet family came outside to greet them. Elizabeth immediately noticed that her father appeared to have aged years in a few weeks. There were wrinkles around his eyes and a weariness in his movements that she had not noticed before. Giving her a hug and a kiss, he seemed genuinely pleased—and relieved—that she had returned.

Jane was delighted to greet her but expressed concern about Elizabeth's wan complexion and her weight loss. The Gardiners had passed along the news of her illness from the letters they had received from Darcy. Elizabeth spent some time reassuring her family that she felt well and was making a good recovery; however, preoccupied as they were with Lydia's plight, no one asked much about her travels—and she was not eager to volunteer many details. When her sisters did mention it, she implied that her journey had been difficult, and she wished to avoid talking about it, which appeared to satisfy them for the present. Elizabeth desperately wanted to confess everything to Jane but knew she had an obligation to tell her father first.

Mrs. Bennet also expressed concern about Elizabeth's appearance and muttered about the Gardiners' deficient care of their niece. She attempted to explain that none of it was the Gardiners' fault, but her mother would hear nothing of it. As soon as he was able, Mr. Bennet retreated to his study while the state of Mrs. Bennet's nerves required her to return to her chambers.

Aunt Gardiner went to her room to rest while Kitty and Mary departed for a visit to Meryton. This left Elizabeth and Jane alone in the drawing room. Elizabeth settled into a chair, happy to be back in familiar surroundings, although, she thought with a pang of regret, she would not be at Longbourn very long.

Elizabeth asked about their father, and Jane confirmed that he spent much of his time in his study and even took some meals there. Their mother, Elizabeth learned, mostly stayed in her chamber, attended by the servants and her daughters.

"I am so happy you are returned," Jane said with a gentle smile. Elizabeth could see dark shadows around her sister's eyes, but apparently Jane was just as concerned about her. "Are you certain you are completely recovered from your illness?" she asked anxiously.

"Indeed," Elizabeth replied, attempting to appear hale and hearty. "I am quite well again." Jane did not look convinced.

Elizabeth was happy she could give Jane one piece of information that would brighten her countenance. "I do have some good news. Mr. Bingley will be returning to Netherfield on Thursday."

Jane's face lit with a broad smile, which she quickly schooled into her usual serene expression. "That is good news!" Then she sobered. "But perhaps I should not tell mother. I do not want to give rise to expectations that might not be satisfied. After all, the circumstances with Lydia taint the whole family, and I hardly expect Mr. Bingley to renew his addresses."

"I do think Mr. Bingley cares about you and that you are the reason he is returning," Elizabeth assured her with a smile. "I think he departed earlier because of his sisters' persuasion."

"How did you happen to learn that he is returning to Netherfield?" Jane asked. Although she had retrieved her embroidery, it lay forgotten in her lap. "Did you see Miss Bingley in London?"

Elizabeth realized she had inadvertently caught herself in a trap that would necessitate revealing more than she had intended. *Well, I would do it again to see that expression on Jane's face.*

"I saw Mr. Darcy in town, and he told me," she admitted with a small smile, anticipating the advent of further questions.

"Mr. Darcy! He visited you? Was he angry about the disagreement you had in Hunsford?" Jane exclaimed. Her countenance demonstrated both surprise and pleasure, for she had always liked Darcy.

"No, indeed," Elizabeth said with a laugh. "He is perfectly amiable and has been a complete gentleman." She mused that now would be a good time to lay the groundwork for future revelations. "We have seen a great deal of each other in fact."

"And you are happy about it?" Jane said with a grin. "I am so pleased! Tell me, when did you see him?"

Elizabeth decided that she could entrust Jane with some details about her travels. While many people would consider their circumstances compromising, her sister never thought ill of anyone and would accept any explanation for their behavior. "I first encountered him accidentally at a ball in Paris. Then, when news of the breakdown of the treaty reached us, he helped me escape from France."

"Mr. Darcy helped you?" Jane's eyes widened with astonishment. "Did he find you passage on a boat?"

"Nay, nothing that simple," Elizabeth admitted ruefully. "What did Aunt and Uncle Gardiner write home about my departure from France?"

Jane's expression was thoughtful as she tried to remember details. "It was in the middle of all that tumult about Lydia, but I recall that they said you had become separated from them and that a friend was helping you return to England. Then a letter came two days later reporting that you had fallen ill, and so your return was delayed. I so wished that I could go to you! There are such terrible stories about the treatment of English travelers in France! But the Gardiners assured us that their friend was taking good care of you." Jane's face reflected all of the anxiety she had experienced.

Elizabeth was heartily sorry for any worry she had occasioned and silently vowed to reveal their marriage in such a way that did not cause additional anxiety for her family. However, she had to admit that she was unsure of the best way to undertake such a revelation.

"It was Mr. Darcy, Jane. He was the one who cared for me." Jane gasped but immediately hid her shock. Elizabeth continued. "He took me to his friend's house near Montdidier when I was ill. And then he found us a boat to England. I honestly do not know if I would have survived without him." Her sister's face was very grave at this revelation, but Elizabeth felt it was a pleasure to unburden herself of at least this much of the story.

"Oh, Elizabeth! I never realized how much danger you experienced!" Jane exclaimed, completely overcome. "We are forever in his debt! When I think we could have lost you..." Tears welled up in Jane's eyes, and Elizabeth patted her hand reassuringly.

"All's well that ends well," she said. "I am well, and I am here. See?" She displayed a patently false smile, making Jane laugh.

Then a puzzled expression crossed her face. "But we knew nothing of his role from the Gardiners' letters."

"I think our aunt and uncle were trying to protect my reputation." Jane nodded earnestly in understanding. "And protect Mr. Darcy from Mama," Elizabeth said with a sly smile.

Jane covered her mouth as she laughed in appreciation. "At ten thousand a year, she would certainly insist that he *had* to marry you!"

"Precisely!" Elizabeth said. "I would not have his kindness repaid with such treatment."

"But Elizabeth," Jane observed, "he must still be violently in love with you to show you such dedication."

"I believe that he is," Elizabeth admitted, disliking the necessity of deceiving Jane. Her sister would never reproach her, but that somehow made Elizabeth feel even worse. At least this conversation would mean it was easier to tell Jane the entire story later. "He was most distressed when I was ill. And,

Jane, he risked his own life. The French were arresting Englishmen and imprisoning them. I wanted him to leave France without me, but he refused."

"Oh my!" Jane seemed overwhelmed with this tale of Darcy's devotion. She took Elizabeth's hand in hers. "Has your opinion of him changed?"

Elizabeth nodded, not trusting herself to speak. A rush of love for Darcy swept over her, and she missed him very acutely. Finally, she choked out some words. "He is indeed a very good man. I will be happy to see more of him when he arrives at Netherfield." *That should give Jane an idea of how my sentiments have changed without revealing too much.*

Mrs. Gardiner stayed only two nights with the Bennets and then returned to London and her children. Over the next three days, the inhabitants at Longbourn fell into easy rhythm, although the atmosphere was clouded by anxiety over Lydia and the consequences of her behavior. They rarely spoke of it, but the subject cast a pall over the entire house. Elizabeth noticed at once that they enjoyed far fewer callers than before; clearly many in the neighborhood thought it best not to associate with a family experiencing such disgrace. When the sisters visited Meryton, they noticed stares and whispers following them, and Elizabeth soon found excuses not to visit town.

Elizabeth and Jane kept the household functioning while their mother mostly remained in her chamber, complaining about her nerves. Mary walked about the house moralizing about female virtue to anyone who would listen—and a few who would not. Finally, Elizabeth asked her to refrain since she was only reminding them of circumstances they would prefer to forget. Kitty often went into Meryton, but her father insisted that she could not go unescorted, so Mary was often pressed into duty.

Elizabeth tried several times to speak with her father and tell him about Mr. Darcy, at least to describe how Darcy had returned her safely to England; however, Mr. Bennet seemed disinclined to conversation when Elizabeth encountered him alone. When she did initiate a discussion, he contributed very little, and she soon abandoned the effort. Perhaps, she hoped, the circumstances would improve when Darcy arrived.

***

On the day following Elizabeth's arrival, her mother bestirred herself from her chambers to greet one special guest. His name was Thomas Fenton, and Elizabeth recalled meeting him at a dance before her departure for France. He was a widower with a small estate in Surrey who was visiting his sister, Mrs. Campbell, who lived not far from Longbourn. Mr. Fenton, Elizabeth soon learned, had seven children, aged from two to twelve, whom, fortunately, he left in the care of his sister when he visited Longbourn.

The majority of Mr. Fenton's visit was occupied by his monologue about his house, his hounds, and his horses. He thought very highly of all three and boasted of his many triumphs in buying horseflesh and breeding hounds, saying far less about his children. Elizabeth was at a loss to understand why her mother paid such lavish attention to the visitor. She encouraged his conversation, hanging on his every word, plied him with sweets, and seemed endlessly complimentary of everything about him.

The mystery of Mrs. Bennet's solicitude was solved, however, when she let slip something about the widower's need for a new wife. Elizabeth realized with dismay that her mother hoped he would choose a wife from among her daughters. As before with Mr. Collins, Elizabeth knew Mrs. Bennet would steer the man away from Jane because of her attachment to Mr. Bingley, so Mr. Fenton's attention would almost certainly turn to the second oldest daughter. Kitty and Mary would likely be considered too young to manage a household of seven children.

Indeed, Elizabeth was alarmed to find Mr. Fenton frequently attempting to engage her in conversation, although any dialogue between them usually devolved into a monologue. She was also the recipient of many warm looks from that quarter. No doubt her mother had been telling Mr. Fenton how Elizabeth would welcome his attentions and extolling her virtues as the future mistress of a house. Attempting to quell her unease, Elizabeth reminded herself that Darcy would soon arrive, and his presence would hopefully discourage any thoughts Mr. Fenton might have about initiating a suit.

Unfortunately, Elizabeth did not anticipate how quickly Mr. Fenton could make up his mind. On the third day after her return to Longbourn, Mr. Fenton came to call once more, and Mrs. Bennet insisted that Elizabeth walk with him in the garden. Elizabeth requested that Jane accompany them, but after a few minutes outside, Hill was sent to fetch Jane on the pretext of reading to her mother. Once alone with Mr. Fenton, Elizabeth started thinking of an appropriate reason to return inside immediately. However, Mr. Fenton was too quick for her.

Jane had hardly disappeared from sight before he grabbed Elizabeth's hand. As she tried to extricate it from his grasp, he cried, "Miss Elizabeth, please relieve my mind! Tell me you will be my wife!"

Her heart sinking, Elizabeth stopped struggling and instead focused on the conversation. "Mr. Fenton, I assure you—"

"But I am too hasty, I know. I told myself not to be, but here I am running away at the mouth. That is just how I am! Before I came over here, I told myself I should describe to you the advantages that should be yours when you accept me. You know I have an estate in Surrey. Quite a good one, if say so myself! It is nearly forty acres. And it produces prodigious amounts of wheat and corn every year. And I own two carriages, one is a barouche landau, which I may have mentioned before. The other is not quite so fine, but it is quite serviceable. My stable has ten, well elevennow, horses in it. I have three for my own use. One, Scout, is an excellent hunting horse. And of course, I have quite a decent pack of hunting hounds, I do not mind telling you. Sir Richard Marlin himself told me, 'No one in the county has hounds like yours. They are quite the best I have seen.'"

"Mr. Fenton, I thank you for the honor, but—" Elizabeth forcefully reclaimed her hand and took a step back so that she was almost standing in the roses.

"No need to thank me, m'dear. But here I am jabbering away, and I have neglected the most essential item" he paused dramatically, "the house itself." Elizabeth stifled a laugh; she had been certain he was about to declare his attachment to her, but apparently he thought that irrelevant to the conversation.

"It is quite a good house, I do not mind telling you. The roof is sturdy and walls quite thick. It has thirty-two windows. My little Maggie counted one day. So, you see, it is quite the elegant abode. It is perhaps not in the latest style. However, after living *here*, I can hardly believe you would care about such things."

Elizabeth colored at the insult to her childhood home. "Mr. Fenton, I have not yet given my answer—" Attempting nonchalance, she walked further down the garden path, but he kept pace with her—far too closely for her comfort.

Fenton rattled on as if Elizabeth had not spoken at all. "And of course, I can give you pin money. I know women must have their hats and dresses and such. It would not do to neglect such things." Enraptured by the sound of his own voice, Fenton accidently brushed against a bush full of prickly thorns and had to spend a moment disentangling himself, but nothing stopped the flow of his monologue. "My estate, your mother may have mentioned, is worth three thousand a year. Not quite as good as your sister's suitor, Mr. Bingley, eh?" He winked at her. "Still, I flatter myself to think that it is not too easily dismissed."

At first Elizabeth had thought she would have an opportunity to speak when Mr. Fenton ran out of topics of conversation, but now she was uncertain that would happen before nightfall. Although she had been attempting to speak, he simply refused to stop talking. Walking away was an option, but her mother would be most unhappy if she was quite so rude. She would be distraught enough when she learned Elizabeth had refused another "eligible" suitor.

If only I could tell her about William, Elizabeth thought. *She would never consider Mr. Fenton in a favorable light again!*

Elizabeth turned her attention back to Mr. Fenton, who was now waxing poetic about his hunting rifles. She decided that she would have to interrupt him, but then he switched to describing his children, a topic Elizabeth found of some interest.

"I have neglected to mention the children. They are such loveable dears, although the boys have been running quite wild for the past two years. Of course, they need a mother, which is one my primary reasons for marrying. Having a woman about the place will be just the thing to tame the children." He did not seem concerned about whether Elizabeth had the qualities of a *good* stepmother. Nor did he stop to wonder how she felt about his children. Idly, she wondered what his first marriage had been like. This had to be the most cold-blooded proposal Elizabeth had ever encountered; he said nothing about love or even affection. At least Mr. Collins had attempted to fake such sentiments. Then it occurred to her with some bemusement that she was becoming quite a connoisseur of proposals!

Mr. Fenton was going on about little Tommy's misadventures in a pile of manure, when Elizabeth finally put a stop to the soliloquy. "Mr. Fenton? Mr. Fenton! Mr. Fenton!" Finally, he fell silent, and before he could draw breath again, she hurriedly spoke. "I thank you for the honor of your proposal, but it is impossible to accept it."

"Impossible? Nonsense!" He shook his head with a grunt. "Your mother assures me that you are a most sensible girl who will see the advantages of such an arrangement—and you have no prior attachment."

"I do not believe we would be happy if—"

"Oh, we shall be happy enough; do not worry your pretty head about that." He waved away their future felicity with one hand.

"Nonetheless, I do not believe I can accept—"

"Of course you can, m'dear!" He startled her by clapping her heartily on the back. "Your mother has given me her permission and blessing!"

"And my father?" Elizabeth felt she was desperate, expecting her father to rescue her from this determined man, but if Mr. Fenton would not listen to her, he might give more weight to her father's words.

"Oh, your father told me anything you will agree to, he will give his consent for."

Elizabeth could well imagine her father saying such a thing in an offhand way, knowing she would never accept someone like Fenton. But she wished, for once, that he was less amused by such irritating people and more interested in exercising some authority.

"And I am *not* agreeing," she said emphatically, trying to hold her anger in check.

"Nonsense, m'dear. I know you will. Do not play coy! Your mother and father want it. I told myself you might be a little shy; why, I almost expected it. Young girls like you never know their own minds—or what is good for them." Elizabeth closed her eyes, trying to suppress the desire to lash out at this man. He was too stupid to know how much he has insulted her.

Although she spent the next few minutes trying to convince Fenton that her refusal was in earnest, he would not believe it. Finally, she insisted that she must return to the house. "Very well. But we must discuss it further. We have many plans to make if we are to organize a wedding." Fenton smiled complacently. "I have but a fortnight left at my sister's before I return home." Elizabeth did not know how to address this man in terms he would understand. *He literally will not take "no" for an answer!*

On that note, Elizabeth turned on her heel and strode into the house. Shaking with anger, she immediately climbed the stairs, having no wish to confront her mother, and did not stop until she reached her room. Miserably, she recalled that her mother had invited Mr. Fenton to dinner that night, so she would have to suffer through more of his conversation.

When William arrived, she reasoned, all would be put to rights. Once she explained the situation to him, he would undoubtedly have some thoughts about how to deter such an obtuse suitor. She sighed as she pictured his face in her mind. He could not arrive soon enough.

***

The next day, Bingley and Darcy arrived at Longbourn earlier than expected. The roads were good, and they made very good time. Darcy could hardly contain himself, imagining Elizabeth's face when she saw him, the shine in her eyes, and the smile gracing her lips. He busily concocted schemes to obtain some time alone for just the two of them. Bingley was no less excited to see Jane but was more anxious about his reception. Before even considering a proposal, he would have to prove his devotion to her.

Hill showed the two gentlemen to the drawing room and announced them, but to their disappointment, only Mary and Kitty were present, conversing with a gentleman Darcy did not recognize, whom Mary introduced as Mr. Fenton. She further explained that their mother was too indisposed for visitors and had sent Jane and Elizabeth on an errand in Meryton. They were expected back soon.

The news was a blow to Darcy. Although he would not have to wait long for Elizabeth's return, every second seemed to weigh on him. Bingley looked similarly unhappy. However, the gentlemen did not want to miss the opportunity to see the ladies as soon as they arrived, so they acquiesced to Mary's rather awkward invitation to sit. A servant brought in tea, and they participated in desultory conversation about the weather and the state of roads.

Neither Kitty nor Mary was a good conversationalist. Kitty did tease Bingley a bit about giving another ball at Netherfield, but she was in awe of Darcy and dared not address any remarks to him. Darcy's black mood prevented him from devising good topics for conversation, so it fell to Bingley to engage the other guest. They established that he had an estate in Surrey and was in the area visiting his sister.

What the deuce is he doing at Longbourn? Darcy wondered. *He can hardly have paid a call on Elizabeth's parents since they are not present. Does he have some affection for Mary?* He observed the two and saw no signs of particular regard.

Fenton was rather quiet when the gentlemen were first introduced but warmed up as Bingley asked him questions about himself. In fact, his conversation became downright plentiful, but he never seemed to say anything of substance. They heard a great deal about the state of the crops on his estate and the names and lineages of his horses. Bingley was too polite to stem this flow of self-absorption and so continued to ask questions. At one point, Bingley asked him if he lived alone at his estate.

"No," the other man replied. "I have seven lovely children. I am, alas, a widower. My darling wife died two years ago. My sister, Hortense, said to me, 'Two years is long enough to mourn. Go find a wife.' That is what she said all right. Now, I don't always do what my sister says; in fact, truth be told, I usually do the opposite, if you take my meaning! But this time I said to myself, 'Maybe she has the right of it! I should take a wife.' But there aren't many unmarried women in my part of Surrey. So my sister says, well, she wrote it in a letter, 'Come visit me. There are the Bennet girls—five and all unmarried. And many other pretty girls in the neighborhood.' So I came and met all five—hearty girls, too!" He smiled as he paused for dramatic effect. "And now I am engaged to Miss Elizabeth!"

Chapter 11

Darcy felt his eyes go wide with shock, and his jaw literally dropped open. Bingley's head swiveled toward his friend, horror written on his face. Then Darcy started to laugh. As he attempted to smother the laugh behind his hand, it sounded more like a cough. Mary hurried to pour him more tea, which Darcy drank more to cover his smile than to quell his nonexistent cough.

Darcy supposed if he had been merely courting Elizabeth, Fenton's pronouncement would have been distressing, but he knew Elizabeth could not have possibly have accepted this man. He could not even be jealous of him. Everything about him was so ridiculous and overbearing that he would never hold Elizabeth's interest. How had this man fallen under the delusion that he was engaged to her?

He took another sip of tea to quell his faux coughing fit and gazed levelly at Fenton. "May I ask when this felicitous event took place?" Darcy now noticed that Mary and Kitty seemed a little surprised at Fenton's announcement, although they did not contradict it.

"Yesterday afternoon, right over there in the garden!" Fenton exclaimed rapturously. "She is quite a sensible woman. She will fulfill the requirements for lady of my manor admirably." *I suppose that is high praise in Fenton's mind. How romantic.* Fenton went on to describe how Elizabeth would care for his seven children and leave him to the business of running the estate—and to go hunting as often as he wished. *He does not want a wife; he wants an unpaid governess!* Darcy realized.

"And I told her last night at dinner—I was sitting next to her, you understand—I would utter

not one word of reproach about her parents'
neglect." *How generous of him*, Darcy thought.
Fenton carried on pompously. "Neglect which
allowed her sister to behave so shamefully. It is the
weakness of the parents, not the sister, that should
be faulted." Darcy wondered how the two Bennet
girls felt hearing their parents described thus. Kitty
shifted uncomfortably in her chair, but Mary's
expression was unreadable. Darcy wanted to
castigate the man for even raising the subject,
although it was obviously on everyone's mind. "It is
a shameful business, but I reassured her that no one
in Surrey will have heard of it." *What an
insufferable boor; I am sorry Elizabeth had to
endure even one dinner with him.*

Bingley frequently shot sympathetic looks at
Darcy, believing the other man to be heartbroken
over losing Elizabeth. Darcy returned smiles, trying
to indicate there was no cause for worry, but
Bingley only frowned in confusion.

Given free rein on the conversation, Fenton
took to boasting about his property and his house.
He knew from the Bennets that Bingley had only
leased Netherfield, and in Fenton's mind, that made
him the better man. Ancestral lands, he declared,
were the backbone of England. He then turned to
Darcy, apparently hoping to best him as well, so
Darcy took great pleasure in describing Pemberley
and his holdings. Fenton admitted to having heard
of Pemberley and then appeared a bit awed of
Darcy. He soon turned the conversation to another
topic.

Finally, Mrs. Bennet came downstairs, effusing
over Bingley and Fenton. She spared little attention
for Darcy, who recognized her encouragement of
Fenton as a probable reason the man thought

Elizabeth might accept him. The irony struck him forcefully as he thought how differently Mrs. Bennet would behave if she knew how matters truly stood. On the other hand, perhaps he was better off if she remained unaware; he should enjoy her neglect while he could.

Mrs. Bennet made a fuss over serving tea to Fenton but then fell victim to a monologue about his latest fox hunt. Bingley took the opportunity to lean over and speak with Darcy in a low voice. "What a shame you had your hopes for a future with Miss Elizabeth dashed in this way. Though I must say you are taking it remarkably well. Perhaps you did not have that great an attachment to her?"

Darcy's smile was unperturbed. "I am completely unconcerned about this man's claims. I know that Elizabeth would not accept him. He is mistaken."

"It is not the sort of topic one is usually mistaken about," Bingley said tentatively.

"Unless one is a fool," Darcy responded.

"You seem very certain about Miss Elizabeth. Do you have some sort of secret understanding with her?" Bingley asked with a suspicious look at his friend.

Darcy realized he must reveal some information to the other man. "Something like that."

Bingley shook his head. "Even so, I do not know how you can be so certain. If he had said that about Jane, I would be heartbroken." Darcy shrugged, knowing he could reveal nothing more, and Bingley was soon drawn into the conversation about hunting.

Soon thereafter Elizabeth and Jane returned from Meryton. They were very surprised to see Darcy and Bingley already in the drawing room speaking with their mother and Mr. Fenton. Darcy could not tear his eyes away from Elizabeth and reveled in the complete rapture on her face as she gazed at him.

The men rose when the sisters entered the room. Elizabeth curtseyed to Darcy and Bingley, coloring a little. It was all he could do to refrain from grabbing her and kissing her right there, so acutely had he missed her. As he continued to stare, Bingley coughed slightly, and Darcy realized everyone was sitting down once more.

Elizabeth seated herself next to her mother on a small settee. Darcy wanted to sit on the other side, but her mother made a show of having Fenton take that spot, placing him far closer to Elizabeth than Darcy was comfortable with. On the other hand, he would not have been happy until Fenton was in a different house. Although he did not see Fenton as a serious rival for Elizabeth's affections, that did not stop him from wanting to punch the man in his smug face and warn him away from her for the rest of his life.

Darcy ground his teeth in frustration, attempting to content himself with sitting across from Elizabeth and gazing on her. Everything about her was enchanting: her laugh, the unruly curl that fell over her forehead, and her long eyelashes veiling her eyes. Knowing firsthand how passionate she could be only made it harder for him to be so tantalizingly close but unable to touch her.

Although he did not wish Elizabeth any unhappiness, he was pleased with her obvious dislike of Fenton's presence. His boorish conversation made her wince, although he did not dominate the discussion as much as he had in a smaller group. She avoided talking to him or looking at him; at one point in the gathering, Fenton leaned closer to her, and she pulled away. All of this was not lost on Darcy. He had no doubts about Elizabeth's fidelity, but Fenton's presumption was testing his self-control. He wanted to smash that supercilious expression off the other man's face!

Unable to bear it any longer, Darcy finally said, "After being confined in the carriage at such length, I experience a need to stretch my legs. Mrs. Bennet, I would like to take a turn in your garden." She nodded curtly, uninterested in what he did.

"Mr. Darcy, would you mind if I joined you?" Elizabeth asked.

"Not at all." He smiled warmly at her, wondering if there was any chance they could find a secluded spot.

"Nonsense, Child!" Mrs. Bennet cried. "You just returned from a walk to Meryton. What need have you for exercise?"

"I would like to show Mr. Darcy the roses. They are particularly fine now, and I was telling him about them when I saw him in London at my aunt and uncle's," Elizabeth said.

"Very well, if you must!" Mrs. Bennet washed her hands of her second daughter, but then a thought occurred to her. "Mr. Fenton, perhaps you would like a turn in the garden as well?"

Darcy cursed inwardly; his entire design was to avoid Fenton's presence—especially since the man was one of the topics he needed to discuss with Elizabeth. He saw his dismay mirrored in her eyes.

"I am not much interested in gardens," Fenton said. "I prefer woods. So I think I will forego this excursion." *More the fool you*, Darcy thought, exhilarated at the reprieve. Fenton would never win

Elizabeth's regard that way, but then he seemed more interested in wedding her than wooing her.

Bingley had been gazing silently at Jane, trying to discern her mood. He stood as well. "I think I will join you. It *was* a long carriage ride. Miss Bennet, will you do me the honor of accompanying me?"

Jane readily assented, and the four of them set off. Once outside, the two couples split apart by tacit agreement, although Bingley gave Elizabeth some anxious glances to reassure himself that she welcomed Darcy's attention. Elizabeth led Darcy to the roses that neither had any interest in. Knowing that they were still in view of the house, Darcy turned his broad back to the windows, shielding Elizabeth from view entirely. Then he took her hand and kissed it tenderly.

"How I have missed you! The hours passed so slowly," he said heatedly.

She nodded agreement and gave him a heart-stopping smile. "I hope we never have to be separated like that again. But I am very happy you are here now."

"I am as well. Apparently, I am arrived in time to prevent you from committing bigamy. Mr. Fenton told us that you are engaged to him."

"He said that?" Her hand flew to her mouth in dismay. "That fool!" She stamped her foot as embarrassment gave way to anger. "I—I refused him yesterday, but he would not accept it. He thinks that my mother's approval is all that is required." Her eyes met Darcy's. "I am so sorry, William, for any pain it caused you."

"I must admit that his announcement came as something of a shock. And poor Bingley was afraid I would die of a broken heart right there in the drawing room. But then I almost burst into laughter. After all, the whole situation is entirely ridiculous."

Elizabeth returned his smile. "It is humorous. The man droned on about his house and his horses and simply would not believe me when I told him no!" She gazed up at him with a twinkle in her eye. "I had thought that being married would mean I would receive no more offers of marriage. How silly of me!"

"Well, madam, I do hope that you will not expect to receive more proposals during our marriage," he said with a smile.

"I do not know. I am accumulating quite a collection of them. Perhaps only one or two a year would suffice," she said flirtatiously. "If you do not mind, sir?"

The playful expression on her face was too much for Darcy. "I must object quite adamantly!" He pulled her behind a tree, kissing her as thoroughly as he had wanted all day. She returned his kisses with equal passion. When they stopped, gasping for breath, Elizabeth said, "I am afraid we must return to where we are visible from the window or my mother will come seeking us—or worse, send Mr. Fenton."

He gave her one last kiss, and then they strolled out from behind the tree. She took his arm, and they walked about as if admiring the flowers, but the only beauty that held Darcy's interest was his wife's. She sighed. "I wish I knew what to do about Mr. Fenton. He would not listen when I told him no— and I cannot reveal the one reason that would discourage him permanently. A more sensitive man might notice my partiality for you, but I am certain he is blind to it." She shuddered. "I hate to think what he has been saying in Meryton. Soon the entire neighborhood will believe I am marrying him!"

Darcy felt a surge of anger toward Fenton for causing her any distress, but then he thought of a solution. "My love," he said with a wicked grin, "leave this to me. I am happy to be of service to you in this regard."

"What do you plan to do?" she asked, returning his smile.

"You shall see," was all he would say. They spied Jane and Bingley standing near the entrance to the garden and walked over to join the other couple. Soon they were engaged a humorous conversation about Mr. Fenton's misconceptions. Even Jane, who never thought ill of anyone, had to admit that the man's failure to accept Elizabeth's refusal made him somewhat ridiculous. In that moment, it was all Darcy could do to avoid revealing the truth of his relationship with Elizabeth.

Jane soon admitted to being chilled, so she and Bingley returned to the house. Darcy was loath to relinquish Elizabeth so quickly, and she was happy to delay facing the odious Fenton, so they walked to the far side of the garden, admiring the late summer flowers. They were holding hands and conversing quietly with their heads bowed when Darcy spied Fenton emerging from the house. Darcy immediately placed his arm around Elizabeth and gave her a light kiss. It was not the thorough, deep kisses they had enjoyed earlier, but it was unmistakably a kiss. After they separated, Elizabeth glanced at Fenton, who was frowning over Darcy's liberties with his "fiancée."

"William, what if he says something to my father?" Elizabeth asked.

Darcy replied to her but gave Fenton a long, steady look. "I have a plan, my love. You go into the house. I must converse with Mr. Fenton." Elizabeth was curious as to what the plan entailed, but she went to the house without another word. Before she entered the house, she turned back and saw Darcy sauntering over to where Fenton stood near the roses.

Elizabeth joined Jane and Bingley in the drawing room, and after a few minutes, Darcy also arrived but volunteered nothing about his conversation with Fenton. Unable to contain her curiosity, Elizabeth ventured into the hall, ostensibly in search of her mother.

Surprisingly, Fenton had already departed, but her mother stood in the hallway, wringing her hands in agitation. She rounded on her second oldest daughter when she emerged from the drawing room. "Oh, what did you do? Mr. Fenton says he was too hasty! He says he needs to talk to your father about the engagement but did not want to do it today. What happened?" Mrs. Bennet fluttered around the hallway. "Oh, my poor nerves! Things were going so well. What did you do to put him off? Did you have a row? Perhaps there is still some hope of repairing the damage!"

Elizabeth replied truthfully that she had not spoken to Mr. Fenton at all in the garden and that his behavior was a mystery to her. Returning to the drawing room, she wondered what Darcy could possibly have said to him; however, there was no opportunity for a private conversation.

***

All too soon the sun was growing lower in the sky, and it was time for the gentlemen to leave for Netherfield. Elizabeth and Jane walked out with them to their carriage. Bingley and Jane soon fell to murmuring to each other. As they stood on the sweep of the drive, Elizabeth turned to Darcy. "What did you say to Mr. Fenton?"

Darcy gave a small smile. "I merely reminded him that he did not have your *father's* permission to marry you and that he should not be so quick to announce an engagement without it."

"That cannot be the whole of your conversation! What did he say about the kiss?"

"We did not discuss it directly, but he realizes if he tells anyone about the kiss, your father will say I have to marry you. I do not believe he has given up hope of you, but now he knows there is competition. So he shall be more discreet in his courtship."

"You, sir, are ▮▮▮▮▮▮!" Darcy merely grinned. "Of course, what I wish is not for him to be discreet but to leave Hertfordshire and never return, but we cannot have everything. He will soon learn he cannot compete with you."

His eyes shone brightly as he kissed her hand and murmured, "It is my pleasure to discourage other men from proposing to my wife." The kiss sent a thrill down Elizabeth's spine, turning what could have been a flippant statement into an endearment.

Too soon the men had said their goodbyes and climbed reluctantly into the carriage. Elizabeth walked with Jane back into the house, their feet crunching on the gravel of the drive. She missed Darcy already.

By the time dinner had ended, Elizabeth had had enough of her mother's harangues. She took tea to her father in his study, hoping he would offer her temporary shelter. Her exasperated expression made him smile as he put down his book. "At least your mother knew better this time than to ask me to advocate for Mr. Fenton. She knows I would never attempt to compel you against your will."

"I know, Papa. I appreciate that you trust my judgment." She sighed in frustration. "I just wish Mr. Fenton would stop his visits. Today, he told Mr. Darcy and Mr. Bingley that we are engaged!"

Mr. Bennet laughed despite the chagrin on Elizabeth's face, and she found herself wishing he did not see everything as a source of humor. He shook his head. "I would hope Bingley had the sense not to believe such a tale. And who cares what Mr. Darcy thinks? His opinion of you is already so low."

Elizabeth winced at this sentiment but recognized an opportunity to discuss her change of heart as she seated herself in a chair opposite her father's desk. "Actually, I believe Mr. Darcy improves upon further acquaintance."

"Truly, Lizzy?" Her father regarded her skeptically over the top of his glasses.

"Yes. I saw him in Paris, and he was quite amiable. He danced with me at a ball and invited us to see the sights with him on a number of occasions."

"Indeed? Well, he must have found the society in Paris somewhat thin to stoop to visiting with someone who is only tolerable, eh?" His smile invited her to share the joke.

"I do not believe that to be the case." Elizabeth attempted to display all the earnestness she could muster. Not for the first time she wished she had been less vociferous in sharing her previous opinions about Darcy.

However, she recognized a losing battle when she was faced with it. Her father's eyes were drifting down to the book open on his desk. He never had a long attention span for this type of conversation, and clearly it had been exhausted.

"I will leave you to your book." He nodded absently to her, and she left the room, hoping she had made a little progress in changing her father's opinion of Darcy but recognizing how far they still had to go.

***

The next day, Darcy and Bingley joined the Bennets for luncheon. Elizabeth knew her mother had only invited Darcy because she could not politely exclude Bingley's guest. Nor clearly did Mrs. Bennet suspect his regard for Elizabeth because her mother seated him as distantly from her as possible. As they sat to eat, Darcy gave her a hopeless look, and she rolled her eyes in sympathy, but there was no recourse.

Frequently, when she glanced up from her meal, she observed Darcy's eyes on her and knew he experienced the same longing she did. His eyes held so much love and desire that Elizabeth thought surely he had betrayed their secret to the others. She did notice Bingley's eyes traveling from Darcy to her with raised eyebrows, but no one else seemed to pay them any mind.

After luncheon, her mother retired to rest her nerves, and Kitty and Mary left for a visit to Maria Lucas. In the drawing room, Darcy managed to secure a seat next to Elizabeth, but her father was on the other side, so they dared not attempt any form of intimacy. By now Elizabeth had an almost palpable sense of yearning for his touch and reassurance, and from the glances he bestowed on her, Elizabeth was certain Darcy was feeling the same.

She was surprised that her father was still with them in the drawing room; most days after luncheon he had already retreated to the library. Why had he had decided to stay?

Her consternation increased when her father addressed Darcy. "Mr. Darcy, I did not realize until recently that you had encountered Lizzy in Paris." A careful glance at her father's face suggested to Elizabeth that he had a deeper purpose behind seemingly casual questions.

Darcy inclined his head. "I did have that pleasure. We met quite by chance at a ball."

Mr. Bennet turned his attention to his second daughter. "Well, I realized that we have heard very little of your trip to France and your daring escape," her father said genially, but she sensed the hint of steel in his tone.

"I have hardly had an opportunity to discuss it," Elizabeth responded. "The whole household has been in a bit of an uproar since I returned." Although Darcy and Bingley knew of Lydia's situation, she felt it would be indelicate to refer to it in front of her father.

"The only news we had of the Gardiners was that you had to leave in a hurry without their company and that you were detained for a time at the home of a friend because of an illness. There must be more to the story than that." He regarded her sharply. Elizabeth felt a flutter of panic; this was neither the time nor the place she would have selected to share these facts with her father.

"I shall tell you another time," she demurred. "I do not wish to bore everyone with such details."

"Come, come." Her father smiled. "Do tell. I daresay we could all do with a little diversion." Elizabeth wondered if he suspected Darcy's role in her misadventures. Her conversation with him the previous day must have piqued his curiosity, but she was uncomfortably aware that it would be difficult to relate the story without giving the impression that Darcy had compromised her reputation.

"Yes, Lizzy, tell us," Jane said quite innocently. "I would like to hear more of your travels. I am certain they were very interesting."

Elizabeth realized she could not avoid telling the tale and rapidly reviewed which portions she could relate and which she must omit. Her eyes darted to Darcy, and he shrugged slightly as if to say, "Might as well."

"How did you escape the city?" Her father's tone was casual, but his eyes were unusually intent. "Did Mrs. Radnor arrange for transportation?"

"Well…she attempted it, but few carriages were available. Everyone was trying to leave Paris at the same time. Nothing was available for hire," Elizabeth admitted, knowing what was coming next.

"So how did you leave?" Her father seemed a little irritated at having to drag the story out of her.

"Mr. Darcy was kind enough to hire a carriage and offer me transportation." Elizabeth tried to keep her voice nonchalant, but even Bingley's eyebrows raised at this information.

"Mr. Darcy!" Her father's eyes swung to Darcy. "Did Mrs. Radnor accompany you?"

"No," Elizabeth said in a neutral tone. "She sent a maid to accompany me, but Mr. Darcy could only hire a curricle, so we did not have space for the maid and sent her back to Radnor House." She hoped that their attempt to accommodate a chaperone would mitigate some of her father's anger.

"So you and Mr. Darcy left Paris together? In a curricle?" Her father's voice was rising, and Elizabeth knew he was struggling to stay calm.

"Yes, but when I fell ill, it was apparent that I could not travel all the way to Calais, so Mr. Darcy took me to the house of a friend of his, Mr. Whitmore." She found herself staring at her hands because she did not want to meet her father's gaze, but the moment she realized this, she lifted her head, reminding herself that they had done nothing wrong. Their behavior had been unconventional, perhaps, but not wrong.

"Whitmore is a friend of mine from Oxford," Darcy interjected for the first time in the exchange. "He took orders soon after we graduated, but he has since moved to France to be with his wife." Her father seemed a little mollified at the thought that Elizabeth had been staying at the home of a married clergyman.

"Mr. Whitmore and his wife took very good care of me, Papa," Elizabeth continued, seeing this as an opportunity to demonstrate Darcy's good judgment in caring for her. "They made sure I had everything I needed. And so did Mr. Darcy. "

"And what did Mr. Darcy do for you, pray tell?" Her father's eyes flashed with anger again. *We did nothing wrong*, Elizabeth reminded herself. However, she felt guilty about what she was *not* telling her father, and he probably sensed she was holding something back. She felt her face turn red. *I probably look extremely guilty.*

"He found a doctor, gave me medicine, got me food…" Belatedly, Elizabeth realized how these actions could be misinterpreted.

"He was in your room?" her father said sharply. Bingley and Jane had identical expressions of shock on their faces.

"I was ill! He was helping to take care of me…with the maids and Mrs. Whitmore…" She stopped; if she protested too much, her father might think they were concealing something.

"Why was I not informed of this situation?"

"He wrote to the Gardiners and kept them informed. They did not pass the details along to you because they did not want to distress you about a situation you could do nothing to change." Elizabeth spared a look for Darcy; she was mortified about her father's behavior—about what he was implying. Darcy was sitting very still with little expression on his face, a pose she now recognized as betraying his anger.

"How dare they decide—?" her father almost shouted. Jane and Bingley appeared to wish they were anywhere else but did not dare to leave.

Elizabeth closed her eyes briefly, trying to quell her anger with her father. "It was in the midst of the distress about Lydia. They did not want to worry you about another daughter. Mr. Darcy took very good care of me—"

"I am certain he did!" Sarcasm laced his words.

"I was very ill! Nothing improper took place." Her father launched himself from his chair and paced the room, his face redder than she had ever seen it. "Our situation was quite perilous; surely the ordinary rules of propriety do not apply. If Mr.

Darcy had not been willing to take me from Paris without a chaperone, I might *never* have left." Her father's unreasonable anger was raising her own ire. A glance over at Darcy revealed that he, too, was close to the breaking point.

"Why did you conceal all of this from me? I believed Mrs. Radnor escorted you, and a friend of hers cared for you! You and the Gardiners deliberately deceived me!" Elizabeth thought wryly that they were lucky he did not know what else they were concealing.

"Mr. Bennet!" Darcy stood and towered imposingly over her father. "Elizabeth will not tell you this, sir, but she almost *died* in France! Her fever was so high, and her breathing was so labored that there were several days when the doctor did not think she would recover. Surely you have noticed the cough that still lingers and how easily she is fatigued?" Darcy's voice had risen. He swallowed and lowered it to a more socially acceptable level, but the intensity of his sentiments kept everyone's attention focused on him.

"She also has been protecting you from the knowledge of how we were almost killed by brigands in Paris and nearly arrested in Dunkirk! She knew you were anxious about being unable to protect her in France and sought to spare you the guilt. But you are demonstrating that she need not have bothered. You are not concerned about her well-being, only that she did not commit the smallest appearance of impropriety! You should be grateful you still have a daughter whose reputation you can worry about!"

Mr. Bennet's face reflected outrage at the rebuke. Jane and Bingley stared in amazement at Darcy, apparently attempting to assimilate this new information. Darcy turned on his heel and strode out of the drawing room. Every eye turned to Elizabeth.

Then her father's gaze returned to the door through which Darcy had exited, and she knew he was trying to bring his anger under control. Finally, he glanced back at her. "Lizzy, are these things true?" he asked in a small voice.

"Yes, Papa," she said simply. Then she stood and followed Darcy.

As Elizabeth suspected, Darcy had exited the house and was standing outside the front door. When she came out, he walked over to her but did not dare to even take her hand for fear that they were observed through the windows.

"I am sorry I lost my temper," he said softly. His eyes were full of anxiety as he gazed steadily into hers. *Does he truly believe I would condemn him for responding to such provocation?* She reminded herself that their marriage was still new, and he was often more unsure of himself than he appeared.

"Do not apologize. Your vexation was completely understandable given what my father was implying about your character." After glancing back at the house to see if they were observed, she daringly brushed his hand with her fingertips. The effect was electric; Darcy shivered slightly.

"I also apologize that my actions gave him cause for suspicion in the first place." Darcy glanced away from her face as if unable to meet her eyes. "I should have put more effort into locating a proper chaperone. In the moment, the thought of spending time alone with you was very appealing, but I should have realized it would lead to such difficulties. In my defense, I can only say that I apparently do not possess much self-control when it comes to you."

She laughed a little. "Then it is fortunate indeed that we are married."

"Not that it does us a lot of good," he growled.

"No." she sighed with regret, focusing on his thick dark hair and thinking how it would feel if she could run her fingers through it. "But, William, you take too much on yourself. I decided to leave with you. It was not your doing alone. I do not, for one moment, regret that decision, despite what my father thinks." This declaration won a warm smile and an expression of relief from Darcy. "I just wish we could reassure him that your intentions are honorable, but it would be a horrible lie to say we are engaged."

Darcy nodded regretfully. "Perhaps we should simply tell your father the truth. He would be angry, but my intentions would be unexceptionable." He finally succumbed to the temptation of taking her hand in his.

Elizabeth shook her head emphatically. "Our deception has angered him; now is not the time to relate additional deceit. That would be a very difficult beginning to your relationship with him."

"More difficult than it is now?" Darcy inquired with a raised eyebrow.

"We should give him time to calm himself— and to know you further."

"As you wish." Darcy fell silent for a moment, then spoke reluctantly. "I should leave so you may speak to your father in private. Please tell Bingley I will see him back at Netherfield."

"Very well." She was loath to have him leave, but the situation was fraught with difficulties. Her father was probably furious that she was outside speaking with Darcy instead of inside explaining herself to him.

Despite her concerns about her father, she felt the effects of Darcy's nearness. He was so tantalizingly close, but she could not act on her impulses. Perhaps it *would* be best to remove the temptation of his presence.

"Tell me, are you still in the habit of taking early morning strolls?" he asked, regarding her from the corner of his eye.

"Yes, I often walk toward Oakham Mount. But, Mr. Darcy, surely you are not suggesting an assignation! That would be highly improper!" she replied archly but kept her voice low.

He leaned over and whispered teasingly in her ear, "I can think of few things that are more proper, except perhaps having you in my bedchamber, Wife." His hand caressed hers in a sensuous way, sending shocks of energy throughout her body.

"I do take my wifely obligations seriously." She smiled flirtatiously.

"Your dedication to your duty is one of the things I love about you." She laughed, and he kissed her hand. As she smiled, she willed her eyes to demonstrate all of the passion she could not express any other way. "Elizabeth," he said fervently, "you have no idea what effect such a look has on me. I am quite undone…but I should depart before I do something your father would find objectionable. Tomorrow cannot come soon enough."

She walked him over to his horse and waited while he mounted, not returning to the house until he had disappeared from sight.

***

Elizabeth knew her father would not let the matter rest, so she was not surprised when he summoned her to his library that evening. He started without any preamble. "I am sorry I suggested that anything improper occurred between you and Mr. Darcy, but you have to admit the circumstances certainly could be misconstrued. I shudder to think what would happen if the gossips of Meryton heard even a hint of that story, but your Mr. Darcy does not seem likely to spread rumors. However, I am very disappointed that you chose to conceal the truth from *me*."

"I am sorry, Papa. I was concerned how you would react given Lydia's situation." She strove to sound more contrite than she actually felt. "I did not wish to cause you additional vexation."

Her father scrutinized her face. "Is there anything else about your visit to France you would like to share with me?" Undoubtedly, he hoped she would explain her relationship with Darcy.

She considered her response before she spoke. "I would be happy to share the details of my adventures, but I assure you that Mr. Darcy was a perfect gentleman."

Her father gazed at her steadily for a moment before speaking again. "I know that he is a gentleman and that you are capable of defending your own honor," he said. "But remember: Mr. Collins informed us that Mr. Darcy is engaged to his cousin. You cannot hold any hopes that he might propose to you."

Elizabeth fought the desire to laugh at the idea that Darcy might never wish to marry her. "He is not engaged to his cousin."

"Did he tell you that?" Mr. Bennet's tone was sharp and suspicious.

"Yes, but—"

Her father shook his head rather emphatically. "He could be denying a previous betrothal merely to encourage you to believe his intentions are honorable." His index finger stabbed into his desk for emphasis.

Anger surged through her. "He would not do that!"

Irritation colored her father's tone as well. "You do not know what men are capable of. See how we were deceived by Wickham!"

"Mr. Darcy is not like Wickham!" she insisted.

"If he cares for you, why has he not requested my permission to court you or asked for your hand? And do not tell me there is nothing between you! Your mother may be blind to it, but I am not!" Her father stood abruptly and spread his hands on the desk. "Mr. Darcy may have some fondness for you, but he has not acted on it. Either he thinks you are beneath him or his intentions are less than admirable."

"He is not—"

"Lizzy," her father sounded suddenly tired. He sank back into his chair and rubbed his face. "I have heard of high-born gentlemen who impose themselves on women, compromising their reputations so thoroughly that they have no choice but to become their mistresses."

Indignation coursed through her once again. "Mr. Darcy would never do such a thing!" Her father's face held infuriating compassion at her ignorance. "I know his intentions toward me are honorable!"

"Then why has he not declared himself? He has had ample opportunity by this time." Her father looked at her sadly. "I have learned my lesson. We cannot trust that any man's intentions are proper. I failed to protect Lydia, but I will not make such an error again."

"He had ample opportunity to compromise my reputation in France and did not take it!" Elizabeth cried, feeling the injustice of the situation.

Her father rubbed his hands together, trying to calm himself. Then he turned and poured himself a brandy before responding. "I am pleased you have such faith in him. I do not know the whole truth of what occurred in France, but I suspect you are concealing something from me." Elizabeth said nothing in response. "I hope you know you can always turn to me if you find yourself in distress of any sort."

The pain and fear in her father's voice made her wish to confide the truth right then. But she knew she could not do so without talking to Darcy, so she merely said, "I am not at all distressed for myself. I am perfectly content with my situation." Far from reassured, her father merely shook his head sadly at this declaration. "I am only concerned about Lydia."

Her father sighed and stared at his brandy glass. "As are we all," he said. "The poor, foolish girl."

Elizabeth made a move to depart, but her father stayed her with a hand. "You and Mr. Darcy have concealed the impropriety of your travels in France admirably, but I hope I hardly need to warn you that you must be properly chaperoned here in Hertfordshire."

She murmured, "Of course," and walked toward the door, thinking that the definition of "proper" chaperonage was flexible given the circumstances.

Before she exited, her father called to her, "And, Lizzy, I had not realized how ill you were in France. I cannot tell you how grateful I am that you are still with us." Tears sparkled in his eyes. "And I intend to thank Mr. Darcy for taking such excellent care of you the next time I lay eyes on him."

Elizabeth smiled and nodded to her father, then left the room.

**

As Elizabeth set out for her walk the following morning, she thought guiltily that she was violating the spirit, if not the letter, of her promise to her father. She would be with Darcy without a chaperone, but because they were married, they would not truly require one.

The summer days had been warm lately, but the early mornings were still cool. Mist rose from the fields as the first rays of early morning light shone on the plants. Elizabeth walked more briskly that usual, excited at the prospect of being with Darcy alone.

As she proceeded along the path to Oakham Mount, she soon noticed a tall figure on horseback. When he reached her, Darcy slid quickly off his horse and embraced her so tightly she could hardly breathe. Scarcely less eager, Elizabeth tilted her head up to receive a kiss, responding with ardent desire as he pressed his lips on hers. She never wanted the kiss to end, but at the same time, it only stoked additional desires that mere kisses could not satisfy. Darcy's hands traced her curves, enflaming desire wherever they touched; every inch of her body ached for him.

When at last they separated, panting, Elizabeth said, "Mr. Darcy, I believe you have compromised me."

He gave a short laugh. "This location *is* rather exposed." His fingers played with one of the curls left visible by her bonnet. "Did you have another place in mind, my love?"

Her smile was impish. "Let me show you one of my favorite hiding places as a child." He tied his horse to a tree, and she took his hand, leading him along the bank of the stream. He followed her into a secluded copse, a grassy area rendered private by the surrounding fir trees. The sun shone brightly through the ring of gray-green branches, creating an intricate pattern of light and shadow.

"This is delightful!" Darcy gasped, turning in a circle to fully appreciate the beauty. "Thank you for sharing it with me."

"As a child I only viewed this as a perfect spot to hide from my sisters. I never realized what a wonderful lover's bower it would make!" Darcy laughed at her playful tone.

As she returned his laugh, her eyes lit with pleasure, and Darcy thought again how incredibly fortunate he was that she had agreed to be his. Once she was surrounded by family and friends at Longbourn, he had worried she would regret her impetuous decision to marry him. After all, she must be thinking that marriage to him would inevitably lead her to leave Hertfordshire and everyone she loved, but she gave no indications of remorse now. Apparently, she wished to be with him as much as he wished to be with her; his heart swelled with love all over again.

He kissed her again, pouring all of his love and passion into that one kiss. As he did so, his hands, moving of their own accord, started to undo the buttons at the back of her dress. Once finished, he realized that Elizabeth's hands had unbuttoned his waistcoat and pushed it over his shoulders and down his arms. *How had she learned so quickly how to undress me?* he wondered absently. *Not that I am not grateful.* Her eagerness excited him even more.

Darcy turned back to Elizabeth and quickly divested her hair of its hairpins, causing her glorious curls to cascade around her shoulders. "I wish you could wear your hair down every day of your life," he murmured. "But I want to be the only man to see it."

"I do believe you are jealous," she whispered coyly.

"Always," he whispered. He laid his coat on the grass and then laid her on top of it, kissing her with a passion borne of many nights of separation.

A long time later, he reluctantly helped button up her dress and watched as she twisted her hair up into a simple knot. He gently kissed the nape of her neck, and she shivered. She had related the substance of her conversation with her father. "How long do you think we can maintain this pretense without betraying ourselves?" Her expression was pensive.

"You, my dear, are a very good actress." He put his arms around her waist. "But I am afraid that if any other men demonstrate an interest in your charms, I may respond rather inappropriately."

"You managed Mr. Fenton well, but I shall endeavor to avoid other eligible young men." She gave him an impudent smile. Then she examined the angle of the sun and sighed. "I am afraid I need to return to Longbourn. I do not want to create additional concern, especially now that my father is so suspicious of your motives." He nodded reluctantly. "Will I see you later today?" she asked.

"Bingley expressed an interest in visiting Longbourn early, so he may already be there. I could join him. The thought of remaining away for so long is simply unbearable."

"For me as well," she said softly. "I will look forward to your visit."

***

When Elizabeth returned to Longbourn, she found that Bingley was closeted with her father in his library. A radiant Jane explained to Elizabeth that he had proposed, and she had accepted. Elizabeth could not have been happier for her sister.

Later in the day, Darcy came to call and had the privilege of being one of the first to congratulate the newly affianced couple. Fortunately, he was spared Mrs. Bennet's effusions on the subject since Elizabeth's mother had gone to Meryton to share the good news with anyone who would stand still long enough to listen.

Bingley and Jane sat close together in the parlor, but during one moment when Jane was engaged in a conversation with Mary and Elizabeth, Bingley confided in Darcy. "I had thought to take a couple more days at this courting business so I would not seem overly hasty," he explained in low voice. "But I received a letter from Caroline yesterday informing me that she will be arriving tomorrow. I knew she was coming because she wanted to prevent my engagement to Jane. I thought if it were a *fait accompli*, she would not argue so much about it. I will have to endure some sour looks, but she will understand that she cannot dictate my actions."

"Indeed," Darcy said. "That was clever."

Bingley managed a grim expression for a whole minute at this prospect before a glance at his fiancée restored his good cheer. "There is one benefit of Caroline's arrival, however," Bingley continued. "I will be able to invite Jane over to Netherfield." He smiled tenderly, but then looked uncertainly at Darcy. "And perhaps Elizabeth if you would like?"

"Yes, I would like it. Very much," Darcy said with a small smile. *If only there were a reason she would need to stay overnight.*

Caroline Bingley arrived the next day, and Bingley wasted no time in extending an invitation for Elizabeth and Jane to dine the following day. Miss Bingley was greatly vexed to learn that the engagement she had thought to prevent had already taken place and was even less pleased to find that her presence facilitated a visit by both Bennet sisters. However, Bingley bore her black mood with equanimity. Nothing perturbed him as long as he would see Jane.

Elizabeth and Darcy had discussed the possibility of her staying overnight at Netherfield, but neither could find a plausible reason. Elizabeth imagined her mother would probably encourage any behavior in pursuit of Mr. Darcy, but she was concerned about her father's suspicions.

***

Jane and Elizabeth arrived in the late morning and stayed for luncheon. Elizabeth found herself seated as far from Darcy as possible while Miss Bingley had placed herself at his right hand. As they took their seats, Elizabeth smiled to herself at the transparency of Miss Bingley's maneuvers—and their futility. *If she only knew the truth, she would probably seat me in the kitchen.*

Once everyone was seated, Miss Bingley shot Elizabeth a look of triumph, which she received with a smile that quite disconcerted her hostess. When Miss Bingley turned to Mr. Darcy, she was even less pleased to see his gaze and smile alighting on Elizabeth.

Conversation was stilted at the table. Jane and Charles were preoccupied with each other, reviewing everything which had occurred since they last saw each other—a mere twelve hours previously. Elizabeth was too far away from Darcy to easily converse with him, and he replied in monosyllables to all of Miss Bingley's conversational forays.

Miss Bingley had clearly devoted much thought to how she could separate Elizabeth from Darcy during the visit. After luncheon, she dragged him off to the music room on the pretext of asking him to help her translate an Italian love song that she was practicing, but once the translation was complete, she demanded that he remain to turn pages for her.

Although Elizabeth missed Darcy's company in the drawing room as she sat with Bingley and Jane, she had to admire Miss Bingley's sheer unwillingness to recognize a lost cause. When Darcy finally prevailed on her to rejoin the others, she insisted that he read to her from a volume of love sonnets. Although he humored her for a few minutes, every time he glanced up from the page, he gazed at Elizabeth as if he read only to her. Miss Bingley's frustration increased every minute as her scheme to capture Darcy's attention had the opposite effect.

Darcy finished the final sonnet and quickly— before Miss Bingley could devise any other schemes—suggested that they all take a turn in the garden.

As they departed the house, Miss Bingley was detained by the housekeeper on some business, so Elizabeth was able to take Darcy's arm unencumbered. They deliberately fell behind Jane and Bingley so they could enjoy a private conversation. Low clouds hung in the sky, and Darcy studied them anxiously, fearing a sudden cloudburst would ruin their walk and force them back inside.

"I do believe you were laughing at my distress," Darcy said in an accusing tone.

"You are too severe upon me, sir," she said playfully. "I merely thought I had monopolized your company long enough. It is incumbent upon me to share."

He shook his head in mock anger. "No, you were enjoying watching me in her clutches. Or else you would have rescued me."

"Must ladies rescue gentlemen now?" she responded with a playful gleam in her eye. "I failed to see the need."

He laughed at this sally, but then his face turned unexpectedly earnest. "I do need rescuing. I have attempted to discourage her in every way possible within the bounds of propriety. I do not wish to be uncivil, but I do not know how long I can suffer her attentions in silence."

"Very well," Elizabeth said with a sincere smile for her husband. "In the future I will be alert for signs of distress and will mount a rescue attempt immediately."

"Thank you." He stopped walking and stared deeply into her eyes. He wished desperately that he could kiss her, but their location was too easily visible, and Miss Bingley might happen upon them at any moment.

Elizabeth glanced up at the dark and foreboding clouds hovering over them. "Oh my, it might storm. It *would* be a shame if the roads were too dangerous for us to return to Longbourn tonight."

Darcy regarded the sky and then Elizabeth with a sly smile. "Yes, that would be shame."

"Which room are you staying in here at Netherfield?" she asked.

"I believe they refer to it as the Blue Room," he replied. "Why?"

Elizabeth smiled. "I was just wondering."

At that moment, Miss Bingley, having ridded herself of the housekeeper at last, rushed up to them and attached herself to Darcy's other arm, so all sensible conversation was at an end.

The three of them were returning to the house when Bingley called to them, and they joined him in an out-of-the-way corner of the garden. Jane was sitting on a bench, and Bingley was holding her foot, examining it. Jane was obviously in pain but trying to conceal it. Elizabeth rushed over to her sister. "What happened?"

"Oh, it was silly. I was hurrying to keep up with Charles, but my shoe slipped on some loose stones, and I took a fall. Do not trouble yourself. It is nothing." Watching her sister's drawn face, Elizabeth was quite sure it was something indeed.

"I beg to differ with your sister," Bingley said, an anxious expression on his face. "She took a bad fall and has certainly turned her ankle and perhaps wrenched her knee as well. She can barely put weight on her foot."

As she struggled to a standing position, Jane shook her head. "Charles, it is not—" But even as she said this, she stood on the foot and involuntarily winced with pain.

"That is quite enough!" Bingley said, with a determination that Elizabeth had never seen before. "I am sending for the doctor!" Without so much as a glance at Jane for her permission, he swept her up into his arms and carried her into the house.

So it was that Elizabeth did not need a thunderstorm to keep her at Netherfield. Bingley would not hear of Jane's removal to Longbourn, despite the doctor's assurance that her injuries were not severe. The doctor bound up her ankle and knee and told her to stay off her feet for a week. Jane protested that she could rest her leg just as easily at her home, but Bingley could not bear to have her leave that night. Elizabeth mused that his insistence might stem, in part, from a desire to spend more time with Jane—but she was far from objecting.

Naturally, he asked Elizabeth to stay and keep her sister company. Although Elizabeth was certain she could do little for Jane under these circumstances, she readily consented to remain. The deep contentment on Darcy's face was all the persuasion she required. A messenger was dispatched to Longbourn with the news and returned with extra clothing for the two women.

***

Darcy dismissed his valet for the night and finished donning his robe; his thoughts, as always, turned to Elizabeth. Reclining on his room's large four-poster bed, he pondered his next step. Although he had longed for them to be under the same roof, he was not sure how they could act on their unexpected good fortune. Her bedroom was several doors down, and visiting her would create the risk of his being seen traversing the hallway. He had noticed that the floors of Netherfield were noisy, creaking with every step. Even if he waited until everyone was abed, a light sleeper might hear his footsteps, but it was too great an opportunity to ignore. It had been too long since their interlude in the copse of trees, and he longed to hold her in his arms again. Just knowing how near she was made him want to throw caution to the wind and race to her door.

Sternly, he reminded himself that he would do her no favors by compromising her reputation, especially in the eyes of Caroline Bingley. They were no closer to revealing their marital status to her father, and therefore they must be above suspicion. Mr. Bennet must be unhappy enough that the two of them were spending the night under one roof. He punched his pillow in frustration. He must see her somehow! Walking to the window, he pressed his hands on the cool glass, wondering for the thousandth time how he had ended up in such a bizarre and frustrating situation.

Then he heard a slight noise behind him and turned to behold Elizabeth in the corner of the room near the bed! "My love!" he gasped. Crossing the room in two strides, he enfolded her in his embrace. "But how did you come to be here?"

Clad only in her nightgown and dressing gown, she smiled impudently. "You forget that I know Netherfield quite well. The Staunton sisters were friends of our when their family owned this house, and I spent many happy hours playing in its corridors. There is a secret passage between this room and the Rose Room, where I am staying." She indicated a small doorway designed to resemble a section of the wall, which was almost invisible when closed.

He buried his hands in her loose curls and kissed her soundly. "You, my dear, are a marvel!" he murmured against her lips. "But how was it that you happened to be assigned the Rose Room?"

She batted her lashes in mock innocence. "I told Bingley's housekeeper this afternoon that I had fond memories of the Rose Room from my childhood. Since no one was using the room, she was more than happy to accommodate my wishes."

He ran his arms up and down her body, wanting to touch every inch of her. "I cannot tell you how happy I am."

She regarded him through her eyelashes. "So, would you care to visit the Rose Room and see if it meets with your approval?"

His smile was fond and indulgent. "I would, but I am already quite certain I will approve of it." She turned toward the door, but he clung to her hand, unwilling to break contact with her for one moment. Tugging softly on his hand, she led him through the concealed door.

Much later, Darcy was lying in the Rose Room's bed gazing at Elizabeth, fast asleep in the crook of his arm, thinking how pleasant it was just to watch his wife sleep. She was so angelically beautiful, her dark lashes vivid against her pale skin.

He, however, fought sleep, knowing that, above all, he could not be in Elizabeth's room come the morning. As much as he longed to lie beside her all night, he knew he needed to return to his own room soon. Already a sense of yearning gripped him at the thought of leaving her.

He had taken the precaution of locking the door so that if he inadvertently fell asleep, they would not be surprised by one of Bingley's maids in the morning. But Darcy's valet might visit his room and wonder where he was. In addition, he had noticed that the lock on Elizabeth's door was old and had not latched well. He could not be certain that it would keep the maid out, or even that she would realize the door was supposed to be locked.

Steeling himself against the pain of separation, he sat up in the bed. Elizabeth sighed and reached for him. "Shhh, my love," he whispered. "I need to return to my room, but I will see you in the morning."

She settled back on the bed, and he pulled the blanket up around her shoulder. As he shrugged on his robe, he enjoyed one last lingering glance at her.

Suddenly, he heard footfall outside the door and a quick knock. "Miss Elizabeth?" *Bingley!* Darcy thought in a panic and rushed to the concealed door. Bingley fumbled with the doorknob. "Miss Elizabeth? Forgive the intrusion, but Jane's ankle is paining her, and she was hoping you—"

The door sprang open even as Bingley was talking. Bingley stood framed in the doorway, staring right at Darcy, who was mere inches from the secret door. "Darcy!" Bingley exclaimed, completely bewildered. "I thought this was Elizabeth's—"

He glanced toward the bed, where Elizabeth was just beginning to sit up, rubbing sleep from her eyes. Then Bingley turned back to Darcy, his look of astonishment rapidly evolving into anger.

Chapter 12

Elizabeth looked from a perplexed Bingley to Darcy, who was completely paralyzed with mortification. Bingley's face grew more furious by the second. Turning bright red, Elizabeth hid her face in her hands.

They stood frozen in a tableau for what seemed an eternity to Darcy. Bingley was the first to recover. "Darcy, might I see you in my study? Miss Elizabeth, Jane was hoping you might know of something that might alleviate the pain in her ankle. Can you go to her?"

Her face still buried in her hands, Elizabeth whispered a muffled, "Yes." Darcy followed Bingley out of the room, trying not to feel like a schoolboy who was about to be paddled.

Bingley stalked down the hallway in complete silence. As they entered the study, Darcy tried a preemptive explanation. "Bingley, you do not—"

But Bingley's low, level voice forestalled him. "How could you? She is under my roof! Under my protection!" Darcy thought he had never seen his ordinarily placid friend so furious. Bingley threw himself into the desk chair and glared at his friend. "What am I going to tell her father? What am I going to tell Jane? Good Lord!" He slapped the arm of the chair in frustration. "Damn, Darcy, I never thought you would do something like this!"

Bingley finally fell silent, frowning fiercely as Darcy sank into the facing chair.

"I am sorry this has caused you consternation—" Darcy began. Bingley made an angry gesture as if to respond, but Darcy forestalled him. "Damnation! Will you listen to me? We are married. Elizabeth and I are married."

Bingley sat up so quickly that his arm inadvertently knocked some papers off his desk, but he spared them no notice. "Married?" he said incredulously.

Darcy nodded. "In France."

"France?" Bingley echoed in a stunned tone. "You mean all this time you have been—?" Darcy merely nodded again, giving his friend time to assimilate the news. The other man shook his head in amazement. Darcy explained the circumstances of their marriage and why they had concealed it.

"I had been hoping I could produce Lydia and Wickham—preferably married—before explaining to Mr. Bennet that *we* married without his knowledge or consent," Darcy finished up. "But we may not be able to wait much longer."

"You are in a deucedly awkward position." Bingley shook his head slowly in sympathy. Then he laughed unexpectedly. "No wonder you were so certain she had not accepted an offer of marriage from Fenton!"

Darcy chuckled. "Yes, that was one thing I could be sure of in this whole situation."

Bingley poured brandy for them both. "You are married." Bingley shook his head in disbelief. "Before you left for Paris, I did not even know you held any special regard for Elizabeth. Now I find you have beaten me to the altar."

Darcy nodded knowingly. "Yes, I can hardly believe it myself."

***

After the men left her room, Elizabeth took several breaths to recover her composure and remind herself that she and Darcy had done nothing wrong. She might feel like a misbehaving schoolgirl, but she was a married woman who was entitled to spend the night with her husband.

Feeling a little better, she climbed out of bed and donned her robe. She walked down the hall to Jane's room, knocked lightly on the door, and then pushed it open. Jane sat up in bed, her head and shoulders propped on some pillows, and her swollen ankle resting on another one. Although Jane's face showed some strain and exhaustion, she did not seem to be in overwhelming pain. She put aside the book she was reading and regarded Elizabeth with chagrin.

"I am sorry, Lizzy." Her beautiful face was anxious. "I did not wish to disturb your sleep, but Charles was beside himself. He had left a maid to watch over me. Then he could not sleep, so he came to discover how I fared, and she told him I was in pain. He wanted so much to be of use to me! So I told him that sometimes you made a poultice that eased Papa's rheumatism. He insisted on rousing you to make it for me. But if you would rather sleep, you may do it in the morning."

Elizabeth had to smile at this rather long, self-effacing speech. "Truly, I want to be of any comfort I can. I will make the poultice if that will help."

"It does not hurt so very much, but I am having trouble sleeping. Perhaps if you could read to me a little, that would help."

Elizabeth pulled a chair to her sister's bedside and took her hand. "I will do whatever you desire. But first I believe I must tell you something." As she had walked down the hall, Elizabeth wondered about Darcy's conversation with Bingley and realized that in all likelihood, Darcy would reveal the truth about their marriage. Elizabeth felt it only fair to divulge the same to Jane. Indeed, she had found it quite painful to conceal the truth from her closest sister. Although she felt an obligation to tell her father, she felt the most desire to confide in Jane and receive sisterly advice.

"What is that?" Jane's eyes were wide and curious.

"I think I can help you forget about the pain in your ankle, at least for a little while," Elizabeth smiled at her sister. "I wanted to tell you…that is…I…we—" Elizabeth stopped and took a breath. This was more difficult than she had anticipated, perhaps because she was anxious about Jane's reaction. Then she realized that Jane's face was furrowed with concern. "It is nothing bad," she assured her sister. She took a deep breath and said the rest in a rush. "Mr. Darcy and I are married. We were married in France."

Jane's hands flew to her mouth as her jaw dropped open. She was struck dumb with surprise.

"I hope you are not too shocked," Elizabeth went on, "but after I recovered from the illness, I felt that I did not want to wait."

Jane nodded. "I remember that Mr. Darcy said you almost died," she whispered.

"Yes. I–we decided to become engaged, and we knew it would be easier to travel if we were married, so—" Elizabeth's words were halting as she gazed at Jane's face. If Jane did not understand, she had little hope of explaining her actions to the rest of her family.

"I understand," Jane said gently, patting Elizabeth's hand. "It makes complete sense."

Elizabeth felt tears prick her eyes. "You are too good to me. Not one word of reproach for marrying without you or for concealing the truth all this time?"

"How could I reproach you for following your heart? When I see you with Mr. Darcy, it is clear he is deeply in love with you. How could I begrudge you the same happiness I have with Charles?" Jane's expression had regained its usual serenity.

Elizabeth had to wipe her eyes with a handkerchief. "My biggest regret was not having you there to share the joy with me. I wanted to tell you when I returned, but William and I had agreed to tell Papa first and—"

"I comprehend perfectly why you could not reveal all. But I knew, Lizzy." Jane smiled. "I knew something had happened between you and Mr. Darcy, although I thought it might be a secret engagement."

"Were we so bad at concealing our affection?" Elizabeth asked with chagrin.

Jane shook her head gently. "I noticed since I know you so well. I am certain no one else was paying such close attention."

"I hope you are right." Elizabeth sighed. "Papa should be the first—well, among the first—to know. I know we shall have to tell him very soon. After tonight, there will be two more in our confidence."

"Two?"

"Oh, I forgot to explain what precipitated my revelation." Elizabeth laughed, a little embarrassed. "When Bingley came to my room to fetch me, he found William there. He was very angry."

"Oh no! Poor Charles." Jane covered her mouth to stifle a smile. Then the two sisters burst into laughter, and it was some time before they recovered their composure.

Jane's eyes sparkled. "And you know, Lizzy, you were right. You did make me forget all about my ankle!"

***

The next morning, they all gathered for a late breakfast. Darcy had already been for a ride and Elizabeth for a bracing walk around the Netherfield grounds, and if they entered the house at the same time, there was no one present to notice. Bingley had spent the morning fussing at the staff to ensure Jane had all the pillows, blankets, and tasty morsels she might need. When she insisted on going downstairs for breakfast, he acquiesced, but only upon the condition that he would carry her. Laughing a little at the impropriety, Jane agreed.

He deposited Jane in a chair next to his sister, who sniffed a bit at his boisterousness but said nothing. Darcy regarded Miss Bingley closely for a moment, afraid that she had heard some of the nocturnal comings and goings the previous night, but her expression seemed much the same. He seated himself next to Elizabeth, a fact which seemed to frustrate Miss Bingley, who had arrived first and had hoped Darcy would be next to her. At a signal from Bingley, one of the serving men provided a full champagne flute for each guest. Miss Bingley looked askance at her brother. "Champagne for breakfast? Has the engagement muddled your head, Charles?"

Bingley merely laughed and said, "I simply felt like celebrating. Jane's ankle is improving, and we are enjoying some of the finest company in England!" He raised his glass in a toast but arched an eyebrow at Elizabeth and Darcy, who knew that his friend was toasting their marriage without revealing anything to his sister. Elizabeth smiled warmly at Bingley, appreciating the gesture.

Everyone fell to eating the fine repast, but they were soon interrupted by Bingley's butler, who brought an express post to Darcy. Darcy scanned the sender's address and raised his eyebrows. "Please excuse me for reading this at the table," he addressed his host and hostess, "but it is a matter of some urgency."

All eyes were on Darcy as he scanned the lines of the short missive. A stormy expression on his face, he folded it up again. Elizabeth knew such a mien meant the matter was quite serious. She touched his arm gently and asked, "Is it something very disturbing, William?" She heard Miss Bingley's hiss of indrawn breath and realized she had unwittingly displayed too much familiarity. Their hostess observed Darcy, expecting him to rebuke Elizabeth.

Darcy, deep in thought, did not seem to notice Elizabeth's slip. "No, I will tell you later." Elizabeth suspected that the note had something to do with Lydia and Wickham but could not ask more in front of Miss Bingley. Now that Jane and Bingley knew their secret, Miss Bingley's presence was most awkward.

Shortly thereafter, the breakfast party broke up, although Darcy and Bingley lingered to exchange some private words while Jane waited for her fiancé to carry her upstairs once more. Elizabeth left the room and found herself in the hallway with Miss Bingley, who turned to her with a completely false air of solicitude. "A word of advice, Eliza. Mr. Darcy is a very proper man. I have known him many years, and he has never invited me to use his

Christian name. Although he is too well mannered to say anything, I could tell that he was quite alarmed by your excessive familiarity."

"Surely that is for Mr. Darcy to decide," Elizabeth said with some asperity.

Some of Miss Bingley's false amiability slid away. "I know you are trying to entice him by pretending a familiarity which does not exist, but let me assure you that such an approach will not succeed with Mr. Darcy."

"How do you know it does not exist?" Elizabeth asked sweetly, attempting to conceal her anger.

Miss Bingley's mouth fell open at this rather brazen question, but she was saved the necessity of a reply by the arrival of the man in question. Darcy swooped out of the dining room and approached the two women. "Elizabeth!" he cried. "Just the person I was hoping to see. Would you take a turn with me in the garden? I must discuss the contents of this letter with you."

Elizabeth took his arm, and they swept out. She turned back to see Miss Bingley still standing in the hallway, paralyzed with shock and mouth agape.

Once they were outside, Elizabeth could no longer contain a smile, and as she gazed up at her husband, he was grinning broadly. "That was very wicked!" she exclaimed. "Did you overhear what she was saying to me?"

"Yes, I admit it. I heard through the dining room door. It is excessively difficult not to eavesdrop when one hears one's name mentioned. Once I understood what she was saying to you, it was even more difficult not to emerge and administer the chastisement she richly deserves. But I feared revealing too much."

"The approach you chose had the benefit of being subtle yet effective," Elizabeth observed, smiling. "And vastly more entertaining."

"Not to mention satisfying." He grinned, lengthening his stride to create more distance from the house.

They walked for a minute in silence, but Elizabeth could wait no longer. "Is the letter about Lydia?"

"Yes, it is from Mr. Scott, one of the investigators I hired. They have found Lydia." Elizabeth regarded him with a mixture of anxiety and hope about what he would say next. "They are not married, but your sister appears unharmed."

Elizabeth sagged under the combined weight of relief and fresh cause for concern. Darcy put his arm around her shoulders to support her. "What of Wickham?" she asked.

"My investigator did not find him, and Lydia does not know where he is. They reached a coaching inn about a day's ride from London. But Lydia says Wickham left one morning and did not return. That was several days ago." Darcy guided her to a low stone bench, and they sat.

Elizabeth covered her mouth with her hand, and tears came to her eyes. "Oh, poor Lydia! He truly had no intention of marrying her."

"No, indeed," Darcy agreed, handing Elizabeth his handkerchief. "Since Lydia had no money to pay for her room at the inn, she agreed to return to London with Mr. Scott. He has taken her to the Gardiners."

Elizabeth dried her eyes with the handkerchief. "I am pleased she is unhurt. The Gardiners will be kind to her."

Darcy nodded. "Lydia did give the investigator some ideas about where to seek Wickham, so they may find him soon enough."

"But what shall induce him to marry Lydia?" Elizabeth twisted the handkerchief in her hands.

Darcy gazed over Bingley's lovely gardens for a moment before answering. "It is not hard to work on Wickham," he said finally. "All it takes is money." Elizabeth felt an immediate sense of relief. Although she chafed at the unfairness of Darcy paying off Wickham, she was reassured by the thought that there was a potential resolution of the dilemma. "There is no possible way he could have known of our marriage," Darcy continued. "But he could not have picked a better way to pursue his vendetta against me—unless, of course, he had eloped with *you*." Darcy impulsively took her hands in his and kissed them both, as if hoping that his affection might help lift her spirits.

"There was no chance of that happening." Elizabeth laughed. "I have more sense than Lydia. And I was never in love with him."

Darcy regarded her intently. "You cannot know how the thought of you with Wickham plagued me. Especially after I knew the lies he had told you."

She shook her head. "I was blind to his lies; that is true. However, I would like to believe I would have discerned the true nature of his character eventually."

"I know you would have." Darcy's strong reaction to Wickham seemed to fire his passion, his eyes practically smoldering as he regarded her. He drew her up off the bench and over to the shade of some small trees near the garden's wall and kissed her very thoroughly. Although they had been together the night before, Elizabeth felt she needed his kisses like a thirsty man needs water in a desert, wanting to drink deeper and deeper. All too soon it came to an end. Darcy scanned the area to ensure that they were not observed and returned them to the well-trodden path once again.

They resumed walking; the romantic interlude had soothed Elizabeth's agitation somewhat. Darcy said grimly, "I must talk with your father today. He is likely to discover Lydia's plight from the Gardiners, and I can no longer conceal my part in the investigation."

Elizabeth glanced at him with some concern. "You need not be so anxious. I am sure Papa will be grateful for the assistance."

Darcy shook his head. "No man likes to be in another man's debt. He is also likely to question me about my interest in this matter. He may not believe me if I say I am merely acting as a friend of the family."

Elizabeth placed her hand on his. "Perhaps the time has come to tell him the truth."

Darcy ran his free hand through his hair. "I fear that our behavior will resemble Lydia's and Wickham's too closely for your father's comfort, and he will undoubtedly be angry that we have deceived him. I was hoping to commence my relationship with my father-in-law on a better footing."

To his surprise, Elizabeth chuckled. "That may be too much to hope for under the circumstances. He will not be pleased no matter what."

"I suppose." Darcy sighed. "Hundreds of fathers in England would be overjoyed to find that I had married their daughter."

Elizabeth shrugged eloquently. "You did not wish to marry a fortune hunter, sir. My father is not mercenary either. You must live with the attendant disadvantages."

"Your sympathy is most heartwarming," he said wryly. She merely laughed.

***

An hour later, Elizabeth and Darcy took Bingley's coach to Longbourn for a visit. Bingley insisted that Jane remain at Netherfield to recuperate, so Elizabeth and her sister would stay there again that night.

When they arrived at Longbourn, Elizabeth went to find her mother and give a report of Jane's condition and to collect clothing for the sisters during their continued stay at Netherfield. Darcy made his way to Mr. Bennet's library.

Mr. Bennet greeted him with some surprise but invited him to take a seat. After Darcy had done so, he saw that the older man regarded him suspiciously; he knew Mr. Bennet mistrusted his intentions regarding Elizabeth. *He is expecting a request for Elizabeth's hand—or at least courtship. Nothing less will satisfy him*, Darcy thought with dismay. It was almost enough to make him wish he was in a position to make either request, but he would not have given up the last weeks for all the world.

Deciding that a straightforward approach was best, Darcy said without preamble, "I have found your daughter, Lydia. Or, rather, my investigators have found her and taken her to the Gardiners' home in London. She is unharmed, but Wickham has abandoned her."

Mr. Bennet stared at him agog then blinked rapidly several times in succession. It took a

moment for him to collect his wits. "Am I to
understand that you undertook to hire investigators
to search for my daughter?"

"Yes, sir."

"By what right have you interfered in my
family's affairs?" Darcy winced at the anger in the
older man's tone.

"I thought—"

"I do not recall asking for your assistance, Mr.
Darcy!" Darcy could see that the older man's
embarrassment at the situation was turning to anger
and tried not to react.

"When we returned from France, the Gardiners
told us the whole story. Miss Elizabeth seemed so
distressed that I thought to provide what assistance I
could. I only regret it has taken my men so long to
discover her." Darcy strove to keep his tone even.

They were frozen in a tableau for a moment,
then Mr. Bennet dropped his head into his hands. "I
apologize. I do not mean to seem ungrateful. I have
not accustomed myself to the public nature of this
misadventure."

"That is completely understandable, sir. I will,
however, tell you that I am not disinterested
Wickham's misdeeds. I have had some unpleasant
dealings with him in the past. Less than a year ago,
he attempted something similar with my sister to
what he has done with Miss Lydia."

Mr. Bennet beheld him in fascination. "Indeed?
I had wondered why you wanted to involve yourself
in this situation."

Darcy nodded, slightly guilty for concealing
some of his motives. "I am to blame for not having
revealed Wickham's true character before this. If I
had, then this could not have taken place."

Mr. Bennet shook his head slowly. "You take too much on yourself. And I fear you underestimate the stupidity of my youngest daughter, but be that as it may, I am grateful for your help."

"I am sorry my investigators have not uncovered more about Wickham's whereabouts. But I have confidence they will find him," Darcy assured him.

"Thank you. Knowing that Lydia is safe does much to ease my mind." He gave an ironic smile. "Although, of my daughters, I had not thought she was the one you were interested in."

Knowing that they were venturing into dangerous territory, Darcy said, "Miss Elizabeth was most upset about Lydia's disappearance. I must admit I hoped to ease her mind."

"I see. That is very noble of you," Mr. Bennet said with a small smile as he regarded Darcy expectantly.

The silence hung between them. Darcy considered revealing the whole truth to Mr. Bennet but was loath to disturb the fragile peace that had developed between them. He stood. "I have trespassed on your privacy long enough. However, I will bring word if I hear more from my investigators." He saw disappointment—and maybe some anger—flash across the other man's face. But it was soon replaced by Mr. Bennet's customary amused detachment.

Mr. Bennet stood as well. "Thank you, Mr. Darcy. I shall write to my brother Gardiner right away."

***

Mrs. Bennet was relieved to hear Elizabeth's news about Lydia but immediately started fretting about what could be done if Wickham could not be made to marry her. She wanted "poor, dear Lydia" to return to Longbourn, but Elizabeth pointed out that Lydia's arrival without Wickham would only confirm the worst suspicions about her behavior. Her mother eventually conceded the point and, after an attack of nerves, took to her bed.

Thus relieved of her responsibility to her mother, Elizabeth went to the drawing room to await Darcy's emergence from his conversation with her father. She hoped her father would be grateful rather than angry at Darcy's assistance.

She had taken up her needlework when Hill arrived to announce, "Mr. Fenton, miss." This was swiftly followed by the man himself. *Good Lord! What is he doing here?* She believed he had given her up and had been quite content at the thought. Perhaps, she mused hopefully, he had fixed his attentions on Mary or Kitty since any marriageable female would do for him, although she would not wish him on anyone.

She stood as he entered and was about to ask Hill to invite her sisters to be chaperones when Fenton took her hand rather violently. "I am so happy to find you alone!" Thinking to be discreet, Hill shut the door to the drawing room, leaving them truly alone. Elizabeth tried to pull her hand from Fenton's, but he would not let go. *How many proposals from the man must I turn down?*

"Mr. Fenton, I—"

He continued as if she had not said anything. "I must admit I was quite shocked. Quite shocked, I tell you, at that Darcy fellow's implications. It took me several days—and quite a few whiskeys, I don't mind telling you—to get over the surprise."

"That really was not necessary," Elizabeth murmured, but he barreled on, not hearing her.

"But then I thought to myself, 'Robert, what does it matter? Maybe this rake has stolen a few kisses. I mean, I would have if I had had the opportunity.'" Here he leered at her in a most unbecoming way. "'So what if he imposed himself? That isn't her fault. He may have been warning me away from her, but it's not like he would marry her! A fellow like that!'" He laughed as if he had made quite a joke.

Elizabeth was losing count of the ways in which the man had insulted her and Darcy. "Mr. Fenton, I must insist—!"

It was as if her words were the buzzing of flies. He paid no mind. "I am here to tell you that I am willing to take you back. The engagement is not broken. All is forgiven. So what if he has sampled the wares? I would not mind that myself, I tell you—"

Elizabeth had slowly backed away as far as the room would allow, but he crossed it quickly and pulled her to him roughly. She tried to tear herself away, but his hands were like vises on her shoulders as his lips came down on hers. Closing her mouth tightly, she attempted to twist her face away, but he bore down, his lips cold and wet and insistent. No matter how she turned her head, his lips followed her. She tried again to pull away, but he was strong, and her struggles only made him grasp her more tightly.

Suddenly, Fenton was wrenched away from her. She opened her eyes just in time to see Darcy spin Fenton around to face him. He pulled his arm back and punched the other man squarely in the jaw. Fenton was not as tall as Darcy, but he was burly and solidly built. Nonetheless, he crumpled to the floor. Darcy hauled him up by his collar and punched him again, causing Fenton to cry out. Darcy hauled back to hit him again, but Elizabeth called out, "William, enough!" Darcy started at the sound of her voice and then allowed Fenton to slip to the floor.

A moment later, Mr. Bennet strode through the door, his eyes flashing in agitation. He took in the scene: Fenton's nose was bloody, and his eye was beginning to swell. Darcy stood over him, looking murderous. Elizabeth was flushed and trying to hold back tears.

"What, may I ask, has been happening in my drawing room?" Mr. Bennet asked.

Darcy glared down at Fenton fiercely. "He kissed Elizabeth."

"I see." Mr. Bennet's gaze sought his daughter's.

"I tried to stop him," she explained, two tears escaping down her cheeks. "But he keeps insisting we are engaged even though I said I would not marry him." Darcy's attention was now riveted on Elizabeth's face. Abandoning Fenton, he crossed the room to her.

From the floor, Fenton said, "Darcy warned me away from her. He's been sampling the wares, he has! Right here in your garden! I saw them! He's been kissing her and probably more!" His voice was somewhat muffled by the handkerchief he held to his bloody nose. Elizabeth did not think she had ever experienced so much mortification in her life, but Darcy's arms around her were an inexpressible comfort. At that moment, she did not care what her father thought. Mr. Bennet had been watching Fenton, but when he looked back at his daughter, his eyes narrowed.

"Somehow I am not finding that part of your story hard to believe, Mr. Fenton," Mr. Bennet said dryly. "Lizzy, am I to take it that you find Mr. Darcy's kisses welcome while Mr. Fenton's are unwelcome?"

Darcy dropped his arms from around Elizabeth but did not move away from her. Blushing, she replied, "Yes, Papa." She grasped the back of a chair for support.

Mr. Bennet turned back to Fenton, who had finally dragged himself up from the floor with the aid of a chair. "Well, I am afraid it is a hopeless business, Mr. Fenton. She does not prefer your kisses."

"But, but it is highly improper—he should not be—they are not engaged! They should—" spluttered Fenton.

Mr. Bennet shot the couple a sharp look, then turned back to Fenton. "Yes, well, be that as it may, I think it is time for you to depart." Firmly, Mr. Bennet took the other man by the elbow and ushered him from the room, ignoring Fenton's torrent of indignant protests. Elizabeth hoped his exclamations were not enough to draw her mother from upstairs, knowing her presence would only worsen the situation.

Once Mr. Bennet had exited the room, Darcy immediately resumed his embrace of Elizabeth. "Are you all right, beloved? I am sorry I did not come sooner. If I had known—!"

"I am fine." She wiped her hand across her mouth. "If I could only wipe the memory of that kiss from my mind! Uggh!"

Elizabeth could hardly blame him. She now wished
that she and Darcy had been more discreet, but she
could hardly have anticipated Fenton's actions.

"I sincerely apologize for creating a scene in
your house. It was not my intention," Darcy said at
once.

Mr. Bennet shifted uneasily in his chair. "Yes,
well, I appreciate your defense of Elizabeth's honor,
but," he skewered Darcy with an angry glare, "I am

not certain *you* can be entrusted with the care of her reputation either. I want to know your intentions toward my daughter, sir."

Darcy's reply was calm, but Elizabeth noticed a muscle in his jaw clench as he struggled to control his agitation. "My intentions are honorable."

Mr. Bennet stood and started pacing behind his desk. "Truly, sir, I find that hard to credit!" Darcy started a little at this insult but said nothing. "I have been waiting for you to declare your intentions, to ask for permission to court Lizzy or marry her, but you have not taken the opportunity. You compromised her reputation in France but seem to exhibit no concern about it. And now I find out that you have been kissing her in my garden! While I am grateful for your efforts on Lydia's behalf, that hardly gives you permission to—"

"Mr. Bennet—" Darcy began, but the other man was on a roll.

"And you, Lizzy!" He rounded on his daughter. "I thought you had more sense than Lydia! What do you think you are about, allowing these kinds of attentions? When word gets out about your sojourn in France and your behavior here, any remaining shreds of respectability our family enjoys will be completely destroyed! And, believe me, they will learn of it one way or another! Do you think our friend Fenton will keep quiet for long? Bingley will withdraw his offer for Jane. Kitty and Mary will never make respectable marriages!" His anger was so ferocious that Elizabeth found herself drawing back from him instinctively.

"Mr. Bennet!" Darcy's commanding voice compelled Elizabeth's father to shift his attention. "It is true that we have been concealing something from you. But I have a good reason why I could not seek your permission to marry Elizabeth—"

"Because you are already promised to your cousin?" Mr. Bennet said with a low growl.

"No!" Darcy replied firmly. "It is because—" Darcy swallowed convulsively. "Because Elizabeth and I are already married. We were married in France."

For the second time that day, Mr. Bennet stared at Darcy with his mouth agape. He sought his chair with one hand, sinking into it while staring at Darcy and Elizabeth. "How...how...?" he repeated weakly. Then he took a deep breath and seemed to find his voice. "How dare you? How dare you!" he shouted, pounding his fist on the desk.

"Are you telling me her reputation was already so thoroughly compromised that—?" Suddenly, all the fire went out of him, and he collapsed further into his chair. He beheld Elizabeth sadly. "That must be it. For I know you have always disliked this man. Forgive me, Elizabeth, your uncle and I have failed you."

"No, Papa!" Elizabeth blushed with equal measures of anger and mortification. "Mr. Darcy would never—he was a perfect gentleman." She was struck by an odd desire to comfort her father even as he glared at her. "No one has failed me. I made this decision of my own free will."

Mr. Bennet shook his head, apparently heedless to Elizabeth's words. Then his expression grew even more horror-stricken as he turned to Elizabeth. "Is it that you are with child?"

"No!" Elizabeth was sure her cheeks must be flaming red by now.

"Mr. Bennet," Darcy intervened, "I told you that Elizabeth nearly died in France. Because of that experience, she had no desire to wait to be married. I proposed, and she accepted, but she...did not wish to wait any longer..." As he said the words, Darcy realized how inadequate their reasoning sounded now. Why would his father-in-law ever believe such a justification?

"This is reprehensible!" Mr. Bennet banged his desk with the flat of his hand. "You have been deceiving me under my own roof!"

"I am sorry, Papa," Elizabeth said softly. "We had thought to tell you as soon as we returned but then were greeted by the news about Lydia, so we believed it would be better to wait. Perhaps that was not the best plan."

Mr. Bennet rubbed his forehead with one hand. "When word of this escapes, our whole family shall be the laughingstock of Meryton!"

"Papa!" Elizabeth said sharply, drawing herself up more fully in her straight-backed chair. "While I admit that these circumstances are not what you would have chosen, the fact that I am married to a highly eligible man is hardly cause for shame. It cannot be placed in the same category as Lydia's elopement with a debt-ridden militia officer!"

"Yes, but there will still be gossip." Mr. Bennet glared at her. "A hurried wedding always occasions talk—doubly so following Lydia's escapades."

Darcy cleared his throat. "May I point out that very few people know of our marriage? If you would prefer, we can conceal it for the present. At least until Wickham can be located and made to marry Lydia. Such would be my preference as well. For reasons of their own, my family would be happier with a delay."

"Hmm…" Mr. Bennet mulled this over, staring intently at his hands. "How many other people are aware of your scandalous behavior?"

Ignoring this jibe, Elizabeth replied, "William's cousin and sister. And we told Jane and Mr. Bingley last night. Also, a couple of people in France."

"But what about Fenton?" Mr. Bennet asked. "He has no incentive to keep quiet about what he saw in the drawing room."

Elizabeth was at a loss, conceiving of no way to work on such a man, but Darcy spoke. "I will pay Mr. Fenton a visit later. I think I can persuade him to remain discreet." Elizabeth was not sure what kind of pressure Darcy would apply, but if he was confident of success, that was enough for her.

Finally, her father appeared to be calming himself. "If it is possible to stem the gossip even temporarily…that would be well."

Darcy took advantage of Mr. Bennet's improved mood. Slowly, he pulled out some papers from his coat pocket. "While I was in London, I had my solicitor draw up settlement papers for our marriage. They arrange a sum of money to be settled on Elizabeth and provide for her should I die without an heir. I do regret that circumstances would not allow you to approve them before the ceremony. Would you like to peruse them now?"

Elizabeth regarded Darcy with surprise; this was the first she had learned of a settlement, although they were a customary part of many marriages. Wordlessly, Mr. Bennet held out his hand with a resigned air. Darcy placed the papers in her father's hand. They both watched his face as he inspected them—and as his belligerent expression turned to one of surprise. Finally, he frowned at Darcy. "This is exceedingly generous. Are you certain you can spare the money for such a settlement?"

Elizabeth knew Darcy would be loath to discuss his financial affairs with anyone, but he was aware such a conversation might partially alleviate some of his father-in-law's distress. "I know that all of Hertfordshire has been talking of my ten thousand pounds a year; I never felt it necessary to correct that impression. The truth is that my holdings amount to far more." Elizabeth's eyes opened wide at this news. They had never had cause to discuss his assets. As he continued to talk with Mr. Bennet, he gazed steadily at her. "The settlement will not cause any hardship, and it is no less than Elizabeth deserves." She seemed doomed to blush her way through the day, she thought, as she felt her cheeks grow warm once more.

Mr. Bennet put down the papers and sighed. "Very well, young man, I can see that your intentions toward my daughter are honorable, and your affection for her is genuine. I only wish you could have conducted your affairs in a more orderly fashion."

Elizabeth turned her attention back to her father and grinned impishly. "What else would you expect of me, Papa?"

Mr. Bennet shook his head at his second-oldest daughter. "I should have known that strict observance of propriety was beyond your capabilities, my dear, but I do believe you have a fair chance of happiness."

"As do I, Papa." She smiled sweetly at him.

"Very well, off with you, lovebirds! I believe I need a glass of brandy and a book to recover from today's events." With that dismissal, Darcy and Elizabeth exited the room.

Elizabeth and Darcy retired to the empty drawing room. Darcy exhaled a long breath. "That was not as terrible as it could have been." Elizabeth looked at him in disbelief; he quirked an eyebrow at her. "Well, he could have challenged me to a duel." She laughed but sobered immediately as soon as the door was closed.

"If you were not regretting marrying me before, you surely are now." She said it with a smile on her face, but Darcy saw a flicker of concern in her eyes.

Darcy did not sink into a chair but instead turned to Elizabeth and pressed her up against the door. "When will you start believing me? I have said this before: *nothing* could make me regret marrying you," he said hoarsely. Placing a hand on either side of her head, he leaned in for a fervent kiss.

When he pulled back to gaze on her, her eyes were half drugged with passion, and he was certain the expression on his face was much the same. "Can I come to you again tonight at Netherfield?" he whispered.

She nodded. "But I do not know how I will survive until then."

Darcy shook his head ruefully. "I know. Perhaps we should sit down—on separate pieces of furniture." Elizabeth gave a shaky laugh and seated herself in a chair while Darcy chose a slightly worn settee.

There was a long pause. "We have been enjoying very fine weather lately," Elizabeth said with the disinterested air of hostess addressing an acquaintance. Darcy laughed at her tone and impudent smile. *What an impossible situation we find ourselves in!* "The roads will be in good condition."

Darcy stood and started pacing. "That is just as well since I believe I must leave for London tomorrow."

"Tomorrow?" Elizabeth was unable to mask her disappointment. "You have only been in Hertfordshire for a handful of days."

"My love, it cannot be avoided. The investigator believes Wickham may have returned to London. I must be present in person to 'encourage' his marriage to Lydia."

"Then I will come with you." Elizabeth's tone was matter-of-fact.

"That would be lovely, my dear, but you know you cannot. Your reputation would suffer from spending the night at the house with a supposedly unmarried man."

"I shall not be visiting *you*," she said in mock indignation. "I have a letter from Georgiana inviting me to stay at Darcy House whenever I like. There is nothing untoward in accepting her invitation."

Darcy came to a halt directly before her chair; he meditated on her proposal for a moment. "Georgiana is staying with my aunt and uncle Fitzwilliam, but I could retrieve her for your visit. She would be pleased to see you, and her companion, Mrs. Annesley, will be there as well. I suppose that would be acceptable to your parents. More importantly for my purposes, she would prove to be a very lenient chaperone."

Elizabeth's face clouded over. "Oh, but your aunt and uncle! They did not want you to be seen with me. Perhaps I could stay with my aunt and uncle Gardiner. Although they are already hosting Lydia…"

For a long moment, Darcy said nothing as he stared at the space over her left shoulder. "No," he said abruptly. "I have played by my aunt's rules long enough. It is not as if my visit to Hertfordshire is a secret. Eventually, the members of the *ton* will learn where my interests lie."

"Are you certain?" Darcy nodded curtly. She stood, threw her arms around his neck, and kissed him. "No doubt this will be a visit to remember."

It was all arranged very expeditiously. Mr. Bennet had no objection as long as the *appearance* of propriety was maintained. Elizabeth was certain that his concerns over the swift resolution of Lydia's dilemma played a part in his acquiescence. Still oblivious to Darcy's interest in Elizabeth, Mrs. Bennet seemed dubious about the plan until Elizabeth pointed out that Miss Darcy would undoubtedly know many wealthy and eligible men. This idea transported Mrs. Bennet into such raptures that she started thinking about how Kitty could accompany them until Elizabeth noted that her sister had not been included in Georgiana's invitation.

Jane's ankle had healed sufficiently, so she could return to Longbourn after Elizabeth departed Netherfield. Darcy sent Georgiana an express advising her of the change in plans and made a very quiet visit to Mr. Fenton to ensure his silence, although Elizabeth never learned exactly what he said to the other man. The next day found them on the road to London, accompanied by a maid Bingley had spared from Netherfield to act as Elizabeth's "chaperone."

***

Mrs. Green, the housekeeper at Darcy House, was accustomed to the master's comings and goings,

so she was not surprised to see him appear in the
front hall. However, at the sight of Elizabeth, she
seemed somewhat flummoxed. Without any words
of explanation, Darcy said, "Mrs. Green, this is
Miss Elizabeth Bennet. She will be staying in the
Yellow Room."

Mrs. Green blinked rapidly in surprise. "The Y-
yellow Room, sir?"

"As I directed. I would hope you can have it
prepared by the time she retires. I also expect there
will be absolutely no talk among the servants." This
was Darcy at his most imperious, and the
housekeeper blanched.

"Y-yes, sir."

Darcy escorted Elizabeth into the drawing
room. "Why is the Yellow Room special?" she
asked as they settled into the room's elegant
embroidered chairs.

"It has not been used since my mother's death.
It adjoins the master's chambers."

"They will believe you brought home a
mistress! Why not spare the poor woman the shock
and tell her the truth? I am certain she would keep
her own counsel if she values her position."

"Yes, but I am not certain all of the servants
may be trusted. I will tell her in time," Darcy said
imperturbably.

"I do believe you are enjoying shocking the
servants!" she said with a laugh. "You wish them to
believe you might do something as out of character
as bringing home a mistress."

Darcy shook his head but did not deny the
charge. "I cannot endure having you here at *our*
house and not having you occupy the mistress's
chamber. Anywhere else would be too far away
from me."

Elizabeth considered for a moment. "I am not certain this is how I would care to begin my tenure as the mistress of the house since the servants do not know me. Perhaps I should stay in another room."

Darcy's eyes flashed fire. "Absolutely not! We have compromised much for the sake of secrecy; I am tired of the sacrifices." Then he sighed and ran his fingers through his hair. "I will make the circumstances clear to a few key servants whom I can trust. The others must remain confused for the time being."

After a moment, he smiled provocatively at her. "Mr. Darcy?" Elizabeth asked archly.

"It has just occurred to me that you are too far away, and my lap is very empty." He gave her a crooked grin.

When the maid brought them refreshments, she said nothing, but upon her return to the kitchen, she reported in scandalized tones that the Bennet woman was on the master's lap with the top buttons of her dress undone—and the master had on neither his coat nor his cravat! Mrs. Green goggled a little at this news but soon recovered and informed the maid frostily that there was to be no talk about it.

***

Georgiana returned home later that afternoon, thrilled to spend more time with her new sister. Elizabeth was no less pleased, and they soon settled in Georgiana's sitting room. Darcy was happy to have his two favorite women for dinner and anticipated many pleasant evenings with the three of them at Pemberley. That first night at Darcy

House gave him even more reason to look forward to their nights.

Less pleasant was Elizabeth's obligatory visit to the Gardiners' house the following morning. Lydia was unrepentant about the anguish she had occasioned her family and insensible to the damage she had done to her reputation. Elizabeth marveled at the naiveté with which her sister expressed confidence that Wickham would return to her.

"But he will still expect me to be at the Three Crowns," she explained to Elizabeth peevishly. "I don't see why I had to come away from the inn. He may have difficulty finding me." Elizabeth reminded her sister that she had needed to leave the inn because she had no means of paying for her room. She also tried to instill a sense of gratitude toward the Gardiners, but Lydia was immune to such hints, only complaining about not being allowed to return to Longbourn. Elizabeth left with the knowledge that her sister was as silly as always and that her unwarranted faith in Wickham was unshakable.

Elizabeth did, however, have a more pleasant visit with her aunt Gardiner, and as they walked in the park, she revealed the secret of their marriage. Her father had agreed that her aunt should know and could be trusted to share it with no one but her uncle. Mrs. Gardiner expressed surprise at the marriage itself but no shock at all about the depth of Darcy's affection for Elizabeth. His love for their niece had been quite evident to the Gardiners even before he risked life and limb to rescue her from France.

When Elizabeth returned to Darcy House, she learned that they had been invited to Darcy's aunt and uncle's house for dinner that evening. Darcy regarded the small family party as an opportunity for his new wife to get to know his family—even if most of them did not know they were already related. Elizabeth was a little apprehensive, but Darcy assured her that she would be brilliant as always.

He felt a great sense of contentment as he escorted his two favorite women to the carriage that evening. It was such a relief to be with Georgiana and act like a married couple. He handed Georgiana into the coach while resting his hand on the small of Elizabeth's back, but once Georgiana was in, Darcy could not resist the temptation to pull his wife against the side of the coach for a long, lingering kiss. Fortunately, the street was deserted. The coachman raised his eyebrows but wisely said nothing. Darcy handed Elizabeth in, climbed in himself, and they were away.

***

None of the party noticed a man lingering in the shadow of a tree near a house some way up the street. Although it was growing dark, he had seen everything very clearly. *Oho!* thought George Wickham. *Darcy nurtures a passion for Elizabeth Bennet!* Most likely Darcy would only make her his mistress, but he *was* very proper, so there was the possibility they were planning marriage. Rules of polite society considered kisses between the affianced acceptable—and Darcy was so very honorable.

Wickham had learned that Darcy was seeking him and had returned to London to discover why; there was always a chance there was some money in it for him. Now that Wickham realized how closely

connected Darcy was to the Bennet family, he knew
that most likely Darcy was only going to be
tiresome about Lydia and demand that Wickham
marry her. Wickham thought gleefully that he
would make Darcy pay richly for his cooperation,
but then an even better idea occurred to him—a
plan that would let him avoid getting shackled to
that chit. He knew someone who would pay
handsomely for information about Darcy and
Elizabeth, and he intended to be the first one to
supply it.

***

Over the next couple of days, the inhabitants of
Darcy House settled into a comfortable routine.
After the first morning, when Darcy's valet, Keans,
had been shocked to find Elizabeth in his master's
bed, Darcy let him in on the secret. He took pity on
Mrs. Green the same day and took her into his
confidence as well; the housekeeper had informed
the more discreet members of the household staff
one by one.

They did little socializing, although Darcy took
every opportunity to have Elizabeth visit his family.
His aunt and uncle had been displeased when he
brought her to the family dinner, but he insisted
they must become acquainted with her. Assuming
that an engagement was imminent, they bade
Elizabeth welcome to their home with less than
complete sincerity. The earl and countess had been
wary of Elizabeth at first, viewing her as a fortune
hunter—and one with a scandalous family as well.
Darcy's aunt had been frosty, and his uncle barely
civil, but they had warmed to Elizabeth's lively
manner and intelligent conversation.

Darcy said little all night, simply allowing Elizabeth to shine. His aunt and uncle were not at the point of giving the match their blessing, but they seemed more accepting of her role in Darcy's life. While Lady Alice had not completely recovered from the scandal over their son's marriage, the event had not proven as socially devastating as she had feared, so she had grown more forgiving of Darcy's choice.

The newlyweds treasured an early morning breakfast as private time together before the business of the day began. After breakfast, Darcy would retire to his study to conduct estate business. Elizabeth sometimes joined him there, reading a book or learning about the estate by helping Darcy with his correspondence and other tasks. Although no one would expect her to help run the estate, she was eager for opportunities to better understand how it functioned. Everything she learned only made her more curious to see Pemberley for herself.

Some afternoons Elizabeth walked in Hyde Park while others were spent shopping with Georgiana. Shopping was not an activity she particularly enjoyed, but it was essential that she have a new wardrobe commensurate with the social position she would soon assume. Georgiana took her to a *modiste* far more elegant and expensive than any she had frequented before. Having Darcy pay for an "unmarried" woman's clothing would be a gross breach of propriety, so he had supplied Elizabeth with some cash for the purchases. If the shopkeepers assumed she was buying her clothing with a rather generous allowance from her father, who was she to dissuade them?

The sheer volume of the items Georgiana thought were essential overwhelmed Elizabeth.

Gloves, hats, shoes, and stockings were ordered in a flurry of activity. Georgiana loved shopping, and Elizabeth allowed the younger woman's good taste to guide her in many of her selections. When her new sister insisted that Elizabeth needed nine new gowns immediately, she protested. However, Georgiana enumerated all of the occasions that would require various gowns; Elizabeth conceded defeat, realizing that she would need far more than nine eventually.

Other afternoons, Elizabeth called on the Gardiners and Lydia, though without Georgiana. Although her new sister knew of Lydia's connection to Wickham, Darcy did not want her exposed to any heedless talk from the youngest Bennet.

The days were pleasant, but Darcy was unhappy at the lack of progress in discovering Wickham. They had returned to London on the strength of some promising information, and Darcy had believed they were on the verge of locating the man, but the leads yielded no results. Darcy hired additional investigators, who had found nothing as of yet. Wickham apparently was moving from place to place rather frequently, and the investigators were always one step behind him. Darcy was eager for the business to be resolved so he and Elizabeth could announce their marriage and retire to Pemberley for a long stay. Weary of the town, he longed to be in Derbyshire. Elizabeth, too, wished for a swift conclusion of the matter and a chance to live as husband and wife for the first time.

Then, approximately a week after their arrival in London, Thomas, the footman, brought Darcy a card with the name "George Wickham" on it.

Chapter 13

Although Thomas had been dubious of Wickham's claim that Darcy would be glad to see him, the master did indeed ask that the rather disreputable-looking guest be brought to his study.

At last! thought Darcy. *We can conclude this business and go home.* At the same time, he knew that Wickham was likely to be a wily negotiator and would require a great deal of persuasion to honor his promise to Lydia—plus he was likely to be contrary just to pique Darcy. He was grateful, however, that Elizabeth was at the Gardiners, and Georgiana was out shopping, so there was no need to expose either of them to Wickham's nastiness.

Schooling himself to patience, Darcy watched while Wickham sauntered through the door and seated himself opposite the desk as though he owned the place. "Hello, Darcy," Wickham said with his usual impertinence, not bothering with any pleasantries. "I received word that you were seeking me out."

"Indeed, I was." Darcy surveyed Wickham coolly. Although the other man pretended to be in good spirits, Darcy noticed signs of anxiety around his eyes. His clothes were well made but beginning to become threadbare. Good. If he needed funds badly, Wickham would be easier to persuade.

"You must marry Lydia Bennet." Darcy saw no need for idle chatter.

"The hell I will!" Wickham exclaimed with force but little emotion. Surely he was unsurprised that this was Darcy's goal. "I'm weary of the chit. And she comes with practically no dowry!"

"You have compromised her reputation, and it is your duty as a gentleman to marry her," Darcy insisted. Wickham's insolent laugh was the only response. "I am prepared to grant you a financial settlement to start your new life. Plus an officer's commission—perhaps somewhere in the north, such as Newcastle."

"And pay my debts?" Wickham asked quickly.

Darcy sighed. "Yes, I will pay your debts as well."

Wickham eyed him keenly. "How much of a settlement?"

Darcy had had many days to ponder this. "Eight thousand," he said without hesitation.

Wickham laughed. "Come, Darcy, you must do far better than that. Fifteen thousand."

Darcy shook his head emphatically. "Ten thousand and not a penny more. For much less than that I could buy Lydia a respectable husband who will not cheat on her and gamble away the money."

Wickham did not even bother to deny Darcy's allegations. "But Lydia will not take someone else. She wants me." His face displayed great confidence. Then Wickham's eyes narrowed. "What's your interest in this? Why do you even care if the wench gets married?"

"I am a friend of the Bennet family and do not wish them to suffer because of your actions." Darcy kept his tone as casual as possible.

"Are you truly a friend to the *whole* family or are you only 'friendly' with Elizabeth?" Wickham asked slyly.

Darcy had hoped that word of his relationship with Elizabeth would not reach Wickham's ear but was not surprised that the other man had learned it somehow. "That is not your business." Darcy tried not to allow his dismay to show on his face. "Returning to the topic of—"

Wickham interrupted. "I know you have your hooks in her. I suppose I should not be surprised." Wickham idly picked up a glass paperweight off the desk and gazed absently at it. "You've always wanted what's mine..."

"She is not yours!" The explosive exclamation was out before Darcy could censor it. *Damn, I am permitting Wickham to goad me already!* Taking a deep breath, he tried to calm his anger.

Wickham leaned forward in his chair, grinning. "She fancied me, and you knew it. So you swooped in and took her. I should be very angry at you."

"Elizabeth never cared about you!" Darcy snarled.

Wickham shrugged. "Believe that if you want. But the truth is she longed for my company. She searched for me at the Netherfield ball; she asked my friends for my whereabouts. She *wanted* me. And if I had any money, she would be in my bed, not yours."

"That is not true. Elizabeth is not mercenary!" Darcy kept his voice low, but he did rise out of his chair, calling on every shred of his self-control to avoid punching Wickham in his smug face.

"*Elizabeth* is it?" Wickham asked silkily, brushing a speck of dirt from his jacket sleeve. Inwardly, Darcy cursed himself for the slip. "How much is she costing you? Or did you give her carte blanche?"

Darcy wanted to strangle Wickham for implying that Elizabeth was his mistress. He could not stop his voice from rising. "Out, Wickham! Leave before I have you thrown out."

Wickham made no move to depart, continuing to speak as if he had not heard. "Not that I blame you. She is a toothsome morsel. I wouldn't mind getting my hand on that…" He gestured obscenely with his hands.

Darcy saw red, and his hands clenched into fists, but he maintained his self-control—just barely. "If I were you, I would be wary of angering the man whose good opinion stands between you and your fortune," he growled.

Wickham met his eyes as Darcy leaned menacingly across the desk. His tone was more mocking. "I wager Elizabeth never told you that she kissed me."

"You are lying," Darcy said quickly.

"So she did not mention it! Not surprising. It was in the garden at Longbourn just before she departed for Kent. Quite a good kiss, for all that she *said* it was her first. Very passionate. It was her idea, too. She wanted me to have something to remember her by while she was gone. But when she returned from Kent, you had twisted her opinion of me. She would not speak to me, but I could still see the desire in her eyes. I am certain it is still there."

Suddenly, Darcy stood on the other side of the desk. "She never wanted you!" He hit Wickham square on the jaw.

Wickham staggered a little but did not fall. As he cradled his jaw in his hand, he smiled at Darcy's anger. "It's amazing how ten thousand a year increases a man's attractiveness. But you'll start to bore her quickly enough."

Darcy laughed derisively. "And you believe she would prefer the man who ruined her sister?"

With a shrug and a grin, Wickham waved away this concern. "Oh, she would be angry with me at first, but she wouldn't stay that way for long."

"You delude yourself," Darcy ground out, but the other man merely laughed.

Darcy gritted his teeth, restraining his rage with difficulty and reminding himself that it would not serve his purposes to strike Wickham again. *Stay in control!* he told himself. *Do not let Wickham get the better of you!* Moderately more contained, Darcy stepped behind his desk and rang for a footman.

"You are leaving, Wickham. My offer stands at ten thousand. I expect to hear from you in two days' time, or I will seek out someone else who will be happy to take the money—and Lydia." Darcy's voice was harsh from the effort of controlling himself.

"Oh, I am sure you will pay more before we're done. Far more." Wickham still fingered his jaw but had recovered his smirk.

Thomas appeared, looking at Darcy inquiringly. "Take out the rubbish," Darcy said tersely, gesturing at Wickham before taking up his quill to resume his work.

Once the two men were gone, Darcy set it down again. *Was it true that Elizabeth had once preferred Wickham?* He knew she had been friendly with the erstwhile militia officer—that was how Wickham had managed to feed her so many lies—but had she truly been seeking Wickham at the Netherfield ball? Had she actually kissed him in the garden at Longbourn?

Clearly she had severed ties with Wickham after her visit to Kent, once she understood his real character. But was she still attracted to him? Many women were, he knew, drawn to men with a dash of wickedness—even men they knew they should not like. There certainly were plenty of *men* infatuated with women who they knew were not good for them.

Darcy shook his head and crossed to the window, wishing he could go for a ride to clear his head. *This is Elizabeth,* he reminded himself sternly. *She loves me! If she only wanted my money, she would have accepted my proposal at Hunsford.* But had she rejected him in part because she harbored affection for Wickham? After all, at that point she had not known of the militia officer's true wickedness.

He thought about their travels in France. No, such love was not possible to counterfeit. *Even if she once entertained an attachment to Wickham, she married me.* But he visualized Elizabeth kissing Wickham. He pictured the garden, imagining what she was wearing and how the garden would appear at that time of year, seeing Elizabeth giving Wickham a pert smile, their lips meeting. He could not shake the image from his mind.

***

Darcy had insisted that Elizabeth use the carriage rather than walk to visit the Gardiners. Although that area of London was quite safe, Darcy worried that it would not be difficult for a lone miscreant to attempt to hurt her. Elizabeth had sighed and agreed, but she thought the precaution quite unnecessary.

After a two-hour visit with her relatives, she returned to Darcy House and wanted to see her husband. She alighted from the coach and was at the bottom of the steps before she realized who was emerging from the front door. Wickham was next to her on the bottom step before she could push past him into the house. "My dear Miss Bennet! What a pleasure to see you again!" He made a great show of gallantry and kissed her hand before she could react; however, his smile was set in a leer that belied any gentlemanly manners.

"The pleasure is all yours, Mr. Wickham," she said icily.

"Now we shall not quarrel, shall we?" He put on an air of wounded innocence that made her want to laugh. "We were always friends."

Then she did laugh. "A strange idea of friendship you have! Seducing my sister and ruining her reputation. What could possibly induce me to continue harboring friendly sentiments for such a man?"

Wickham smiled insolently. "You are one to speak! Is your reputation then so pristine, *Miss Bennet*?" The way he said her name was almost an insult, causing her to gasp at his audacity. He leaned closer to her. "I know what you and Darcy are about. You didn't do so badly for yourself after all, did you?"

The man's impudence knew no bounds! "You know nothing of what you are talking about! I am a guest of Miss Darcy's." She kept her voice low to preserve the privacy of their conversation. "Mr. Darcy is the most moral, upstanding—"

Wickham laughed knowingly at her. "Has he promised marriage, then? He will not follow through, you know. The damned Darcy pride. Your family is not nearly exalted enough for him."

For a moment, Elizabeth wanted to fling the fact of their marriage in Wickham's face just to see his reaction, but she restrained herself; she did not need to give the man more leverage over Darcy than he already had. "He is, in every way, a better man than you. You are not fit to lick his boots!" She mounted the stairs hurriedly and went into the house before Wickham could respond. Not at all distraught at the conversation, he sauntered away, whistling cheerfully as he made his way down the street.

Upstairs in Darcy House, Darcy stepped away from the window. Viewing the encounter between Wickham and Elizabeth had done nothing to quell his sense of disquiet. For much of the conversation, Darcy had been unable to see her expression because her bonnet hid her face, but the meeting seemed friendlier than he would have anticipated. At one point, she had tilted her head up, and he noticed that Wickham had made her laugh, followed by a whisper in her ear. Wickham also appeared quite pleased with how the meeting had gone.

Stop your preoccupation with Wickham's insinuations! he told himself. *She married you. She loves you. But what if she really had kissed Wickham? And what had he whispered to her?* These doubts would not release their hold on him. Before he knew what he was doing, his feet carried him away from the study, but he could not escape his thoughts.

***

Darcy arrived at luncheon strained and unhappy. Elizabeth noticed at once and put her arms around him for a comforting kiss that did serve to soothe some of his anxiety. Although she volunteered that she had seen Wickham as he was leaving, she said nothing about their conversation except that it was unpleasant. Afraid he might hear evasion in her voice, Darcy did not press her for details.

Elizabeth attributed his foul mood to Wickham's visit, of which Darcy had related little—only that he was attempting to convince the other man to marry Lydia and that Wickham was demanding more money. She had long since resigned herself to the idea that nothing except cash would induce Wickham to the altar. When Darcy explained that Wickham would return in two days to give his response, Elizabeth merely sighed and said, "Poor Lydia."

Try as he might, Darcy could discern no traces of affection, or even tolerance, for Wickham. By the end of the meal, his mood had improved considerably. After all, why should she bear affection for the man who had ruined her sister? The idea was absurd!

Georgiana returned from shopping just as Darcy and Elizabeth were finishing their luncheon. Darcy said a silent prayer of thanks that she had not been home when Wickham was there. Elizabeth suggested that Georgiana play her new Mozart piece for them in the drawing room. Georgiana had been practicing it diligently but was still anxious about performing before others. Elizabeth offered to act as her audience so she could rehearse her performance, and Georgiana eagerly complied.

As Darcy and Elizabeth sat holding hands, the afternoon sun slanted through the windows, and music filled the room. Darcy mused that this was the sort of future he had envisioned with Elizabeth, enjoying her company in the privacy of their home. He thought about all the estate work he should be addressing in his study, but it was just too pleasant to bask in their domestic peace. After the agitation occasioned by Wickham's visit, the reassurance of Elizabeth's presence was a balm to his soul.

It was shattered by the sound of a woman bellowing in the hallway. "I will show myself in! I know the way."

Georgiana's playing faltered and then halted. Darcy closed his eyes briefly in dismay. He recognized the voice: Lady Catherine de Bourgh. *First Wickham, then Aunt Catherine. What a difficult day it was turning out to be.* All that was necessary was a visit from Caroline Bingley to make his joy complete.

Lady Catherine de Bourgh burst into the room like an avenging angel, her long cape flapping behind her. She halted just inside the doorway, surveying the room, and when her eyes rested on Elizabeth, she regarded her like a spider she had found on her pillow. Elizabeth returned her gaze unflinchingly, stoking Darcy's pride that she remained unbowed.

Lady Catherine strode across the room and settled herself imperiously in a brocaded chair. Darcy's beleaguered footman followed behind her. "Lady Catherine de Bourgh, sir."

"Thank you, Copley," Darcy replied. "I believe some tea would be in order." Copley left without another word.

There was a long pause as Darcy waited for his aunt to explain her visit, but she seemed content to sit and glare haughtily. After a moment, he sighed. He was fairly certain he knew the answer to his question, but he asked it anyway. "To what do we owe this unexpected pleasure, Aunt Catherine?"

"Do not pretend ignorance with me," she barked. "You can be at no loss to understand the purpose of my journey."

At this sign that it would be a contentious meeting, Georgiana excused herself and fled the

room. Darcy wished he could do likewise, as it
promised to be an unpleasant scene.

"I am completely at a loss," he said stonily. She
would receive no assistance with *this* conversation.

"A report of an alarming nature reached me
yesterday—"

Darcy wondered who had betrayed him to his
aunt. It was almost certainly someone who did not
know the whole story. "From whom?"

"That is not pertinent," she said dismissively. "I
instantly resolved on setting off for London to have
this rumor contradicted. I was told that you had
made an offer of marriage to that woman." She
pointed a bony finger peremptorily at Elizabeth.

"Why should that alarm you?" Darcy wished
that he could tell his aunt the real truth and have
done with it. Then she would return to Kent in high
dudgeon, and they would be rid of her; instead he
would have to endure her attempts to dissuade him
from committing an act he had already committed.

"Why?" she echoed in amazement,
straightening herself in her chair. "Are the shades of
Pemberley to be thus polluted? Is such a girl to be
your wife?"

As he prepared a heated response, he noticed
Elizabeth shifting on the settee. "Mr. Darcy is a
gentleman. I am a gentleman's daughter. So far we
are equal." Elizabeth's eyes blazed with anger.
Irrelevantly, Darcy noticed how becomingly her
eyes flashed when she was furious—as long as she
was not angry with him.

"But who was your mother? Who are your
uncles and aunts? It is not to be borne!" Lady
Catherine exclaimed.

"If your nephew does not object to them, they can be nothing to you," Elizabeth replied with some warmth.

Abandoning Elizabeth as a lost cause, Lady Catherine rounded on Darcy. "What of the obligations owed to our family? What of your engagement to Anne?"

"Neither Anne nor I wish to marry. You know that well enough." He wondered how often he had said those words to his aunt. Apparently, he must be married before she would believe him.

"It was the fondest wish of your mother." She flung out this declaration as if it decided the argument.

"Be that as it may, I am my own man, and neither you nor my mother may choose a wife for me." Although Darcy was flushed with anger at his aunt's manner, he managed to maintain a measure of rationality in the conversation; however, he did not know how long he would be able to maintain his self-control. It had been a trying day.

Lady Catherine drew herself up to her full height and glowered at Elizabeth. "Tell me once for all, are you engaged to him?"

It was hard to avoid a giving an answer to such a direct question. "I am not," Elizabeth finally admitted, giving Darcy an ironic smile. His aunt might experience relief at this answer, but only because she had failed to ask the correct question.

Lady Catherine glared at Darcy triumphantly. He could not bear to see her smug expression, nor could he allow her to leave believing she had cowed them into submission. "I would not have you labor under a misapprehension. Although we are not formally engaged, Elizabeth *will* be part of our family. You should accustom yourself to that notion."

Lady Catherine gasped. "Her arts and allurements have made you forget what you owe to yourself and your family!" She gestured to Elizabeth dismissively. "Such fortune hunters can be quite sly in creating a moment of infatuation—"

A wave of fury enveloped Darcy, and he launched himself off the settee. "Elizabeth is not a fortune hunter!" he yelled, momentarily stunning his aunt with the vehemence of this retort. He continued in a more conversational but still forceful tone of voice. "If she was merely seeking my fortune, she would have accepted my offer the first time I proposed. I am fortunate indeed that she has granted me another opportunity to change her mind." He gazed at Elizabeth and saw gratitude in her eyes at this defense.

"She refused you?" His aunt's tone was colored by disbelief.

"Yes, at Hunsford in April." Darcy felt some of his anger drain away as he saw a corner of Elizabeth's mouth quirk up at the memory.

"At Hunsford?" Lady Catherine's voice was shrill as she turned to Elizabeth. "Is this your gratitude for my attentions to you last spring?" She glared at Darcy. "You have conspired under my roof with this–this–chit!"

Darcy had had enough. Closing the gap between them, he towered over his aunt. "You have insulted me and Miss Bennet quite sufficiently, madam. I must ask that you depart!"

Lady Catherine turned unexpectedly conciliatory. "Very well. However, this discussion is not finished, Fitzwilliam. Have someone show me to my room. It was a long and wearying trip."

Elizabeth regarded Darcy with alarm. The idea of Aunt Catherine at Darcy House also caused him consternation. Fortunately, he had no hesitation in exerting his influence as master of the house.

"You are not staying here." His tone was firm though less angry

"What? Turned away from Darcy House?" Lady Catherine appeared truly shocked. "You are lost to all reason. That girl—"

"Elizabeth has behaved like a perfect lady," Darcy said. "Your own actions have brought this upon your head. You cannot be trusted to be ladylike—or even civil—to her. I will not request that *she* depart, so you must be the one to stay elsewhere. I daresay my uncle Fitzwilliam has some guest chambers available."

"But I always stay at Darcy House when I am in town." Her voice had grown bewildered at this unforeseen turn of events.

"You will not be a guest under my roof until you can treat Elizabeth with civility," Darcy said coldly as he rang for the footman. "Copley, show Lady Catherine out."

Before Copley could move, Lady Catherine swept past him. "I can find my own way out!"

"And, Copley," Darcy added once she was out of earshot, "Please tell the staff that Lady Catherine is not to be admitted unless I specifically authorize it."

Copley's eyes went wide at this order. "Very good, sir." He followed Lady Catherine into the hall and closed the door.

Instantly, Darcy's arms went around Elizabeth. "I am so sorry, my love, that you must endure such abuse from my family."

She leaned her head on his shoulder. "Well, you have endured a great deal of unpleasantness from my family as well." She smiled impertinently at him. "If we always apologize for the misbehavior of our families, we will spend the rest of our lives in nothing but contrition. Perhaps for the sake our sanity, we should forsake the apologies now."

Darcy laughed outright, very pleased she could jest about it; however, he sensed her continued uneasiness and tightened his hold around her shoulders. The visit from Lady Catherine had cost her some measure of peace of mind. For that, he could not forgive his aunt.

"Perhaps we should have an early supper and retire for the night, dearest?" she said, smiling enticingly. *Very well,* Darcy thought. *If that will ease some of her distress, I am happy to oblige.*

He smiled down at her. "I do not know, my love…" His voice took on a teasing quality. "Having ejected two people from my house today, I am becoming quite practiced at it. Perhaps we should simply stay in the drawing room and await the appearance of someone else we can banish."

Now it was Elizabeth's turn to smile. "I doubt we could find another person so capable of giving offense. Mr. Collins is still in Kent!" They shared a laugh.

***

They passed a quiet evening at home. The following morning, Darcy worked on estate matters, and Elizabeth kept him company in the study. After luncheon, Darcy returned to work, and Elizabeth took her usual afternoon stroll, deciding to visit Hyde Park.

It was a beautiful day, and Elizabeth tipped her head back so the sun could shine on her face. Her mother would tell her she should avoid getting a tan, but the warmth felt so lovely, she could not forgo it. She had visited Hyde Park many times already and was quite familiar with the route. The day was rather warm, so the street was traversed by few other travelers.

A block from the park, Elizabeth found her way unexpectedly obstructed by a rather big man. She attempted to navigate around him, but he grabbed her arm to stop her. His grip was like an iron shackle on Elizabeth's upper arm; she could not pull it free. Outraged, Elizabeth looked up and saw that her captor was Wickham!

Before she could say anything—before she could barely form a thought—he covered her mouth with his hand. She struggled fiercely to break free from him, but even as she did so, another man approached behind her and clamped her arms tightly by her side, effectively paralyzing her. Together the two men lifted her as if she weighed nothing and pushed her through the open door of a carriage that was waiting by the curb. Wickham did not remove his hand from her mouth until the coach had started to move, by which time any screams Elizabeth made were drowned out by the clatter of the carriage. The entire occurrence had taken less than a minute, and nobody on the street had noticed anything untoward.

Chapter 14

It was around five o'clock when Colonel Fitzwilliam responded to an urgent summons to Darcy House. He found his cousin glaring at a map of London spread on a table in the house's front hall. One glance at Darcy and the colonel knew something was seriously wrong. His cousin's usually impeccable hair was a mess, his cravat was untied, and his face was gray with anguish.

Losing no time on greetings, Fitzwilliam asked, "What is it?"

"Elizabeth is missing! She went for a walk this afternoon and never returned." Darcy's voice was harsh with anxiety.

"Perhaps she lost track of the time or went to visit a friend?" Fitzwilliam inquired, attempting to restrain his own sense of panic.

Darcy shook his head vigorously. "She knows few people in London beyond the Gardiners, and they have not seen her today. My men and I have combed Hyde Park for her to no avail. She would never be so irresponsible as to remain away this long without sending word." Darcy turned back to the map, clutching the edge desperately. "I have not the faintest idea where to begin searching for her. She could be anywhere! I only hope she is still in London." He banged his fist on the table so hard that a vase of flowers quivered.

"I will summon some of my friends from the garrison to help," Fitzwilliam said at once.

Darcy shot him a grateful look. "Thank you. I have asked for assistance from the Bow Street Runners, but they do not have many men, and there is a lot of city to search." The colonel scribbled a hasty note, and Darcy rang for a footman to take it.

Fitzwilliam regarded Darcy, who peered intently at the map; one hand tightened convulsively around a corner of the paper, crushing it. "Why did I not send a footman with her?" he moaned.

Fitzwilliam spoke levelly. "We must think rationally. If she is not with friends or on her own, we must consider the possibility of foul play."

Darcy's expression darkened, but he did not glance up from the map. "Believe me, I have."

His cousin continued in a measured tone. "It is doubtful she would be subject to random violence between here and Hyde Park during daylight hours. I suppose a careful abduction might be conducted without raising suspicions. But who?"

"I cannot imagine. No one knows of our marriage, so she is unlikely to be the target of a ransom demand." Darcy's eyes narrowed. "Of course, Aunt Catherine is in town."

Fitzwilliam grinned. "I think she would have trouble overpowering Elizabeth. Although she is so desperate over your 'engagement' that she might hire someone."

Darcy shook his head slowly. "No, I do not believe she could be involved in something so nefarious."

"Who else, then?"

"Wickham!" Darcy exclaimed.

"Wickham is in town?" Fitzwilliam cried. "Why did you not tell me?"

"I saw him yesterday," Darcy said tersely. "I am attempting to persuade him to marry Lydia Bennet. But what would he have to gain by kidnapping Elizabeth?"

"I can think of three dozen things off the top of my head. Beginning with the opportunity to avenge himself on the man he has always hated and ending with the likelihood that you would pay him any amount of money to recover Elizabeth."

Darcy's grimace confirmed that statement, but then he shook his head. "I find it difficult to believe Wickham is capable of this kind of evil. He might lie and cheat or take an opportunity that comes his way, but he has never stooped to actual criminal behavior."

"Maybe he encountered Elizabeth on the street and seized an opportunity for mischief." Darcy was still shaking his head. "He is the most plausible perpetrator. It is either him or a completely unknown villain. At least with Wickham we have some ideas where he could be found."

Darcy ran his hands over his face. "I suppose. I could pay Mrs. Younge a call and discover if she knows where he might be."

Suddenly, a door at the back of the hall opened with a bang, and Darcy's cook rushed in with a piece of paper in her hand. "If you please, sir. A boy just left this at the back entrance. The back entrance! I told him messages should be delivered at the front, but he ran away before I could ask him where he come from."

Fearing the worst, Darcy ripped the message from the cook's hand and tore it open. Wide-eyed, she quickly retreated down the hall and back into the kitchen. Fitzwilliam watched Darcy as he hurriedly read the letter. When he was finished, the paper simply fell from his fingers as Darcy froze with an expression of pure horror on his face.

"What is it?" Seeing that no answer would be immediately forthcoming, Fitzwilliam retrieved the note from the floor.

Dear Darcy,

Seems I was right. Elizabeth does prefer my company to yours. I encountered her by chance on the street, and she begged me quite eloquently to take her away from you. I could not, in good conscience, refuse. She has asked me to tell you that she hopes you will not search for her. It would only cause a scandal, and she does care about you a little after all. Just not enough.

Yours,

George Wickham.

Fitzwilliam read the letter through again and snorted a laugh, the unexpected sound bringing Darcy to life. "As if you would actually believe she would elope with George Wickham!"

"You think the note is untrue?"

"Untrue? Of course it is—" Fitzwilliam stopped and carefully regarded his cousin's frozen visage. Darcy had turned his head toward his cousin, but his gaze seemed more inward than anything else. "You do not believe any part of this, do you?"

Darcy walked back to the table, turning his back on Fitzwilliam and staring blankly at the map of London. "When Wickham was here yesterday, he reminded me that back in Hertfordshire there was a time when Elizabeth preferred him to me."

"But that was before she knew his true character!"

"He said he had kissed her in the garden at Longbourn and that he knew she still harbored a passion for him."

Fitzwilliam shook his head. "You are an idiot! To believe those lies after everything Elizabeth has been to you. I have never seen a woman so besotted in all my life. She barely notices that other men exist!"

Darcy glanced at his cousin briefly to ascertain how deeply his cousin believed his words. Then he returned his gaze to the map. "But if not for my fortune—"

"She cares nothing for your fortune. She loves *you*. I have never been more certain of anything in my life." Darcy's head remained bowed over the table, and Fitzwilliam could not see his face, but he decided to attempt another strategy. "See here, if Elizabeth had decided to elope with Wickham, why would she have him write the letter for her? He probably attempted to have her pen such a letter, but she refused, so he had to do it. And the letter mentions nothing about your marriage. It is written as if you and Elizabeth are engaged. Eloping after marriage is quite a different matter from breaking off an engagement. Divorces are very difficult to obtain."

"That is true." Darcy straightened up.

"Elizabeth is a very clever woman," Fitzwilliam continued. "She would not believe she could escape your marriage so easily—if she wished to, which I am certain she does not."

The colonel paused for a moment, allowing these words to sink in. Darcy's eyes were closed, and his face was etched with pain, but then he shook his head emphatically as if to clear out the negative thoughts. Fitzwilliam clapped him on the shoulder. "Wickham knows you entirely too well. He knows exactly where you are most vulnerable. You should not allow him to manipulate you."

Darcy combed his fingers through his hair. "You are right. I *am* being an idiot."

"Of course. I am always right." Fitzwilliam tried to focus his cousin on the task at hand. "This note is good news. We can narrow our search to those places frequented by Wickham or places accessible to him. It will be far simpler than searching the whole of London."

Darcy returned to the desk and penned a quick note. "I am sending word to Bow Street now. They have been investigating Wickham for a long time. They know his haunts." Darcy rang for a footman to take the note, and the man left. "And you and I should visit Mrs. Younge." Darcy started toward the door.

Fitzwilliam stopped him with a hand to his arm, his eyes bright with concern. "You and I know that Wickham's note lies. He and Elizabeth are not eloping. But have you considered his true motivation? He could wrest quite a bit of money from you in ransom. Money is usually behind his every action, but this letter does not mention it."

"True. Perhaps he is attempting to shake my confidence and then demand money."

Fitzwilliam nodded slowly, lost in thought. "Perhaps. Or perhaps he has a completely different motivation."

"You mean seduction?" Darcy asked, his face grim.

Fitzwilliam nodded. "But we can be confident she will not respond to his 'charms.'"

Darcy's expression was thunderously dark. "And what will he do when she refuses to be seduced? Good Lord, we must locate her immediately!"

****

Elizabeth stared out the window again, but it was too high to climb down. It could be opened, she had discovered, but if she climbed out, there would be nothing between her and the ground. She was not that desperate—yet. After trapping her in the carriage, Wickham and his henchmen brought Elizabeth to a town house in a part of the city she did not recognize and locked her in a musty attic room on the third floor, most likely a former servant's room. They had not been rough or threatening; in fact, Wickham talked very smoothly, but she was not fooled. She was a prisoner.

It had been at least four hours since her kidnapping; the sun was starting to set. *William must be frantic with worry*, she thought. He would have no idea where she was or if she was all right.

Elizabeth turned her thoughts once more to the problems of her captivity, reviewing the contents of the room for anything that might help her escape. But the small room only contained two mismatched wooden chairs, a rough table, and a narrow bed. The table held the remains of a simple meal they had provided, but Elizabeth's anxiety had extinguished her appetite, and she had not touched the bread and cheese.

What did Wickham want with her? Would he demand a ransom from Darcy? Was it some plot to revenge himself on her husband? She roamed around the small room, turning these questions over in her mind again and again, but unable to guess at the answers.

Suddenly, the knob turned, and the narrow door was opened by Wickham himself. Elizabeth was actually happy to see him. Unlike the other men, she knew Wickham and thought it was more likely that she could induce him to answer her questions.

Wickham glanced at the table. "Was the food not to your liking? I know it's not what you have grown accustomed to at Darcy House, but it was the best we could supply on short notice." He oozed charm and faux sincerity. It was disgusting.

"It was fine," Elizabeth said tightly. How dare he act so nonchalant? Playing the perfect host with her under these circumstances!

He sauntered over to the table and poured two glasses of wine; she had wondered why they had provided her with another wine glass. He handed one to her as if they were sharing a simple dinner in the home's dining room. Willing to play along, she took it and drank a sip, attempting to control the revulsion she felt toward this man; she needed to avoid provoking his anger unnecessarily. Appearing very much at home, he settled into one chair, and she sat in the other.

Since Wickham did not seem inclined to start a conversation, Elizabeth decided on a direct approach. "Why have you abducted me?" She had asked him in the carriage, but he had said they would discuss it later.

"We have not abducted you. You are merely our guest for the night; we will not harm you. You will be free to leave in the morning." His voice was silky, and he smiled at her in a very intimate way that made her skin crawl.

"Why should I believe you?" she asked sharply.

"Why would I lie about that?" he countered.

Wickham was the most accomplished liar she had ever met, and his every word was suspect. If he told her it was raining, she would not believe it until she was soaking wet. "Please trust me, Elizabeth." He leaned toward her, staring earnestly into her eyes. "I promise you will not be harmed."

"You still have not said why you brought me here." She tried to soften her tone so it was not too antagonistic. If Wickham believed she had relaxed her attitude toward him, he might lower his guard a little, giving her an opportunity to escape.

"Do I need a reason to crave your company?" His eyes ran lasciviously over her body; it made her want to slap him.

"There are more polite ways of getting it," she said tartly. "For instance, you might marry my sister. Then we could see each other at family occasions."

A shadow crossed his face, and she knew instantly that she had made a mistake, but her anger over his treatment of Lydia had overcome her better judgment. "I do not want to talk about your sister," he said with irritation. There was a silence. Toying with the stem of his wine glass, Wickham seemed to be deciding on his next move. Finally, he raised his eyes to her, giving her a gaze filled with desire. "She is but a girl. You are a woman." Wickham's voice was low and seductive. "A very attractive woman."

Now we get to the heart of the matter, thought Elizabeth. *Seduction is, after all, one of his specialties.* She was aware that he desperately wanted to avenge himself on Darcy, and seducing the woman everyone assumed was Darcy's fiancée would be revenge indeed. The thought made her want to retch, but she had to appear cooperative or there would be no opportunity for escape.

"Thank you." Elizabeth cast her eyes down at the floor, trying to seem flattered by the compliment. "But surely you need not go to such lengths to flatter me."

"Not with Darcy around. He would never let me within a hundred yards of you." Wickham stood and walked over to her chair, staring down at her. "Not that I blame him. If you were my fiancée, I would never permit you to leave the bedroom." Elizabeth suppressed a shudder of disgust.

With Wickham towering over her, she felt very vulnerable, so she stood as well. But now they were standing very close. Uncomfortably close. She could smell the wine on his breath—and the fact that he had not bathed in a while. *Do not show your revulsion,* she told herself sternly. *It will not serve you.*

Wickham ran his hand down her bare arm below the short sleeve of her dress. *Pretend you like it.* "You always were my favorite, you know. I wanted Mary King for her money, but you…with you…it is desire." He lifted her hand to his lips, but his eyes were locked on hers. "You are so very beautiful. Your eyes…so expressive…and I am sure there is no other woman with hair that is quite so lustrous." As he touched a curl, Elizabeth schooled herself not to flinch.

Apparently unable to control himself any longer, Wickham pulled her toward him rather roughly and kissed her. She endured the kiss, thinking that if she appeared cooperative, perhaps there would be an unguarded moment when she could escape. However, she could only conceal her antipathy for so long; when Wickham grabbed her breast, her control shattered.

She pushed Wickham away and wiped her mouth on her sleeve. "How dare you! You have no claim on me! No right! I am in love with Darcy. And he is searching for me! *When* he discovers you, you will be lucky if you do not hang for this."

"By the time he finds *you*, it will be too late," Wickham growled threateningly as he abandoned all pretext of seduction and made a lunge for her. She backed away but quickly bumped into the wall.

The room was simply too small to allow her to avoid Wickham for long. As he got closer, she slid sideways along the wall, putting the small table between them. He swept the dinner tray onto the floor with a clang and the tinkle of broken crockery and grabbed her arm. Twisting it out of his grasp, she rushed to the door but turned the knob in vain.

Wickham laughed. "What a shame I have the key." He patted his coat pocket. "That door isn't opening until you give me what I want." She backed away as he lurched toward her, but the backs of her legs bumped up against the room's narrow bed.

I cannot escape him in a room this small, she thought desperately. *Time for a new plan.* She stood still and allowed him to approach her. He grinned at her apparent acquiescence and prowled toward her like a large cat. As he pushed up against her, the buttons on his waistcoat pressed into the front of her dress, but she did not resist when he placed his hands on her shoulders. He bent his head down toward hers, and she willed herself to stand still. "That's right. It will be easier for you if you do not fight me," he purred, closing his eyes for a kiss.

Now! Elizabeth stamped the heel of her shoe down hard on Wickham's foot. As he winced in pain, she jerked her knee up as hard as she could between his legs. It connected with a satisfying jolt. Wickham doubled over with a wordless shout of pain as he fell to the floor, writhing. Elizabeth's hand darted into his jacket pocket and found the key. Before he was upright, she had unlocked the door and was fleeing down the narrow wooden stairs.

"Stop her! Beecham, Carr, you idiots! Stop her; she is getting away!" Wickham bellowed as Elizabeth flew down the second set of stairs. Now on the first floor, she glimpsed the front door of the house. Only steps away from freedom! She raced for it. Four steps. Three steps—but then one of Wickham's burly cohorts rushed out of the front parlor and tackled her. They fell into a heap. Even as she strained to get up, he held down her arms with his big, beefy hands that might as well have been steel bands. "There, there, missy," he yelled. "Stop yer struggling, and I won't have ter hurt you!" The other thug arrived from the kitchen, ready to lend assistance.

I cannot escape both of them. Recognizing defeat, Elizabeth went limp. "Good girl," the man said. Elizabeth thought he was Beecham. Then he hoisted her over his shoulder as if she weighed no more than a sack of grain and carried her up to the attic room.

Elizabeth saw with some satisfaction that Wickham stood in a hunched-over position with his hand on the sloping wall of the attic, holding himself up. Beecham dumped her on the bed and looked over at Wickham. "You hurt?"

Wickham waved away his concern in irritation, glaring at Elizabeth. He then crossed the room to stand over her in the bed. "You are fortunate I never hit women because you sorely tempt me. Try anything like that again, and I *will* hit you!" Fury was etched in every line of his face. Elizabeth had no trouble believing what he said and shrank back against the wall.

Wickham smiled in satisfaction at her reaction and walked to the door, still stooped and moving with a funny hitch in his step. There would be no further attempts to get her into bed again—at least for tonight—Elizabeth realized with relief. Beecham followed his boss, closing and locking the door. They talked as they strode away, and she rushed to the door to press her ear against the keyhole.

"You said this would be easy work," Beecham complained.

"I thought so. I did not realize we would be kidnapping a hellcat," Wickham growled. Elizabeth smiled to herself as she pressed her face to the smooth wood of the door. "No matter. We only need to concern ourselves with her until morning. I want you stationed near the front door in case she somehow escapes the room again."

"When does the lady pay us?" asked Beecham.

"*She* doesn't pay us, you idiot. Her agent will. Tomorrow, after we release the woman. But we have to let her go precisely at nine, remember." The voices receded as the men thumped down the second set of stairs, and Elizabeth heard no more.

Elizabeth seated herself once more on the bed, her hands brushing the rough wool blanket, and puzzled over what she had heard. It was a tremendous relief to hear that they truly planned to release her the next day, but she could not understand the reasoning behind it. Obviously, Wickham had been interested in seduction—or worse—but that was not his primary purpose. With a shudder, she realized that if rape was their goal, Beecham would do as well as Wickham, but it appeared they were now prepared to let her alone for the night.

Why were they keeping her here? Wickham hated Darcy, but she was certain that antipathy alone would not have spurred him to such action without some hope of material gain. She had expected Wickham to extort a ransom from Darcy, but he had said nothing of it to Beecham—and if they wanted money, surely they would not release her until it had been paid.

No, apparently someone else had paid Wickham to perform an abduction, but that made no sense. Why would someone else want Wickham to kidnap Elizabeth? No, she realized with a start. The question was: why would someone want Wickham to keep Elizabeth in his house for the night?

They were attempting to ruin her reputation! To accomplish that, Wickham need not be successful in his seduction. If she was seen leaving Wickham's house in the morning, it would be assumed they were conducting a love affair. That is why they needed to release her precisely at nine. They must plan that witnesses would be present to see the evidence of her debauchery. She felt sick to her stomach.

Who would go to such lengths to ruin her? It must be that someone sought to prevent her from marrying Darcy! Whoever masterminded this plan did not know they were already married and was hoping to prevent the wedding. Wickham had referred to the person who hired them as "she," a mysterious lady who must assume that Darcy would call off the wedding if he believed his fiancée was carrying on with Wickham. In fact, whoever had devised the plan probably thought it would not matter if Darcy actually believed in an affair with Wickham; he would be forced to abandon her no matter what he truly thought. Elizabeth had her suspicions about who might have devised this plan, but it could also be someone she had never met: a woman who had hopes of Darcy's hand and wanted to prevent him from marrying someone else.

Elizabeth lay back on lumpy bed with a groan. The problem with the plan was that it could work.

Even understanding their strategy would not help Elizabeth thwart it. The members of Darcy's social circle would not care that she had refused to be seduced or that she had fought off Wickham's advances. Whoever the witnesses were, they would certainly have been selected for their social standing or ability to gossip—or both. They would not believe a farfetched tale about abduction, not when it was far simpler to believe that Darcy's love had been caught in a compromising situation and was inventing a story to cover her loose behavior.

The news that Darcy's supposed fiancée had been carrying on with a disgraced militia officer would be all over the *ton* within a day. Elizabeth closed her eyes against the thought. Of course, the plan would not have the desired effect because they were already married, and she briefly considered revealing this information to Wickham. It might lead his employer to call off the kidnapping, but, she thought with a sigh, part of Wickham's motivation was revenge on Darcy—and that he would not give up. He might try to seduce her again or ransom her or extort Darcy to keep quiet about the whole affair. If she conveyed the news of their marriage to Wickham, he might be pushed into more rash behavior.

The unfortunate fact was that their married status would be no proof against scandal. If the *ton* knew they were already married, nothing would be accomplished except to besmirch the Darcy name and make him even more of laughingstock. What newlywed woman would seek someone else to warm her bed so soon?

Tears trickled from her eyes. It was bad enough to think of enduring such embarrassment, but the thought of Darcy's humiliation was almost unbearable. He was so proud of the Darcy name, but here she would be disgracing it within a month of their wedding! What would he do? Would he send her away, have them live separately to escape the scandal? And her family! They had not yet recovered from Lydia's wanton behavior, and now they would be facing an even worse scandal. It would destroy her father.

An even more horrible thought struck her: What if Darcy believed that she *wanted* to run away with Wickham? She had no idea what lies Wickham had told Darcy about her. Had he sent Darcy a letter? It would be like him to rub salt in the wound. She had been assuming that Darcy would be frantically searching for her, but what if he believed that she wanted to elope with Wickham? *No*, she told herself. *He knows I hate Wickham. And he knows I love him. He is searching for me, but will he find me in time?* London was an enormous city, but she was sure Darcy would find her eventually; however, it might be too late.

Gazing at the cracked plaster over her head, she thought that she might thwart Wickham's plan in other ways. Perhaps she could refuse to leave the house; the irony was not lost on her. But it would not be hard for Wickham to force her out the door. Perhaps she could fight Wickham in front of the witnesses, but the man had a glib tongue and could probably explain it away as a lovers' quarrel to anyone watching.

Tears trailed across her cheeks, and Elizabeth attempted to stifle sobs. Humiliation and disgrace seemed guaranteed.

Chapter 15

Elizabeth had thought she could not sleep, but the events of the day had exhausted her, and sleep crept upon her sometime after midnight. She was awakened by a scraping and scratching sound at her window. Had she been at home, such noises might have alarmed her, but in this place they gave her hope. Maybe someone had found her! She rushed to the window and saw a dark shape the size of a person, and although she could barely distinguish the outline, she pushed the window open.

"Elizabeth! Thank God!" Darcy climbed through the window and embraced her fervently. In the circle of his arms, she released all the tears she had been holding in since the abduction, relief washing through her as his crushing embrace seemed to express all the desperation of their last hours. Then he held her away a little to scrutinize her face. "Are you hurt?" She shook her head, but he continued to examine her, inspecting every inch of her face and arms. Elizabeth took the opportunity to examine him, noting the dark circles under his eyes and how his normally neat hair hung in his face. "I was afraid that Wickham would try—" He made a choked sound as if the words were stuck in his throat.

"He tried to seduce me, but I, um…kicked him in—where—" She blushed, unable to finish the sentence. "Then he left me alone."

Cradling her head at his chest, he barked a laugh. "Would that I had seen that! I should have had more faith in your fighting skills." Relief colored his every word.

Elizabeth shrugged with a small smile. "He angered me. I do have a temper sometimes." In answer, Darcy kissed her desperately and at great length. There was an edge of anguish in his lips, as though he could never bring her close enough to him, but she was his equal in desperation, wishing that he would never release her.

When they finally separated, Elizabeth was surprised to see Colonel Fitzwilliam standing by the window, watching them with a mixture of relief and humor. "Well, Darcy, I suppose this is the correct room?"

"Yes." Darcy's voice was hoarse. "Your instincts were sound. Thank you." Elizabeth regarded him inquiringly. "When we were surveying the house, Richard considered the attic and said if he had a prisoner, that is where he would put one," Darcy explained. "So we sent up a rope with a grappling hook and decided to enter the house here."

"What about the front door?" Elizabeth asked.

"We were concerned that if we entered there, Wickham might get to you and hurt you before we could stop him," Darcy said, stroking her hair. "Your safety was most important." Elizabeth felt unshed tears pricking her eyes.

"Thank you," Elizabeth said simply, watching both Darcy and Colonel Fitzwilliam. "But how did you find this house?"

"Once we knew Wickham had kidnapped you, it was simply a matter of finding his friends and prying information out of them with money or threats," Darcy explained. "We discovered a Mr. Easton, who related that Wickham had borrowed his townhouse for the night in lieu of repaying a debt. He told Easton he would be throwing an exclusive party."

To Elizabeth's surprise, another man climbed through the window. "Goodness! How many men did you bring?" Darcy shifted Elizabeth to a more comfortable spot by his side but kept a protective arm around her shoulders.

"Ten in all," answered Darcy, "between some Bow Street Runners and Richard's army friends." Elizabeth's eyebrows rose in surprise.

Elizabeth recognized the colonel's friend, Lieutenant Preston, and thanked him for his part in the rescue while Fitzwilliam set about picking the worn lock on the bedroom door.

"My, what useful skills one picks up in the King's service," Darcy observed wryly as he watched.

"I learned to pick locks because a certain cousin was forever locking me in unused rooms at Pemberley when we were children." Fitzwilliam's voice was acerbic.

"I am so happy I helped you acquire new skills," Darcy said with a laugh.

The lock clicked, and Fitzwilliam tested the knob by carefully turning it without opening the door. "How many men does Wickham have in the house?" he asked Elizabeth.

"There are only three, including Wickham. I do not know where they are in the house, but I believe one has been stationed by the front door to prevent me from attempting to escape again."

"Again?" Darcy squeezed her shoulders with pride. "You *have* been busy." Fitzwilliam gave him a quizzical look. "She also kicked Wickham in the groin," Darcy said by way of explanation.

"Good for you!" Fitzwilliam exclaimed. But his eyes flickered to Darcy's apprehensively. Elizabeth understood the question he feared to ask.

"He thought he could seduce me—"

"I will kill him!" growled Darcy. Elizabeth put her hand on his arm to calm him down.

"No harm was done—at least not to *me*."

Fitzwilliam shook his head. "I must remember never to tangle with you." Pride and relief warred on Darcy's face. Fitzwilliam opened the door a crack. They were all silent for a minute as he listened; hearing nothing, he shut the door softly again. "Do the men have pistols?" he asked Elizabeth.

Elizabeth nodded. "Wickham has two, and each of the other men has one apiece."

"It turns out your wife is an excellent advance scout," Fitzwilliam said to Darcy with a smile. "I think we should attack now." Darcy nodded curtly in agreement, and Fitzwilliam waved his hand at Preston. "Give the signal. We will descend the stairs from here. The others can enter through the front door. No need to knock." Preston leaned out the window and made some hand gestures. Darcy and Fitzwilliam both pulled pistols out of their coats.

Elizabeth caught her breath; she had only seen Darcy with a gun once before. Part of her wanted to beg him to remain with her so he would be safe, but she knew he must confront Wickham. It was a matter of honor. The relief she had experienced when he appeared at the window washed away in a new flood of anxiety. *I wish I could go with him and help, but I would be of no use.* She caught his arm. "William, please be careful." He pulled her to him roughly with one arm and kissed her fiercely.

"I will," he promised. Fitzwilliam opened the door just as Darcy released Elizabeth. He turned to Preston, "Will you stay here and guard Elizabeth? If one of those blackguards gets away—"

Preston nodded. "No one will get past me."
With one last glance at Elizabeth, Darcy was gone,
and Fitzwilliam was close on his heels. She
immediately felt bereft. Pulling out his pistol,
Preston positioned himself in the doorway.

Down below, Elizabeth heard shouts and
bumps. A shot rang out, and she started. She sank
onto the rickety, narrow bed. Now there was
nothing to do but wait.

As Darcy stepped onto the tiny third floor
landing, he reminded himself that it was best not to
enter a fight in a white hot rage. He tried to temper
his anger at Wickham with relief that Elizabeth was
unharmed. Still, he had seen that haunted
expression in her eyes and knew that, despite her
attempt at good spirits, the experience had been
terrifying. She had been roughly handled, he had no
doubt. Her clothing was wrinkled and torn in places,
and her hair was half undone. A lesser woman
would have been hysterical in his arms.

Thinking of the hands that were responsible for
her disheveled state renewed Darcy's rage. He
charged down the stairs, his pistol held at the ready
and Fitzwilliam at his heels. Once on the second
floor, he opened the door to the first bedroom he
came to. It was empty. Fitzwilliam did the same
with the next door. The noises from below told
Darcy that the rest of their men had begun their
assault on the first floor.

Then the two men came to a door that was
locked. It took Fitzwilliam mere seconds to pick the
lock, and Darcy kicked the door open. Inside, the
room was small and dark, but they could see
Wickham at the open window in his nightshirt
framed by the gray moonlit sky.

Darcy and Fitzwilliam pushed through the doorway and into the room. Whirling at the sound of the door opening, Wickham raised his pistol and shot at Darcy. Darcy's own shot was one second behind. Wickham's bullet flew past Darcy's head and buried itself in the doorframe. Darcy's bullet lodged itself in Wickham's shoulder; the impact knocked Wickham up against the window frame.

Before Darcy had time to react, Wickham pulled out his other pistol, although his hands were shaking with the effort. Darcy tried to shoot, but his gun only fizzed and popped. A misfire! He dove to the floor as he heard Wickham's pistol go off. The shot went wild and buried in the wall. "Damn you, Darcy!" Wickham shouted as he staggered upright and threw one leg over the sill of the open window.

He must not escape! Darcy thought, but Wickham, dividing his attention between the window and Darcy, had lost track of Fitzwilliam. Prowling around the edge of the room, the colonel pounced, knocking Wickham's gun to the floor. Darcy crossed the room in two strides and grabbed hold of the front of Wickham's shirt, dragging him back into the room. Once Wickham was leaning back on the window frame, Fitzwilliam slammed the window closed. Only then did Darcy indulge himself by landing a resounding punch on Wickham's jaw. He folded to the floor.

Darcy took an extra pistol that Colonel Fitzwilliam offered and pointed down at Wickham's head. His whole body shook with rage. "I would love to have a reason to shoot you."

"I yield! Damn, Darcy, don't kill me!" Wickham looked exhausted and greatly aggrieved. As he clutched his wounded shoulder, bright red blood oozed out between his fingers, but his terrified eyes were fixed on Darcy.

Darcy hauled Wickham up by the neck of his shirt, his face only inches from Wickham's. "If you ever touch my wife again—if you ever talk to her again—if you ever glance in her direction again—I *will* kill you!"

Wickham's eyes went wide. "Your wife? I didn't—"

Darcy's fist connected resoundingly with Wickham's stomach. Wickham fell back, hit his head on the sill, and slumped to the floor, unconscious. Darcy stood over the man, breathing hard. Fitzwilliam grabbed his arm to keep him from hitting Wickham again, but Darcy felt his fury dissipate as he realized the threat from Wickham had ended.

Fitzwilliam stepped out of the room to descend the stairs and talk with their men downstairs. When he returned to the room, Darcy was tying Wickham's hands together using the man's own discarded cravat. "Our men have secured the downstairs. They captured Wickham's men; one was knocked out, and the other is tied up. None of our people were hurt. They are preparing to deliver those two to the jail. Do you want them to take Wickham, too?"

Darcy gazed at their captive in disgust. "Not yet. I suppose we should get a doctor for his shoulder. Send a man for one and have someone come up and guard Wickham. Have them notify me when Wickham is awake. I have some questions for him; there is more to this story than it first appears."

Fitzwilliam nodded slowly. "I am afraid you are right."

After a man arrived to take charge of Wickham, Darcy bounded up the stairs to the attic bedroom. Preston stood in front of the door but gave way quickly to Darcy, who encouraged the soldier to go downstairs and help with the mopping up. Before he opened the door, Elizabeth rushed out. "I was so worried Wickham would kill you!" She flung her arms around his neck.

"I am all right, my love," he assured her. With a strength he had not known she possessed, Elizabeth pulled him into the attic room, pressing him up against the cracked plaster of the wall and kissing him with an eagerness that rendered him breathless. "I should rescue you more often," he said after she finally released his lips.

"I am certain there will be no need!" Elizabeth said emphatically. Then she leaned into him once more for another demanding kiss.

Half an hour later, Darcy, Fitzwilliam, and Elizabeth were sitting in the home's small parlor. The Bow Street Runners had taken away the two hired ruffians while some of the soldiers were upstairs guarding Wickham as the doctor treated him. Darcy had drawn Elizabeth into his lap as he sat on the room's rather worn, overstuffed loveseat, and Elizabeth leaned into his chest, reassured by the warmth of his presence. It had been a long day. Fitzwilliam was seated across from them, and the two men were discussing the details of their operation, including how to ensure that Wickham and his cronies were properly prosecuted.

Silence fell for a moment, only to be broken by Fitzwilliam. "What I do not understand is why Wickham undertook this scheme in the first place." The colonel glanced from Darcy to Elizabeth. "As attractive as Mrs. Darcy is, Wickham went to an awful lot of trouble just to seduce a beautiful woman."

Darcy nodded. "I have been puzzling over that as well."

Elizabeth settled next to Darcy, but he kept his arm about her. "I believe I have some pieces of that puzzle." First recounting the conversation she had overheard between Wickham and Beecham, she then described the conclusions she had reached. Both men nodded in agreement, but they appeared sickened.

"Good God!" Darcy exclaimed in a strangled voice when she had finished. "The thought that someone would resort to such actions to ruin your reputation—it is appalling!"

"What a clever plan," Fitzwilliam said with disdain. "Your reputation is ruined simply by having spent the night in the wrong house. Clever and disgusting."

"Do you believe my conclusions are wrong?" Elizabeth asked.

Darcy stood and started pacing. "No, unfortunately I believe you are correct in every supposition. The question is: who would do such a thing? Who would hate you that much, desire my hand to that extent, and have the means to pay Wickham? It must have been a handsome sum since he did not demand a ransom from me. He is always one to wring the maximum profit from any situation."

Fitzwilliam shook his head sadly. "There is only one probable suspect: Aunt Catherine."

Darcy froze in his tracks. "She has the motive and the means." He looked sickened at the thought. "I would rather find another candidate, but you are right, Richard. She is the likeliest culprit."

"Would she do that to her own family? Her nephew—?" Elizabeth asked.

"I am afraid family is the reason she *would* commit such an act," Darcy said. "Her misplaced sense of pride and her insistence that I marry Anne. She can be ruthless in achieving her goals. Unfortunately, I *can* believe she would stoop to this."

"She also does not consider you part of the family yet," Fitzwilliam pointed out to Elizabeth. "It is that eventuality she thinks to prevent."

"But does she even know Wickham?" Elizabeth's expression was perplexed as she rested her head against the faded back of the loveseat.

Darcy stopped pacing and tightly gripped the back of a wooden chair. "Yes, Wickham would have met her when she visited Pemberley, and he knows she wishes me to marry Anne. He must have warned her about you."

"So they concocted this scheme. Wickham seizes the opportunity to seduce Elizabeth and humiliate you, all for a princely sum, and Aunt Catherine assumes that once Elizabeth is 'ruined,' you will drop her and go running to Anne," Fitzwilliam said.

"How horrible!" Elizabeth said. "To imagine them devising such a plan—"

Darcy settled onto the loveseat next to her and placed his arms around her. "It is despicable, but they did not succeed. Rather than spend the night in Wickham's borrowed townhouse, you will spend it with me, your legally wedded husband."

Comforted, Elizabeth let her head drop to Darcy's shoulder. "I wonder who the witnesses are that Lady Catherine arranged," she murmured.

Now it was Fitzwilliam's turn to stand and pace. "I have a horrible suspicion it might be my parents."

Darcy's breath hissed between his teeth. "You think they are involved?"

"No, not at all," Fitzwilliam hastened to assure him. "They would never be party to such a scheme. But they would certainly be unimpeachable witnesses—and more importantly, they would keep quiet. Aunt Catherine is not necessarily seeking to create a scandal; she just wants the threat of disgrace to separate you from Elizabeth."

"Your parents would never accept her as my wife if they saw her leave Wickham's. I would have to choose between her and my family," Darcy said, shaking his head slowly. "It is a clever plan, but my aunt does not understand me at all." Elizabeth squeezed his hand in acknowledgement of his tacit endorsement.

"I am certain Aunt Catherine will invent some plausible reason for them to be here at nine o'clock tomorrow morning." Fitzwilliam's pacing was on the verge of wearing a hole in the carpet. "Perhaps she will tell them she 'has heard tell that Miss Bennet is not quite as virtuous as she appears.' If they catch you leaving this house in the morning, it certainly will appear that your reputation is compromised."

Darcy saw tears welling up in Elizabeth's eyes and held her close. "Do not worry, my love; we will ensure that any rumors will be crushed."

"But how?" Elizabeth asked Darcy. "Even if your aunt and uncle do not see the evidence, Lady Catherine's insinuations will be enough to poison their opinion of me, which is already tenuous."

"Well," said Fitzwilliam, falling back into his chair, "we simply need to ensure there is nothing here for them to see."

"No," Darcy said. "I have a better idea."

The next morning a little before nine o'clock, Darcy and Elizabeth were standing in the foyer of the small town house. They had returned briefly to Darcy House for a change of clothes and a few hours of sleep.

When first questioned, Wickham had been defiant, but after Darcy outlined their suppositions about the scheme, he had finally admitted that he was working for Lady Catherine. Colonel Fitzwilliam had gleefully taken the prisoner to the jail himself; he had thought Wickham deserved punishment ever since Ramsgate. The soldiers and Bow Street Runners had left, and now the house was empty.

As they waited, Darcy encircled Elizabeth with his arms. His anxiety over her almost-abduction had not completely abated, and he wanted to keep her close. As if reading his mind, she murmured, "I assure you I am fine."

"I know, my dearest, but I cannot help being overly protective." His hold on her tightened. "The thought of losing you—I do not know how I would survive."

"I know what you mean," she said feelingly, "but all is well." Reassured by his presence, she laid her head on his shoulder, reminding herself that once this business was finished, they could return home and rest.

He heard the sounds of a carriage approaching. "It is time," he murmured to Elizabeth. She smiled mischievously at him and then opened the door. As he stood in the shadows, he could see her clearly illuminated by the bright morning light, and she would be quite visible to anyone on the street. The carriage stopped opposite the house's door, so Darcy knew it was the one they had been awaiting.

Time for him to play his part. Darcy reached out his hand and pulled Elizabeth back toward him, so they were both mostly in the shadow of the house's vestibule. Then he kissed her very thoroughly as she melted into his arms. This was the enjoyable part of their little charade, he thought, as he sensed the softness of her lips on his and felt passion coursing through him, almost forgetting they had another purpose at the moment.

The carriage's door banged open, and he heard his aunt declare, "I tell you, it *is* Miss Bennet. She spent several weeks in Kent. I would know her anywhere. I knew those rumors were true!" Hearing the note of triumph in her voice, he had to restrain his impulse to denounce her right away.

At the sound of Lady Catherine's voice, Elizabeth turned toward the street while Darcy faded back into the shadows. Nobody on the street could have seen his face. "Lady Catherine! W-what are you doing in this part of town?" Darcy admired his wife's acting skills, she sounded very much like a woman caught misbehaving. Darcy maneuvered himself until he could catch a glimpse through the crack between the door and the frame, and he could see Lady Catherine descending from the carriage. As Richard had predicted, Darcy's aunt and uncle Fitzwilliam were also in the coach. The Earl of Matlock followed his sister out of the carriage.

Lady Catherine was at her imperious best, striding across the street as if she owned it. Darcy knew she was enjoying every moment of her supposed triumph—putting this "upstart country

miss" in her proper place. His anger flared at the
thought that she was prepared to ruin Elizabeth's
reputation to serve her own purposes. Well, she
would regret it.

"Who were you kissing there? I saw you!"
Lady Catherine bellowed at Elizabeth.

"K-kissing?" Elizabeth sounded convincingly
anxious, and Darcy knew his aunt would have no
trouble believing Elizabeth had been caught with
Wickham.

"Yes, kissing! I demand to know who you have
been carrying on with! Who is in that house?" The
older woman was glorying in her victory.

This is the moment, Darcy thought. He walked
around the open door and stepped into the doorway.
Lady Catherine blinked rapidly and then gaped at
him. His uncle drew level with his sister on the
sidewalk and gazed up the steps, his face revealing
less shock than confusion. "You have caught me,
Aunt. I am afraid it is my bad judgment that has
provoked this incident," Darcy said, hoping his tone
sounded more embarrassed than angry.

"Darcy!" His uncle Fitzwilliam exclaimed.
"What are you doing here?"

"Elizabeth and I came to visit a former servant
from Darcy House. Mrs. Clement is sick, and we
thought to cheer her up," Darcy said, trying to
sound as nonchalant as possible. He and Elizabeth
descended the steps to the street and drew level with
his relatives. "She had been kind enough to visit
Mrs. Clement without me, but this time I had the
chance to accompany her." *There. That would
account for any tales his aunt had spun about
witnesses seeing Elizabeth leaving this house
previously.*

"Your...former servant...lives here?" Lady Catherine asked, bewildered.

"Indeed." Darcy gave her a level look. He knew she dared not contradict him without revealing that she knew whose house it truly was, so he turned an amiable smile on his uncle. "What are you three doing going for a ride at this time of day?"

Now his uncle appeared rather embarrassed, and Darcy rather enjoyed seeing him attempt to devise a reason for their presence. They could hardly admit they hoped to discover their nephew's love displaying her debauched behavior. "Um...Catherine thought to show us a faster way to get to Hyde Park from our town house...but it seems rather roundabout to me. I do not believe we shall use it again." Guilt was written all over his face, and his eyes lookedeverywhere but at Darcy. Still, he had to admire his uncle's quick wits.

His aunt Alice had emerged from the carriage and joined the others, eyeing Darcy with frank disapproval. "Fitzwilliam, your father would be ashamed of you! Such wanton behavior! And practically on the street!"

Darcy attempted to appear appropriately chagrined. "I apologize for my breach in conduct. You are absolutely correct." Elizabeth glanced down at her feet, red staining her cheeks. While he had not minded, she was probably genuinely embarrassed about being caught kissing in public— even though that had been part of the plan.

Now that the initial shock was over, his uncle had recovered his sense of propriety. "You have compromised the young lady. You must do right by her!"

Lady Catherine opened her mouth to object, saw Darcy's murderous expression, and closed it again. Darcy put his arm around Elizabeth's waist. "No, actually I do not." He rather enjoyed the shock on his aunt and uncle's faces. "You see, we have something to tell you—"

Lady Catherine could contain herself no longer. "You cannot get engaged to this woman. It is unsupportable!" she bellowed.

"Your opinion on this match has been sufficiently expressed." Darcy leveled his gaze at her until she looked away. "In any event, your concern is misplaced," Darcy continued. "I wish to explain that we are not announcing our engagement; we are already married."

"Married!" Aunt Alice cried. Lady Catherine appeared so horrified that Darcy thought she might have a seizure in the street.

"Yes, we actually were married in France a month ago, but Elizabeth's father asked us to delay the announcement." Darcy strove to keep his tone casual but felt a glimmer of triumph when he gazed at Lady Catherine's scandalized face.

"Indeed!" Uncle Fitzwilliam sounded more surprised than dismayed. "You have been married this whole time?"

"Yes." Darcy regarded Aunt Alice. "So I fear that any attempt to persuade me to consider any other women has been wasted effort. I apologize." There was a long pause while Darcy's relatives considered this information. Lady Alice regarded Darcy in shock while his uncle watched her to see her reaction.

Lady Catherine was the first to recover her voice. "Marriage in France? I am certain it could be annulled! You could escape this trap she has laid for you."

Darcy experienced a rush of rage but attempted to restrain it. Shouting at his aunt on a public street would only damage the family's relationships. "The wedding was performed by a Church of England priest with all due ceremony, and we have no desire to have it annulled."

After a brief pause, Aunt Alice took a step toward Darcy, regarding him with an ironic gleam in her eye. "Well, this was quite impulsive of you, Fitzwilliam, and I must say I regret wasting my matchmaking efforts on you. But I enjoyed your Elizabeth's company at dinner the other night. You could have done far worse." She turned to Elizabeth with a warm smile. "Welcome to the family, my dear." Darcy sighed with relief at the sign that his aunt had bowed to the inevitable.

"Thank you," Elizabeth responded with a heartfelt smile. Lady Catherine did not appear disposed to follow her sister-in-law's example but instead glared at Darcy.

Darcy's uncle shook his head. "Apparently, you are as impulsive as your father when you set your mind to it," he said finally. "Congratulations to both of you!" After contemplating them in bemusement for a minute, he announced, "As interesting as all these revelations are, I would like to continue on to Hyde Park before the day grows too warm." He offered his wife his arm.

"Yes, indeed," Aunt Alice seconded. "Darcy, let me know when the announcement will appear in the newspaper. Then we shall throw a ball in your honor so we may introduce your young lady properly."

Darcy smiled broadly; such an event would go far toward establishing Elizabeth in London society. "Thank you." Darcy gave her a kiss on the cheek.

His aunt and uncle ambled back toward the carriage, accompanied by Elizabeth. Darcy could hear her explaining the circumstances surrounding the wedding to them. Lady Catherine turned to follow the Fitzwilliams, but Darcy caught her by the elbow. "Aunt Catherine," he hissed, all pretext of civility gone, "do not make the mistake of believing I am unaware of your role in Wickham's misadventure."

"I–I do not know of what you are speaking," she said in a quavering voice.

"Wickham confessed all to me before Richard carted him off to jail. Be thankful that you are my aunt. That is the only thing preventing me from having you named as a conspirator in my wife's kidnapping!" He drew closer to her so she was forced to gaze up at him.

"Kidnapping! I never—she–she was not to be harmed—" Lady Catherine broke off suddenly, realizing she had already revealed too much.

"You schemed to ruin an innocent woman's reputation," Darcy continued relentlessly. "You should be ashamed of yourself, but I know you are incapable of such sentiments. Instead I want you to ponder what would have happened if Wickham had succeeded in his ploy to drag Elizabeth's name through the muck. It would have been the name of *Darcy* that would have been besmirched. You would have caused the very event you thought to prevent!"

These words made Aunt Catherine blanch more than any other, but she remained silent. "Currently, no one else knows of this conspiracy, save

Wickham, Richard, and Elizabeth," Darcy said. "However, should you be anything less than supportive of my marriage to Elizabeth, it will not remain that way."

"You would never go public with such a tale—" she scoffed.

"I do not need to. Would you like me to share the tale with my aunt and uncle? Or perhaps your daughter? Or the Bennets?"

Lady Catherine gritted her teeth. "No."

"Very well, then here are my demands. You will stay away from Elizabeth and me. You will not visit us. We will not visit you. When we see each other at social events, you will be unfailingly polite to Elizabeth. You will not say one word against her to our family or anyone else. If you fail to meet these terms, I will not rest until *everyone* in our family knows the story of your misbehavior. Do you consent to these stipulations, or should I save time and tell them now?"

"I agree," she ground out. "Now, let me pass! I have had enough of this!" She pushed past Darcy and marched toward the carriage where the Fitzwilliams awaited her. Darcy let her go. They had reached an understanding. It was enough. Lady Catherine climbed into the carriage, and it immediately began rolling down the street, the sounds of the horses' hoofs echoing in the morning quiet. Elizabeth strolled back to Darcy, and he put his arms around her shoulders.

"I can promise that you will never again experience difficulties with my aunt Catherine," he said softly.

"Thank you." She leaned against him, clearly exhausted. The morning sun glinted off the soft curls of her hair.

He touched a single curl tenderly. "Now, my love, it is time to go home."

Epilogue

The atmosphere in the Bennets' drawing room was very festive. The bride shone with joy, and the groom smiled sunnily at everyone he saw. The bride's sisters chattered happily about nothing in particular, causing the bride's father to roll his eyes.

All is right with the world, Elizabeth mused as she poured tea for the guests at the Bingleys' wedding breakfast. The new Mrs. Bingley was resplendent in white satin ornamented with just the right amount of lace. Elizabeth was pleased to see her sister laughing and happy; she deserved it. At her side, Mr. Bingley conversed animatedly with Sir William Lucas while Mrs. Bennet, clearly in her element, related an amusing anecdote to Lady Lucas. The Gardiners talked with Mrs. Phillips and Mr. Bennet. Kitty abandoned her position near Mary and cornered poor Colonel Fitzwilliam, the only man present in regimentals, who seemed extremely uncomfortable. *When I am finished with the tea, I will have to rescue him.*

Lydia, as usual, talked too loudly with a crowd of male admirers, but this time she did so in the company of her new husband: Frederick Denny. It had been something of a shock when he had arrived in London to propose to Lydia, but she had been thrilled to accept him. Elizabeth suspected that Denny had received word—perhaps from Lydia herself—of the substantial dowry Darcy was offering upon her marriage. They had married very quickly thereafter—only weeks after the kidnapping episode—and Denny had left the militia in favor of a career in law.

Elizabeth and Darcy had kept the story of the abduction from the Bennet family, who only knew that Wickham had been taken to jail six weeks ago for unspecified crimes. Elizabeth smiled to herself while watching Denny and Lydia, musing that he would be a far better husband for her than Wickham. Although he was a little flighty, he did not gamble or drink to excess. Already he was a steadying influence in her life, refusing to indulge the behavior that her mother had condoned.

Seeing Lydia brought Elizabeth's thoughts inevitably to Wickham, who had died in prison, murdered by a fellow prisoner whom he had offended. Wickham's henchmen had been wanted for other crimes and were immediately transported, so the kidnapping story had never been revealed in a courtroom, for which Elizabeth was profoundly grateful. Lydia had mourned the tragedy of Wickham's life cut short but had quickly recovered and sought out other companions, remaining unaware of her first love's true perfidy.

Sensing some movement from the corner of her eye, Elizabeth turned to see Darcy deftly extricating Colonel Fitzwilliam from Kitty. Good for him. She watched as the two men strolled away to a far corner of the room, knowing that poor Darcy had been uncomfortable with the public visibility of standing up for Bingley during the wedding ceremony. Elizabeth had glanced his way several times to see the muscles in his jaw clenching spasmodically. He truly did not like crowds. *Just as well that we married as we did. He would have detested a large ceremony.* Although Jane's wedding had been beautiful, Elizabeth was not sorry she herself would never go through the arduous process of planning such an event.

Darcy glanced around the room. When his eyes alighted on her, he smiled with heart-stopping brilliance, and she felt her insides melt with warmth. Fitzwilliam was now talking with Bingley, so Darcy wove his way through the crowd toward her. They had only been separated for a few minutes, but she felt as though an invisible thread tugged her toward him.

Unfortunately, just before he could reach her, he was intercepted by Caroline Bingley, who latched onto his arm. "Lovely ceremony, was it not?" she asked in an unnaturally sweet voice. Bingley had told Jane that Caroline had been asking him questions about Darcy and Elizabeth's relationship, and apparently she took some hope from the absence of a formal engagement announcement. Still pouring tea, Elizabeth was close enough to hear everything.

"Indeed," Darcy said noncommittally. "Charles appears very happy. I daresay they will do well together."

"Naturally, we are all delighted about having Jane in our family." The falsity of her tone belied her sentiments. At that moment, Mrs. Bennet let out a shriek of laughter in reaction to something Mrs. Long had said, causing Elizabeth to wince with embarrassment. "Of course, marrying into such a family is not to *everyone's* taste," Miss Bingley continued snidely. Elizabeth shook her head in amazement at the woman's transparency. Although Miss Bingley spoke in a confidential tone, Elizabeth knew the other woman meant her to overhear what she hoped would be Darcy's disavowal of her family.

Darcy regarded Miss Bingley with a stony expression. "I suppose not...." he said very deliberately, "although I have recently come to the conclusion that finding the right woman should take precedence over any behavior by her family. Do you not concur?"

"Oh, indeed, but—" Miss Bingley was still spluttering in surprise as Darcy excused himself to refill his teacup. While Elizabeth poured the tea, he gave her an ironic smile.

Aware that Miss Bingley was watching, Darcy leaned over to whisper in her ear, "I cannot wait to get you alone, Mrs. Darcy. You look quite fetching in that dress and will look even more fetching out of it." She ducked her head to conceal her blush, thus missing the sight of Miss Bingley flouncing away in disgust. Over the next few minutes, they enjoyed some quiet conversation, standing a shade closer than was acceptable for an unmarried couple and earning a disapproving glare from Sir William. Servers, hired for the occasion, now circulated, distributing glasses of champagne to the guests. Elizabeth knew what was coming next.

Then she heard her father's voice calling for everyone's attention. Standing at one end of the room, he led a toast to the health and happiness of the new couple, and everyone joined in enthusiastically. When the murmuring died down, he declared he had another announcement to make, and Elizabeth steeled herself and glanced up at Darcy, who was clenching his jaw once more. Surreptitiously, she felt for his hand, taking comfort in its strong grip. They had known what her father planned; Jane and Bingley had not minded the idea, but Elizabeth was still anxious about the reaction it would receive.

"As many of you know, our daughter, Elizabeth, recently traveled in France," Mr. Bennet began. Some curious faces turned toward Elizabeth, wondering what her travels could have to do with

Jane's wedding. "You may not know that Mr. Darcy was instrumental in getting Elizabeth safely out of France when political and health considerations made it quite difficult. We are most grateful to Mr. Darcy for saving Elizabeth's life." Many heads nodded at this sentiment.

"However, most people do not know that Elizabeth and Mr. Darcy fell in love and were married in France." There were gasps from the crowd, and now every eye was on the couple. Miss Bingley appeared to choke on her champagne, and Mrs. Hurst had turned so white that she seemed in danger of fainting. The members of the Bennet family, however, were smiling for joy. She and Darcy had told her mother and sisters the previous evening, trusting them to keep a secret for one day.

"Various family considerations made it necessary for us to conceal the happy event for a few months." Elizabeth looked over at Lydia, but her sister was giggling and whispering in Denny's ear, seemingly oblivious to her father's implications. "We now want to take the opportunity to welcome Mr. Darcy into our family. A toast to the happy couple: Mr. and Mrs. Darcy!"

As everyone raised their glasses, Elizabeth felt Darcy's arm encircle her waist. It was skirting the standards of public propriety even for a married couple, but Elizabeth knew Darcy was simply expressing his relief at being able to act like a husband in public. Sharing the unspoken sentiment, she leaned a little against his warm body.

Elizabeth watched her father, seeing genuine warmth in his eyes. As he had become aware of Darcy's role in bringing about Lydia's redemption, Mr. Bennet had been increasingly impressed with his new son-in-law. Although he still seemed bemused by the whole affair, he no longer treated Darcy with distrust and, at moments, seemed quite pleased with their marriage. Her mother, on the other hand, treated Darcy with an embarrassing amount of deference. The younger Miss Bennets were so intimidated by him that they said little to him at all.

An announcement would appear in the London newspapers the next day to ensure that the whole world would now be in on their secret. Fortunately, Darcy's aunt and uncle had become quite welcoming to Elizabeth and had plans to schedule a ball at which they could introduce her and help the *ton* grow accustomed to the idea of Darcy as a married man. But these events were in the future; for now they could simply enjoy each other's company.

The past weeks had given the couple a well-deserved respite at Pemberley. Elizabeth was a fair way to loving the estate as Darcy did; already it felt more like home than Longbourn. Of necessity, the population at Meryton had believed that Elizabeth was in London enjoying the Gardiners' hospitality, but when they returned to Pemberley after Jane and Bingley's wedding, they would do so as husband and wife.

The Darcys were immediately mobbed by well-wishers and curious friends who wished to know the nature of their courtship and marriage. It made for a thrilling tale that both Elizabeth and Darcy told many times. The crowd finally thinned, and Elizabeth had an opportunity to glance at her husband, who was clenching his jaw again; he could not tolerate much more.

As she surveyed the room, she saw no one who needed their immediate attention. Turning to Darcy, she whispered in his ear, "My love, would you like to take a turn around the garden?"

With an expression of great relief, Darcy simply nodded. Taking his hand, she led him from the room.

Once outside, they sat on the bench admiring the garden, which was still beautiful in early fall. Leaning against Darcy, Elizabeth sighed contentedly. "What is it, darling?" Darcy asked.

"I am happy to have all of our secrets out in the open now. We no longer have to conceal our attachment or our relationship."

"Yes, it will be a great relief." He smiled gently. "It will be easier on Bingley as well. He was constantly anxious that he would inadvertently reveal the information to someone who did not know."

"Oh, poor Charles!" Elizabeth exclaimed with a little giggle. "Now he can go on his wedding trip without it weighing on him."

They sat in silence for a little while. Darcy's hand caressed her neck and promised greater pleasures later when they were truly in private.

"I have another reason for being grateful the story of our marriage is public," Elizabeth finally said.

"Oh, what is that?" Darcy's tone was distant, his mind on other things as he gazed at the garden.

"I am increasing," Elizabeth said matter-of-factly.

Darcy's hand jerked suddenly to her waist, and then he turned to her in amazement. "Elizabeth! A baby? Are you certain?"

Her face wreathed with smiles, Elizabeth nodded emphatically. "Yes, and so is Mrs. Reynolds, and she would know." The housekeeper at

Pemberley had liked the new Mrs. Darcy from the start.

"She did not tell me!" he said in mock indignation. "I knew this would happen. The staff likes you better than me." They both laughed. Darcy pulled her to him and embraced her fiercely, inhaling the delicious smell of lilac. "When will the baby come?"

"Seven months."

He shook his head in wonder. "Seven months, and I will be a father...I cannot believe it." He released Elizabeth, and she could see his thoughts turning inward. "A mere five months ago I despaired of any of this coming about."

Elizabeth covered his hand with hers. "I am sorry I caused you so much pain, William."

He shook his head but still stared out into the distance. "No. If you had accepted me at Hunsford, you would have deprived me of time I needed to learn some valuable lessons." Suddenly, he barked a laugh.

"What is it?"

"We should give Richard a present every year on our anniversary. Perhaps a bottle of my best French brandy..."

"Why Richard?"

He finally turned to look at her. "I do not suppose I ever told you the story, but he convinced me to go to France. I had not been planning to—not at all."

Elizabeth tilted her head, regarding him curiously. "How did he convince you?"

"He told me Paris would help ease the pain of being rejected by a certain woman at Hunsford." He smiled at her, and she chuckled a little.

Elizabeth gave him an arch look. "And did it work as predicted, sir?"

He shook his head in mock sorrow. "I do not believe I can ever get over her."

She matched his playful tone. "I am so sorry to hear that."

Leaning in for a kiss, he gazed deeply into her eyes. "I have never been so happy to have my plans thwarted in my life."

"Perhaps we should send the Gardiners a bottle of brandy as well. If they had not taken me to France, none of this would have come about."

He nodded solemnly. "Perhaps brandy and an invitation to Pemberley to celebrate our anniversary. No thanks are sufficient for the people who brought us together."

The End

Thank you for purchasing this book.

Your support makes it possible for authors like me to continue writing.

Please consider leaving a review where you purchased the book.

Learn more about me and my upcoming releases:

Website: www.victoriakincaid.com

Twitter: VictoriaKincaid@kincaidvic

Blog: https://kincaidvictoria.wordpress.com/

Facebook: https://www.facebook.com/kincaidvictoria

Please enjoy this exclusive excerpt from Victoria
Kincaid's *Mr. Darcy to the Rescue*:

Mr. Darcy to the Rescue

When the irritating Mr. Collins proposes marriage,
Elizabeth Bennet is prepared to refuse him, but then
she learns that her father is ill. If Mr. Bennet dies,
Collins will inherit Longbourn and her family will
have nowhere to go. Elizabeth accepts the proposal,
telling herself she can be content as long as her
family is secure. If only she weren't dreading the
approaching wedding day…

Ever since leaving Hertfordshire, Mr. Darcy has
been trying to forget his inconvenient attraction to
Elizabeth. News of her betrothal forces him to
realize how devastating it would be to lose her. He
arrives at Longbourn intending to prevent the
marriage, but discovers Elizabeth's real opinion
about his character. Then Darcy recognizes his true
dilemma…

How can he rescue her when she doesn't want him
to?

Excerpt

"…And now nothing remains for me but to
assure you in the most animated language of the
violence of my affection!"
It must be admitted that Elizabeth Bennet's
attention had drifted a little as her cousin, Mr.
Collins, had enumerated at great length his reasons

for choosing to marry and why he had very
rationally selected Elizabeth for this "honor."

Now as Elizabeth focused on his words, she
had to stifle a laugh at the idea that his affection for
her was violent or deep or anything more than
nonexistent. In fact, he had not even managed to
produce any "animated language." Instead, he had
merely assured her that his language was animated.
It was a bit like having someone declare it was
raining when you stood in bright sunshine.

Oh, merciful heavens, he was still talking!
"To fortune I am perfectly indifferent, and you may
assure yourself that no ungenerous reproach shall
ever pass my lips when we are married." As he
drew breath for another long-winded speech,
Elizabeth knew she must say something—and
quickly!

"You are too hasty, sir! You forget that I
have not yet made an answer—"

Mr. Collins waved his hand airily. "We may
dispense with these formalities. We both know how
you shall respond."

"We do?" Elizabeth expected smoke to be
streaming from her ears by now.

"Yes, I have spoken with your most excellent
father, and he assured me how felicitous he found
this event." He graced her with a smile, which
presumably was intended to be charming, but oozed
insincerity.

"He did?" Elizabeth found these words hard
to credit.

"Indeed. I assured him that our union is
already a foregone conclusion since we are united
of one mind and one heart."

"We are?" Elizabeth could not stay silent
any longer. "Pray, sir, when did that happen?"

Mr. Collins merely looked bemused. "I…do not believe I can supply you with the exact date.…"

Elizabeth shrugged. "I keep a journal. I shall have to go back to see if I recorded it." She tapped her lip with her finger. "I hope it did not escape my notice."

Her erstwhile suitor blinked rapidly, fiddling with his cuffs. "Your father did caution me that you should speak with him first before making any decision regarding my most generous offer." He shrugged. "I do not see the necessity since we both know that another offer of marriage may never be made to you… Miss Elizabeth?"

Mr. Collins had been so caught up in the sound of his own voice that it took him a few moments to realize that Elizabeth was halfway across the drawing room floor. He hastened to catch up with her. "Where are you going, my most precious love blossom?"

The sound of this ridiculous pet name almost stopped Elizabeth altogether, but she had a more urgent mission. "I must speak with my father," she muttered.

"Why?"

"To assure myself his wits are in order."

"Hmm?" Mr. Collins's tone was quizzical. "I assure you he was of quite sound mind this morning when I spoke to him."

Briefly, Elizabeth considered the possibility that Mr. Collins was so stupid he was incapable of being insulted. Elizabeth would be tempted to laugh if the situation were not so dire. Why would her father give Mr. Collins the impression he wanted her to marry him?

She opened the door to her father's study rather more forcefully than she intended, and it banged against the wall. Her father looked up from his desk as Elizabeth closed the door, preventing Mr. Collins from entering.

"Ah, Lizzy, I thought I might receive a visit from you." Elizabeth's father removed his spectacles and regarded his daughter with a grim smile.

Elizabeth sat in the chair opposite the desk but perched on the edge, unable to relax. She expected Papa to smile and laugh or at least regard her with an ironic twinkle in his eye. Instead, he merely looked worn and solemn. "Mr. Collins has made me an offer of marriage." Her voice trembled with uncertainty.

"And you listened to him?"

"I suppose I must be amenable to people's wishes some of the time, or I run the danger of becoming predictable."

Such banter usually drew a chuckle from her father, but today, it merely produced a rather wan smile. Fingers of anxiety crept up Elizabeth's spine. "Papa, is there something amiss?"

Her father's hands fiddled with his spectacles. "The last thing I wanted was to burden you with this. If Mr. Bingley had... Well, it is of no matter."

Elizabeth said nothing. Everyone in the family had been disappointed when Mr. Bingley had abruptly left the neighborhood two days earlier. Jane tried to hide her melancholy, but the loss still haunted her eyes. Elizabeth still believed that Mr. Bingley would return, but his sister's latest letter to Jane had held little hope.

Papa rubbed his hand over his forehead wearily. "Do you recall when Mr. Bartlett was here a week ago?" Elizabeth nodded. She had sent for the doctor herself after her father experienced pains in his chest. "I may have misled your mother about how severe he believes the problem to be."

Elizabeth's breath caught.

"Mr. Bartlett believes my heart is weakening. And it is only a matter of time until it fails." Papa's voice was calm, but his hands moved restlessly over the surface of the desk.

Elizabeth covered her mouth to muffle her gasp. "Oh, Papa!" Tears spilled out of her eyes and ran unchecked down her cheeks.

Her father nodded slowly. "I know. I am not a young man. I had hoped for more time, but..." His hands once again worried the frame of his spectacles. "For my own sake, I have made peace with it, but I do wish you girls could be safely married." He ran his hand through the thinning hair over his forehead; many strands of gray had recently joined the strands of brown. "I had intended to father a son. And when it became clear that was not to be..." He bowed his head, showing the weight of his years. "I should have run my business affairs more carefully. That is the truth."

"Oh no, Papa!" Lizzy cried. She jumped up and hurried around the desk so she could kneel beside her father's chair. "'Tis nothing but the vagaries of fate! Our situation can scarcely be laid at your door."

"If it pleases you to say it...." Her father patted the hand she laid on his arm. "I must confess to being a coward as well. I have not shared this news with your mother. I did not wish her to worry—or shriek." Elizabeth and her father exchanged a knowing look.

Elizabeth stood, leaning against the desk for support. "Do not be anxious for our future. The solution has been presented to us just in time." She swallowed hard. "I shall marry Mr. Collins and then when you…" She noticed a tremor in her voice. "And then Mama and my sisters will not be forced to leave Longbourn. It is the perfect solution."

Her father leaned back into his chair, looking very frail. "Yes, indeed, it would be perfect if Mr. Collins were a sensible person. If he were not living proof that the Good Lord has a sense of humor. But I would not ask you to make such a sacrifice! I would have you marry for love." The corners of his lips, indeed his whole face, seemed to be dragged down by the weight of his burdens.

"You are not asking; I am offering. Yes, I had hoped for love, but I have always known the chances of finding it were never very great. I am much too outspoken, and I have little dowry. I love Longbourn and my family, so I would be marrying for a different kind of love." She attempted to catch her father's eye, but his head remained bowed.

"Perhaps Mr. Collins's affections might be transferred to one of the other girls…"

Elizabeth took her father's cold hand in hers, touched by how much he cared for her. "Mary has stated more than once in Mr. Collins's presence that she has no intention of ever marrying. Kitty and Lydia are too young and silly. And Jane… I could not ask that of her." Elizabeth wanted to believe Mr. Bingley would return for Jane, and nothing should stand in the way of her sister's happiness.

"But—"

Elizabeth formed her lips into a semblance of a smile. "My marriage will bring happiness to you and Mama and the family. And it will ensure our future. That will make me very happy indeed." Kneeling again, she tried to radiate an air of calm acceptance, although it was not one of her strengths. *Perhaps Jane can give me lessons.*

Her father placed his other hand on hers. "I must confess it would set my mind at ease to know the family future would be secured."

"It will be." Elizabeth squeezed his fingers briefly.

Papa shifted in his seat, looking at the window. "I have said nothing of my health to anyone. I think it best if it remains that way."

"Yes, of course," Elizabeth said. Even with the promise of security through her marriage to Mr. Collins, her mother would be beside herself with anxiety. "Your health might continue to be good for quite a time. No need to worry about it now."

"Yes, just as Mr. Bartlett said." He turned his gaze back to Elizabeth. Tears glistened in the corners of his eyes. "Oh, my darling girl, you have ever been a comfort to me."

She gave her father a watery smile. "And you have been my strength, Papa."

Her father discreetly wiped his eyes and straightened in his chair. Elizabeth stood.

"Now, go and give Mr. Collins the good news. It is far more than he deserves." Her father picked up his book. "I am nearly to the end of this book, and I mean to finish it today." He managed to smile at her before lowering his eyes to the book, but he blinked rapidly as he commenced reading.

Before opening the door, Elizabeth wiped her eyes with a handkerchief, wishing to avoid awkward questions about red-rimmed eyes and blotchy skin. *Although Mr. Collins would certainly interpret them as tears of joy.*

But no, she must not be bitter. She must only dwell on the good things about the marriage. This union will make her father happy, her family happy, Mr. Collins happy. Only one person would not be happy.

But that does not matter, she told herself firmly and opened the door.

About Victoria Kincaid

As a professional freelance writer, Victoria writes about IT, data storage, home improvement, green living, alternative energy, and healthcare. Some of her more…unusual writing subjects have included space toilets, taxi services, laser gynecology, bidets, orthopedic shoes, generating energy from onions, Ferrari rental car services, and vampire face lifts (she swears she is not making any of this up).

Victoria has a Ph.D. in English literature and has taught composition to unwilling college students. Today she teaches business writing to willing office professionals and tries to give voice to the demanding cast of characters in her head. She lives in Virginia with her husband, two children who love to read, a hyperactive dog, and an overly affectionate cat. A lifelong Jane Austen fan, Victoria confesses to an extreme partiality for the Colin Firth miniseries version of *Pride and Prejudice*.

Victoria Kincaid's other books:

Darcy vs. Bennet

Elizabeth Bennet is drawn to a handsome, mysterious man she meets at a masquerade ball. However, she gives up all hope for a future with him when she learns he is the son of George Darcy, the man who ruined her father's life. Despite her father's demand that she avoid the younger Darcy, when he appears in Hertfordshire Elizabeth cannot stop thinking about him, or seeking him out, or welcoming his kisses....

Fitzwilliam Darcy has struggled to carve out a life independent from his father's vindictive temperament and domineering ways, although the elder Darcy still controls the purse strings. After meeting Elizabeth Bennet, Darcy cannot imagine marrying anyone else, even though his father despises her family. More than anything he wants to make her his wife, but doing so would mean sacrificing everything else....

384

When Mary Met the Colonel

Without the beauty and wit of the older Bennet sisters or the liveliness of the younger, Mary is the Bennet sister most often overlooked. She has resigned herself to a life of loneliness, alleviated only by music and the occasional book of military history.

Colonel Fitzwilliam finds himself envying his friends who are marrying wonderful women while he only attracts empty-headed flirts. He longs for a caring, well-informed woman who will see the man beneath the uniform.

A chance meeting in Longbourn's garden during Darcy and Elizabeth's wedding breakfast kindles an attraction between Mary and the Colonel. However, the Colonel cannot act on these feelings since he must wed an heiress. He returns to war, although Mary finds she cannot easily forget him.

Is happily ever after possible after Mary meets the Colonel?

Pride and Proposals

What if Mr. Darcy's proposal was too late?

Darcy has been bewitched by Elizabeth Bennet since he met her in Hertfordshire. He can no longer fight this overwhelming attraction and must admit he is hopelessly in love. During Elizabeth's visit to Kent she has been forced to endure the company of the difficult and disapproving Mr. Darcy, but she has enjoyed making the acquaintance of his affable cousin, Colonel Fitzwilliam.

Finally resolved, Darcy arrives at Hunsford Parsonage prepared to propose—only to discover that Elizabeth has just accepted a proposal from the Colonel, Darcy's dearest friend in the world. As he watches the couple prepare for a lifetime together, Darcy vows never to speak of what is in his heart. Elizabeth has reason to dislike Darcy, but finds that he haunts her thoughts and stirs her emotions in strange ways.

Can Darcy and Elizabeth find their happily ever after?

52325441R00214

Made in the USA
Lexington, KY
24 May 2016